"[AN] EXCITING NOVEL OF DETECTION AND ESCAPE . . . [A] FAST-PACED THRILLER."
—*Dallas Morning News*

"Perry is so skillful with the old chase-and-pursuit routine, creates such interesting characters, and writes about them so tellingly, one wants more immediately, not next year—Right Now."
—*The Boston Globe*

"Excellently plotted and executed . . . Jane Whitefield's third appearance is eagerly awaited."
—*The Orlando Sentinel*

"Explosive . . . The plotting is a miracle of unrelenting tension; the breathless, knowing prose is pitch-perfect; and Jane's fierce righteousness is perfectly balanced by a mind-boggling wealth of detail about how to plunder trusts, defraud banks, and disappear."
—*Kirkus Reviews* (starred review)

Please turn the page for more reviews . . .

By Thomas Perry:

THE BUTCHER'S BOY
METZGER'S DOG
BIG FISH
ISLAND
SLEEPING DOGS*
VANISHING ACT*
DANCE FOR THE DEAD*

*Published by Ivy Books

DANCE FOR THE DEAD

Thomas Perry

IVY BOOKS • NEW YORK

An Ivy Book
Published by Ballantine Books
Copyright © 1996 by Thomas Perry
Excerpt from *Shadow Woman* copyright © 1997 by Thomas Perry

http://www.randomhouse.com

Library of Congress Catalog Card Number: 96-94984

ISBN 0-8041-1425-0

This edition published by arrangement with Random House, Inc.

Manufactured in the United States of America

First Ballantine Books Edition: April 1997

10 9 8 7 6 5 4

For Jo

with love to
Alix and Isabel

The common aim of all war parties was to bring back persons to replace the mourned-for dead. This could be done in three ways: by bringing back the scalp of a dead enemy (this scalp might even be put through an adoption ceremony); by bringing back a live prisoner (to be adopted, tortured, and killed); or by bringing back a live prisoner to be allowed to live and even to replace in a social role the one whose death had called for this "revenge."

Anthony F. C. Wallace, *The Death and Rebirth of the Seneca,* 1969

The tall, slim woman hastily tied her long, dark hair into a knot behind her head, planted her feet in the center of the long courthouse corridor, and waited. A few litigants and their attorneys passed her, some of them secretly studying her, more because she was attractive than because she was standing motionless, forcing them to step around her on their way to the courtrooms. Her chest rose and fell in deep breaths as though she had been running, and her eyes looked past them, having already dismissed them before they approached as she stared into the middle distance.

She heard the chime sound above the elevator thirty feet away. Before the doors had fully parted, three large men in sportcoats slipped out between them and spun their heads to stare up the hallway. All three seemed to see her within an instant, their eyes widening, then narrowing to focus, and then becoming watchful and predatory, losing any hint of introspection as they began to move toward her, one beside each wall and one in the middle, increasing their pace with each step.

Several bystanders averted their eyes and sidestepped to avoid them, but the woman never moved. She hiked up the skirt of her navy blue business suit so it was out of her way, took two more deep breaths, then swung her shoulder bag hard at the first man's face.

The man's eyes shone with triumph and eagerness as he snatched the purse out of the air. The triumph turned to shock as the woman slipped the strap around his forearm and used the momentum of his charge to haul him into the second man, sending them both against the wall to her right. As they caromed off it, she delivered a kick to one and a chop to the other to put them on the floor. This bought her a few heartbeats to devote to the third man, who was moving along the left wall to get behind her.

She leaned back and swung one leg high. The man read her intention, stopped, and held up his hands to clutch her ankle, but her back foot left the ground and she hurled her weight into him. As her foot caught him at thigh level and propelled him into the wall, there was the sickening crack of his knee popping. He crumpled to the floor and began to gasp and clutch at his crippled leg as the woman rolled to the side and sprang up.

The first two men were rising to their feet. Her fist jabbed out at the nearest one and she rocked him back, pivoted to throw an elbow into the bridge of his nose, and brought a knee into the second man's face.

There was a loud slapping sound and the woman's head jerked nearly to her left shoulder as a big fist swung into her cheekbone. Strong arms snaked around her from behind, lifted her off her feet to stretch her erect, and she saw the rest as motion and flashes. The first two men rushed at her in rage, aiming hard roundhouse punches at her head and face, gleeful in the certainty that she saw the blows coming but could do nothing to block them or even turn to divert their force.

Two loud, deep voices overlapped, barking for dominance. "Police officers! Freeze!" "Step away from her!" When her opponents released her and stepped away, she dropped to her knees and covered her face with her hands. In a moment, several bystanders who had stood paralyzed with alarm seemed to awaken. They were drawn closer by some impulse to be of use, but they only hovered helplessly nearby without touching her or speaking.

The judge's chambers were in shadow except for a few horizontal slices of late-afternoon sunlight that shone through the blinds on the wood-paneled wall. Judge Kramer sat in his old oak swivel chair with his robe unzipped but with the yoke still resting on his shoulders. He loosened his tie and leaned back, making the chair's springs creak, then pressed the PLAY button on the tape recorder.

There were sounds of chairs scraping, papers shuffling, and a garble of murmured conversation, so that the judge's empty chamber seemed to be crowded with invisible people. A female voice came from somewhere too close to the microphone. "This deposition is to be taken before Julia R. Kinnock, court stenographer at 501 North Spring Street, Los Angeles, California, at ten . . . seventeen A.M. on November third. The court's instructions were that if there is an objection to the use of a tape recorder, it will be turned off." There was silence. "Will the others in the room please identify themselves."

"David M. Schoenfeld, court-appointed counsel to Timothy Phillips." Schoenfeld's voice was smooth, and each syllable took too long to come out. Judge Kramer could almost see him leaning into the microphone to croon.

"Nina Coffey, Department of Children's Services, Los

Angeles County, in the capacity of guardian for a minor person." Kramer had read her name on a number of official papers, but he had never heard her voice before. It was clear and unapologetic, the words quick and clipped, as though she were trying to guard against some kind of vulnerability.

"Kyle Ambrose, Assistant District Attorney, Los Angeles." As usual, the prosecutor sounded vaguely confused, a pose that had irritated Kramer through six or seven long trials.

Then came the low, monotone voices that were at once self-effacing and weighty, voices of men who had spent a lot of time talking over radios. They started quietly and grew louder, because the last part of each name was the important part.

"Lieutenant James E. Bates, Los Angeles Police Department."

"Agent Joseph Gould, Federal Bureau of Investigation."

There was some more shuffling of papers and then Julia Kinnock said, "Mr. Ambrose, do you wish to begin?"

Ambrose's parched, uncertain voice came in a beat late. "Will you state your name for the record, please?"

There was some throat clearing, and then the high, reedy voice of a young boy. "Tim . . . Timothy John Phillips."

Schoenfeld's courtroom voice intoned, "Perhaps it would be a good idea to ask that the record show that Lieutenant Bates and Agent Gould here present have verified that the deponent's fingerprints match those of Timothy John Phillips, taken prior to his disappearance."

The two voices muttered, "So verified," in the tone of a response in a church. Amen, thought Kramer. Schoenfeld had managed to sidestep onto the record with the one essential fact to be established in the case from Schoenfeld's point of view.

Ambrose's voice became slow and clear as he spoke to the boy. "You are to answer of your own accord. You are not to feel that you are in any way obligated to tell us things you don't want to." Judge Kramer could imagine Ambrose's dark eyes flicking to the faces of Schoenfeld, the lawyer, and Nina Coffey, the social worker. It was a confidence game, as Ambrose's legal work always was. The kid would have to answer all of the questions at some point, but Ambrose was trying to put the watchdogs to sleep. "Mr. Schoenfeld is here as your lawyer, so if you have any doubts, just ask him. And Mrs. Coffey will take you home if you're too tired. Do you understand?"

The small, high-pitched voice said, "Yes."

"How old are you?"

"Eight."

"Can you tell me, please, your earliest recollections?" Judge Kramer clenched his teeth.

"You mean, ever?"

"Yes."

"I remember . . . I guess I remember a lot of things. Christmas. Birthdays. I remember moving into our house in Washington."

"When was that?"

"I don't know."

A male voice interjected, "The lease on the Georgetown house began four years ago on January first. That was established during the murder investigation. He would have been four." The voice would be that of the F.B.I. agent, thought the judge.

"Do you remember anything before that, in another house?"

"No, I don't think so."

"When you moved in, was Miss Mona Turley already with you?"

"I don't know. I guess so."

"Who lived there?"

"My parents, me, Mona."

"Did you have relatives besides your parents? Cousins or uncles?"

"No, just my grandma."

"Did you ever see her?"

"Not that I remember. She lived far away. We used to send her a Christmas card every year."

"Did you?" There was the confusion again, as though Ambrose were hearing it for the first time and trying to fathom the implications.

"Yeah. I remember, because my daddy would put my handprint on it. He would write something, and then he would squish my hand onto a stamp pad and press it on the card, because I couldn't write yet."

Ambrose hesitated, then said gently, "Do you remember anybody else? Any other grown-ups that you were with?"

"You mean Mr. and Mrs. Phillips?"

"Yes."

"I know about them. I don't think I ever saw them."

"So when you say your 'parents' you mean Raymond and Emily Decker?"

"They were my mother and father."

Judge Kramer's brows knitted in distaste. This was typical of Ambrose. Get on with it, he thought. An eight-year-old's distant recollections weren't going to get

Ambrose anything in a criminal investigation. Such meticulous, redundant questioning had bought him an inflated reputation as a prosecutor—laying the groundwork for an unshakable, brick-hard case. It looked like magic to juries, but to Judge Kramer and the opposing attorneys who knew where he was going, it was like watching an ant carrying single crumbs until he had a hero sandwich.

"So you lived in Washington from the time you were four until . . . ? We'll get back to that. Tell me what it was like in Washington. Did you like it?"

"It was okay."

"Were your parents . . . nice to you?"

There was a hint of shock in the boy's voice. "Sure."

"How about discipline? Rules. Were there rules?"

"Yeah."

"Can you tell me some?"

"Ummm . . . Pick up the toys. Brush your teeth. My father always brushed his teeth when I did, and then he'd show me his fillings and tell me I'd need some if I didn't brush the ones in the back."

"What happened when you didn't follow the rules?" Ambrose was casual. "Did they hit you?"

Now the little voice was scandalized. "No."

"Did you go to school?"

"Sure. The Morningside School. It wasn't far, so sometimes we walked."

"So life was pretty good in Washington?"

"Yeah."

"What did you do when you weren't in school?"

"I don't know. Mona used to take me to the park when I was little, and then later sometimes I'd go with my friends. She would sit in the car and wait for me."

Ambrose paused and seemed to be thinking for a long

time, but then Judge Kramer recognized the sound of someone whispering. After a second exchange it sounded angry. He knew it was Nina Coffey. The lawyer Schoenfeld said, "I must point out that this is not an adversarial proceeding, and this part of the story adds no new information to any of the investigations in progress. Miss Coffey has consented to this questioning because she was assured its purpose was for the safety and future welfare of the child. She has a right to withdraw the consent of the Department of Children's Services if she feels this is unnecessarily traumatic. The child has been over this ground several times with the psychologist and the juvenile officers already. Perhaps we could depart from our regular habits of thoroughness and skip to the recent past."

Ambrose sounded defensive. "Then would one of you care to help us in that regard to make the record comprehensible?"

Nina Coffey said, "Timmy, tell me if anything I say isn't true."

"Okay."

"Timmy was raised from the time of his earliest recollections until the age of six by Raymond and Emily Decker. They hired Miss Mona Turley as a nanny when they came to Washington, D.C. He has no direct knowledge of earlier events. He was told he was Timmy Decker. From every assessment, he had a normal early childhood. It was a loving home. Miss Turley was a British citizen and a trained nanny, a legal resident alien. There are no signs of physical or psychological abuse, or of developmental difficulties that would indicate deprivation of any kind." She said pointedly, "This is all covered in the caseworker's report, so it already is part of the record."

Judge Kramer felt like applauding. His finger had been

hovering over the FAST FWD button, but he knew that he wouldn't have let it strike. Either you listened to all of it or you were just another politician in a costume.

Ambrose went on. "All right. Now, Timmy, we have to talk about some unpleasant things, and I'll try to keep it short. What happened on the afternoon of July twenty-third two years ago?"

"I don't know."

Schoenfeld prompted. "That was the day when they died."

"Oh," said Timmy. "Mona and I went to the shoe store after school. Usually we came home at three, but that day we didn't. After we bought the shoes we walked in and everything had changed. I remember Mona opened the door, and then she stopped and went, 'Uh!' Like that. Then she made me wait outside while she went in alone. She was inside a long time. I thought it was a surprise, and she was telling my parents I was there so they could hide. So I went around to the side of the house and looked in the window. And I saw them." His voice cracked, and the judge could hear that he was trying to keep the sob from coming out of his throat in front of all these strange adults, so it just stayed there, with the muscles clamping it in place. Judge Kramer had heard a lot of testimony that had to be forced out through that kind of throat, so he had become expert.

"They were covered with blood. I never knew so much blood came out of a person. It was everywhere. The walls, the floor. I could see Mona was in the next room on the telephone. Then she hung up and walked into my bedroom. I ran around to that window, and it was broken. All my stuff was gone."

"What do you mean 'stuff'?"

"My toys, my clothes, my books, everything. They stole my stuff. She kept looking around my room and frowning."

"What then?"

"She looked up and saw me. She ran out of the house and grabbed me. She took me to the car and we drove away."

"What did she say about it?"

"She started to say that my parents were called away, but I told her I saw them."

"What did she say then?"

"She said that awful things sometimes happen, and a bunch of stuff about how they wanted me to be safe more than anything. I didn't hear a lot of it because I was crying and wasn't really listening."

"Where did she take you?"

"She had a friend. A man. He used to come to the house to pick her up sometimes. She said he was a lawyer. She took me to his house."

"For the record, do you know his name?"

"Dennis."

"Was his last name Morgan?"

"Yes."

"Do you know the name of the street?"

"No. It wasn't anyplace I ever was before. We drove a long time on a big road, and then at the end there were a lot of turns. By then it was night."

"What happened there?"

"She put me to sleep on the couch, but I could hear them talking in the kitchen."

"What did they say?"

"She told him about my parents. She said it looked like an abuttar."

Abattoir, the judge translated. No wonder Nina Coffey was all over Ambrose. This kid had looked in his own window and seen his parents—or the ones he knew as parents—lying on the floor butchered, and Ambrose was asking him about spankings and dental hygiene. The man was a dangerous idiot.

"What did he say?"

"He said she did the right thing to call the police, and the wrong thing to leave. Then she said a lot of things. She said it looked as though whoever came in wasn't even looking for them. They were looking for me."

"What made her say that?"

"They broke into my room at a time when I was usually home and my parents weren't. She said it looked like they tried to make my parents tell them something. And then the only things they took were my stuff, and all the pictures."

"What pictures were those?"

"My father used to take a lot of pictures. Like when we were at the beach . . ." Here it comes, thought the judge. The sob forced its way out, and there was a squealing sound, and then the tears came in volume.

"Come on, Timmy," said Nina Coffey. "Let's go take a break."

Amid the sounds of chairs scraping and feet hitting the floor, Ambrose said redundantly, "Let the record show that we recessed at this point."

There was another click, and the recording began again. "We will continue now. It is six minutes after eleven," said the stenographer.

Ambrose said, "Timmy, I'm sorry to ask so many sad questions."

"It's okay," said the little voice. There was no conviction behind it.

"You were at the lawyer's house. They didn't agree, right?"

"He told her to go to the police. Mona said they would just make me stay in a place where I wouldn't be safe. They talked for a long time, and I fell asleep."

"What happened when you woke up?"

"The lawyer—Dennis—he was talking on the telephone. I couldn't hear what he was saying. When he hung up, he and Mona talked some more. He gave her some money. He had a lot of money inside of books on the bookshelf, and some in his pocket. He gave her that too."

"Then what?"

"The phone rang and Dennis answered it, and talked to somebody else. Then we all got in the car and Dennis drove. This time we drove all night and all the next day, almost. Then we got to Jane's house."

"What is Jane's full name?"

"I don't know."

"Where does she live?"

"I don't know."

"Tell me about her."

"We went to her house. She put us in a room upstairs, and we went to sleep. When I woke up, she made us breakfast. Mona was already awake."

"I mean about Jane. What was she like?"

"I was afraid of her at first."

"Why?"

"She was tall and skinny and had long black hair, and she seemed to listen to people with her eyes."

Ambrose paused. "I see. What did she do?"

"She and Mona talked for a long time. Then I heard her say she would make us disappear."

"Is that why you thought she was scary?"

"No . . . maybe."

"How long did you stay with Jane?"

"A long time. I think Mona said it was three weeks, but it seemed like a year. Then we all got in Jane's car and she drove us to Chicago."

"What did she do then?"

"She stayed for a day or two, and then one morning I woke up and she was gone."

"Was Mona surprised?"

"No. Mona acted like it was normal, and didn't talk about her again. Mona and I lived in Chicago after that. Mona was Diana Johnson, and I was her son. She wanted me to be Andrew, but I didn't like it, so I got to stay Tim."

"How did you live?"

"Like people do."

"I mean, did Mona have a job—did she go to work?"

"Yes. While I was in school."

"They called you Tim Johnson at school?"

"Yes."

"When did you start—what grade?"

"Kindergarten. I had already been in kindergarten, so it was the second time."

"And you're in the second grade now?"

"Yes."

"Were you afraid in Chicago?"

"At first I was. It was different. I was afraid the bad people would get Mona, and then I would be all alone. But after a while I made some friends, and got used to it, and I didn't think about that part much anymore. I was sad sometimes."

"And Mona pretended to be your mother for over two years?"

"I guess so."

"What else did she do? Did she still see anybody you knew from Washington?"

"No. She used to talk on the phone a lot."

"To whom? Jane?"

"No. Dennis."

"Did you ever hear what she said?"

"Once in a while, but it wasn't really okay. She would go in her bedroom and talk to him. Sometimes she would tell me what she said."

"Then a little over a week ago something changed, didn't it?"

"Yes. Everything."

"You found out who you were, didn't you?"

"Yes."

"Excuse me, Mr. Ambrose." It was Schoenfeld's resonant voice again. "Maybe we should let Timmy tell us exactly what happened in his own words from here on. I believe you've done an admirable job in laying the groundwork, but now we're in new territory, and I have no objection to letting Mr. Phillips speak freely and tell us whatever he can that will aid in the possible prosecutions." Of course not, thought the judge. Schoenfeld could be magnanimous. He had already established that Timmy was Mr. Phillips, and nothing else that anyone said or did from there on was of any consequence for Schoenfeld.

"Thank you," said Ambrose. "Timmy, tell us what happened."

"I came home from school, and Mona was there, and so was Dennis the lawyer, and so was Jane. Dennis said he had spent two years trying to figure out why anyone would want to hurt my parents and me, and now he knew."

"This was in Chicago?"

"Yeah," said Timmy. "He told me that when my mother died they had special doctors look at her, and that she had never been to the hospital to have a baby. He said he got to look at a copy of the birth certificate they had at my school, and it wasn't real. He said I wasn't adopted. They just drew a picture of a birth certificate and said it was mine. He said that the reason they did that was because they loved me very much and had always wanted a little boy."

Judge Kramer stopped the tape and backed it up to listen to the last exchange again. It was a hell of a way to explain a kidnapping. In spite of everything, he had to admire Dennis Morgan. After what he had seen, this little boy was going to be an annuity for the psychiatrists for the next fifty years. There was no reason to make it worse.

The tape kept running. "Then he told you about your other parents?"

"Yes. Mr. and Mrs. Phillips. They died when I was one."

"And your grandma?"

"I knew about her already, but I didn't know she had died like all my parents. She had been dead for three years."

"Did Mr. Morgan tell you that she had left you some money?"

"Yeah. He said that when Mr. and Mrs. Phillips died she put all the family money in a big pot and said it could only go to me. And when I was gone she hired a company to take care of the money and keep looking for me forever."

"Did she say what they were called?"

"Trusty."

Judge Kramer prayed that Ambrose wasn't about to drag an eight-year-old on a field trip through a morass of legal terminology. What could the child possibly know about trustees and executors?

"What happened last week to change that? Did he tell you?"

"He said that the Trusty had gotten tired of looking and waiting, and they were going to say I wasn't alive anymore. So he called Jane again."

"I'm very curious about this Jane. I understand about Mona. She was your nanny, and she loved you. The lawyer, Mr. Morgan, was a very close friend of Mona's, right?"

"Yeah. They were going to get married when the people came and got my parents. Then they couldn't because we'd get caught. That was why he looked so hard to find out where I was really supposed to be—so Mona could go back to being Mona and marry him."

"But why was Jane doing it? Did she know your parents?"

"No. Mona had to tell her about them that time when we went to her house. Mona thought they worked for the government, so the people who hurt them must be spies. It took Jane a long time to find out that my parents didn't work for the government."

"Then Jane was Mona's friend?"

"I don't think so. Dennis was the one who called her."

Judge Kramer could imagine the F.B.I. agent. He was going to make his career sorting all this out. Not the least interesting question was why a prominent Washington defense attorney had the telephone number of a woman who made people disappear. They would be going over the record of Morgan's former clients right now to see if there were any on their Most Wanted List.

Even Ambrose seemed to sense that he had crossed the trail of an unfamiliar creature. "The lawyer knew her?" he repeated. "Did he pay her?"

"No. Dennis said he tried, but she had decided that so many people loved me that I must be a fine boy."

"Hmmmm . . ."

Judge Kramer had a vision of Ambrose's raised eyebrows, as he had seen them during cross-examinations.

"Did anybody say anything else about her?"

"Dennis. He said that from then on we had to do everything that Jane said, exactly. It didn't matter what anybody else said, we should listen to her."

"So she was the boss."

"He said that he had done everything he could to find out things, but the only way to solve this was to walk into court and surprise everybody and say who I was. He said the bad people knew I must be alive, so they would be expecting me to come. Jane was the one who knew how to get us past them."

"So you all took an airplane to California?"

"No. Jane said we had to drive all the way or the bad people might see us. Every day we got a new car. She would go to a place where they rented them, and then drive all day and then leave it and rent another one. Then we were in California."

"What then? Did you stay in a hotel?"

"No. Jane said that if people were after me, they would be watching hotels near the courthouse, because they would be expecting us to do that. So we went to the courthouse right away."

"What time was it?"

"About dinnertime. Jane opened the lock on an office and we stayed there all night. I fell asleep on a couch."

"What happened when you woke up?"

"I heard Dennis come into the office. He had been out in the building by himself. He said they had pulled a trick on us, and now we had to go to a different building. So we ran out and got into our car and drove again. Jane said on the way that it didn't feel right."

"Did she say anything else?"

"She asked Dennis if there was any way of doing this besides actually showing up in court. Could we call and ask for a delay or something. He said that he didn't know who was honest and who wasn't. A phone call wouldn't stop the case for sure, but it would tell the bad guys I was coming for sure. Then he said if they fooled the judge they could do something that day, right away. I don't know what. Jane drove for a long time without saying anything. Then she said, 'Is there any way to know what's in the building?' "

"What did she mean by that?"

"She said, 'We want to fade in. If Timmy's the only boy in the crowd, we're in trouble.' She said something about adoption and custody."

"I see," said Ambrose. "Did Mr. Morgan know the answer?"

"We stopped at a phone booth and he looked in the book and made a call. He came back and got into the car and made Jane scoot over, so he could drive. He said he and Mona would be getting a divorce before they got married, and Jane would carry his briefcase like she was their lawyer. But we would go to Courtroom 22 on the fifth floor instead."

"Did Jane agree?"

"At first. But then we got near the courthouse, and Jane said two men in a car were following us. They kept coming faster and faster, and then they tried to get in front of us, and they bumped the car."

"What did Mr. Morgan do?"

"He got all nervous, and kept trying to go fast and keep the car straight. Jane said to him, 'Well? What's it going to be?' and he said, 'I can't get them into the building. It's got to be me.' He was scared. He looked pale and sick and sweaty."

"And Jane?"

"She was quiet. He drove to the parking lot and stopped. Mona kissed him, and Jane yanked me out the door and we started running."

"Did you see what Mr. Morgan did after you were out of the car?"

"I heard this loud bang, and I turned around and it looked like what he had done was go backwards into the other car. One of the men jumped out and started hitting him. He tried to fight but he wasn't good at it. And the other man got out of the car and ran after us, so Dennis tried to tackle him, but the man kicked him, and the first one grabbed him around the neck. I didn't see any more because Jane and Mona and I were running and I tripped, but Jane held my hand and kept me from falling. We ran up the steps."

"Did anyone try to stop you?"

"There was a man on the other side of the glass door, and he saw us and put his foot against it so it wouldn't open. Jane didn't stop. She let go of me and hit it with her shoulder and stuck her purse in it when it opened a little. The man put his arm there to push the purse out, but as soon as his arm was in there she jerked the purse out by the strap and shut the door on his arm. When he pulled the handle to get his arm out, she pushed the door into his face and we ran on."

"Anybody else?"

"There were men right by the elevator, and they started coming toward us. We ran up the stairs. I counted four flights, but there was a door and it only had a two on it. We ran through it, and when we passed the elevator Jane pushed the button and ran to another staircase, and we got up to the third floor. We got to the fourth floor, and we heard a door below us slam open against the wall, and some men were running up after us. Mona was breathing hard and then she was crying too. She touched my arm at the top of the next landing and said, 'This is my stop. Keep going. I love you, Timmy.' "

"What did Jane say?"

"Nothing. She just looked at her, and then we ran up to the fifth floor. Just when we got to the top, I looked back and saw Mona on the stairs. She was holding on to both railings and kicking at these men. I saw one of them reaching out like he was trying to hug her. But right then, the door that said five swung open right in front of us. It was one of the men that was by the elevator. He looked surprised, and Jane just punched him and kept going."

"She hit him in the jaw?" The judge could sense Ambrose's raised eyebrow again.

"No. In the neck. Then we were on the fifth floor, and we ran down this long hallway. When we got to the corner I could see 'TWENTY TO THIRTY' painted on the wall with an arrow pointing to the left, but the door we had used to get there opened up again and three big men were running after us. Jane jerked me around the corner and said, 'Run to the room that says twenty-two. Don't stop for anybody until you're right in the front where the judge sits, and yell, "I'm Timothy Phillips." ' I tried to say something, but she said, 'Don't talk, just run.' "

Judge Kramer pushed the STOP button and sat in his dark office. He had been on the bench when the little boy had burst through the doors and run up the aisle screaming. The bailiff had made a reasonably competent attempt to head him off, but he had actually touched the bench and yelled, "I'm Tim Phillips." What had happened in the hallway Judge Kramer had heard from one of the policemen who had piled out of the adjoining courtrooms to quell the disturbance.

Judge Kramer pressed the intercom button on his telephone.

"Yes, Judge?" came his assistant's voice.

"Where are they holding this 'Jane' woman?"

"I think they took her for medical treatment to County-USC. I'll find out if she's in the jail ward and let you know."

"No," Kramer said. "Just call the precinct and tell them I want to see her."

"Would you like a conference room at the jail?"

"Have them bring her here."

The male police officer was tall and rangy, and the female was short and blond with her hair drawn up in the back and cinched in that way they all knew how to do. The department never had all-male teams transport a female prisoner anymore, so the judge should have been used to it, but the pairs still seemed to him like married couples from a planet where people wore uniforms. They ushered the prisoner into his chambers. When her face came into the light he felt his breath suck in. He had never gotten used to seeing a young woman's face with bruises and cuts and blackened eyes. He tried to see past them.

She was not quite what he had heard described on the tape. She was tall, as tall as he was if he stood up, and this realization made him intuit that it was better not to, so he stayed down behind his big desk. Her hair was black and hung loose to a place below her shoulder blades, but that probably wasn't the way she wore it; they had combed it out because they always searched women's hair. He could see that Timmy's description was not wrong, just uninformed. This woman had the strange, angular beauty he associated with fashion models: it was striking, but geometric and cold. The judge's taste ran more to women like his late wife and the little policewoman, who looked round and soft and warm. The woman's hands were cuffed in front of her instead of behind, which meant they weren't taking all the precautions, but the police officers were wary: the policewoman kept a hand at her left elbow, and the man was a step behind and to her right, leaving just enough room to swing his club.

Judge Kramer said, "Thank you very much, officers. We've got some coffee in the outer office, and I keep soft drinks in the little refrigerator under the water cooler. I'll be finished with the prisoner in about fifteen minutes."

The policewoman said, "Your Honor, we should mention—"

He interrupted, "I know. I spoke with the arresting officer. Has she hurt anyone since she's been in custody?"

"No."

"Then I'll chance it."

The prisoner held out her hands, and the male officer unlocked the cuffs, took them off, and said to no one in particular, "We'll be right outside."

When they had closed the door, Judge Kramer said to her, "Sit down, please."

The woman sat in the chair in front of the desk.

Judge Kramer probed for a way to break the silence. "I hear you're one of those people who could kill me with a pencil."

She said simply, "If I am, then I wouldn't need a pencil." She looked at the tape recorder on his desk. "Is that running?"

He said, "I want to assure you that no record will be made of this conversation. I just listened to a deposition of Timothy Phillips, and I decided that the only person left who can answer the questions I have is you. Mona Turley and Dennis Morgan are dead."

She nodded silently and watched him.

"What do you know about the child's situation?"

"Who are you? Why are you the one who has questions?"

His eyes widened involuntarily, as though someone had thrown a glass of water in his face. "I'm sorry," he said. "When you've been a judge for a few years, you're used to being the only one in the room everyone takes at face value. My name is John Kramer. I'm the judge who was presiding in Courtroom 22. We hadn't gotten to the petition to declare Timothy Phillips legally dead when he ran in and disrupted my court. For the moment, the matter is still undecided, and I've left it that way."

"Why?"

"First I had to recess while the officers took you away. Then I had to adjourn for a few days to give time to the authorities who can verify Timothy's claim. In a day or

so, oddly enough, I have to set a date to give the petitioners the opportunity to refute the claim—fingerprints,
blood tests, and all. Then I have to rule on it."

"Will you be the one who decides what happens to him
after that?"

He shook his head. "Not directly. At the moment he's
in the care of a very protective woman from Children's
Services named Nina Coffey. After a time there will be
criminal cases—probably several of them. There will be a
family court case to decide who is granted guardianship
of Timmy. There will be some sort of civil action to
settle the disposition of the trust. I can influence the
direction some of those cases take if I find out the truth
and get it on the record so it can't be ignored. I'm asking
what you know because I don't have much time and I
need to know where to begin. Once I rule on the petition
that's before me, it's out of my hands."

"Is any of this legal?"

"What I'm doing is so contrary to legal procedure that
it has no name."

She sat erect in the chair and met his gaze steadily
while she decided. "He was a ward of his grandmother
because his parents were killed in a car crash. She was
old at the time—about eighty. Whoever she hired to
watch him didn't. Along came Raymond and Emily
Decker, and he disappeared. I have no way of knowing
what was going on in their minds at the time. They may
have been kidnappers who stalked him from birth, or
they may have been one of those half-crazy couples who
create their own little world that doesn't need to incorpo-
rate all of the facts in front of their eyes. If you read the
old newspaper reports, it sounds as though maybe they
just found him wandering around alone in a remote area

of a county park, picked him up, and then convinced themselves that he was better off with them than with anybody who let a two-year-old get that lost. I've tried to find out, and so did Mona and Dennis, but what we learned was full of contradictions."

"What sorts of contradictions?"

"Timmy says they sent pictures of him to his grandmother, sometimes holding a newspaper, sometimes with his fingerprints. He doesn't know what the letters said. If the Deckers knew where to send the letters, then they knew who he was. But I can't tell whether it was a straight ransom demand or they were trying to keep him officially alive so he could claim his inheritance when he grew up, or whether they were just being kind to an old lady by letting her know her grandson was okay."

"What do you know about the grandmother?"

"From what Dennis Morgan said, the police stopped looking. That means they never saw the letters. Grandma kept looking, so maybe she got them. She must have believed he would turn up eventually, because she tied up all the family money in a living trust for him and made a business-management firm named Hoffen-Bayne the trustee. She died a few years ago."

"Before or after Raymond and Emily Decker?"

"Before. But I'm not the best source for dates and addresses. I'm sure if you don't have it in the papers on your desk yet, it'll be in the next batch. Anyway, I don't think she hired somebody to kill them for kidnapping her grandson."

"You're the only source of information I have right now. Who did kill them?"

"I don't know."

"Who do you *think* did it?"

"When someone killed the Deckers, they also stole all of Timmy's belongings, every picture of him, and a lot of paper. If you're looking for somebody, you would want the photographs. But they took his toys, clothes, everything. That's a lot of work. The only reason I can think of for doing that is to hide the fact that he was alive—that a little boy lived there. Maybe they did such a good job of wiping off their own prints that they got all of his too, as a matter of course. I doubt it."

"Who would want to accomplish that?"

She hesitated, and he could tell she was preparing to be disbelieved. "What I'm telling you is not from personal knowledge. It's what Dennis Morgan told me. This company, Hoffen-Bayne, got to administer a fortune of something like a hundred million dollars. They would get a commission of at least two percent a year, or two million, for that. They also got to invest the money any way they pleased, and that gave them power. There are some fair-sized companies you can control for that kind of investment. As long as Timmy was lost, the trust would continue. You're a judge. You tell me what would happen if Timmy turned up in California."

"The court would—will—appoint a guardian, and probably in this case, a conservator, if you're right about the size of the inheritance."

"That wouldn't be Hoffen-Bayne?"

"We don't appoint business-management companies to raise children, or to audit themselves."

"Then the power and money would be in jeopardy."

"Certainly they would have to at least share the control."

"And they did try to have him declared dead."

"That's a legal convenience. It relieves them of responsibility to search for him, and also protects them if someone were to ask later why they're administering a trust for a client who hasn't been seen for seven years."

"Then it would have been even more convenient if he were really dead. They wouldn't have had to go to court at all."

"Filing a motion is a little different from hiring assassins to hunt down a six-year-old and kill him."

"Maybe. I think filing the motion was a trap. I think Dennis Morgan was poking around, and somebody noticed it. It's not all that hard to find out what you want about people; the trick is to keep them from knowing you're doing it. Dennis was a respected lawyer, but investigating wasn't his field; lawyers hire people to do that. I think they sensed that if a Washington attorney was interested, then Timmy was going to turn up sometime soon."

"And you—all of you—got caught in the trap?"

"Yes." She stood up. "You asked me what I think, so you would know where to begin. I've told you. Dennis couldn't find anybody but Hoffen-Bayne who would benefit from Timmy's death—no competing claims to the money or angry relatives, for instance. Nobody tried to break the will during all the years while Timmy was missing. But I don't know what Dennis got right and what he got wrong, and I can't prove any of it. I only saw the police putting handcuffs on four of the men in the courthouse, and there won't be anything on paper that connects them with Hoffen-Bayne or anybody else. I know I never saw them before, so I can't have been the one they recognized. They saw Timmy." She took a step toward the door. "Keep him safe."

The judge said, "Then there's you." He watched her stop and face him. "Who are you?"

"Jane Whitefield."

"I mean what's your interest in this?"

"Dennis Morgan asked me to keep Timmy alive. I did that. We all did that."

"What are you? A private detective, a bodyguard?"

"I'm a guide."

"What kind of guide?"

"I show people how to go from places where someone is trying to kill them to other places where nobody is."

"What sort of pay do you get for this?"

"Sometimes they give me presents. I declare the presents on my income taxes. There's a line for that."

"Did somebody give you a present for this job?"

"If you fail, there's nobody around to be grateful. My clients are dead." After a second she added, "I don't take money from kids, even rich kids."

"Have you served in your capacity as 'guide' for Dennis Morgan before?"

"Never met him until he called. He was a friend of a friend."

"You—all three of you—went into this knowing that whoever was near this little boy might be murdered."

She looked at him as though she were trying to decide whether he was intelligent or not. Finally, she said, "An innocent little boy is going to die. You're either somebody who will help him or somebody who won't. For the rest of your life you'll be somebody who did help him or somebody who didn't."

The judge stared down at his desk for a few seconds, his face obscured by the deep shadows. When he looked up, his jaw was tight. "You are a criminal. The system hates people like you. It has special teeth designed to grind you up."

As she watched him, she could see his face begin to set like a death mask. He pressed his intercom button. "Tell the officers to come in." He began to write, filling in lines on a form on his desk.

The two police officers swung the door open quickly and walked inside. The man had his right hand resting comfortably on the handle of the club in his belt.

The judge said, "I've finally straightened this out. Her real name is Mahoney. Colleen Anne Mahoney. She was attacked by those suspects on the way into the courthouse. Apparently it was a case of mistaken identity, because she had no connection with the Phillips case. I'm giving you a release order now, and I want all records—prints, photographs, and so on—sealed . . . no, destroyed. Call me when it's been done." He handed the female officer the paper. "I want to avoid any possibility of reprisals."

"Will do, Judge," said the policewoman. Kramer's instinct about her was confirmed. She had a cute little smile.

The policeman opened the door for Jane Whitefield, but this time nobody touched her. She didn't move. "You should have those teeth checked."

He shrugged. "The system was never meant to rule on every human action. Some things slip through."

She stared at him for a second, then said simply and without irony, "Thank you, Your Honor," turned, and walked out of his office.

2

Jane Whitefield drove her rental car down Fairfax past the high school, the old delicatessens and small grocery stores and the shops that sold single items like luggage or lamps, beyond the big white CBS buildings and then into the hot asphalt parking lot at Farmers' Market, where she found refuge from the Southern California sun in the cool shadow between two tour buses. The market was crowded on Saturdays, and it took her a few minutes of threading her way among the hundreds of preoccupied people to find the pet store. There were two glass enclosures out front where puppies lay sleeping with their smooth little potbellies in the air.

She bought two cubical birdcages that had one side that could be opened for cleaning, and a two-pound bag of bird feed that was peppered with sunflower seeds. She walked across the market to a craft store where people bought kits for making bead jewelry. She drove out of the market and headed northward toward the hills, but then stopped only a few blocks up when she saw a secondhand store that looked as though it might have the right kind of teddy bear. Then she drove the winding road over Laurel Canyon to the San Fernando Valley, and on across the flats to the campus of the California

State University at Northridge. She had been past the school once years ago, and carried a picture of it in her mind. It was the right kind of habitat.

Jane had not done this in years, but she was very good at it. She drove around the nearly empty campus until she found a long drive with a row of tall eucalyptus trees beside it and a few acres of model orchard beyond them. She parked her car in the small faculty parking lot behind some kind of science building and carried her cages to the eucalyptus trees. Nearly everyone on campus seemed to be in a library or dormitory, so she had the luxury of silence while she worked.

She propped open the sides of the cages with sticks that had fallen from the trees, took the food cups from their slots on the bars and filled them with bird feed, then ran thin jewelry wire from the cups to the sticks. She balanced a stone on the open wall of each cage so it would come down fast and stay shut. She sprinkled a handful of bird feed over the carpet of fallen eucalyptus leaves in front of the cages, and went for a walk. She used her sense of the geography of university campuses to find the Student Union, and sat at a table in the shade of a big umbrella at the edge of a terrace to drink a cup of lemonade.

Even at this time of year, Southern California seemed to her to be parched and inhospitable. The broad lawns in public places like this were still a little yellow and sparse from the eight-month-long summer, with its hundred-degree stretches. Back home people would be telling each other stories about years they remembered when the snow didn't stop until May, and wondering if this would be another one. When her lemonade was finished she walked back across the campus to the row of eucalyptus trees. Before she turned the corner of the science building she heard a squawk, and then some fluttering, and she thought about the difference between birds and human beings. No matter how many times it had been done, each new generation of birds flew into the trap as though it had never before happened on earth. Maybe they weren't so different.

She approached the traps, but they didn't look the way she had expected. One of them was just as she had left it, and the other one had two big blue scrub jays in it together. When she moved closer she could see that one was a male and the other female, slightly smaller with more brown on top and less blue. As she stepped to the cage, the questions began. *"Jree?"* asked the male. *"Jree?"* The female scolded, *"Check check check!"*

They weren't like the birds at home, but they were quick and greedy for survival, so territorial and aggressive that they had probably crowded in together without hesitation. It was too late in the year for them to be feeding hatchlings, and having one of each seemed right. They were already mated.

She poured in some more seed to give them something to think about, lifted the cage, put it in the back seat of the car, and covered it with a silk blouse from her suitcase.

Jane drove to the county office building and wiped her face clean of the thick makeup she had been using to hide the bruises, then walked to the Department of Children's Services. The people in the office were busy in a way that showed they had given up hope of ever doing all they were supposed to do but were keeping on in the belief that if they worked hard enough they would accomplish some part of it. There were two empty desks for each one that had a person behind it, so they moved from one to another picking up telephones and slipping files in and out of the piles like workers tending machines in a factory. She waited for a minute, then saw a woman hang up her telephone and pause to make a note in a file.

Jane stepped forward. "Excuse me," she said. "I need to leave something for Nina Coffey."

The woman's eyes rolled up over the rim of her glasses and settled on Jane; her head, which was still bent over the papers on the desk, never moved. Jane could tell that her bruises had identified her as an abused mother. "How can I help you?"

"It's this teddy bear," said Jane. "Timmy Phillips left it in my car."

The woman showed no recognition of the name. She snatched a gummed sticker out of the top drawer and put her pen to it. "Spell it," she said.

"P-H-I-L-L-I-P-S. I'd appreciate it if you got it to her, because it's important to Timmy." Jane handed the woman the small, worn brown teddy bear.

The woman turned her sharp gaze through the glasses at the bear. "I can see that," she said. "Don't worry. I'll give it to her."

"Thanks," said Jane warmly.

The telephone rang and the woman held up one finger to signal that Jane was to wait while she answered it, but Jane turned away. She heard the woman call, "Mrs. Phillips?" but she was out the door.

Jane waited down the street from the parking garage. She had seen the row where the employees' parking spaces were, and now she parked at the curb where she could watch them.

It was not long before she saw the woman she had been waiting for. Nina Coffey was in her forties and very

slight with red hair that was fading into a gray that muted
it. Jane saw that she had the habit of holding her keys in
one fist when she came out of the elevator, so she suspected that this was a woman whose profession had
given her a clear-eyed view of the planet she was living
on. In her other hand she held a hard-sided briefcase and
a teddy bear.

Jane waited for her to start her car, drive to the exit,
and move off down the street before she pulled her own
car out from among the others along the block. She followed Nina Coffey at a distance, and strung two other
cars between them so she wouldn't get too accustomed to
the sight of Jane's. Coffey turned expertly a couple of
times, popped around a corner and then up onto a freeway ramp, and Jane was glad she had put the other cars
between them so that she had time to follow in the unfamiliar city.

She pushed into the traffic and over to the same lane
that Coffey chose and stayed there, letting a couple of
other cars slip in between them again. Coffey turned off
the freeway in a hilly area that the signs said was in
Pasadena, and Jane had to move closer. There seemed to
be stoplights at every intersection, and Nina Coffey was
an aggressive driver who had a knack for timing them.
After the third one, Jane had to stop while Coffey dimin-
ished into the distance. She turned right, then left, then
sped up five blocks of residential streets that had no
lights, turned left, then right again to come out three
blocks behind her.

Finally Nina Coffey came to a street where she had to
wait to make a left turn, and Jane caught up with her
again. When Coffey stopped in front of a modest two-
story house with a brick facade, Jane kept going. As she

passed, she studied the car that blocked the driveway and knew it was the right house. The car was a full-sized Chevrolet painted a blue as monotonous as a police uniform.

The authorities had done exactly as Jane had hoped they would. They were protecting Timmy from everybody, without distinction—the people who wanted him declared dead, the reporters, people who were sure to search the family tree to suddenly discover they were relatives—and without comment. They had put Timmy in the home of a cop while the mess around him was sorted out.

She spent fifteen minutes driving around the neighborhood to look for signs that anyone else had found the house. She saw no parked cars with heads in them, no nearby houses with too many blinds drawn, and no male pedestrians between twenty and fifty. She came back out on Colorado Boulevard satisfied and drove up two streets before she found the place where she wanted to park her car.

She had to climb over the fence at the back of the yard and crouch in the little cinderblock enclosure where the pool motor droned away and stare in the back window until she saw Timmy. She watched him eat his dinner in the kitchen with two other children, and then begin to climb the carpeted stairway to the second floor. Upstairs, a light went on for a few minutes and then went out. The other children weren't much older than Timmy was but they were still downstairs. She supposed he was still living on Chicago time, where it was two hours later.

The sun was low when Jane decided how she would do it. She walked quietly to the back of the house. In a moment she was up the fig tree and on the roof of the garage. She walked across it to a second-floor window of the house, tied a length of the jewelry wire into a loop, inserted it between the window and the sill, and slowly twirled it until she had it around the latch. She gave a sharp tug to open the latch, quietly slid the window up, and slipped into the upstairs hallway.

When she opened the bedroom door Timmy was lying on his side looking at her, his coffee-with-cream eyes reflecting a glint of the light coming from the hallway, his child-blond hair already in unruly tufts from burrowing into the pillow. Somebody had bought him a new pair of pajamas with pictures of fighter planes in a dogfight all over them, and had at least looked at him closely enough to be sure they fit his long legs. He held the teddy bear on the sheet beside him. "Jane?" he said.

"Hello, Timmy," she whispered. "Can't sleep?"

"I'm tired, but it's still light, and I keep thinking about them. Mona and Dennis."

"I thought you might want to go to their funeral."

"I did want to, but they said I couldn't."

"So we'll have our own."

The shadows of the trees at the edge of the vast cemetery were already merging into the dusk, but the sky to the west had a reddish glow. Jane had sent two big displays of white roses in case she and Timmy arrived after dark, but the flowers weren't necessary. It was still light enough to find the two fresh graves on the hillside.

The bodies of Dennis and Mona would be shipped to London and Washington for burial, but Jane had searched the funeral notices in the newspaper and found a pair of brothers who had been killed in a car accident and had been buried today. As they walked up the hill Timmy said, "What are we going to do?"

Jane shrugged. "We can only do what we know. The kind of funeral I know best is the kind my family did for my father, my mother, and my grandparents."

They stopped at the head of the graves. Jane said, "One thing we always did was to have close friends or relatives say something to them."

"How?"

"Just talk to them."

Timmy looked down at the two mounds of dirt for a moment, then said, "I don't know what to say."

"Then I'll go first," Jane said. "Dennis and Mona? We're here to say goodbye to you, and to tell you that there are people who know and understand who you were and what you did. We saw it. You spent your lives protecting and caring for people who needed help: little children, and people who were going to court and didn't have anybody to speak for them. You died fighting enemies you knew were bigger and stronger, trying to give us time. We're here because we want you to see that we're okay. You won." She nudged Timmy. "Ready to say something?"

Timmy said, "Mona, I'll . . . I'll miss you. It's lonely here. I didn't know you weren't coming back. I would have said something . . ." His voice trailed off.

"What would you have said?" asked Jane.

"I . . . guess . . . 'I love you.' "

"That's good."

"And I would have thanked her. But I can't now. It's too late."

"You just did," said Jane. "Those are the two things that had to be said."

Jane knelt on the grass and used her hands to dig a hole

in the soft mound of earth over the first grave. Then she reached into her purse.

"What are you doing now?"

"Well, the Old People believed that after somebody died, he had to make a long trip to a place where he would be happy all the time. They figured it took a long time to get there, so they tried to give him presents that would make the trip easier. Weapons, food, that kind of thing."

She held up a new Mont Blanc fountain pen and said, "This is like the one Dennis carried in his briefcase, but the police have that. We'll let it stand for the weapon." She pulled out a credit card and put it beside the pen. "This is the way people travel now."

At the other grave she dug a second hole and placed a credit card and four granola bars in the bottom.

"What's that?" asked Timmy.

"Mona wasn't the sort of person who thought much of weapons. She loved to feed people, so she would like this better." Jane stood and brushed the dirt off her hands. "Now cover them up."

As Timmy worked to pack the dirt over the little holes, Jane went to the car and brought back the birdcage.

"What's in there?"

She took the blouse off the cage and the scrub jays glared around them suspiciously, the white streaks above their shining black eyes looking like raised eyebrows.

"Birds!" said Timmy.

"The Old People did this, so maybe it works." She spoke to the birds. "Mr. and Mrs. Bird, we have the souls here of two very brave and noble people. They had a lot of reasons why they must have wanted to run away from danger, because they loved each other very much, just like you do. But they did the hard thing instead. I want you to carry them up to Hawenneyugeh. Will you do it?"

The birds jumped back and forth on the perches calling *"Check-check-check,"* uneasy about the low level of the sun.

Jane said, "Mona, it's time to go. Have a short trip. You did your work well. You were a wonderful woman." She grasped the female scrub jay gently, holding her on her back and stroking her breast feathers as she stood over the grave, then tossed her into the sky. She fluttered about and then flew fifty feet to light on a limb of a magnolia tree.

Jane reached into the cage again and caught the male. "Dennis," she said, "you were a great fighter. Now I wish you peace. Mona is waiting."

The scrub jay flew up and joined the female on the branch of the magnolia. They looked down at Jane and Timmy for a few seconds as though they wanted to be sure there was no plan afoot to molest them further, then flew off to the west toward either the setting sun or the college campus.

"Goodbye," said Timmy. He waved as the birds flew, and kept waving long after they were invisible.

"Ready to go now?"

"I guess so."

They walked back to the car in silence, got inside, and coasted down the hill and out of the cemetery.

"Do you think they heard us?" asked Timmy.

"There's no way to know," said Jane. "The Old People will tell you that they do. What I think is that it doesn't really matter. Funerals aren't for the dead."

"They're not?"

"They're for us, the ones who have to go on."

"You did all this for me, didn't you?"

"For you and for me." She drove on for a few seconds, then admitted, "But mostly for you. For somebody your age you've seen a lot of heartache. Some of it you don't remember already, but you'll remember this. I wanted to be sure you remember it right."

"What should I remember?"

"That you got to live when there were still heroes. Real heroes that feel scared and bleed, and that's the part that gets left out of the books. That's a privilege. Nobody has to read you a story. You saw it."

"I wish they hadn't done it," said Timmy.

"Me too."

Timmy started to cry. At first it was just a welling of tears, but Jane knew the rest of the tears that he had been too exhausted to cry were behind them. She drove to the freeway and kept going beyond Pasadena into bare and unfamiliar hills. After half an hour Timmy stopped crying, and Jane drove until he spoke again. "What's going to happen? They're all gone."

"You don't have to worry about that, because some very smart people are spending all their time taking care of it. Judge Kramer said the court would study your story, learn all they can about you, and appoint somebody to take care of you."

"Will it be you?"

"No," she said. "It will be a family. Somebody like the people you're staying with now. Are they nice?"

"Yes," he said.

Jane let out a breath before she realized she had been holding it. "Well, I've got to get you back there so you can get some sleep."

"Will I see you?"

"Probably not for a long time."

She drove back to Pasadena and parked behind the street where the policeman and his family lived. She climbed to the top of the fence, lifted Timmy and lowered him to the lawn. She could see that the other two children were still watching television downstairs. She led him to the tree, hoisted him to her back, and climbed. When they walked to the open window, Timmy was seized with a panic. "I don't want you to leave."

"I have to, Timmy," she said.

"But what am I going to do? I mean after you're gone."

Jane hesitated, then accepted the fact that she had to try. "Go to school. Make friends. Play games. Try to grow up strong and decent and healthy. That's plenty to do for now." She helped him in the window and sat on his bed while he put on his pajamas.

"But what happens after that? What will I be then?"

"I think that's why it takes so much time to grow up. You don't really make a decision; you just find out when the time comes."

"What would you do?"

Jane shook her head and smiled sadly. "I'm not a good one to ask."

"Who is?"

Jane had an urge to tell him everything she knew, because this would be the last time. No words came into her mind that were of any use, but she had to push him in the right direction. "Well, when I was in college I knew a boy who was in a position sort of like yours. He didn't know what to do, but he knew that if he wasn't careful, he would be lazy and wasteful and selfish."

"What did he decide?"

"He decided to become a doctor. It was the hardest

thing he could think of to be, so he knew that would force him to study. And when he had done enough studying, he would know how to do something worthwhile. At the time I thought he was being very sensible. I still can't find anything wrong with the idea."

"Is he a doctor now?"

"As it happens, he is, but that isn't the point. The real reward was that he got to be the kind of person he wanted to be. It doesn't matter whether he ended up a doctor or something else. He had decided to try. That made him special."

There were noises. She heard the first complaints from little voices downstairs. The children were being sent to bed.

"I've got to go now or I'll get caught," she said. She leaned down and kissed his cheek. "Sleep well, Timmy. Remember that people have loved you before and others will love you again, because you're worth it."

As she slipped out the window she heard a whisper. "Jane?"

"Yes?" She stopped and leaned on the sill.

"Thanks for the bear. I knew it was from you."

"I thought you would."

"Are you one of the people? The ones who love me?"

"Of course I am."

"Will you marry me?"

"Sure."

She drifted across the garage roof like a shadow, and seemed to Timmy to fly down the tree without moving a leaf. He watched the back fence, but even in the light of the moon he didn't see her go over it. After listening for a few minutes, he fell asleep.

3

Jane returned the car to the airport rental lot and caught the shuttle bus to the terminal. As she stepped off, she smiled perfunctorily at the efficient skycap offering to check her luggage through to her destination and shook her head. She didn't have luggage and she didn't have a destination. She had made a stop at a Salvation Army office on the way to the airport and disposed of the clothes that had remained in her suitcase that weren't torn or bloodstained, and then had donated the suitcase too. She had known that she would never wear any of the clothes again because they would have reminded her of all that had happened.

She had spent her three days in the county jail ruminating on failure, and her nights remembering the faces of dead people. She should have been quick-witted enough to save Mona and Dennis. There had to be some better way to stop a court case. If nothing else had come to mind, she should have called in a bomb threat to make the police evacuate the courthouse, then arrived during the confusion and attached Timmy and Mona to a squad of policemen. She had not thought clearly because she was so busy trying to get Timmy to the building on time;

she had not seen the ambush because she was too busy dragging her clients into it.

In the nighttime, after a day of reliving her failure in her mind, gripped by the shock over and over again as each of her mistakes was repeated, old ghosts crept into her cell. The one she knew best was Harry the gambler. She had hidden him, then made the mistake of believing that the man who had been his friend would not also be his killer. Harry had visited her so often over the years that he had almost become part of her.

One of the ghosts was a man she had never met. She kept remembering the newspaper picture of John Doe. The police artists had needed to touch it up so much that it was more a reconstruction than a photograph. A cop had found him three years ago sprawled among the rocks below River Road. He had five thousand dollars in cash sewn into his suit, a pair of eyeglasses with clear glass lenses, a brand-new hairpiece that didn't match his own hair, and three bullet holes in his head. Jane had watched the newspapers for months, but the police had never learned who he had been or why he was running. Maybe he had not been trying to reach her; perhaps he was just heading for the Canadian border. But his death within a few miles of her house still haunted her.

On the third day in jail, one of the ghosts came to life. The guards had let Jane out into the exercise yard with the other prisoners and she had seen Ellery Robinson. Years ago Jane had taken Ellery Robinson's sister Clarice out of the world to escape a boyfriend who was working his way up to killing her. Jane could remember Ellery's eyes when she had tried to talk her into disappearing with her sister. Ellery had said, "No, thank you. He's got nothing to do with me." For the next few years

Jane had often thought about those clear, innocent eyes. Ellery had waited a couple of days while Jane got Clarice far away, then killed the boyfriend. Later Jane had made quiet inquiries for Clarice and learned that Ellery's life sentence meant she would serve four to six years.

After the six years, Jane had kept the memory quiet by imagining Ellery Robinson out of the state prison and living a tolerable life. But here she was, back in county jail. In that moment ten or twelve years ago when Jane had not thought of the right argument, not said the right words, not read the look in those eyes, Ellery Robinson's life had slipped away. Jane looked at her once across the vast, hot blacktop yard, but if Ellery Robinson recognized her, no hint of it reached her face. After that, Jane had not gone out to the yard again. Instead she had sat on her bunk and thought about Timothy Phillips.

As she stepped into the airport terminal she had a sudden, hollow feeling in her stomach. She still had not freed herself of the urge to take Timmy with her. She had recognized the madness of the idea as soon as she had formulated it. The whole purpose of this trip had been to bring Timmy under the protection of the authorities. They weren't going to let him disappear again easily. Even if she succeeded in getting him away, it might be exactly the wrong thing to do. It might make her feel as though she had not abandoned him, but Timmy would lose all that money, and with it, the protection. Maybe in ten years he would hate her for it—if he lived ten years. Jane had not even been good enough to keep Mona and Dennis alive. No, Timmy was better off where he was, with the cops and judges and social workers. She was tired, beaten. It was time to go home, stop interfering, and give the world a vacation from Jane Whitefield.

She walked to the counter and bought a ticket for New York City because it was the right direction and there were so many flights that she didn't expect to have to wait long to get moving again. She used a credit card that said Margaret Cerillo. As the man at the counter finished clicking the keys of the computer and waited for the machine to print out the ticket, she noticed his eyes come up, rest on Jane's face for an instant, and then move away too fast. Jane explained, "I had a little car accident yesterday. Some idiot took a wide left turn on La Cienega and plowed right into me." The last time she had looked, the makeup had covered her injuries well enough, but with the heat and the hurry, the scrapes and bruises must be showing through.

"It must have been . . . painful," said the man.

"Pretty bad," said Jane. She took the ticket and credit card and walked up the escalator and through the row of metal detectors. She kept going along the concourse until she found an airport shop that had a big display of cosmetics. She selected an opaque foundation that matched her skin tone and some powder and eye shadow. When she caught a glimpse of herself in the mirror at the top of a revolving display, she reached below it and picked out a pair of sunglasses with brown-tinted lenses. Then she took her purchases with her into the ladies' room. Her face was still hot and tender from the punches she had taken, and her right hand was aching from the hard blows she had given the men in the hallway, but a little discomfort was better than being noticed.

She looked under the stalls and found she was alone. She was glad, because she wouldn't have to pretend that what she was doing was easy. She leaned close to the mirror and dabbed on the foundation painfully. The result looked tolerable, but it stung for a few seconds. She stopped until the pain subsided a little, and had just begun to work on her eyes when she heard the door open and a pair of high heels cross the floor behind her. She had a pretty vivid black eye from the big guy with the yellow tie who had piled in at the end. It was hard to cover it and make both eyes look the same with a hand that hurt.

"Can I help you with that?"

Jane didn't turn around, just moved her head a little to verify what she guessed about the woman behind her in the mirror. She wasn't surprised that the woman was attractive. Makeup was a personal issue—not quite a secret, but almost—and you had to be pretty spectacular to have the nerve to tell somebody you could do her makeup better than she could. This one was tall—almost as tall as Jane—and almost as thin, but her face had that blushing china-figurine skin that women like her somehow kept into their forties. They were always blond, or became blond, like this one. Every last one of them had switched to tennis after their cheerleading coaches had put them out to pasture, but they must have played it at night, because their skin looked as though it had never seen sunlight.

Jane said, "No, thanks. I can handle the painting. It's the repairs that are hard."

"You don't remember me, do you?" There was tension in the voice.

"No," said Jane. "If I should, then you must be good at this. Maybe I should let you do my makeup after all."

The woman whispered, "I was in the county jail when you were."

Jane turned to look at the woman more closely, this time

with a sense that she ought to be watching her hands, not her face. "Well, congratulations on getting out."

Jane waited for her to leave, but the woman just smiled nervously and waited too. "Thanks."

Jane decided that she could do the finishing touches in another ladies' room or even on the plane. "Well, I've got a plane to catch."

"No, you don't. It doesn't leave for an hour. Four-nineteen to New York. I'm on it too. My name is Mary Perkins."

"Are you following me?"

"I was hoping to do better than that."

"What do you mean?"

"There's not much to talk about when you're in jail. There was a girl who had been in court when you were arrested. There was a rumor you had hidden somebody. That sounded interesting, so I asked around to find some-body who could introduce us, but sure enough, all of a sudden they were letting you go under another name. How you managed that I don't want to know."

"You don't?"

"No. I want you to do it for me."

"Why?"

"When I got arrested there were some men follow-ing me. That was thirty days ago. I just saw two of them here."

"Why do they want you?"

The woman gave her a look that was at once pleading and frustrated. "Please, I don't have time to tell you my life story and you don't have time to listen to it right now. I have to get out of Los Angeles now—today—only they're already here, and it can't be a coincidence. They're looking for me."

"But who are you?"

"The short answer is that I'm a woman who needs to disappear and has the money to pay whatever it is you usually get for your services."

Jane felt exhausted and defeated. Her head, face, hands, and wrists were throbbing and weak. She looked at the woman who called herself Mary Perkins, and the sight of her face made Jane tired. She had said almost nothing, but Jane was already picking up signs in her eyes and mouth that she had lied about something. She was genuinely afraid, so she probably wasn't just some sort of bait placed in the airport by the people Jane had fought outside the courtroom. But if men were following her at all, they were undoubtedly policemen. Jane thought, No. Not now. I'm not up to this. Aloud, she said, "Sorry."

"Please," said the woman. "How much do you want?"

"Nothing. You have the wrong person. Mistaken identity."

Mary Perkins looked into Jane's eyes, and Jane could see that she was remembering that Jane was injured. "Oh," the woman said softly. "I understand." She turned and walked toward the door.

As she opened the door, Jane said, "Good luck." Mary Perkins didn't seem to hear her.

Jane looked at her face in the mirror. The bruises were covered, but the thick makeup felt like a mask. When she put the glasses on, they reminded her that the side of her nose had been scraped by the buttons on the big guy's sleeve when he missed with the first swing.

She walked out to the concourse and strolled along it with the crowds until she was near Gate 72. She saw the woman sitting there pretending to read a magazine. If she was being hunted, it was a stupid thing to do. Jane walked closer to the television set where they posted flight information. Mary Perkins's eyes focused on Jane, and then flicked to her left. Jane appreciated not being stared at, but then the eyes came back to her, widened emphatically, and flicked again to the left. Jane stopped for a moment, opened her purse, turned her head a little as though she were looking for something and studied the two men to Mary Perkins's left. If they were hunters they were doing a fairly good job of keeping Mary Perkins penned in and panicky. The short one was sitting quietly reading a newspaper about fifty feet from Mary Perkins, and the big one was pretending to look out the big window at the activity on the dark runway. She could see he was watching the reflection instead, but that wasn't unusual. Her eyes moved down to the briefcase at his feet. It was familiar, the kind they sold in the gift shop where she had bought the makeup.

The smaller man had no carry-on luggage. He sat quietly with his newspaper, not looking directly at Mary Perkins. He had to be the cut-off man, the one she wasn't supposed to notice at all until the other man came for her and she bolted. They couldn't be cops, or they would already have her. She had already bought her ticket, and a plane ticket was proof of intent to flee.

Jane felt spent and hopeless. She admitted to herself that if she got home safely she would find herself tomorrow going to a newsstand and picking up a *Los Angeles Times* and the New York papers to look for a story about a woman's body being found in a field. These two were going to follow Mary Perkins until, inevitably, she found herself alone.

Jane walked back down the concourse, raising her eyes

to look at the television monitors where the departing flights were posted, never raising her head and never slowing down. By the time she had passed the third monitor she had made her selection. There was a Southwestern Airlines flight leaving for Las Vegas five minutes after the flight to New York. She went down the escalator, walked to the ticket counter and paid cash for two tickets to Las Vegas for Monica Weissman and Betty Weissman. Then she returned to the gate where Mary Perkins was waiting. She sat down a few seats from her, counted to five hundred, then stood up again.

She walked close to Mary Perkins on the way to the ladies' room. As she did, she waggled her hand behind her back, away from the two watchers.

She waited inside the ladies' room in front of the mirror until Mary Perkins came in. "Did you check any luggage onto the plane for New York?"

"I don't have any," said Mary Perkins. "As soon as I got out I came here."

"Good," said Jane. "When we get out of here, stay close but don't look at me. You never saw me before. One of those guys will be standing between you and the exits. The other one will have moved to a place where he can see his buddy signal him." She handed Mary Perkins the ticket for Las Vegas.

She looked down at the ticket. "Las Vegas? How does this change anything?"

"Just listen. When it's time to board, one of them will go to a telephone to tell somebody at the other end that you're on the plane. It's a five-hour flight with a stop in Chicago, and that gives them time to do everything but dig your grave before we get there. The other will sit tight until the last minute."

"But what are we going to do? What's the plan?"

Jane looked at her wearily. "The plan is to go to Las Vegas and make them think you've gone to New York. Now give me about the time it takes to sing the national anthem before you come out. Then go sit where you sat before."

Jane swung the door open. Instead of looking toward the waiting area, she glanced behind her for the one watching the exit. The man with the paper was loitering a few yards away at the water fountain. She turned and saw that the other one had taken a seat where he could watch his friend. There was a certain comfort in seeing that they were predictable.

Jane sat a few yards behind the man with the briefcase and studied him. He couldn't be armed with anything worse than a pocketknife. Three inches or less, if she remembered the regulation correctly. They weren't going to do anything in an airport anyway. People you didn't know wouldn't commit suicide to kill you. These were hired help for somebody.

The woman at the boarding desk was joined by a second woman, who said something to her. Then the one who had given Jane her boarding pass picked up a microphone and cooed into it, "Flight 419 for New York is now ready for boarding." People all over the waiting area stood up. "Will those passengers with small children, or who need help boarding, please come to the gate now. . . ."

That invitation seemed to apply to no one, so as the woman went on—"Passengers in rows one through ten may board now"—the taller man walked to the row of telephones beside the men's room.

Mary Perkins stirred, but Jane gave her head a little shake and picked up a newspaper someone had left on a seat near her. The woman went on calling out rows of seats, then said, "Passengers in the remaining seats may board now." Still Jane sat and stared at the newspaper. There were four minutes left. When there were three minutes, she closed the newspaper and began to walk toward the gate.

In her peripheral vision she saw Mary Perkins stand up and follow, then saw the taller man hurriedly punch some numbers into the telephone. Jane stopped to glance up at the clock on the wall, and saw the smaller man walking along behind Mary Perkins. The man at the telephone had hung up, and he walked straight to the gate, handed the woman his ticket, and entered the tunnel. Jane walked a few feet past the last set of seats in the waiting area slowly, letting Mary Perkins catch up with her. At the last second, she turned to her.

"Why, Mary," she said. "It *is* you."

Mary Perkins stopped and stared at her in genuine shock. "Well . . . yes."

"You don't remember me, do you?"

The man who had been following Mary Perkins stopped too, standing almost behind them. Jane seemed to notice him for the first time. "Oh, don't mind us. Go ahead." She pulled Mary Perkins aside. "It's me, Margaret Cerillo. I thought I recognized you before, but I wasn't sure . . ."

The man hesitated. He obviously had orders to follow Mary Perkins onto the airplane, but he also had been instructed to be sure he wasn't caught doing it. He could think of no reason to stand and wait for these two women while they talked, so he stepped forward, handed his ticket to the woman at the door, and stepped past her into the boarding tunnel.

Jane moved Mary Perkins away from the gate casually. "Slowly, now, and keep talking," Jane whispered. "You seem to be worth a lot of expense."

"I guess they think I am," said Mary Perkins.

"If you have something they want, you'll never have a better time to come up with it. We can go right into the plane and make a deal. The lights are on and everybody's been through metal detectors. There's no chance of other people we can't see."

"If I had anything to buy them off with, what would I need you for?"

Jane stopped and looked at her. "I'll still help you shake them afterward in case there are hard feelings."

"Thanks, but I can't get rid of them that way."

"What did you do?"

Mary Perkins turned to look at Jane, leaning away from her as though she had just noticed her there and found it displeasing. "Why do you assume I did something?"

"I know you did. If you didn't, what would you need me for?"

Jane began to walk again. Any woman whose claim to trust was that she had picked up some gossip in the L.A. county jail didn't inspire much confidence, and this one struck her as a person who had done some lying professionally. But Jane could see no indication of what she was lying about. She was being followed by two men who had not taken the sorts of steps that anybody would take if they wanted to stop her from jumping bail or catch her doing something illegal. They had seen her waiting for a flight to a distant state, and they had gotten aboard. The local cops couldn't do that, the F.B.I. wouldn't be prepared to do it on impulse, and if none of them had stopped her from leaving the county jail, then they didn't know of any reason to keep her there.

Jane had to admit to herself that the only possibility that accounted for the way these men were behaving was that they wanted to keep her in sight until there weren't any witnesses. "A little faster now," she said. "We've got a plane to catch."

They started across the waiting area and Jane caught a peculiar movement in the edge of her vision. A man sitting at the far end of the waiting area stood up, and two men who had been conferring quietly at a table in the coffee shop did the same. It wasn't that any of them would have seemed ominous alone. It was the fact that their movements coincided with Jane's and Mary's starting to walk fast. "Did you hear them announce a flight just now?"

Mary winced. "Please don't tell me you hear voices."

"I don't. There were two men on that flight. Do you have some reason to believe there wouldn't be others?"

"Well . . . no."

Jane's jaw tightened. "Let me give you some advice. Whatever it is you've been doing that makes people mad at you, cut it out. You're not very good at getting out of town afterward."

Mary Perkins let Jane hurry her along the concourse in silence until they reached Gate 36. They slipped into the tunnel with the last of the passengers, just as the man at the gate was preparing to close the door. Jane heard running footsteps behind her, so she stopped at the curve and listened.

"I'm sorry, sir," said the airline man's voice. "You'll need a ticket. We aren't permitted to accept cash."

"Can't I buy one?"

"Yes, sir, but you'll have to go to the ticket counter. I have no way to issue a ticket."

"But that's way the hell on the other end of the airport. Can you hold the plane?"

"I'm sorry, sir, but passengers have to catch connecting flights, and we have a schedule. There are five flights a day from LAX to McCarran. You could—"

Jane walked the rest of the way up the tunnel and through the open hatch, and she and the woman took their seats. Mary Perkins said, "What do you call that?"

"Airport tag," said Jane. "I haven't played it in years." She sat back, fastened her seat belt, and closed her eyes. "I hope I never do again."

4

"What are you thinking?" asked Mary Perkins.

"I'm not thinking. I'm resting," said Jane.

"Does resting mean you've already thought, and you have a plan? Because if it does, I'd sure like to know what it is."

"No, it means I want you to be quiet."

Jane closed her eyes again. The plane was flying over the Southwest now, toward the places where the desert people lived: Mohave, Yavapai, Zuni, Hopi, Apache, Navajo. Some of them believed that events didn't come into being one after another but existed all at once. They were simply revealed like the cards a dealer turned over in a blackjack game: they came off the deck one at a time, but they were all there together at the beginning of the game.

What Jane needed to do now was to find a way to reveal the cards in the wrong order: go away, then arrive. She reviewed all of the rituals that were followed when an airplane landed. The fact that they were known and predictable and unchanging meant that they already existed, even though the plane was still in the air. The flight was a short one, and she felt the plane begin to descend almost as soon as it had reached apogee. It was just a hop over the mountains, really, and then a long low glide onto the plateau beyond.

Jane reached into the pocket on the back of the seat in front of her and examined the monthly magazine the airline published. She leafed past the advertisements for hotels and resorts and the articles on money, cars, children, and pets. At the back she found the section she was looking for. There were little maps of all of the airports where the airline landed, so people could find their connecting gates. She studied the one for McCarran, then tore the back cover off, reached into the seat pocket in front of Mary, and tore that back cover off too.

"What are you doing?" asked Mary.

Jane pulled her pen out of her purse and began printing in bold capital letters. "Here's what you have to do. When the plane lands, everybody is going to get off except you. You take as much time as you can. You're sick, or your contact lens fell out. I don't care what it is."

"How long?"

"Try to stretch it out long enough to get at least one flight attendant to leave the plane first. It may not work, but I've seen it happen, and when it does, people watching for a passenger get confused."

"Okay," said Mary. "Then what?"

"Then you come off the plane. Walk out fast, don't look to either side. Head for the car-rental desk. Rent a car. Make it a big one, not a compact. Something fat and luxurious and overpowered. They'll probably have lots of them in Las Vegas. Drive it around to the edge of the building where you can see the Southwest baggage area. When I come out the door, zoom up fast and get me."

"What if something goes wrong?"

Jane was busy going over and over the printing on her

two sheets, making the letters bigger and bolder. "Here's what it will be. They'll follow you to the car desk. They'll stick around long enough to be sure what you're doing, and then they'll leave to try to get to the lot before you do. The lot will be the first time you're alone and away from airport security. They'll want to get into the car with you."

"Then what do I do?"

Jane looked at her in disappointment. "As soon as they're gone, cancel the car and go to the next desk, of course. Rent from a different company. They'll take you to a different lot."

"Just let me get it straight. Stay on the plane, get off quick, rent a big car, pick you up at baggage."

"Right." She looked up at Mary critically. "Come to think of it, even if you don't spot anybody behind you at the rental counter, cancel the car and go to the next desk anyway."

"You don't think I'll see them, do you? That's it, isn't it?"

Jane stuck the two magazine covers into her belt under her coat at the small of her back. Then she leaned back and closed her eyes again. "Bet your life on it if you want. Either way I'll come out of the baggage door and look for you. If you don't come, I can probably find a cab."

When the pilot's voice came on the intercom and said something inaudible that contained the words *Las Vegas*, Jane opened her eyes. People ahead of her in the plane were looking out their windows and nudging each other. Probably they were beginning to see the lights. Flying into Las Vegas after dark was always a strange experience. The world below the plane was as black as the sky above it, and then suddenly, with no warning, there was a light like a frozen explosion in the middle of it: not just a lot of dull yellowish bulbs like the lights of other cities, but crimson, aquamarine, veridian, gold, and bright splashes of white. As the plane descended, the lights moved, blinking, flashing, and sweeping, and a line of fan-shaped beams of car headlights were visible flowing up and down in the middle of it. The explosion had gotten even crazier in the past couple of years, she noticed.

Mary was staring out the window like the others. "God, I love this place," she said. "Are we going to be here long?"

"Not unless you're held over by popular demand," said Jane, and closed her eyes again. She listened and let her body feel the machinery of the plane work. The ailerons moved to tilt and swing the plane around, and then the right one went down with the left and the plane leveled to skim over the desert. There was the odd whistling noise of the wind holding the plane back, and the engines cut down, and then the noise seemed to get louder for no reason she had ever understood, and then the hydraulic system pushed the wheels down until they locked with a thump, and there was the long sickening feeling of the plane losing altitude. She said, "You okay on everything?"

"Yes," said Mary.

Jane nodded. The best part of the plan was that if Mary Perkins, or whatever her real name was, panicked and ran, they would both have a pretty good chance. Mary Perkins would be behind the wheel of a big, fast car with a good head start. Most of the watchers would still be following Jane.

The plane bounced along the runway, slowed, and taxied to a stop at the terminal. Jane stood up and joined the line of impatient people opening overhead compartments and shuffling along between the seats. She stepped into the boarding tunnel and picked out a man a few paces ahead of her. He was tall and in his mid-forties and had the preoccupied, bored look of a salesman making his rounds.

She hurried until she was at his side, then matched his pace to make it look as though they were together. As soon as they were out of the tunnel and around the corner she separated herself from him and ducked into the gift shop. She took two steps past the entrance and found a baseball cap with LAS VEGAS on the crown in sequins and gold thread, and a sweatshirt with a picture of a hand holding five aces. She walked across to the other side wall and picked out a pair of running shorts. The little store didn't sell shoes, but it had some foldable slippers for people whose feet bothered them on long flights. The whole shopping spree took less than a minute, and then she was at the cash register.

She came out the door with her bag of purchases and slipped into the ladies' room. She changed in the stall, dropped her clothes into the trash can, picked up her magazine covers, and then came out again, this time to join the crowd going toward the arrival gates.

As she walked, she checked her watch. Only four minutes had passed since she had stepped off the plane and come out of Gate 10 with the salesman. This time she was in her shorts and sweatshirt, two and a half inches shorter than she had been in her high heels, her tinted glasses gone and her hair in a ponytail through the back strap of her Las Vegas baseball cap.

She moved to Gate 12, directly across the open hallway from Gate 10. The sign over the desk at Gate 12 said, ARR: NORTHWEST FLT 907 LOS ANGELES. She sat down in the side row of seats where other people were waiting for Flight 907 to arrive and put the sign she had made on her lap, where it could be seen if somebody were looking. It said in big, black letters, MARY PERKINS.

She saw the two men notice her. They were in the positions they should be in—apart, but watching the people coming off the Southwest flight from Los Angeles at Gate 10. They both wore sportcoats that might have covered the guns they couldn't have on them now. They noticed Jane within a few seconds. They kept glancing across the hallway at her, but neither moved.

At last Jane saw two stewardesses come out of the tunnel at Gate 10 and walk past the two watchers. They were wearing their little uniform jackets and were towing their overnight bags on little carts. Jane's heart began to beat more quickly. Whatever Mary Perkins had done to delay getting off the plane must have been good. If she could only hold out a little longer, Jane would be able to tie the knot in time.

The two men were staring at each other now, silently conferring. The departure of the flight attendants struck them as evidence that they had already watched all the passengers get off the plane at Gate 10. The two women they had been told to watch for had not been among them. But there was a person waiting at Gate 12 holding a sign that said MARY PERKINS. A second flight from Los Angeles was going to arrive at that gate any minute. Obviously they had been given the wrong airline and flight number. The men silently agreed. First one man went to the drinking fountain. When he came back up the concourse, it was to Gate 12, where Jane waited. She pretended not to see him. She looked at her watch, at the clock on the wall, at the carpet.

At last the second man moved. He walked along the

window, pretended to see something out on the runway, and moved closer to get a better angle. Then, without seeming to have made a decision, he was in Jane's waiting area. He guessed maybe he hadn't seen anything after all. He looked at his watch and sat down.

Now there was only one more thing. If they were trained, or even if they had an instinct for this sort of work, they would be anxious not to spook her. A woman limousine driver who picked up strangers at airports probably often drove alone at night, and she would be careful to avoid being stalked. The sensible place for them to be was behind her, and fairly far away.

Jane turned to face Gate 12, so the men would move to the spots where she wanted them to be. She let her eyes go up under the brim of her cap and used the reflection in the darkened window to check. Yes, they were perfect now, watching her from behind, not able to see the first gate at all.

She picked up movement behind them. Mary Perkins was not a novice. She was coming out of the accordion tunnel fast. Ten steps across the waiting area, around the corner, and gone.

Jane needed to keep their attention on her, so she stood up and walked toward the gate. She sat down in the closest seat she could find to the gate and held her sign in her lap. She felt her heart begin to beat more slowly. Now time had a little knot in it, and the longer the rest of it took the better. The men were convinced that Mary Perkins's plane was about to arrive, but she was already on her way down to the car-rental counter.

A woman much like the one who had presided over the arrival of Jane's flight announced, "Flight 907 from Los Angeles will be arriving at Gate 12 in approximately four minutes." Jane could already see the lights of the plane shimmying along at the end of the runway. She kept her head motionless so the two men wouldn't get the urge to move again. She could see that the plane was a big one, and this improved her chances considerably.

The plane slowly rolled to the terminal and nuzzled up to the doorway. The ground crew chocked the wheels, the boarding tunnel extended a few feet to touch the fuselage, and the engines shut down. People near Jane began to stand up and congregate near the doorway. Most of the passengers flying into McCarran were strangers, so the crowd of relatives and friends was small.

Jane stood among them. She held up the MARY PERKINS sign while she watched the first few passengers come out. There were some middle-aged couples, some men traveling alone, a couple of grandmothers. Then there were about ten people of both sexes who seemed to be the age of college students, and she remembered there was a college here. Then she saw a pair of women in their early thirties, and one of them was blond.

She had been cradling the MARY PERKINS sign under her chin, and now she flipped the sign over without letting the move be visible from behind. She stepped out where the two women could not help seeing her, and tried to look at them winningly. They read her new sign: PRIVATE LIMO: ANY HOTEL, THREE DOLLARS.

The blond woman stopped and asked, "Three dollars for both of us, or three each?"

Jane smiled. "If you're both going to the same place, I'll take you for four."

The blonde said, "Caesar's."

"No sweat," said Jane.

The three women walked down the concourse quickly.

Jane didn't look behind her to see if the men were following. She knew they were. She said, "You've been to Vegas before?"

The blonde had appointed herself to do the talking. "Once in a while. Just when we get really sick of behaving ourselves. We gamble, stay up late, and never grade a single paper."

"You're teachers?"

"Yes," said the other one, who had curly brown hair. "As if you couldn't tell by looking."

Jane felt guilty about what she was going to do next, but the truth was that both of them were attractive in a scrubbed-and-deodorized way. "No," she said. "Everybody comes to Vegas. I just drive them around. Once you're here, you're whoever you say you are—at least until your money's gone. I wouldn't have guessed teachers, though. Most people wouldn't."

"Sure," said the blonde.

"Really. Those two guys who gave you the wall-to-wall and roof-to-foundation when you got off the plane. I bet they don't think you're teachers."

The quiet one said, "That's a laugh." As though to prove it, she laughed.

Jane had put the itch in them, and that was enough. At some point in their walk to the baggage area, each of them would turn and look at the two men, trying very hard and very clumsily to be sure she wasn't caught at it. Looking had nothing to do with real interest. It didn't matter if they were nuns, or lesbians in the tenth year of a lifelong relationship. If they were human, they would look. The idea that they were being watched might frighten them or disgust them or make their weekend, but they would look, and when they did, the two men would be sure.

Jane led them to the baggage claim and waited while they tried to spot their suitcases. The dark one said, "Are those the ones? Don't look."

Jane didn't look. She said, "Tall, muscular guy with dark hair and cowboy boots. Shorter one with curly hair. Both in coats, no ties."

"Yes," said the blonde. "The very ones."

Her companion turned to her in surprise. "You looked?"

"Of course I did," said the blonde. "As soon as I heard about it. But I have a feeling they're not our type. Worse luck."

There was more to the quiet one than Jane had expected. "Maybe my type in Las Vegas isn't the same as my type in Woodland Hills." She was joking, but some part of her mind was agitated.

Jane decided not to let them get too curious. "A lot of ugly things happen in this town. Nobody you want to know hangs around in airports looking for a nice date."

The two bags came down and the blonde soberly scooped them both off the track. Jane picked them up and walked toward the exit with the two women at her back. She used the seconds to prepare herself. If Mary Perkins had failed to rent the car in time, or more likely, had rented it and decided not to drive it back into the light and danger of the airport, Jane was going to be left at the curb with two innocents and some men who might consider this a good opportunity to push them into the back of a car.

She stepped out the door into the cool desert air, set the bags down on the sidewalk, and looked around her. She was careful not to look behind her for the two men, but she knew they must be coming closer. Then a car swung out from the loading zone for United Airlines a hundred yards away and glided toward them. It was a black Lincoln Town Car, and as it drew nearer, she could see Mary Perkins behind the wheel, her face set in an expression of intense discomfort. She stopped two feet from the curb in front of Jane.

The order and economy of Jane's movements were critical now. As soon as the car stopped she swung open the back door and said, "Hop in." As soon as the two women were inside she pushed the button down and slammed the door. Scooping somebody off a curb was easy, but dragging them out of a locked car took time and force. She snatched the suitcases off the pavement, scurried to the back of the car, and banged on the trunk. Mary Perkins leaned out the window and tossed her the key. She set the suitcases inside, closed the lid, and looked around her as she ran to the driver's side. She couldn't see them anywhere, which meant they were somewhere nearby getting into their own car. "I'll drive," she said.

Mary Perkins barely had time to slide to the passenger seat before Jane was inside and wheeling the big car out into the loop. She drove fast to be sure the two men thought it was worthwhile to keep her in sight. She swung to the right on Las Vegas Boulevard. The Strip began just past the airport entrance, and already she was gliding past big hotels: Excalibur, Tropicana, Aladdin, Bally's on the right, the Dunes on the left. They stopped for the light at Flamingo Road, but she still couldn't pick out the car that must be following somewhere in the long line of headlights. The light changed and she drove the two hundred yards with the bright moving lights of the

Flamingo Hilton on her right and Caesar's parking lot on the left, then pulled into the long approach to the front entrance.

The blonde said, "How do you make any money on four dollars a trip?"

Jane shrugged. "Lots of hotels, lots of flights, and nothing shuts down, so we work long hours. We take turns driving." She turned to Mary Perkins. "That reminds me. If you want to take a nap, this is a good time."

Mary took the hint and leaned back in the big front seat. "Thanks," she said. She arranged herself so that her head didn't show over the headrest.

Jane stopped the car at the Caesar's front entrance and ran to open the trunk. The doorman opened the back door for the two passengers while a bellman picked up their suitcases. The doorman made a move to reach for Mary Perkins's door, but Jane stopped him. "She's not getting out."

The blond woman said "Thanks" to Jane, handed her seven dollars, and followed the suitcases toward the lobby.

Jane said to the doorman, "I saw a couple of creeps pick those two out at the airport and follow us. I didn't want to scare them, but you might want to tell Security."

The doorman said seriously, "Yeah. Thanks. I'll do it." He went to his station at the side of the door and picked up a telephone.

Jane slipped behind the wheel and started the car. "Keep your head down," she said. "No matter what happens, stay down and out of sight." She watched for the two men as she glided back along the driveway to the strip. When she saw a dark blue car stop at the side of the building, she kept it in the mirror until she saw the men from the airport get out. They would waste the next few hours trying to find the two women in the enormous hotel complex, then watch them for a while. They would receive no help from anybody who worked at the hotel, and sooner or later two or three polite men in dark suits who had been watching them through the network of video cameras and the see-through mirrors in the ceilings would ask them what they wanted.

"Can I get up yet?" asked Mary Perkins.

"Yeah," Jane said. "I guess it's okay now."

Mary Perkins sat up and looked through the windshield. "That's the airport up ahead. I thought we were going to drive out."

"We're not."

"Why not? It's dark and empty, and we could go a hundred."

Jane sighed. "It's the logical thing to do."

They returned the car to the rental lot, walked into the terminal, and bought two tickets for the next flight out. It happened to be to New York with a stop in Chicago. They had to walk quickly to get to the gate in time. It was almost three A.M. now, and any watchers would have had to be disguised as furniture to escape Jane's notice.

As soon as they had taken their seats, Mary Perkins whispered, "I can't believe it. By now those guys don't know where they are, let alone where we are."

"We're alive," said Jane quietly. "Now I'm going to sleep. Don't wake me up until we're in Chicago."

She closed her eyes and prepared herself for the unpleasant experience of having the past few days run through her mind all over again. There were a few bright, crackling images that flashed in her vision, but they weren't in order or coherent, so they didn't cause her much pain. After she had dozed for a short time, she saw the fist coming around just before she had flinched to take the force out of it. The spasmodic jerk woke her up, but when she relaxed her muscles again, she dropped into a deeper animal sleep that put her in darkness far out of reach of recent memories.

5

When the plane began to descend, the pressure on Jane's ears increased and she woke up. The engines changed their tone, and she pushed the button to let her seat back pop up again. The sleep had left her feeling stiff in the shoulders, but she was alert. The Old People believed that the place to obtain secret information was in dreams. Sometimes a dream would be an expression of an unconscious desire of the soul, and at other times a message planted there by a guardian spirit. Those were two ways of saying the same thing. If there were such a force as the supernatural, then the soul and the guardian both would be supernatural. If there were no such force, then the soul was the psyche, and the guardian spirit was just the lonely mind's imaginary friend.

This time Jane could not remember any impression that had passed through her mind in three hours. Maybe that was the message from her subconscious: enough. She had stored enough tragedy and violence in her memory during the past few days to trip the circuit breaker and turn the lights out. The rest had helped: she was thinking clearly again. As they walked into the terminal at O'Hare she glanced up at a monitor that had the schedule of arrivals and departures on it.

"More tag?" asked Mary Perkins.

Jane kept her moving. "Once a game starts, you have to play to win. That means remembering all the moves. We sent two men to New York with a stop in Chicago. The two we left in Las Vegas can look at the schedule and see that a plane left for Chicago about the time we did. When you start sending the chasers across your own path, it's time to get off the path."

They walked along with the crowd heading for the baggage claim until it passed the car-rental counters, and then Jane led Mary Perkins aside. Within minutes they were in a white Plymouth moving along the 294 Expressway toward Route 80.

Jane drove fast but kept the pace steady, always in a pack of cars that were going the same speed. She counted as she drove: two men fooled into boarding the flight to New York, three left at the gate in L.A., two following the wrong woman in Las Vegas. Seven. The one who had made a phone call before he had boarded the plane to New York must have been reporting to somebody, so it was more than seven. Who were they, and why was Mary Perkins worth all this trouble?

"Where are we going?" asked Mary Perkins.

"Detroit," said Jane. "It's about three hundred miles." She turned her head and pointedly studied the right-hand mirror to check for headlights coming up in the right lane. "In the airport you said you didn't have time to tell me anything and I didn't have time to listen. We've got about five hours."

Mary Perkins sat in silence for a long time. They passed an exit where a blazing neon sign towered above a building much bigger than the gas stations around it. Mary gave a little snort that was the abbreviation for a laugh. "Jimmy Fugazi's End Zone Restaurant. Did you ever notice that all those guys who get too old to play buy restaurants?"

This time Jane did look at her. Mary was probably in her thirties, but she was already paying too much attention to her hair and skin and clothes. "I guess they have to invest their money somewhere," she said.

"All professional athletes want to own restaurants," Mary Perkins pronounced. "It doesn't have to do with money. It has to do with not being able to give up having people look at them and pay attention. Even the dumbest jock in the world knows he can do better by putting bets on any ten mutual funds, but all professional athletes want a restaurant. Every crook already has one. What he wants is a casino. A crook is basically lazy, and that way people come to him to get robbed, and they bring it in cash so he can take it and screw the government at the same time. There's only one game bigger than that."

Jane could sense that Mary Perkins was backing closer to whatever she had been concealing, so she waited patiently.

"What happened to me," said Mary Perkins, "well, not exactly to me—but what happened was that one day in 1982 Congress passed the Garn–Saint Germain Act. It pretty much got rid of all the rules for savings and loan companies. They could charge what they wanted, pay what they wanted, buy and sell what they wanted, take deposits in any amount from anywhere, and then lend it to whomever they wanted, or even forget about lending and invest it themselves. I could see that this was maybe the first great opportunity in American life since the discovery of gold at Sutter's Mill, so I jumped at it."

She glanced at Jane to see if her expression had

changed, but it had not, so she went on. "It wasn't only that the rules had changed, but that there was nobody to enforce them. That was part of the program. If you don't have regulations, you don't have to hire regulators. Reagan was cutting the size of the government payroll."

Jane had finally learned something true about Mary Perkins. She was a thief. But until she knew more about what Mary Perkins had stolen, there would be no way to know who was after her. "What did you have to do with savings and loans?"

"I started working in one right out of college. When I got there, the regulators still knew all the players and all the rules were fifty years old. The money coming in was all from local people with passbooks, and the money going out was for mortgages on local one-family houses."

"I take it you were one of the ones who changed all that?"

"No, not little me. I just came to the party. That's what it was like—a party. You have to understand what was happening. One day the rules change, so each savings and loan sets its own rates. The next day, deposit brokers start taking money from everywhere in the world, breaking it down into hundred-thousand-dollar chips and depositing the chips in whatever institution anywhere in the country had the highest interest that day. So if Bubba and Billy's Bank in Kinkajou, Texas, gives an extra quarter point, suddenly it's got millions of dollars being deposited: Arab oil money, skim-off money from business, drug money from L.A. and Miami, Yakuza money from Japan, money the C.I.A. was washing to slip to some tyrant someplace, and lots of tax money."

"Wait. You did say 'tax money'?" Maybe Jane had been wrong about the men in the airport. If they were federal agents of some kind, they might be prepared in advance to follow a woman like this.

"Sure. You think they keep it in a big box under the president's bed? Say there's a billion-dollar budget for some program. It's got to be in short-term CDs so they can use it when they need it. A loan broker pops it in wherever the interest is highest. Half a year's interest on a billion dollars at eight percent is forty million, right?"

"If you say so."

"And this is money that can't rest. It can't stay put if there's another bank that's offering higher interest. One point of interest on one billion is ten million dollars. There were all kinds of city-government funds, college budgets, whole states that got their money a few months before they spent it. They counted on the timing and figured the interest in as a way to stretch it. And it didn't matter if the money was in the Bank of America or the Bank of Corncob, Iowa, because it was all insured."

"How did this create an opportunity for you?"

"Forget about me for a minute. A few other things had to change first. Glockenspiel City Savings is suddenly a happening thing."

"What's Glockenspiel City Savings?"

"You know, the little storefront with a million in assets built up over twenty years. One day they offer a nice rate on their CDs; the next week they've got four hundred million in deposits. That happened a hell of a lot more often than you'd think. There are little pitfalls, though. They're offering, say, nine percent. That means they've got to turn maybe ten, even twelve to make a profit. There's very little in Glockenspiel City that you can invest in that pays ten percent, and nothing at all that you can invest four hundred million in. So you've got to invest it the way you got it, in the great wide world outside Glockenspiel City."

Mary Perkins was telling all this with relish, as though she weren't sitting in a car speeding across the dark Midwest to keep her alive. She seemed to be calming herself by wandering in territory that was familiar to her, a place that was filled with numbers. Jane let her talk.

"Glockenspiel Savings is run by a guy named Cyrus Curbstone. He goes along for years and years, paying three percent on savings, charging six percent on loans. He knows his limits because they've been written down in a law since the thirties. He's honest. He was born there, and he's got two plots in the cemetery for him and Mrs. Curbstone, right behind Great-grandma and one row over from Colonel Curbstone, who got shot in the ass at Gettysburg. But I know Cyrus Curbstone is vulnerable."

"You said he was honest. What's his weakness?"

"One day Cyrus wakes up and finds himself on another planet. He's got to pay nine percent and charge twelve. His million-dollar bank suddenly has four hundred million in deposits. He can't invest it fast enough in the usual way to make the forty or fifty million he needs to turn a profit. In walks a nice person: maybe me. Maybe I've been referred to him by a deposit broker who's been putting lots of those hundred-thousand-dollar chips in the bank. Or I simply happened to meet one of his regular customers socially. Anyway, I'm a developer, or the general partner in a limited partnership. I've got a piece of land that's been appraised for twenty million, I want to develop it as a resort, and I need a loan of ten million to finance it."

"Is the land real?"

"Sure. That doesn't mean I own it, or that it's worth anything like twenty million."

"Didn't they look at deeds?"

"Sure. The owner is Pan-Financial Enterprises of San Diego, or Big Deals of Boca Raton. I'm an officer."

"How did you make it look like it was worth twenty million?"

"In those days there was no licensing law for appraisers anywhere in the country. So I'd get an appraisal that said what I wanted. Then we'd do a land-flip."

"What's that?"

"Buy it for a million. Sell it to your brother-in-law for six million. He sells it back to you for ten. You sell it to Big Deals, Inc., for twenty."

"That worked?"

"Of course it worked. They've been doing it since the Romans."

"If it was that stale, wasn't it risky?"

"You've heard of the term 'motivated seller'?"

"Yes."

"Well, the day after Cyrus Curbstone starts getting these brokered deposits, he becomes a motivated lender. He's got four hundred million to lend out. If he makes ten percent, that's forty million a year. He pays his depositors nine percent, or thirty-six million, pays his overhead, and he's got maybe two million left in profit. He's part owner, or at least a big stockholder. The others are local people, friends of his. He wants that profit. But if he lets the deposits sit in the vault, he's losing three million a month. That's a hundred thousand a day. That's almost forty-two hundred an hour. I mean, it's costing this guy thirty-three thousand dollars to sleep eight hours."

"You're saying Cyrus fooled himself."

"No. Cyrus had never played for big numbers before, but he wasn't stupid. I was a nice, personable business-woman. I dressed well. I smelled good, I smiled, I had money. I had a hot business and I wanted to expand. Hot businesses need banks. Banks need hot businesses. He got fooled because he was doing exactly what he was supposed to do: for the first few years, a great company looks exactly like the company I was showing him. So he cut a check."

"But what if—"

"What if he said no? If Cyrus didn't bite, I'd leave him to somebody who had a pitch he liked better, and I'd go after his buddy Homer in the next town, who by now has five hundred million to move. But we hardly ever had to do that. Cyrus would have had to hunt pretty hard for a reason to turn me down, and he knew he didn't have time to hunt. He had to find jobs for his dollars."

"So you got a loan. What then?"

"Big Deals, Inc., got a loan. Big Deals spent it: build-ing expenses, salaries, et cetera. But Big Deals neglected to pay the interest."

"What did Cyrus do about it?"

"I'll skip a few phone calls, meetings, and threats. Usually that went on for months. At some point Cyrus sees that he's got a problem. He can do several things. One is to foreclose on the land. Fine with me. I just sold a one-million-dollar chunk of Manitoba for ten million. Another is to accept my excuses and roll over the loan into a new one that includes the interest I owe him. Now it's a new loan for eleven million. Some of these banks carried loans like that for five years."

"What for?"

"Because Cyrus hasn't lost any money until he reports

the loan as nonperforming. If he makes a new loan, he not only hasn't lost the ten million, he can put out another million as an asset. This satisfies the regulators, if any should ever get around to Cyrus with all the work they've got. It keeps the bank looking healthy, so Cyrus has breathing space."

"Why does he need such expensive breathing space?"

"Because he didn't make the forty million he needed to turn a profit. If he was a very quick learner, he made maybe thirty-five million: eight and three-quarters percent. He's still got to pay nine percent to the depositors, so he's maybe a million in the hole at the end of the first year. From one point of view that's not bad. It cost a million dollars to make his bank four hundred times as big as it was last year. But now he's on a treadmill that's going faster and faster. He needs to attract more brokered deposits so he can make more loans. If he gets another two hundred million, he can bring back maybe fifty or sixty million next year and easily absorb the million dollars he lost. As I said, he's not stupid. He knows that he looks great on paper as long as he's moving fast. But if somebody takes a photograph—that is, stops the action and studies it—his bank is insolvent. So now he's interested in keeping the system in motion."

There was still something missing from the story Mary Perkins was telling: who were the seven men following her? "By then he must have known you weren't going to pay the money back."

"In a way they all knew too much. See, Cyrus has been around long enough to have seen problems come and go—the oil crisis and the stock market slide in the early seventies, the inflation after that. He's a survivor. There was no question this wasn't going on forever. If he rode it out, then when it ended he'd be on top of a big company and could count the change later. But if he stopped now, he was out of business. Sometimes these guys would do anything to keep the money moving through—loan anything to anybody and then cook the books to keep the loan from going bad."

"So you got big loans and walked away with the money."

"That was my specialty. There were other people who made a lot of headlines by building screwy empires—lending themselves money to build ghost communities in the desert and paying themselves and their families fifty million in salaries for doing it. But what I'm trying to tell you is that it was all going on a long time, and the ones you've read about weren't the only ones who did it. They weren't even the only ones who got caught. They were just the ones who got convicted. They were very unlucky."

"Why unlucky?"

"It meant that one of these overworked low-level federal accountants had to get around to looking at all the loan papers, spot yours, notice there was something really wrong with the loan, ask questions, get the wrong answers, and convince his supervisor to do something about your loan instead of about somebody else's. Even then the procedures were amazing. That stuff we've all heard about the cold-eyed bank examiners popping in at dawn and padlocking everything is a myth. It never happened that way. Not once."

"You're saying it was staged for the television cameras?"

"No, the pictures were real. What you didn't see was what happened first. The regulator asks questions. Six months go by while somebody at the bank dances around. The supervisor sends his first-level letter."

"What's that?"

"They all have names like Notice of Discrepancy or Letter of Caution or Admonition. The letter describes what they found and says they want it fixed. Another six months go by, and the regulator checks the bank again and sees that you didn't fix it. He looks deeper for other problems, or he forces you to agree to move the loan over to the debit column instead of the credit column. Another six months go by and you get the Caution. Then the Admonition."

"That's ludicrous."

"Of course. The regulating procedures were left over from the days when everybody in the business was Cyrus Curbstone. If he got a letter pointing out a discrepancy, he would have been after it like it was a gaping hole in his own roof. The system was set up to say, 'Please look into this,' then 'Have you fixed it?' then 'Okay, here's how you fix it,' then 'If you don't fix it, I will,' and finally, 'Here I come.'"

"You have to wonder how any of these people got caught."

"It was like being chased by a glacier. You could live a whole life without seeing it get any closer. It was coming, sure. But there was so much time to get out of the way."

"And some waited too long."

"Only a few. About a thousand people actually got to the point where they went to trial. This meant that their savings and loans were so out of control that the government put them at the top of the list for closure. They had to be losing millions a day for that. Then a couple of agents had to figure you were so obviously guilty that it was worth spending four years of their lives preparing the case.

A U.S. attorney had to be sure the case was a slam-dunk, so it wouldn't ruin her won-lost record. Then her boss would have to be convinced that you had stolen so much that when the case was over they could recover enough millions in civil court to repay the millions all this prosecution was costing, and enough millions more to make it look to Joe Taxpayer like they'd gotten his money back, and enough millions more so it would look like they put your head on a pole to scare off the other high rollers."

"How did that work out?"

"Not so great. In order to convict, they had to take the judge and jury through all these loan papers, land-flips, asset appraisals, and files. The average person can barely follow his own taxes. All this paper was written up to fool qualified accountants. The paper made most of these guys look like victims. For all I know plenty of them were. About a third got off, and of the others only about half got convicted of anything that carried jail time. The average sentence was three years."

"You said they were picked so there could be civil suits. Didn't they still have to face that?"

"Sure, but they all said they were broke. Even if they had a hundred million dollars in a box under their bed, they also had papers to show they owed somebody two hundred million."

"I know the government confiscated land and buildings and things. They've been selling them off for years."

"If you read that much, you don't have to ask me how that's going. The savings and loans the government took over were the worst, because that was all they had enough money for. The worst were ones where somebody had pulled land-flips to jack up an acre in the middle of a toxic waste dump from a thousand dollars to a million, and had a shady contractor put a substandard building on it so they could jack up the price of the land all around it."

"It's an interesting story," said Jane, "but it's history. It's been over for years."

"Oh?" said Mary Perkins. "Then let me ask you something. Where is it?"

"What?"

"The money."

"It wasn't real to begin with, was it? If you take something that's worth a thousand dollars and say it's worth a million, and then it goes back to a thousand, nothing happened."

"Something happened. Somebody walked out the door clutching a check for a million dollars he didn't have before, so he got a profit of nine hundred and ninety-nine thousand. The collateral wasn't real, but the money he got from the bank was. He didn't even have to pay taxes on it. A loan isn't income. It's a deduction."

"I forgot about that for a second."

"Sure you did. You're supposed to. Everybody gets used to the idea that money is gooey, flexible stuff. They talk about it inflating and deflating and flowing and being liquid. No reason why it can't evaporate."

"Somebody got it, but if nobody can put his hand on it, then it did evaporate. So that part of it is over."

"It's not over," said Mary Perkins. "We're just moving into the second round now."

"What's the second round? The ten thousand who got away are still doing it?"

"No. Let's say a lull has settled over the borrowing industry. There's no such thing as a savings and loan anymore. The ones that are left are just banks that haven't changed their names yet. That goose has been killed.

Scams always work best in boom times, when everybody's too busy to do much checking, almost any business you say you're in might make a profit, and the value of any kind of collateral is going up. But there's still unfinished business."

"Then what's unfinished?"

"I'll give you another typical case: a guy who got into the borrowing business right after the law changed. He didn't amount to much before that. The government shuts him down in 'eighty-nine or 'ninety when they take over the S and L he was borrowing from. He weasels around during the four years it takes to prepare a noose for him. His lawyer and the prosecutor work out a plea bargain. He'll cooperate in the investigation, do six months for one count of making a false statement on a loan form, and settle for twenty million in damages."

"The government bought that?"

"Would you?"

"No."

"Neither did they. If he's offering twenty, he's got forty. The only way he could have gotten it is by stealing it. They take him to court. He's convicted. He gets his standard three-year sentence and is ordered to repay fifty million dollars. He says he's broke. They say, 'No way is this man broke.' They lock him up and look for hidden accounts, fake names, the rest of it. They find nothing. He serves his three years. Some time during those three years the statute of limitations runs out on everything he did at the bank."

"You mean he's free? Nobody can do anything?"

"He can never be charged again by the government for the crimes he committed in getting the money. Of course he still can't show that he's got twenty or forty or a hundred million. He's still got the judgment against him for that much, and swearing he didn't have it was a new crime. But generally speaking, his legal problems are over. Now he's got illegal problems."

"What are those?"

"Well, let's study this guy. He got only a three-year sentence for the following reasons." She ticked them off on her long, thin fingers, the nails looking like knife points. "He has never committed any offense before. He is clearly not armed or violent or dangerous. He has no known connection with organized crime or the drug trade. Everybody who ever heard his name thinks he's got a fortune, but federal investigators who sniff out money for a living didn't find it. What does all that mean to you?"

"It means he's got the money pretty well hidden."

"Good for you. You win a trip to the Caribbean."

Jane looked closely at Mary Perkins. "I think I know what his illegal problems are."

"Yes," said Mary Perkins. "He's not violent enough to scare anybody off and he's got no connections that are worth anything. If you steal his umpteen million he can't even call the police because he'd have to tell them he had that kind of money, and this time his sentence wouldn't be three years; it'd be more like thirty. He's the perfect victim." After a long pause Mary Perkins added, "He's a lot like me."

6

Jane drove along the dark highway skillfully, sometimes lingering in the wake of a big eighteen-wheel
truck for many minutes if the driver was pushing to make
time, and sometimes moving out into the other lanes
to slither between drifting cars where the truck wasn't
nimble enough to navigate. Always she stayed within a
few miles an hour of the rest of the traffic to keep from
tempting the state police, but almost always she was the
one who was passing. It was difficult to study and recognize the headlights coming up from behind, so she kept
them back there. Now and then she would see one of the
exceptions coming up fast in the rearview mirror, and she
would evacuate the lane he seemed to prefer and find a
space in the center, where she could move to either side
if he swerved toward her, and waited there until he had
gone on his way.

"Why aren't you saying anything?" asked Mary Perkins.

"I'm waiting to hear your story."

"I told you."

"You told me a lot of stuff about how you used to steal
money. You didn't tell me anything about yourself. I
thought you were just warming up to it."

"What do you want to know?"

"What's your name?"

"Mary Perkins," she answered, the annoyance making her voice strain. "I told you that in the ladies' room in Los Angeles."

"Okay," said Jane quietly. She drove in silence for a long time.

"Oh," said Mary Perkins brightly. "You mean the one I was born with. I haven't used it in years, so it sounds strange when I say it: Lily Smith."

"What made you pick Mary Perkins?"

"Well, I was in a business where it didn't seem to be a good idea to use the name on my birth certificate. Smith is okay, but it sounds like an alias. Perkins is the kind of name that makes the mark think good thoughts. Mary Perkins is Mary Poppins, with 'perk,' which is peppy and cheerful instead of 'pop,' which is unpredictable. And 'kins' is sweet and innocent, like babykins and lambkins. Also, all names that end with 'kins' are Anglo-Saxon in a homespun straight-from-the-farm sort of way, not in the my-ancestors-were-on-the-*Mayflower* way."

"And Mary is just from Mary Poppins?"

She smiled. "It's kind of hard to find anything that sounds more innocent."

"The word *immaculate* comes to mind," said Jane.

"Well, there's that side of it, of course," said Mary Perkins. "But there are other things that aren't quite as obvious. First, Mary says 'mother.' In fact, it says 'mother of somebody important.' And it's common and feminine. See, if you're going to rob banks—" She stopped, as though she realized it was going to be hard to make herself understood, then started over. "Did you ever take a look at the way your bank is set up?"

"I think I have," said Jane.

"You've got the open floor, which is just there to make you think the bank is big and solid. Then you see the people. At the tellers' counter there are twenty women and a couple of men too young to shave. Then there are a few desks behind that, where everybody is always on the phone. Those are usually women in their fifties. They look like chaperones, there to supervise the twenty women and two boys up front, and to smooth over mistakes."

"I take it those aren't the people you were trying to impress."

"Not if what you came for is money. When you get behind those desks, there are offices. Sometimes they're not even on the same floor. But somewhere down a long, quiet, carpeted hallway there will be a huge wooden desk with nothing on it except a couple of those old-fashioned black pens that stick up out of a marble slab, and a lamp with a green shade. Behind that desk will be a middle-aged man. See, banks are in layers. You can meet fifty-two senior executive vice presidents, and all of them are women. You've got to resist the temptation to tell them enough so that they can say no, and hold out until you see this man."

"And Mary was for him?"

"Yes. It's straightforward, short, and unpretentious. It's not a nickname. It's not a boy's name that was supposed to be cute on a girl. A lot of women in businesses use initials: M. H. Perkins, or M. Hall Perkins. They think it makes them serious. They're wrong. It does not endear them to that man in the back office, and that is the only game being played."

"It is?"

"You must impress the man who has the power to say yes. He doesn't want to be fooled, or to be in business with any person of either sex who is insecure enough to hide things. The only thing worse is a hyphenated name—the woman is married, which is a fact that has very big pluses and minuses that have to be managed carefully. But the hyphenation implies some kind of nonconformist convictions about men and women that she wants to advertise. The man in the back office is not interested in thinking about that. He's interested in getting more money. He wants to deal with somebody who is going to get lots of money and pay him some of it."

"Okay, so Mary Perkins makes it in the door, and M. H. Perkins doesn't."

"Right. She's at the door now. She's energetic and cheerful and well scrubbed, and she has hair that's a bit on the long side and high heels and subtle makeup, but not so subtle that he can't tell she bothered. She wears good jewelry, but very little of it, and it's small. If Mary is married for this meeting, it's a solitaire diamond that's just a little bigger than an honest banker can afford, and that's all. If she's not, maybe a lapel pin. Why? Because that's the way the women who end up with the most money look. The most common way to get it is still to marry it, so Mary is feminine."

"It doesn't sound as though he's thinking about Mary Perkins as a business partner."

"I'm not talking about the deal. I'm talking about the first impression—unconscious, probably—the five seconds from the door to the chair. Finance is a tough business. The guy is smart, and above all he's patient. He's seen a lot on the way to the corner office. In order to automatically get back ten percent of his loan each year, he has to lend the money to somebody who will win—who will use his money to make fifteen percent. What I'm describing for you is the sort of woman he can be made to believe will win."

"How did Mary Perkins get to the point where people are hunting for her?"

Mary Perkins shook her head as though she were marveling at it. "There was a lot of wild stuff in the papers when I went to trial. My lawyer told me that if I went for the plea bargain, it didn't matter how much I agreed to admit I took, because I was already broke. The prosecutor could use a ridiculous number to help her look good, and I would declare bankruptcy and never have to pay a dime. It didn't work that way. Now people think I was one of the ones who ended up with the big money. They want it. I don't have it."

"Who are these people?"

"That's part of the problem. It could be anybody."

Jane looked at her for a moment. Mary was slouching in the passenger seat, looking out the window at the darkness. When she turned to meet Jane's gaze her eyes were wide with wonder and a touch of injury. What she was saying coincided with the truth in one spot: there was no way of limiting the number of people who might be interested in robbing a woman who had stolen millions of dollars. But this did not alter the fact that Mary Perkins knew who was after her tonight, and that she insisted she didn't. Jane said, "Why were you in county jail?"

Mary Perkins shrugged. "Parole violation. I saw those men and tried to leave town."

Jane stifled the annoyed response that rose to her tongue. Mary obviously was experienced enough to know that the best lies were short and simple. Where did the lie begin? She might have noticed that men were following her, but she had not tried to leave town because of that.

Something else must have happened first—something that told her what they wanted. All of the hours Jane had spent hustling this woman around the country settled on her chest like a weight. "Where do you think you could go where there would be the smallest chance you'd be recognized?"

"Smallest chance?"

"That's what I said."

"Let's see. We just left California, so that's out. Texas is also out."

Jane concentrated on the mechanical details for the next few minutes. At Ann Arbor she took the Huron Street exit. She said, "When was the last time you slept?"

"I slept maybe four hours last night. Jails never seem to quiet down until you start to smell breakfast."

"We'll sleep now."

There was a motel just after the exit. Jane pulled into the lot and walked into the office by herself to rent a room. She opened the door with the key, locked the door, checked each of the windows, tossed the key on the table by the door, undressed, and lay down on the nearest bed without speaking. Mary Perkins had no choice but to imitate her. When she awoke, the sun was glaring through a crack between the curtains and Jane was sitting on the other bed reading a newspaper. Mary sat up and said, "What time is it?"

"Ten. Checkout is twelve. We've got a lot to do."

Mary Perkins rubbed her eyes. "I guess we'll make it." She smiled. "It's not as though we had to pack, is it?"

"No."

Mary Perkins swung her feet to the floor and stood up. She had been surprised to see that Jane was dressed, but the newspaper suddenly caught her attention. "You've been out."

"Yes," said Jane, not looking up. Mary Perkins could see that she had circled some little boxes in the want ads. Jane also had set a medium-sized grocery bag on the table beside the key.

"I never heard you," said Mary on the way to the bathroom. "You must be the quietest person I ever met in my life."

"I figured you needed to sleep."

Mary examined the shower and found that the knobs were hot and the tub was wet. She thought about the woman in the other room. A lot of people could tiptoe around pretty well, just like little cats. But how did this one get everything else to be quiet—appliances and fixtures and things?

Mary Perkins got the water to run warm and stepped under the spray. She felt good, she had to admit. Here she was in a clean room with a clear head a couple of thousand miles away from danger, and taking a shower. Once again whatever it was that had always kept the luck coming had not failed.

But now that she was alert and not particularly frightened, she had time to think about that woman out there on the bed. What she sensed about Jane Whitefield was not comforting. No, the animal wasn't a cat. Just because it looked like it had soft fur and the eyes were big and liquid and it didn't make any noise at all didn't mean it was cuddly and gentle. Mary was not the sort of person who lost fingers at zoos. Whatever this one was, it had that look because it happened to be the female of its species, not because it was something you wanted around the house.

The person who had recognized Jane Whitefield in jail

was a short black woman named Ellery Robinson. The word on Ellery Robinson was that she had been pulled in on a parole violation. That didn't make her seem interesting until Mary learned that the conviction was for having killed a man in bed with an old-fashioned straight razor. She had served six or seven years of a life sentence in the California Institution for Women at Frontera, one of those places in the endless desert east of Los Angeles. She was in her fifties now, small and compact with a short, athletic body like a leathery teenager. She never spoke to anyone, having long ago lost interest in whatever other people gained from listening, and having gotten used to whatever it was they expelled by talking. But sometimes she still answered questions if they weren't personal.

Mary was in the mess hall one morning when another woman pointed out Jane Whitefield and asked Ellery Robinson if she knew anything about her. Ellery Robinson had actually turned her whole body around in the chow line to stare at her before she said, "She makes people disappear." Then the conversation was over. Ellery Robinson turned back to eye the food on the warming tables. When a young woman down the line on her first day inside saw the same food and started crying, she looked at her too for a second, not revealing either sympathy or contempt, but as though she just wanted to see where the noise was coming from.

Mary Perkins had come upon Ellery Robinson sitting in the sunshine in the yard, a headband around her forehead and the sleeves of her prison shirt rolled up to make it fit her child-sized frame. Mary Perkins smiled, but Ellery Robinson said only, "What do you want?"

"I heard you know who that woman is that came in yesterday. Tall, black hair, thin?"

"Yes."

"Is it true that she hides people?"

Ellery Robinson closed one eye and tilted her head up to look at Mary Perkins. "Why aren't you talking to her?"

"I thought I'd better find out what I could first."

Ellery Robinson abruptly lost interest in Mary Perkins. She seemed determined to end the conversation, so everything came out quickly in a monotone. "I heard that if a person is in trouble—not the kind of trouble where the cops take them to court, but the kind where the cops find their head in a Dumpster—the person could do worse than see her."

Mary Perkins stared at Ellery Robinson, but her face revealed nothing. "You sure nobody made her up?"

Ellery Robinson nodded in the direction of the cell-block. "There she is."

"If you know her, why haven't you talked to her?"

For the first time Ellery Robinson's facial muscles moved a little, but it wasn't a smile. "I don't have that kind of trouble. If you do, go meet her yourself."

Mary Perkins looked uncomfortable. "This is all new to me. It's the first time I've been arrested."

"No, it isn't." It wasn't an accusation. There was no trace of reproof or irony. There was nothing behind it at all. Then she seemed to acknowledge that her words were what had made Mary Perkins take a step backward. "Lots of bad girls in here. You aren't the worst." She closed her eyes and moved to the side a little so she would be in the full sun again and Mary's shadow would be gone.

Now Mary stood in the shower in Michigan, feeling safe. She had begun to relax when she sensed something had changed again. She tensed and swung around to see the shape outside the shower curtain.

"Dry off," said Jane, "but leave your hair wet."

Mary turned off the water, snatched a towel off the rack, pulled it inside the curtain with her, and turned away to dry herself. "Why?"

"Why what?"

"Why leave my hair wet?"

Jane reached into the paper bag and pulled out a box with a picture of a fashion model on it. "We'll dry it after it's dyed."

"Dyed? What if I don't want it dyed?"

"Then don't dye it," said Jane. "You've got easy ways to stay lost, and hard ways. Changing the color of your hair is one of the easy ways."

Mary glared at the model on the box. Whatever color her hair had been when the picture was taken, an artist had painted it over a hedgehog brown. "That color?"

Jane set the box on the sink just under the mirror. "What's wrong with it?"

"I've just always been blond."

Jane's eyes lifted to glance at her in the mirror, and then Mary saw them move to the picture on the box. She said nothing, but Mary saw what she was comparing the color on the box to. She angrily snatched another towel off the rack, wrapped it around her and tucked it under her arm like a sarong. "I meant I've always *felt* blond. I've been blond for a long time."

Jane didn't turn to face her. "We've got less than two hours before checkout time. If you want to look different, the time to do it is before you rent an apartment, not later, after everybody has seen you already. I'll be out there. Think it over."

Mary sat on the edge of the tub and stared at the mirror. It was just high enough so that all she could see of herself was the glowing blond hair at the crown of her head. It was bright, shiny, almost metallic when it was wet like this. She walked to the door and called, "Okay, let's get it over with."

Jane came back in, slipped on rubber gloves, pulled a chair up next to the sink, and went to work on Mary's hair. The acrid smells and the mess on the counter were all familiar to Mary, but it had been years since she had endured them outside of a hairdresser's shop.

Jane worked in silence and with extreme care, glancing at her watch every few minutes. Then it was over, and she was brushing Mary's hair out.

Mary said, "You've done this quite a bit, haven't you?"

"Sure," Jane said. "If you do all of the easy things, the hard ones work better. Dyeing your hair, buying new clothes, using glasses to change the way your eyes look—those are easy. You can do all of them in a day, and none of them has any risk. If you think about what you're trying to accomplish, you can do it as well as I can."

"What am I trying to accomplish?"

Jane looked at her in the mirror impatiently. "You put in a lot of time trying to be Mary Perkins. You had it all worked out. Just do it in reverse. For the time being, you have nothing in common with Mary Perkins. She liked Las Vegas. You hate it; the lights give you a headache and everybody on the street looks like a zombie to you. Mary Perkins made businessmen think about her and remember her. Lose everything you did to accomplish that. Be the one who doesn't catch their eye. That's easy to do, and if you don't do at least that much, you're finished. Anybody who wants to find you can knock on doors and show your picture."

Mary Perkins studied her reflection. The effect wasn't as bad as she had expected. The woman who stared back at her wasn't dowdy or mousy. She was mildly, quietly attractive, and with a little makeup she could be made better than that. What she looked most like was a woman who had never existed; she looked like a grown-up version of Lily Smith. "All right," she said. "What do we change next?"

"That will have to do for now. Come on."

Checking out consisted of sitting in the car while Jane went into the motel office and set the key on the counter. When she returned, she started the car and said, "All right. Now we start getting into the hard parts. Do you have identification in any name besides Mary Perkins?"

"Lila Samuels," said Mary.

"Throw her away with Mary Perkins. You've been in county jail. Although you haven't exactly said so, you've been investigated, and probably arrested more than once. The authorities know your aliases, and so can anybody else who wants to."

Mary Perkins said, "I've got to be somebody."

"I've got some papers with me that you can use. Your name is Donna Kester. You're thirty-five."

Mary Perkins stared at her. "You have fake I.D. with you? But you were arrested too. They went through your purse."

Jane pulled the car out of the parking lot and drove up the street. "It wasn't in my purse." Jane had brought the papers for Mona and kept them taped under the dashboard of each car they had used while traveling across the country. After Dennis had wrecked the last car, she had gone to the lot where it had been towed and found the papers untouched. "You can be Donna Kester without worrying about anything for a while."

They looked at three different apartments before they found the right one. It was in a building in the middle of a large modern apartment complex on Huron Street that seemed to contain a high proportion of single people, but it was far enough from the University of Michigan campus to be vacant. The fact that Donna Kester had a credit card was enough to get her a lease that began in two days. The fact that she had no local employer only confirmed her story that she had just gotten to town.

That afternoon Jane checked them into another motel at the edge of Ann Arbor, past the place where Huron Street crossed Route 94 and became Liberty Road. Jane sat in the motel room on the twin bed across from Mary. It was dusk, and the cold wind was beginning to blow outside to announce that the short fall days were fading into winter nights here. The tree branches that scraped and rattled the gutters of the building were bare, and the wet pavement of the parking lot outside the window would be frosted by morning.

Jane said, "This is a good place to be. There are about thirty-five thousand students here, just about all of them strangers. Figure five thousand faculty, all from other places. Most of them are married, so they're really ten thousand, and another five thousand staff. Most of those people just returned here for fall semester. You're one of fifty thousand people who just got to town in a community with a year-round population that can't be much over a hundred thousand."

"Are you trying to sell me a condo?" asked Mary.

"No," said Jane. "I'm trying to teach you something. If

you're going to be a fugitive you'd better get good at it. I've heard a couple of versions of who isn't chasing you, but not who is. It doesn't matter. This isn't the sort of place where they'll look first. That's the best you can do in choosing a place to be invisible. There are always about five likely places to look for anybody. If you're stupid, you'll be in one. Once you move beyond those, every place is about as likely as any other, so the odds of finding you drop dramatically."

"Where would you look? You said five places."

"I haven't studied Mary Perkins as thoroughly as they have. You've been to Las Vegas and liked it. You'd be too smart to go back, and Reno's too close, so I might try looking in Atlantic City. You said you had worked in Texas and California, so people know you. But that leaves lots of cities in between that would appeal to Mary Perkins: I'd try Scottsdale, Sedona, Santa Fe. You like to be around money and sunshine." As she watched Mary, she could see that the list was making her frightened. "The fifth place is somewhere in the South."

Mary Perkins looked like a woman who had paid to have her palm read and heard that she had no life line. "Where?"

"You have just a trace of a southern accent. Since I know you've been arrested, I'd check the arrest record to find the city where you were born. That's always the fifth place."

Mary looked at Jane with an expression that was meant to be intrigued puzzlement, but the surface never set properly; her face only formed itself into pie-faced hurt. "Why is that?"

Jane's eyes were tired and sad. "I don't know. Some people will tell you it's because they know the territory better than a stranger could, but they say that even if every inch of the place was bulldozed and rebuilt the day they left. Some of them say it's because they can get help from friends and relatives, but half the time they don't ask for it when they're there. They go there even if everybody they ever knew is dead and buried."

"You're telling me what you don't believe. What do you believe makes them go back?"

"I'm telling you I don't think the people who do it know why. Maybe it's just some feeling that people have because we're animals too. You go to ground where you once felt most safe, and that's wherever your mother was." She watched Mary Perkins for a moment. "It's a lousy instinct, and it will get you killed."

"So what now?"

"This is a place where nobody is searching for you. You look a little different, and if you work at it you can change more. You have identification as Donna Kester that should hold up. The credit cards are real. You'll get the bills. The driver's license is from New York, but it's good too. Somebody actually took the road test. You can get a new one here with the old one and the birth certificate. That's real too." A man Jane knew had found a job in a small-town courthouse and added forty or fifty birth records that hadn't been there before. He sold about one name a year, so the odds were good that nobody would catch one and start looking into the rest.

Mary Perkins looked increasingly alarmed. "How long do we have to stay here?"

"It's up to you. If you want my advice, I'll give it to you. Spend your time around the university, where there are crowds of strangers of every description and all the thugs wear helmets and shoulder pads. Buy yourself a long, warm coat with a high collar and wear a hat and scarf."

"You're telling me you're cutting me loose, aren't you?" said Mary Perkins with growing anxiety. "I thought you were going to protect me and get me settled."

Jane framed her words carefully, making an effort to keep the frustration out of her voice. "You came to me in trouble, with two men on your back. I got you out of that trouble because you asked me to and I didn't think you could do it yourself. Now you're reasonably safe if you want to be. That's as far as I go with you."

"It's because you think I can't pay, right? Well, I can. I've got money with me, and I can get more when it's safe to travel. Enough to make it worth your time, anyway."

"Keep it," said Jane. She picked up her purse and the keys to the car. "The more you have, the longer it will be before you do something foolish." She walked to the door, stopped, and added, "Take care."

"I have a right to know why."

"No, you don't," said Jane. She stepped outside, closed the door, and walked across the cold lot to the car. She started it and drove around the block and past the motel twice. When she was certain that nobody was watching the motel and nobody had followed the car, she continued straight to Route 94 and headed east toward the junction with 23 to Ohio.

7

When Jane reached Toledo she swung east across the vast flat lake country toward home. In the morning when she passed into the southwestern tip of New York, she felt as though she had left enemy territory. Three hours later, she drove the rented car to the Rochester airport and turned it in at the lot to make it look as though the driver had continued east on a plane. Then she took a commuter flight seventy miles west to the Buffalo airport, where she had left her own car.

She drove up the Youngmann Expressway to Delaware Avenue and turned north into the city of Deganawida in the late afternoon. The sun had already moved to a position in the west where its feeble glow did little to blunt the bite of the wind off the Niagara River. She drove onto Main Street near the old cemetery that had filled up before the Spanish-American War, took the shortcut along the railroad tracks and down Erie to Ogden Street, then turned again to her block. The house was one of a hundred or more narrow two-story wooden buildings placed beside the street that ran the length of the city from one creek to the next one, two miles away.

Jane pulled the car into the driveway and her eyes instantly took in the state of the neighborhood. She had been looking at these same sights since she had first stood upright and been able to see over the hedges to survey the world while she was playing. The houses in this block had been built before the turn of the century for the people who worked in the factories and shipyards that were no longer here, and the trees were tall and thick, their roots pushing the blocks of the sidewalks up into rakish tilts that had made roller skating dangerous. Her front yard looked lush and green and needed cutting, the blades thick and wet from the rain she had missed while she was away. The clapboards of the narrow two-story house always had looked soft and organic to her because the dozens of layers of paint spread on by generations of Whitefields had made the corners rounded. She saw the curtain on Jake Reinert's corner window twitch aside and she knew he had heard the car's engine in the driveway next door.

She walked to her front door, unlocked it, and slipped inside to punch the code on her alarm keypad before the alarm could go off. She left her front door open so Jake would know that she was willing to talk. She walked into the kitchen, poured coffee into the filter of the coffee-maker, opened the freezer and unwrapped a frozen square of corn bread and a package of blueberries, and started to defrost them in the microwave oven.

Jane heard Jake on the porch, his footsteps heavy and a little stiff. "Come on in," she called, then went back to the cupboard for honey. The microwave bell chimed, and she had the corn bread, berries, and honey on the kitchen table before Jake was comfortably seated. She heard him strain a little to ease himself down with his arms.

"I brought your mail," said Jake. He set a pile of letters on the table.

"Thanks. Arthritis acting up?"

"It's just the winters," said Jake.

"Cold nights getting to you?"

"Yeah, too damned many of them."

He watched her bustling around getting cups, plates, and silverware. Nothing escaped his notice. She was wearing heavier makeup than usual, and her right eye was half closed and the high cheekbone on that side seemed tight—not puffy, exactly, but swollen. She still moved quickly and gracefully, but she didn't pick up things in groups: she lifted each one and set it down before she picked up the next. He judged it was probably a sprained wrist.

Jake had known Jane Whitefield for all of her thirty-two years, had known her mother for a few years before that, and her father all his life. He had come into this same kitchen as a child and watched her grandmother lay out corn bread, berries, and honey for him on this same table. Seneca women obeyed some ancient law that said that anybody who came in at any time of the day or night got fed.

He had not merely known Jane Whitefield, he had been around to see her coming, but it had been only two years ago that he had accidentally discovered what little Janie had grown up to do with herself. From the look of her, it had gotten harder lately. He said, "Rough trip this time?" He had suspected he would feel like an idiot if he said it this way, and he did; a woman who made her living by taking fugitives away from their troubles and into hiding probably didn't have any kind of trips but rough ones. He had said it that way because it acknowledged that he knew the nature of her business and implied that he wasn't shocked by it anymore. He considered this a necessary piece of hypocrisy.

To Jake's surprise Jane didn't take the chance he had given her to shrug it off or make a joke out of it. "Yeah," she said. "It was awful." She set a plate of corn bread in front of him and started to eat her own, but then set the fork back down. "I always thought the way it would end was that one day I would get sick of people and decide they weren't worth the trouble anymore. That probably won't be how it happens. I lost two of them, Jake."

"Lost them?" he said. "You mean you can't find them?"

"No." She spoke clearly but with the quiet voice that made him know what she was going to say, because people spoke in low voices about the dead. "I got them killed."

"How?"

"I don't know, exactly. I mean, I know what happened, but not how. We—the three of us—were taking a little boy to California. There was an ambush. I didn't read it in time because it wasn't a dark alley or a lonely road. It was a courthouse. The other two had to stop and buy me time to get the boy inside where he would be safe."

"I'm sorry," Jake said. That was what people said when somebody died. A man his age ought to have thought of something better than that by now, but if he had, he never remembered it when he needed it.

"Somebody outsmarted me. He knew what bait to use, and somehow he must have figured out a way to be sure that this lawyer—the one who died—knew it was there. But the trap he set wasn't for a lawyer. It was for someone like me."

"How do you know that?"

"He knew that I would find a way to get the boy into the courthouse before it opened in the morning, or at least study the building so I knew the entrances and exits and who was supposed to be where. So at the last minute he had them transfer the case to a different court."

Jake ate some of the corn bread and honey, and thought about what she had said. "Who is he, a cop?"

She said, "He was tracking the boy all over the country for years. If you run into a crooked cop, you can almost always avoid him by driving past the city line. There's hardly ever a good enough reason to follow you beyond it. On one side of the line he's just about invulnerable. On the other, he has no legal power and the local police wonder what he's up to. No," she said. "I think he's something else."

Jake stopped pretending not to stare at her face. "How did you get hurt?"

When she lifted her hands out of her lap and picked up her coffee cup he saw her knuckles and fingers. "At the courthouse," she said.

Jake ate his corn bread, drank his coffee, and considered. What she had wrong with her looked like one shot to the side of her face, but there was a lot of damage to her hands and wrists and probably elbows from somebody's teeth and facial bones. It was possible somebody was dead that she hadn't mentioned. "Should I be listening for sirens?"

"No. There was a judge who made sure I got out before it got to that stage." She noticed his puzzled look. "There are people like that. I don't know if I ever told you about that part of it. People who have no reason to take risks will do it. He knew he could get into trouble—

probably get disbarred or something—but he did it anyway."

Jake answered, "People one at a time are a lot more appetizing than you would think if you look at them all at once." He shrugged. "So you came home."

She shook her head. "I was trying, but something else happened on the way home. There was a woman I ran into. She heard somebody talking about me in jail in California. She needed my help to get out of trouble. I started to do it. Then I realized I couldn't. I gave her some identification and some advice and left."

"Was she in danger when you left?"

"No."

"Then that's a good place to stop," he said.

She looked at him over the rim of her coffee cup. He couldn't see her mouth, just the deep strange blue of her eyes against her olive skin. To Jake it was like looking at both of Jane's parents at once. The skin and the long black hair that wreathed her face were all Seneca. But there was her mother too, the liquid blue eyes that had originated somewhere far from here in northern Europe. He tried to talk to the eyes because he had some superstitious feeling that he had something in common with them, some hope of talking to somebody behind them who shared at least one or two assumptions. But even before he began, he knew that it was nonsense. It was like thinking she was her mother because she was wearing her mother's dress. "I don't want to start giving you advice," he lied. "I never have, in spite of the fact that if everybody listened to me they'd all be a hell of a lot less erratic, since I seldom contradict myself. But I know something about how time works. No matter what you do with yourself, the day comes when it ends. You die or go into something else. If you spent your time catching fish, no matter how long you stuck at it, on the day you quit there would still be some fish out there somewhere. Not only can you not go back out and get them, but you shouldn't try."

Jane stood up and changed into the young woman next door again. She picked up the plates carefully, one at a time, and put them in the sink. She stood tall and straight, with her long black hair naturally parting to hang down her back, and began to clean her kitchen.

Jake stood up too and signified that he understood that their meeting was over. "Well, thanks for the snack, but I've got a lot to do in the yard before supper. It gets dark so damned early now, I barely have time to wake up before the streetlights go on."

Jane turned to him and gave him a small kiss on the cheek. "Thanks, Jake."

"I'll be home if you need anything," he said as he walked to the door. "I don't imagine much of what's in your refrigerator bears looking at by now." He stopped and glared suspiciously at the keypad on the wall by the door. "Can I open this without going deaf?"

"Yes," she said. "It's turned off."

He walked outside. "Don't forget to turn it on again."

Jane closed the door and stood beside it to listen to his footsteps going down the wooden steps and scraping on the sidewalk before she moved away. She walked back into the kitchen, washed the dishes, wiped the counters, and turned off the lights. She had cleaned the oven and emptied the shelves of the refrigerator before she had left to pick up Timmy and Mona in Chicago, so she could think of no justification for doing anything more in here. She walked out into the living room. She had given the whole house a nervous cleaning before she had left, and it had been closed tight with the furnace thermostat set to 50 degrees just to keep the pipes from freezing if the winds coming out of Canada turned fierce early, so there wasn't even any dust.

She climbed the old varnished staircase and walked into her bedroom. The telephone answering machine glowed with a steady, unblinking zero. She stripped off the clothes she had been wearing since she had left Michigan, stuffed them into the laundry bag she kept in her closet, then walked into the bathroom. She ran the water so that it cascaded into the tub hot, turned the air steamy, and condensed on the mirrors.

She stepped into the tub and let the water rise until it was close to the rim, then turned it off, leaned back, and closed her eyes. She had slept very little for the past few days, waiting until Mary Perkins was settled and breathing deep, regular breaths before she stood up, moved a chair to the best window, and sat watching the street outside the motel. Whenever she had begun to doze off, she had found herself sinking into a dream about Timothy Phillips.

She sat up, washed her hair, then lay back down and submerged her head to let the hot water soak away the shampoo and sting the bruises and abrasions on her cheek and jaw. She held her breath for a minute and a half, hearing the old, hollow sound of the pipes, feeling her hair floating up around her face and shoulders like a cloud of soft seaweed. Then she slowly lifted her head above the surface and arched her back to let the long, heavy hair hang down her back, draining along her spine. She lay back to feel the water cleaning every part of her body, slowly dissolving away the feeling of dirt, like a stain, that she always felt when she had been locked in a jail. The showers they had in jails could never wash it out. It had to come off in water she found outside.

Jane stayed in the water until it was cold, and then got out and dried herself gingerly with a big, thick towel, wrapped it around her, and brushed out her hair. Her skin was tender now, as though all of her pores had opened and the grime of the trip had been taken away, and then beneath that, a whole layer of skin cells had come off. She felt new.

She put on a clean gray sweatshirt, some soft faded blue jeans, and white socks, then lay on her bed facing the ceiling, her arms away from her body. She consciously relaxed each muscle, first her feet, ankles, calves, knees, thighs, then her fingers, hands, wrists, forearms, biceps, then her back muscles one pair at a time, from the waist to the shoulders, and fell asleep.

Jake Reinert raked the leaves in his back yard and put them into a new bushel basket. The problem with planting trees when you were young was that the damned things got bigger and more vigorous while you got older and stiffer, until you found one day that you were too old to pick up all the leaves. His problem was worse than most, because his grandfather had planted the one over his head right now. It was absurd to keep picking up sycamore leaves, but it was the first task that had presented itself while he was looking for a way to keep himself from thinking about Jane. The problem was that raking took so little thought that he kept coming back to her.

He remembered the day he had started worrying full-time, when Jane was ten or eleven. Jake had been working in the chemical plant up in the Falls. It was good money for those days, but it was heavy and hard, and the danger of it was constant. There were caustic chemicals that would have to be poured from the big vats a few times each day, and tiny droplets might hit your overalls without your noticing it. By the end of the shift there would be men in the shop whose clothes were already disintegrating, with pinholes through their pants and shirts that were getting big enough to meet each other. In those days nobody said much about it because this was a part of the country where most people worked in the heat of open-hearth steel mills, risked their limbs beside drop-forges or hydraulic presses, or worked in the lumber-yards, where anything that made a noise had the capacity to cut you in two.

There were a number of Indian fellows in the part of the plant where Jake worked. There were a few Tuscaro-ras from the reservation in Lewiston, two or three Mo-hawks who came over the Rainbow Bridge before dawn every morning from Brantsford, Ontario, and four Sene-cas—two from Cattaraugus and two from Tonawanda. They were always playing practical jokes on each other and shouting across the shop in their languages and then laughing. At lunchtime they all sat around one of the long workbenches that was covered with butcher paper and played as many hands of euchre as they could in half an hour, slapping cards down so fast that sometimes it was hard to see them. There were about ten in the shop but only eight played, so there were two games going at a time. They made tally marks on the butcher paper to keep score. Euchre usually went to ten, but they played to a hundred.

Jake had watched them for his first couple of shifts on the job when one day he heard an enormous roar of laughter. One of their interminable games had ended. The two losers sat in their places looking as solemn and wooden as any movie fan would have liked. The two winners stood over them and gleefully flipped the cards against their noses while everybody else pointed and laughed. If the loser was caught laughing or even let a muscle of his face change, the penalty was doubled. Jake didn't need to have it explained to him. They were playing for Nosey, just like kids had when he was growing up. Later, after he knew them better, they had corrected him. The name of the game was some Indian word—they all sounded like "yadadadadadada" to him. So he said, "What's it mean?" and one of them thought for a second, and then said, "Nosey."

They accepted Jake without appearing to notice that they had, and during the summer, when people took their vacation time, he would be the one they asked to sit in for the absent player. One late July he had sat down with his lunch and eyed the tally marks on the butcher paper, pretty certain that if he and his partner, Doyle Winthrop, didn't get lucky this was their day to go home with red noses. Or redder, in Doyle's case.

One of the Mohawks came in from the loading dock looking grim. He talked to two of the others in low tones and then one of the others talked to three more on the other end of the shop. Finally Doyle Winthrop looked back at the bench, stared at Jake for a moment, and then came to sit down.

Doyle leaned on his elbows across the table, stared directly into Jake's eyes, and said, "You were a friend of Henry Whitefield's, weren't you?"

After that the details didn't much matter, but Jake listened to them anyway. Henry was an ironworker. He had

been part of a gang, all of them Iroquois, who had been
out west someplace building a big bridge. Doyle said a
cable that was holding the girder Henry was walking on
had snapped, and down went Henry. Theirs was the generation that had fought in Europe and the Pacific, and the
memory of it hadn't gotten hazy in the few years since.
The Iroquois Confederacy had officially and indepen-
dently declared war on Germany, and all of this little
band that had somehow come to include Jake Reinert had
seen friends blown apart by heavy weapons. They were
all acquainted with the feeling, but none of them spoke
again that day.

Jake had gone home early and found his wife, Margaret, already next door with Jane and her mother. Over
the years after that he had tried to be helpful, but they
weren't the sort of women who needed much help. Jane
had been good at schoolwork, and had never had the sort
of critical shortage of boys that would have required a fa-
therly man to come over and tell her the story of the ugly
duckling. She managed to get herself a scholarship to
Cornell and apparently did whatever they required of her,
because they gave her a diploma at the end of it.

Jake had only begun to worry about Jane in earnest
again a year or so after that, when her mother died. Here
she was a young, strikingly attractive girl with a college
degree and the whole world out there waiting for her. She
came back, moved into the old house next door, and lived
there all alone. She had always held jobs in the summers
when she was home from school, but now, as nearly as
he could tell, her movements weren't regular enough to
accommodate any job he had ever heard of. She was not
merely secretive about what she did, she was opaque.

If he managed to plant himself so that he was impossible to ignore while she was out front mowing her lawn and ask her a question like, "What are you doing these days?" she would say in her friendliest way, "Mowing my lawn." Then she would flick the conversation out of his hands, fold it into a joke, and toss it back to him. "When I get done with this one I'm heading over to your house to do yours. You're turning that place into an eyesore and lowering property values from here to Buffalo."

It was around this time that Jake had begun to notice the visitors. Maybe they had been coming for a long time, and he hadn't noticed because he was still going to work every day. But there they were. The strangers would come to her front door. Some were women, but most of them were men. The door would open and they would disappear inside. Sometimes late at night he would hear a car engine and then they would be gone. A lot of the time Jane would be gone too, and not return for a month or more.

After a couple of years of this he pretended he didn't know where the boundary was between small talk and prying. He asked her where she was getting the money to live. She said she had a "consulting business." That pushed Jake four or five steps past the boundary and made him determined to find out what was going on. Various theories suggested themselves. She obviously had plenty of money that she wasn't prepared to account for in a way that might set anyone's mind at ease.

He had worried himself five years closer to the grave before he heard her burglar alarm go off one night. He rushed to his corner window and flipped the switch to turn on the porch light that he used so seldom he wasn't even sure the 250-watt bulb was good anymore. There, caught in the sudden glare, were not one or two but four men. The one nearest him reached into his coat and produced a pistol. It wasn't the standard revolver the Deganawida police carried. It was big and square like the .45 Colts they used to issue in the army. Jake still considered it a great piece of fortune that the man's second reaction to the light had been to turn his face and then his tail rather than to open fire.

After that night he had sat Jane down and demanded answers to the questions he had been asking less and less politely for years. The ones he got weren't the sort that would induce a reasonable person to sleep much better. A man who had the sort of enemies other people only dream about had managed to get himself tracked to her door, and the four of them had tried to break in to see if there was anything in there to help them learn where he was.

Now Jake took his bushel basket and dumped the leaves into the big barrel by the garage. This part of the country was different from other places because the Indians had never left. There were so many differences between groups—the English from Massachusetts who had fought here in the Revolution and seen how much better this land was; the Irish recruited from their bogs to dig the Erie Canal, supposedly because somebody figured they could survive the swamps but maybe because nobody cared if they didn't; the German farmers who arrived as soon as there was enough water in the ditch to float their belongings here on canal boats—that the Indians weren't much stranger to them than they were to each other. After that the rest of the world arrived.

The names of most places stayed pretty much whatever the Seneca had called them, and the roads were just improvements of the paths between them. The cities were built on the sites of Seneca villages beside rivers and lakes, plenty of them with Senecas still living in them, at first just a trading post and then a few more cabins, and then a mill.

Even now things that people thought of as regional attitudes and expressions came straight from the Senecas. When anybody from around here wanted to say they were still present at the end of a big party, they would say they had "stayed until the last dog was hung." Most of them probably had no idea anymore that they were talking about the Seneca New Year's celebration in the winter, where on the fifth day they used to strangle a white dog and hang it on a pole. Nobody had done that for at least a hundred years.

It was easy to forget about Indians as Indians or Poles as Poles most of the time, so people did, but whenever Jake got to the point where he was pretty sure everybody was just about the same, one of them did something that was absolutely incomprehensible unless you compared it with what her great-grandpa used to do.

Jane awoke suddenly in the darkness. Her hands could feel the stitched outlines of the flowers on the quilted bedspread her mother had made. She was puzzled. It took her a moment to remember why she was in Deganawida, sleeping fully dressed. She could tell that her mind had been struggling with something in the darkness, but whatever it was, she had not been able to bring it back with her this time. There was a sound still in the air, maybe left over from the dream, and then she heard it again: the ring of the doorbell.

She stepped to the window and looked down at the front steps. She could see the faint glow of the porch light on Carey McKinnon's high forehead. He was carrying a big brown shopping bag. She hurried to the mirror, turned on the light, brushed her hair quickly, then rushed into the bathroom and reached for the handle of her makeup drawer, but the ring came again. She had no time.

She came down the stairs, crossed the living room, and swung the door open. She stayed back out of the reach of the bright light on the porch and said, "Oh, too bad. I was hoping it was Special Delivery."

"No, you weren't," said Carey. "They don't come at

eleven o'clock at night. I happened to be passing by on the way home from work, and I saw your car was back."

"No, you weren't," she said. "Deganawida is north of the hospital. Amherst is due east."

"I had to stop near here to buy myself these flowers." He opened the bag and held up a dozen white roses. "Since you're up anyway, could you do me a favor and put them someplace?"

"Oh, all right." She reached out and took them. "I suppose you'd better come in while I do it. I don't want you scaring Mrs. Oshinski's Dobermans."

He stepped in and closed the door behind him. She knew she had imagined he had ducked to come through the doorway; he had just looked down to plant his feet on the mat. But he had always given the impression that he was a big boy and still growing, and it had never gone away, ten years after college, when his sandy hair was already thinning a little at the crown.

He followed her into the kitchen. "So how was your trip?"

"Who said I was on a trip?"

"Oh. Then how did your car like its month in the shop?"

"I was on a trip," she conceded. "California. It's pretty much as advertised."

He nodded. "Warm."

"Yeah. What's a doctor doing coming home this late? House calls?"

"Dream on. I'm working the emergency room. Night is the time when roads get slippery, fevers go up, people clean loaded guns."

Jane snipped the stems of the roses and skillfully arranged them in a cloisonné vase that had been her grandmother's, then placed the vase on the dining room table.

"Beautiful," said Carey. "Good place for them, too."

"They're right where you won't forget them when you leave."

"No, you might as well keep them. They're all wet." He pretended to fold up his shopping bag. "Oh, I forgot. They gave me this too." He held up a bottle of champagne. "Two-for-one sale or something. I couldn't understand the lady in the store. Thick Polish accent."

"Your mother was Polish."

"Was she? I couldn't understand her either." He walked to the sink, popped the cork on the champagne, and plucked two glasses out of the cupboard. "Explains a lot. Maybe that's what she was trying to tell me. Nice woman, though."

Jane had to step into the light to take her glass. Carey clinked it gently with his, then followed her into the living room.

"So why are you working the emergency room?" she asked as she curled her legs under her on the couch. "Finally piss somebody off?"

A change came into his voice as it always did when he talked about his work. "I decided I needed a refresher course, so I took over the evening shift a couple of weeks ago. If Jake asks, I've still got plenty of time to check my regular patients for suspicious moles."

"Why does a young quack like you need a refresher course? Doze off in medical school?"

"I guess I should have said 'a reminder course.' It's basic medicine. The door at the end of the hall slides open, and in walks Death. You get to look him in the eye, spin him around, and kick his ass for him. It's exhilarating.

Besides, the regular guy asked me to help him out. E.R. doctors last about as long as the average test pilot, and he's approaching the crash-and-burn stage. They don't always win." He seemed to notice her listening to him. "You look awful, by the way."

"Sweet of you to say so. That's how women look when you wake them up."

He turned his head to the left to call to an invisible person. "Nurse! More light!" Her eyes involuntarily followed his voice, and he turned on the lamp above him with his right. "Wow. Pretty good contusions and abrasions. Finally piss somebody off?"

She knew she wasn't going to get the car accident story past Dr. Carey McKinnon. "I was mugged outside my hotel."

"I'm sorry, Jane," he said, tilting his head to see her more clearly. "What happened?"

"It was nothing, really. He came out from behind one of those pillars in the garage under the hotel to grab my purse. I yelled and the parking attendant came. He got away."

"Is he all right?"

She frowned. "Why would anybody say that?"

"Your hands."

"Oh," she said. "Well, I did resist a little. I'm not dumb enough to die for a purse, but he scared me."

Carey was already on his feet and moving toward the door.

"Where are you going?"

"I left my bag in the car. I always have one with me in case there's a chance to bill somebody."

"You're a dear friend, but I like you because your big

feet tromp my snow down in the winter so I can get my car out. Who said I wanted medical treatment from you?"

"I just need to bring it in. Old Jake probably recognized my car, and he's handy enough to break in for the drugs."

Carey stepped outside. She heard his trunk slam, and then his feet coming back up on the porch. In a moment he was inside, the black bag was open at her feet, and he was sitting beside her turning her head gently from side to side. He took a bottle out of his bag and poured something out of it onto a ball of cotton. He swabbed her face with the cold liquid and then stared into her eyes with a little flashlight. He took her hands in his and studied them, then bent her wrists a couple of times, staring as though he could see through to her bones.

"Doctor?" she said. "Just tell me, will I be able to play the piano?"

"Heard it. You couldn't before." He didn't smile. "The wrist is only a mild sprain," he said. "It'll be okay in a few days. The lacerations on the knuckles look good already—probably because you didn't put makeup on them. You're lucky. Human teeth are an incredible source of infection." He took a small aerosol can out of the bag and sprayed her hands. It felt colder than the disinfectant, but as it dried, the pain seemed to go away. He lifted her hand and kissed the fingertips. "I just like the taste of that stuff." He looked at her cheerfully. "You want to know the truth, it helps things heal. We don't tell people that, of course."

Jane couldn't think of a retort. In all of the twelve or thirteen years she had known Carey McKinnon, they had been buddies. They had kissed hello and goodbye, but he had been the friend she could call so she didn't have to go to a movie alone or eat at a table for one. The champagne was a pleasant surprise, but the roses brought with them a new ambiguity, and it was growing and getting more confusing.

"Stand up," he said. She stood up. He moved her arms and felt the elbows, pressed the radius and ulna between his fingers. He put his big hand under her rib cage and poked her a couple of times with the other. "Does that hurt?"

"Uh! Of course it hurts. Cut it out," she said. At another time she would have poked him back, but now he was being a doctor—at least she thought he was.

"Your liver didn't pop loose, anyway," he said. "You can have champagne without fear of death."

"Oh?" she said. "How long have I got?"

"What do I care?" He sipped his champagne. "I'll have been dead for twenty years. You pamper yourself like a racehorse, and women handle the wear and tear better than men." His eyes swept up and down her body with a frankness that she wasn't positive was detachment. "It's just a better machine."

"Then you must really be walking around in a piece of junk," she said. She stretched her sore arms and rubbed her shoulders.

"That's only muscle pain," he said.

"Well, don't sound disappointed. It's the best pain I can manage right now."

"A big shot of adrenaline comes in and your muscles go from rest to overperformance in a second or two, and they feel the strain. In two days you'll be back out there teaching truck drivers to arm wrestle, or whatever it is you do."

"Consulting."

"Insulting them—whatever," he said. He started to close his bag, but then spotted something. He picked up a clear bottle with a liquid in it that looked like vinegar. "Try this stuff."

"What is it?"

He handed it to her. "Don't look free samples in the mouth. Doctors get an incredible number of them, and once in a while you get something you can give your friends legally. This stuff is terrific."

"What's it for?"

"It's not medicine. It's just glorified massage oil. It's got a very mild analgesic in it, so it puts a deep warmth on sore muscles."

Jane opened the bottle and sniffed it. "You're not lying, anyway. It smells too good to be medicine."

He took it back. "Come on," he said. "Lie down and I'll put some on you."

"Lie down, Carey?" she asked. "Could you be a little more specific, please? Or maybe less specific?"

"I assure you, madam, I am a qualified physician. Board-certified. Climb up there on the board." He pointed to the dining room table.

She walked uncertainly in that direction and stared at the table skeptically. "The table? Are you sure?"

"Well, if I asked you to lie down on your bed, would you do it?"

"Maybe," she said. Then she wondered how much she had actually meant by that. If it wasn't what she was afraid it was, why had she hesitated?

He said, "Okay, if it's not occupied, let's use it." He walked to the stairs.

Jane took a big gulp of her champagne. They had been friends for so long that the possibility of a sudden change was unsettling. She didn't want to lose him. She picked up the bottle and followed. "I was thinking about you a few days ago," she said. "I was talking to a little boy."

"Tall or short?"

"Uh . . . tall, I guess, for his age. He's eight."

"Tell him surgery, then. Dermatologists are short, as a rule. Surgeons are tall."

He stopped at the door of her bedroom, and she edged past him and sat on the bed. She looked up at him. "Are you sure you're not just trying to get funny with me?"

Carey sipped his glass of champagne thoughtfully. "It's crossed my mind. Always does. We never have before, and this may not be the best time to start. I sure don't want to lose you just because we disagreed on how to go about it. It's kind of tricky, and you're a very critical person."

"I am not," she said. "But what if it turned out to be an awful mistake? Would you still be able to call me up when you wanted to go someplace where no respectable person would go with you?"

"It's hard to know. How about you? If you needed somebody to make fun of, would it still be me?"

She stared at him for a moment. "I don't know. I guess we should talk about it sometime when we're not exhausted and the bottle's still corked." She flopped onto the bed on her stomach with her arms bent and her hands under her chin. "Right now I need an old friend who's willing to rub my sore back."

He sat on the bed beside her, lifted the sweatshirt a few inches, poured a little of the oil in his hand, and then slowly and gently rubbed it into the small of her back in a circular motion.

"Ooh," she sighed. "That's good."

He worked patiently, his strong hands softly kneading the sore muscles in exactly the right spots, working up higher on her back now, to the shoulder blades. She could feel the tight, hard knots of muscle relaxing under his touch. The hands kept moving inward toward the tender muscles along the spine. When he stopped to pour more oil into his palm, Jane pulled the sweatshirt up almost to her shoulders, hesitated, then slipped it up over her head and set it beside her. She was naked to the waist now, but it had seemed that making him work under a shirt was idiotic. If Carey saw her breasts, he saw her breasts.

His hands were on her shoulders, and then the connecting muscles to her neck and then along the back of her neck to her scalp. She felt goose bumps and shivered, then relaxed again. She was so loose and at ease now that all the muscles on the top half of her body were on the edge of some kind of sleep, a paralysis of laziness, so happy not moving that they didn't quite belong to her anymore. They were just there waiting for him to touch them again.

Carey said, "How's it going so far?"

"I'm ready to die now," she announced. "Just give me more champagne and keep rubbing, and you can tell them to pull the trigger whenever."

He worked back down her spine, and she began to imagine that she could see him clearly from the position of his hands on her skin. She remembered telling Timmy about him. She had said he was special, and he was. Without warning, the word *angel* appeared in her mind, and she laughed.

"What's funny?"

"Nothing," she answered with the smile still in her voice. "You're being an angel."

"How about your legs?"

"What about them?"

"Do they hurt?"

She considered the implications. He couldn't rub oil on her through a pair of blue jeans. He knew that. "Not at the moment." When she had said it she felt a sense of loss that she didn't have the time to analyze if she was going to fix it. "You can't be too careful, though." She reached under her stomach to unbutton the jeans and give a tug on the zipper.

He slipped the jeans down her legs and off her ankles, and she felt tension in her throat. Then his hands were on the soles of her feet, squeezing them with tiny circular movements, until she began to imagine she was feeling him sending messages up the nerves to her shoulders and neck. The tension didn't go away, but it wasn't unpleasant anymore. He worked up the Achilles tendon, the calves, and very softly the backs of her knees, and then slowly and carefully up the hamstrings. She was calm and happy, and she wasn't thinking at all anymore, just following his touch. But then the circular movement of his hand passed for a moment between her thighs and she caught herself arching her back to spread them apart the tiniest bit.

He kept working on her legs and back, but she could feel that the hands weren't alternating anymore, so he was undressing with the other. Then she felt the panties being peeled off, and he turned her over to gently kiss her bruised face, and they slowly joined in the embrace that she had always known would come.

Everything began with a slow inevitability, a luxurious

ease and simplicity that made her feel warm, then eager, and then glad. But the feeling didn't fade. It built and intensified. After that, every second, every heartbeat expanded into a moment of its own. Suddenly she became aware that she was hearing a woman's voice, and she wondered how long she had been doing that, moaning and making little cries that she couldn't have silenced if she tried. Then she went beyond thinking into a place where every sensation seemed to go up one notch on the scale to the highest frequency—colors, sounds, movements. She was almost afraid when the intensity kept building, and the word *angel* came back to her, but this time she didn't laugh, because everything was bright and fever-clear and immediate, with no distance left at all, no will inside her but his.

The whole night passed without her knowing the time, because she had the sense that she would have to give up something in order to think. They would pause and let their heartbeats slow, lying together still clasped in the same embrace but not the same now, somehow friends simply passing together into sleep. But then one of them would stir, and the other would silently say yes, each time the question and the answer completely different, because every time the last time had not faded or gone away, so it was like going up another step on a stairway.

At dawn they were lying on the bed, eyes closed, when he said, "What do you think about getting married?"

Jane's breath caught in her throat. Have beautiful tall children. Live here—not in this house, but at least close by, in the big old stone one in Amherst with him. Maybe that was where all of this had been taking her, leading her away from death the way she had taken other people. She would never have to tell him what a guide was because it would all be over—already was over when you started losing.

"No answer?" he asked.

"Every girl's fondest wish," she said. "Think the guy who owns the Buffalo Bills might be interested in marrying me? Maybe the one who fathered those quintuplets. There's a guy who knows his way around a diaper."

"I mean it," said Carey. "We should get married."

Jane sat up, then leaned over and kissed him, letting her hair hang down on both sides of their faces like a curtain. She lay back down. "Thank you," she said. "I guess we ought to have a serious talk about it sometime."

"Does that mean yes? That's what you said last night."

"Don't be an idiot."

"Meaning?"

"I've always loved everything I knew about you."

"So why are you saying no?"

"I didn't say no." She sat up again and ran her fingers through her hair to find imaginary tangles. "I said we should have a serious talk sometime. I'll start any time you want to, but I'm not going to say yes right now."

He sat up too. "I can do that."

She sighed. "When was the last time you had sex, Carey?"

He pursed his lips and said reluctantly, "The other night."

"You mean the night before last night. The last time you came off a shift."

"It was a colleague. It wasn't a routine procedure. She's a terrific diagnostician, a person of the highest—"

"I don't want to know."

"What is this? You pry and then pretend you're not interested?"

"You'd make a lousy husband."

"Jane, this thing with my colleague. It's not anything to get jealous about. It was a single, isolated event. Two patients died at the end of the shift after we did everything we could. I think we were just comforting each other. There's something buried deep in the cerebral cortex that gets triggered when you lose a life, some primitive forgotten instinct that says 'Fuck while you can, because one of these times that is going to be you.' It's the practical animal reaction that evolved to keep the species alive after prehistoric kill-offs. She's probably mystified that we did it. Next time we do a shift together we'll be perfectly professional."

"I'm sure you will. You're a good doctor, and you'd know if she weren't. But I assure you, if you had her in the sack, she's not going to let herself get too mystified. She's probably waiting on your doorstep. If she isn't, it doesn't matter, because there will be another along shortly. There is, in fact, isn't there? Me. The world is full of women—an endless supply—and every last one of them has something about her: a little smile that makes you want to smile too, or breasts like two perfect grapefruits. Remember her? That's probably why she hung around your supermarket—so you could make the comparison."

"That's not fair," he said. "You want me to start quoting you?"

"No," Jane answered. "It isn't fair. That's part of what I'm talking about. What we know about each other looks a little different if marriage rears its ugly head. And I'm not criticizing you."

"You aren't?"

"No. I never thought for a second that there was anything wrong with anything you do. I still don't. But the only way it would make any sense to marry you is if I had some reason to believe you had become monogamous."

"You actually think I can't do that?" Carey asked.

She smiled and lay down with her head on his shoulder. It was surprising how good it felt. In a moment she said, "Want some breakfast?" and was up and heading for the kitchen. She slipped her bathrobe on as she walked down the hall. Then she heard the *beep-beep-beep-beep*, stopped, and walked back to the bedroom doorway. He was sitting on the bed staring sadly at the pager attached to the belt on the floor. "Your alarm's going off," she said. "Somebody seems to be breaking into your pants."

Carey picked up the beeper, slipped on his pants, walked to the telephone by the bed, and cradled the receiver under his chin as he dialed. "It's the hospital," he said, and buckled his belt. As she walked back down the hallway she heard him say, "Dr. McKinnon."

Jane went into the kitchen and packed him a little lunch while he talked on the telephone. She could hear him thumping around up there, probably not doing a very good job of making himself presentable. When she heard his feet on the stairs she came out and handed him the little brown bag.

"Sorry," he said. "I'll call you as soon as I'm off and get some sleep."

"Thanks," she answered, then added, "If I'm not around, don't worry. I may have to go out of town."

"See?" He grinned. "Nothing's changed. You always say that." He gave her a long, gentle kiss, picked up his black bag, and hurried out to his car.

Jane thought about what she had said. She had no

plans to go anywhere. It was simply the old habit: never give anyone a reason to ask the police to look for you.

She considered going back to bed, but if she did she would be out of step with the sun and moon, and she hated that feeling more than being tired. She spent the day cleaning her clean house, cutting her lawn, and weeding her flower beds. She tried not to think about what Carey McKinnon was doing, or about being Mrs. Carey McKinnon, or about finding the right way of loving a particular person. What she needed to know wasn't something that could be figured out in advance. She had to wait until she was sure she wasn't taking an old friend and converting him into the consolation prize for failure. It was only after night had come that she went back up to bed and allowed herself to sleep.

9

Jane sat in the kitchen and drank coffee. The sun was beginning to come up, the light now diffused and gray beyond the window. She wasn't sure how long she had been hearing the birds, but they were flitting from limb to limb now, making chirrups. She used the hot coffee and the silence to work her way back through her dream, and she knew where every bit of it had come from.

She had been running at night through the woods, trying to make it to the river. She must have been a child, because her parents were with her. There was something big and dark and ferocious chasing them, but she wasn't able to catch a glimpse of it through the trees. Every time she tried to look over her shoulder it seemed to be closer, but she could only discern a shadow that blotted out some of the stars, or see branches shaking as it trampled through a thicket.

She walked to the middle of the living room and cleared her mind while she began the one hundred and twenty-eight movements of Tai Chi, one flowing into the next without interruption. She decided her muscles weren't as sore as they had been yesterday. Maybe Carey's liniment had worked after all—or something else had. Her body borrowed part of her consciousness as it had learned to do through long years to move through positions with names like "Grasp Sparrow's Tail" and "Cross Hands and Carry Tiger to Mountain," and ended as it had begun, almost floating. Then she slipped on a sweat suit, hung her house key on a chain around her neck, went down the front steps, and began to run.

She started slowly and easily in the cold dawn air and gradually lengthened her strides as her body warmed and her muscles relaxed. She ran down to the river and along the open grassy strip toward the south. Deganawida was alive this morning with people just up and driving along Niagara Street toward their jobs, the men's hair wet from their showers and plastered to their heads, the children dressed in their second-heaviest coats already, their mothers hustling them down the sidewalk and making sure they were at least pointed in the direction of the school when they started off. She ran up as far as the Grand Island bridge and then turned back. The run home would give her just the right stretch of time to shower, change, and eat before the library opened.

Inside the library she walked to the desk and collected all of the past month's issues of the *Los Angeles Times*, then hid in the small room in the corner surrounded by the reference books that nobody ever used unless they wanted to settle a bet, and sat down to read.

The first one that caught her eye was two days old.

INVESTIGATION OF COURTHOUSE DEATHS IS
INCONCLUSIVE

VAN NUYS—In the latest development in the strange saga of Timothy Phillips, kidnap victim and heir to a San Francisco fortune, an L.A. Police spokesman

conceded today that the investigation has so far produced no charges against anyone. The bizarre events at
the Van Nuys courthouse which caused the deaths of
two persons and the arrests of five others last month
are still under investigation, said Captain Daniel Brice.

Details are still sketchy, but the police have put together this much of the puzzle: Just as the courts began
session on the morning of the 15th, attorney Dennis
Morgan, 38, of Washington, D.C., stopped his car in
front of the courthouse to let off his eight-year-old
client, Timothy Phillips, and Mona Turley, 29, the
woman posing as Phillips's mother. The rented car
then apparently slipped into reverse and slammed into
an oncoming vehicle. Driver Harold Kern, 23, and
passenger James Curtain, 26, both of Los Angeles,
suffered minor injuries, but Morgan was (See *Inconclusive*, A 29)

Jane impatiently searched page 29 and found the
rest of the article in the lower left corner.

pronounced dead at the scene.

Kern and Curtain ran into the courthouse, apparently
seeking assistance for Morgan. Mona Turley, police the-
orize, may have believed the two men were pursuing her
with hostile intent. A struggle ensued, in which numer-
ous bystanders took sides. The confrontation erupted
into a fight in a fifth-floor hallway, where bailiffs in a
nearby courtroom responded to the disturbance.

Arrested with Curtain and Kern were Roscoe Hull,
22, Max Corto, 28, both of Burbank, and Colleen Mahoney, 29, of Orlando, Florida.

After police restored order, the body of Mona Turley was discovered at the bottom of a stairwell, an apparent victim of a fall from an upper floor. Police sources confirm that a maze of conflicting allegations have been made, but eyewitnesses have established that none of the five persons arrested could have left the hallway once the fighting began.

Captain Brice explained that in the absence of evidence that any of the combatants had ever met the deceased, had any motive to harm her, or were in the stairwell at the time of her death, they could not be considered suspects. He said that foul play has not been ruled out, but that Turley might have been overcome with anxiety or remorse because of possible kidnapping charges and taken her own life.

Jane sat and stared at the orderly rows of thick volumes on the shelves in front of her. They had killed Mona, but the best she could do was to go into court as Colleen Mahoney, lie and say she saw them, then watch twenty witnesses parade to the stand and say she was wrong. The ones who had been in the car had certainly broken Dennis's neck with a choke-hold after the crash, but she hadn't seen that either.

If the police hadn't found a connection between any of them and the Timothy Phillips case, then they were hired hands. No doubt the police and the F.B.I. were quietly looking for Colleen Mahoney, but there was no reason to let them find her. She was finished.

She looked through the newspapers for more articles about Timothy Phillips. Finally she found one that was only a day old.

HOFFEN-BAYNE NOT SUSPECTED OF
WRONGDOING, D.A. SAYS

A spokesman for the District Attorney's office issued
a statement today denying rumors that Hoffen-Bayne
Financial, Inc., is under suspicion of attempting to
defraud kidnapped heir Timothy Phillips of the multi-
million-dollar estate of his late grandmother.

"The rumor has no merit," said Deputy D.A. Kyle
Ambrose. "All you have to do is read the conditions of
the trust. If Mr. Phillips were deceased, Hoffen-Bayne
did not stand to benefit. All the money was to be donated to charities. I'm convinced that they filed to have
the child declared dead because it was the proper procedure under the trust instructions, and consistent with
the behavior of a good corporate citizen. There's very
little benefit to society from having vast fortunes tied
up in trusts with no beneficiaries. The intent of the
grandmother was to provide for her grandson, not to
build a perpetually-growing pyramid of unused money."
Ambrose noted that Hoffen-Bayne had reason to be
delighted with the news that Timothy Phillips had
been found. "If the estate went to charities, the company would have lost large annual fees as trustee and
executor, which now legally must continue until the
boy reaches eighteen, and could continue as long as he
wishes."

Jane read the article twice. Dennis had been certain
that the men who were after Timmy had been hired by
Hoffen-Bayne. Dennis was a lawyer, and there had been
something in the documents that had convinced him that
Hoffen-Bayne had a rational reason for doing it. But the

Los Angeles D.A.'s office was full of lawyers, criminal lawyers at that. Were they just convinced that companies like Hoffen-Bayne weren't in the business of killing their clients?

She tried to look at it in a logical way. Hoffen-Bayne had chosen this time to have Timmy declared dead. If they were capable of murder, they could have waited until they had actually killed him, left his body where it would be found, and let the coroner do the paperwork. Or they could have waited and filed the papers at the best possible time for them. No, she had to assume that they had already waited, and that this was the perfect time. There was nothing external to make them do it now. There were ten more years until Timmy could take control of the money and fire them, ten more years of the "large annual fee" the D.A. had mentioned.

Jane stood up, walked out to the librarian's counter, and caught Amy Folliger's eye. "Can I make a couple of copies on the machine?"

"Sure," said Amy. "A dime a copy. But I'm afraid you'll have to sign this sheet," she added apologetically. "It relieves the library of liability if you violate a copyright."

Jane glanced at the papers on the clipboard. The first page was a summary of the copyright law of 1978. She signed the second page and handed it back.

"Sorry," said Amy. "Did you ever wonder how we ever got to this point?"

"What point?"

Amy's big eyes widened behind the silver-framed glasses that Jane had never seen her wear except on duty at the library. "Where everything is lawyers. Of course they get to write the laws. Did you ever hear of a lawyer missing the chance to give himself perpetual fees?"

"Once or twice," said Jane. "Maybe if we all behave ourselves for a hundred years, they'll go away." She copied the articles, then walked to the newspaper rack and carefully replaced the stack of *L.A. Times*.

Jane put the copies into her purse and walked out of the library. As she approached her car, she composed the note that she would write to Karen the lawyer to explain what was bothering her, but it didn't feel right. What was bothering her was that she wanted to know now.

Jane passed the telephone booth beside the building and then walked back to it. She dialed the number and said to the secretary who answered, "This is Jane White-field. She knows me. Tell her I'm going to fax something to her."

"Would you like an appointment for a consultation or—"

"No, thanks," she said. "She can call me." Jane hung up and walked up Main Street to the little stationery store that Dick Herman had run for the last few years since his father retired. The growing collection of signs in the window announced there were post office boxes, copiers, and a fax service now.

When she had sent the clippings Jane drove home, walked inside, and heard the telephone ringing. She closed the door and hurried to the phone. Maybe Carey wasn't with the great diagnostician. She snatched up the receiver just as her answering machine started. "You have reached—" said the recording, and clicked off. "Hello?"

"Hi, Jane." It was Karen's voice. The last time Jane had heard it Karen had wondered aloud—in a purely speculative way—whether there was any way to protect a witness who had just saved a client of hers. "I got your message. But what is it?"

"Did you read the articles?" said Jane.

"The second woman—I take it that was you?"

"You don't want to know."

"It's okay. Attorney-client privilege."

"I'm not a client."

"If you're in trouble you are."

"I'm not," said Jane. "I just need advice. How are they stealing the money?"

"I don't have the slightest idea," said Karen. "If it were obvious, I certainly wouldn't be the only one who could figure it out. Without reading the documents that established the trust I'd only be guessing anyway."

"All right," said Jane. "Let me fish, then. What's the statute of limitations on stealing money from a trust fund?"

"That's breach of trust as a fiduciary. Here it's four years. I'd have to look up California."

"Suppose they robbed Timmy the day the old lady died. They have Timmy declared dead and it's over? Nobody can do anything?"

"No," said Karen. "He's a minor, right? The statute time doesn't start running until he's eighteen, when the money goes to him. If he doesn't spot it after four years, they're in the clear, as long as they didn't do anything worse."

"What if he were dead?"

"Then the next heir gets the money—presumably some adult—and the clock starts again. Who is it?"

Jane was silent for a minute. "The charities," she said. "That's it, isn't it?"

"That's what?"

"That's the answer. That's why they wanted Timmy dead—legally or really. So that the heir isn't a person."

"I'm not sure I follow that."

"Timmy's grandmother set up this trust fund. It was supposed to go to her son. The son died. The next beneficiary was her infant grandson. That's Timmy. There weren't any other relatives, or if there were, Grandma wasn't interested. The D.A. mentioned it in that article. The money goes to charities."

"It can't be that. Charities aren't generally run by stupid people. They receive bequests all the time, and their counsel are very sophisticated about making sure they get what the benefactor wanted them to. The charity is a corporation, and that's like a person in law. The charity would have four years before the statute time ran. The lawyers would go over the will and the trust papers the day they heard about it."

"No," said Jane. "The trust doesn't go to the charities. Only the money does."

Karen was silent for the space of an indrawn breath. "Oh, no," she said. "You're telling me the old lady didn't specify the charities?"

"Nobody has ever mentioned any," said Jane. "And Dennis—another lawyer who did read the papers—said it was just 'charities.' He was sure they were going to steal the money, but he didn't say how."

Karen's voice sounded tired, but she spoke quickly, as though she were reading something that was printed inside her eyelids. "Then I can think of a lot of ways to do it. Here's the simplest. Timmy becomes deceased—either in fact or in law—and they get a death certificate. They then disperse the money to a charity of their choice, or even of their own making, which kicks most of the money back in some way: ghost salaries and services, paid directorships, whatever."

"Is that the way you would do it?"

Karen's voice was a monotone. "Thank you very much."

"You know what I mean. Is it the smartest way? They picked this time to have Timmy declared dead. They could have waited forever. There must be a reason why they did it now."

"What I just told you is the dumb way. The smartest way is always to stay as close to legality as possible. If they were sole trustee and executor, they could have been draining the fund since it was started. They could set enormous fees, charge all sorts of costs to the trust, and cook the books a little here and there to show losing investments. They wouldn't steal it all. They would leave a substantial sum in there. How much is there?"

"I don't know. I get the impression it's tens of millions, maybe hundreds."

"Okay. Say it's a hundred million. They could get away with four or five percent a year as trustee and executor. They could also do virtually anything with the principal. There are written guidelines in every state I know of, but they're broad, and they're open to interpretation. They could invest in their friend's chinchilla ranch and have their friend go bankrupt, if nobody knew the connection. If they were smart enough to steal it slowly and vary the investments to make it look inconclusive, they could do a lot."

"Inconclusive?"

"You know. The trust has lots of stock in fifteen hundred companies, twenty million in federal bonds and a five-million-dollar write-off on the chinchilla ranch, and it's tough to prove they were anything but mistaken on the issue of chinchilla futures. Not dishonest."

"So then what?"

"They do it a few more times over the years, always making sure that the proportions are right—nine winners, one loser. They're stealing a lot, but some of it is hidden by the fact that most investments are making money. You have to remember that even the good investments go up and down too, so the bad ones are hard to spot. When they've got all they can, they call it quits."

"How do they call it quits?"

"They fulfill the terms of the trust—that is, they disperse the money to charities. Only now it's not a hundred million. It's twenty million."

"And nobody notices that eighty million is gone?"

"If the trust doesn't change hands, nobody looks. If you have twenty million, you can create quite a splash in the world of charity. You don't write a twenty-million-dollar check to the United Way and close the books."

"What do you do?"

"You divide it into ten-thousand-dollar tidbits and dole it out. Now you have two thousand checks from the Agnes Phillips Trust, which nobody ever heard of. Each year, you send four hundred different charities all over the country ten thousand dollars each. That's more than one a day. You do it for five years. The first year, when the Children's Fund of Kankakee gets a check from the Agnes Phillips Trust, what does it do?"

"You've got me."

"It sends a thank-you note. They're not going to demand an audit of the trust that sent them ten grand. It would never occur to them, and if it did, they couldn't make it stick. They're not heirs named in a will. They're a charity that got a big check at the discretion of the people who sent it. They're grateful. They have no idea of the size of the trust, and they hope they'll get another check next year so they can help more children."

"So at the end of five years, the money is all gone, and the statute of limitations has run on the eighty million they stole?"

"If they get only five percent return on the money while they dole it out, they get a couple of extra years. What's working most in their favor is that during all that time—figure eight years—nobody is asking any questions. That's the main thing. If at the end of that time there's a full-scale audit, the auditors won't be able to find a single instance of mistaken judgment that isn't at least eight years old, and no theft at all. As long as it's more than four since the payout began, nothing much matters."

"So what do I do now?"

"I'll tell you one thing I'd do. I'd make sure Timothy Phillips isn't alone much. None of this works if the heir is alive."

10

Jane went to the pay telephone at a market a few miles from her house, dialed Los Angeles Information to get the number of the Superior Court in Van Nuys, then asked to be transferred to Judge Kramer's office. It was still early in the morning in California and Judge Kramer's secretary sounded irritable and sleepy. "Judge Kramer's chambers."

Jane said, "Could you please tell him it's Colleen?" The last name he had given her had slipped her mind.

"One moment. I'll see if he can be disturbed."

The name came back to her. "Mahoney."

"Pardon me?"

"Colleen Mahoney."

Jane's mind could see the secretary pushing the hold button, walking to the big oak door, giving a perfunctory knock, and walking into the dim room with the horizontal blinds. She allowed a few seconds for the secretary to tell him, but before she expected him to remember and pick up, he was on the line. "Judge Kramer."

"Hello, Judge," she said. "Remember me?"

"Yes. This is an unexpected pleasure," he said. "At least I hope it is."

"I found out something that you need to know."

"What is it?"

"Well, I read that the D.A. has taken a look at Timmy's trust and said Hoffen-Bayne couldn't be anything but honest. He missed something."

"What did he miss?"

Jane spoke with a quiet urgency. "If Timmy was dead, the trust was to go to charities, so the D.A. assumed everything had to be okay. But in the trust Grandma didn't say, 'If Timmy dies, dissolve the trust right away and divide its assets among the following charities,' or 'Let the trust continue forever and the income go to the following charities.' She simply said, 'Give it away.' So there was no specific organization named in the trust who could demand the right to see the books."

"You're saying that someone at Hoffen-Bayne planned to plunder the trust fund, give the residue to charities, and nobody would be the wiser?" he asked. "I don't see how they could imagine they would get away with it."

"A lawyer friend of mine thinks it would have worked fine if Timmy hadn't turned up. If there are no heirs, there's nobody with the right to demand an audit."

"Except the state of California."

"Let me ask you this. When the grandmother died, wouldn't the trust have either gone through probate or been declared exempt?"

"Well, yes."

"And doesn't it have to file tax returns each year?"

"Certainly."

"My friend seems to think that there's no other occasion when the state automatically takes a look, unless the trust changes hands. Somebody with a legitimate reason has to ask. And the statute of limitations for embezzling the money is something like four years."

The judge blew some air out through his teeth. "Your friend seems to have worked this through more carefully than I have. If they filed the standard annual forms, declared Timmy legally dead, and took their time about the disbursement to charities, then yes, they could probably avoid scrutiny until it was too late to prosecute the theft. Your friend must practice in another state. The statute of limitations here isn't four years. It's two."

"Great," she muttered.

"But they can't do what they planned. They never got the death certificate."

Jane spoke slowly and quietly. "If they've already robbed him, then they still need to get one. I think they're committed."

"It's all right. Timmy is under police protection."

"I know," said Jane. "I went into his bedroom, talked to him, took him for a ride, and brought him back."

"I'll order him moved," said the judge.

"Moving him increases the danger. Just tell them you're not keeping him incommunicado, you want him protected, and they'll do their best. I'm sure you know they can't keep somebody from killing him if the person tries hard enough."

"Then what the hell do you want me to do?"

"Remove the motive."

"How?"

"The reason to kill him is to hide a theft, so uncover it. He's a ward of the court. Order an audit of his assets. Open everything up."

"All right."

"And, Judge," Jane said, "can you make it a surprise? You know—like a raid?"

"Yes. I'll have to do some preliminary probing first, and I'll have to find probable cause for a search, but I'll do it. Now what else are you waiting for me to stumble onto?"

"Nothing." Then she added, "But, Judge . . ."

"What?"

"I don't know if it's occurred to you yet, but if they realize you're going to do this, then Timmy isn't the big threat to them anymore. You are."

"I'm aware of that," he snapped. "Now I've got sixty-three litigants and petitioners and all their damned attorneys penned up in a courtroom waiting for me, so if you'll excuse me . . ."

"Keep safe. You're a good man."

"Of course I am," he said. "Goodbye."

Jane hung up the telephone and drove home. She climbed the stairs, opened her closet, and then remembered that she had given the suitcase she was looking for to the Salvation Army in Los Angeles. She went downstairs into the little office she had made out of her mother's sewing room, looked in the closet, and found the old brown one. It was a little smaller, but she wasn't going to bring much with her. She stared at the telephone for a moment, then dialed his number. His answering machine clicked on. "Carey, this is Jane. I'm afraid I was right about the trip. I'll call when I'm home. Meanwhile you'll have to make your own fun. Bye." She walked upstairs to her bedroom and began to pack.

As Jane set down her suitcase and walked through the kitchen to be sure that all the windows were locked and the food stored in the freezer, she saw the pile of letters that Jake had brought her. She had not even bothered to look at them. She leaned against the counter and glanced at each envelope, looking for bills. There were several envelopes from companies, but they were all pitches to get her to buy something new.

Finally she opened the one at the bottom. It was thin and square and stiff, from Maxwell-Lammett Investment Services in New York. Inside was a greeting card. It was old, the picture from a photograph that had been hand-tinted. There was a stream with a deer just emerging from a thicket, so that it was easy to miss at first. All the leaves of the trees were bright red and orange and yellow. The caption said "Indian Summer." When she looked inside, a check fluttered to the floor. The female handwriting in the card said, "You told me that one morning after a year or two I would wake up and look around me and feel good because it was over, and then I would send you a present. I found the card months ago and saved it, but you're a hard person to shop for. Thanks. MaRried and PrEgnant." *R* was Rhonda and *E* was Eckerly, or used to be.

Jane picked up the check and looked at it. The cashier's machine printing on it said "Two Hundred and Fifty Thousand and 00/100 Dollars." The purchaser was the investment company, and the notation said "Sale of Securities." She put the check into her purse and took one last look at the card. Rhonda had probably felt clever putting her name in code. If the people her ex-husband had paid to hunt her had known about Jane they could have identified Rhonda's prints from the paper and probably traced her through the check.

She switched on the ventilator on the hood over the stove, set out a foil pan, lit the card at a gas burner, and set it in the pan to burn. There would come a time when an uninvited guest would go through this house. Maybe it would be some bounty hunter, or maybe it would be the policemen investigating her death. Whoever it was would not find traces of a hundred fugitives and then turn them into a bonanza for his retirement. When the card was burned, she turned off the fan, then rinsed the ashes into her garbage disposal and let it grind them into the sewer. She dropped the rest of the mail into the trash can, picked up her suitcase, set the alarm, and stepped out onto the porch.

As she locked her door and took a last look at her house, she thought about the old days, when Senecas went out regularly to raid the tribes to the south and west in parties as small as three or four warriors. After a fight they would run back along the trail through the great forest, sometimes not stopping for two days and nights.

When they made it back into Nundawaonoga, they would approach their village and give a special shout to tell the people what it was they would be celebrating. But sometimes a lone warrior would come up the trail, the only one of his party who had survived. He would rest and eat and mourn his friends for a time. Then he would quietly collect his weapons and extra moccasins and provisions and walk back down the trail alone. He would travel all the way back to the country of the enemy, even if it were a thousand miles west to the Mississippi or a thousand miles south beyond the Cumberland. He would stay alone in the forest and observe the enemy until he was certain he knew their habits and defenses and vulnerabilities. He would watch and wait until he had perceived that they no longer thought about an Iroquois attack, even if it took a year or two.

It occurred to Jane as she got into her car that Rhonda's present had come at a good time. If she stopped to deposit it on her way to the airport, it would buy a lot of spare moccasins.

11

Jane took a flight to Dallas–Fort Worth under the name Wendy Simmons, and another to San Diego as Diane Newberry. Then she took a five-minute shuttle bus ride from the airport to the row of tall hotels on Harbor Island. She stepped off at the TraveLodge, but walked down Harbor Island Drive to the Sheraton East because it seemed to be the biggest.

She checked in with a credit card in the name of Katherine Webster. She had gotten the card in the same way she had obtained the five others she had brought with her: she had grown them. Now and then she would take a trip to a different part of the country just to grow new credit cards. She would start with a forged birth certificate, use it to admit her to the test for a genuine driver's license, and then would go to a bank and start a checking account in a new name. If the amount she deposited was large enough, sometimes the bank would offer her a credit card that day. If it did not, she would use the checks to pay for mail orders. Within a few months, the new woman would begin receiving unsolicited mail. Among the catalogs and requests for contributions would inevitably be offers for credit cards. She used the credit cards carefully, a new one in each town, so that when Katherine Webster disappeared, she didn't reappear in the next city. Instead, a woman named Denise Hollinger took her place.

The banks that issued their own credit cards were happy to pay themselves automatically each month from her checking account, so all she had to do was to keep the balance high. For the others, she simply filled in the change-of-address section on the third bill and had future ones sent to a fictitious business manager named Stewart Hoffstedder, C.P.A. One of Mr. Hoffstedder's services was paying clients' bills. He had a post office box in New York City to receive the bills, and he issued neatly typed checks from a large New York bank to pay them. The imaginary Mr. Hoffstedder was so reliable that each year most of his clients would have their credit limits increased.

Sometimes Jane would grow a different kind of credit card. It would begin with her opening a joint checking account for herself and her husband, who was so busy that she had to bring the signature card home and have him sign it and return it by mail. Months passed while the husband paid for his mail-order goods with the checks and got his credit card. Then Jane would close the joint checking account and make sure the imaginary Mr. Hoffstedder got her imaginary husband's bills. She could use the man's card to pay expenses if she made reservations over the telephone, and when traveling let people guess whether she was wife, lover, or colleague without having to give herself any name at all.

After Katherine Webster checked into the hotel, she bought the San Diego newspapers, went directly to her room, ordered dinner from room service, and made the preparations she had planned during her long trip across the country. First she ordered a rental car by telephone, the keys to be delivered to her room for Mr. William Dunlavey, and the car left in the hotel parking lot. She spent a few minutes reading the society page of the *San Diego Union*, then set her alarm for six A.M. and went to bed.

When the alarm woke her, she checked the name she had found on the society page again: Marcy Hungerford of Del Mar, co-chair of the Women of St. James Fund-raising Committee and honorary chair of this year's ball, was headed for the family's eastern digs in Palm Beach. That was the best name in the columns. Honorary chairs were either famous or had money, and Marcy Hunger-ford wasn't famous. She was doing fund-raising and was active in that world, so she might have one telephone number that people could find. Jane checked the tele-phone book and found it listed, with the address beside it.

Jane took the stairs to the swimming pool, went out the garden gate, and skirted the building to the parking lot. She had no difficulty finding the rented car. She had told the woman on the telephone that Mr. Dunlavey liked big black cars, and this one had a small sticker on the left rear bumper that had the right rental company's name on it. She walked farther along the line of cars until she found one with an Auto Club sticker, peeled it off with a nail file, and stuck it over the one on her car's bumper.

She drove out to the Golden State Freeway, headed north to the first Del Mar exit, went over a high mesa and came down onto the road along the ocean. The houses on the west side of the street were big and far apart, and she could see vast stretches of flat beach on the other side of them. When she found Marcy Hungerford's house she was satisfied. It was two stories with a long, sloped roof and stilts on the beach side, a four-car garage under it on the street side, and about eight thousand square feet in the middle. She drove past it at thirty miles an hour and studied the exterior. The establishment was too complicated for Marcy Hungerford to have given all of the servants the week off or taken them with her, but they would cause no trouble. By the time they realized something was wrong, it wouldn't be wrong anymore.

At nine A.M. Jane found a little shop in San Diego that rented post office boxes, and she took a key and paid for a month in the name of Marcy Hungerford. Then she drove back to Del Mar and found the post office. She filled out a change-of-address form and had all of Marcy Hungerford's mail sent to her new post office box beginning the next day.

At ten A.M. Jane went to a pay telephone in a quiet corner of Balboa Park and dialed a Los Angeles number. As she put the coins into the slot, she checked her watch again.

"Hoffen-Bayne," said the receptionist.

"I'd like to speak to a representative for new customers, please," said Jane.

"Your name?"

"Marcy Hungerford."

"Please hold and I'll transfer you to Mr. Hanlon." There were a few clicks and a man said "Ronald Hanlon" in a quiet, calm voice. "What can I do for you, Ms. Hungerford?"

Jane said, "It's Mrs. I'm considering new financial management and I'm shopping around. I'd like to know more about Hoffen-Bayne."

Mr. Hanlon said, "Well, we've been in business in Los Angeles since 1948 and handle a full range of financial affairs for a great many people. We offer investment specialists, tax specialists, accountants, property-management teams, and so on. If you could give me a rough idea of your needs, I think I could give you a more focused picture."

That was the money question. "Well," said Jane, "my husband's affairs are managed by Chase Manhattan." This established that she wasn't somebody who had just dialed the wrong number; banks seldom managed anything less than a few million. "But I have some assets I like to hold separately." She kept her voice cheerful and opaque. Maybe there were problems with the marriage, and maybe not. If there were, California was a community-property state, and this meant she might be talking about some money the husband didn't know about and half of what he had at Chase Manhattan. She was giving Mr. Hanlon a small taste. "I'm interested in having somebody I trust manage my money conservatively so that it pays a reliable income each year." "Conservative" meant she didn't need to gamble to make more, and the income was another hint of divorce.

Hanlon rose to the bait slowly and smoothly. "Yes, that sounds wise," he said. "That would mean setting you up with our accountants and tax people, and a financial planner."

"And property management," she added. "Do you have arrangements to handle foreign real estate? France and Italy?"

That did it. He wasn't talking to a lady with a couple hundred thousand in passbooks. "I think the best thing to do would be to make an appointment and we can talk it all over in detail with advisers from some of our departments. When are you free?"

"That's a problem," said Jane. "I live in San Diego and I'm leaving for Palm Beach today." She checked her watch again to see how long she had been talking.

"When will you be back?"

"I'm not sure. It could be a month. I'm asking for information from several companies. I'm going to look it over while I'm away, and when I'm back I'll have the choices narrowed down." The element of competition would help. "I'd like to have you send me whatever material you've got that will help me know whether your company is the right one for me." She decided Marcy Hungerford had no reason to be vague, and making her naive wouldn't help. "I'd like to know the backgrounds and qualifications of your investment people, financial planners, and so on."

Mr. Hanlon seemed a little surprised. Maybe she had gone too far. "I think we have some things we can send you. What's your address?"

"It's 99233 The Shores, Del Mar, California 91182." She glanced at her watch again. She had only twenty seconds left before the operator came on and asked for more quarters.

"Phone?"

Jane gave him Marcy Hungerford's telephone number. The answering machine or the maids would tell him she was out of town.

"Got it," he said. "I'll get that right out to you."

Ten seconds left. "Fine. I'll watch for it. And thanks." She hung up and walked across the lush green grass of the park in the direction of the zoo. She felt satisfied. Hanlon would make a serious attempt to impress her with Hoffen-Bayne's operation. The main issue would be whether he had caught the hint about backgrounds. Whoever had gone after Timmy Phillips had been in the company seven years ago and was still there.

The next morning when Jane went for her run on the beach, she considered the ways of taking the company apart so that she could see what was inside. If Hoffen-Bayne had been around since 1948, then they had almost certainly been sued. She could drive up to U.C.L.A. and hire a student to research the county records for the cases. The least that would give her were the names of the people at Hoffen-Bayne who had been served with subpoenas, and almost any lawsuit would provide a lot more.

But that would mean dreaming up another story to tell the law student that would make him feel comfortable about doing it but not comfortable enough to talk about it freely. It would also place the student in a public building where someone might notice that he had an unusual curiosity about one particular company. He might be helping somebody build a case. That sort of information might easily get back to Hoffen-Bayne. Certainly when Dennis Morgan had been doing his research, somebody at Hoffen-Bayne had learned about it. She decided not to bring anybody else into this mess.

At four o'clock Jane drove back along the Golden State Freeway to Del Mar and stopped at the little store where her post office box was. She saw through the little window that Marcy Hungerford had lots of mail. She sorted through the letters and bills and catalogs until she found the packet from Hoffen-Bayne, then drove to the post office and filled out another change-of-address form so that Marcy Hungerford's mail would start being delivered to her house again.

She considered scrawling "misdelivered" on today's mail and slipping it into the nearest mailbox, but she decided that the safest way was to ensure that there was no interruption in service. She waited until eight P.M., when it was dark along the beach, walked past Marcy Hungerford's house, left the mail in her box, returned to her car, and drove on.

At the hotel Jane opened the packet from Hoffen-Bayne and began to study it. She could see immediately that Mr. Hanlon had not missed any of her hints and that he had been convinced that her account was worth having. There was a printed brochure that included little descriptions of the various arms of the company and a cover with a touched-up photograph of their building on Wilshire Boulevard. Inside were graphs and tables purporting to be proof of high returns for their clients, mixed with a text that promised personal service. Mr. Hanlon had also dictated a cover letter to Mrs. Hungerford, and stapled to it was a little stack of computer-printed résumés.

The next morning Jane checked out of the hotel and drove up the freeway toward Los Angeles. The coast of California had always made her uneasy. The air was lukewarm, calm and quiet, as though it were not outdoors. On the left side of the road the blue-gray ocean rose and fell in long, lazy swells, looking almost gelatinous where the beds of brown kelp spread like a net on the surface. The low, dry, gentle yellow hills to the east always made her sleepy because they were difficult for the eye to define, not clear enough to tell whether they were small and near or large and far. Behind them she could see the abrupt rising of the dark, jagged mountains like a painted wall.

The land along this road always looked deserted. She had to remind herself that it had been the most densely populated part of the continent when the Spanish missionaries and their soldiers arrived. The Indians here had not been at war for centuries the way the Iroquois had, so they weren't fighters. The first Europeans they saw herded them into concentration camps where they forced them to build stone missions and work the fields, and then locked them up at night in barracks, the men in one and the women in another. They were chained, whipped, starved, tortured, and executed for infractions against the priests' authority, and they died from diseases that flourished in their cramped quarters until they were virtually exterminated.

California was a sad place, a piece of property that had begun as a slaughterhouse and could never be made completely clean. It was perpetually being remodeled by new tenants who could not explain why they were doing it. They bulldozed the gentle hills into flat tables where they built hideous, crowded developments that encrusted the high places like beehives. They gouged and scraped away at the surface and covered it with cement so that every town looked like every other town, and the rebuilding was so constant that every block of buildings in the state seemed to be between ten and twenty years old and just beginning to show signs that it needed to be bulldozed and rebuilt again.

Jane drove along the Golden State Freeway for three hours until she came to the Hollywood Freeway, took the exit at Vermont, then swung south again for the few blocks to Wilshire Boulevard, where the tall buildings that sheltered corporations instead of people rose abruptly out of the pavement.

The things that had been happening had a very impersonal quality to them: a respected corporation had managed an account, and it had decided it was time to file a
petition to declare a client deceased. But somewhere behind the opaque and anonymous veneer there was a person. Money was stolen by human beings. Sometimes
thieves worked together and sometimes separately, but
most successful embezzlers worked alone. It was time to
find the man.

12

In the late afternoon, Jane began to watch the Hoffen-Bayne building from the window of a restaurant across Wilshire Boulevard. It was small for this part of Los Angeles, only five floors. The bottom floor was rented out to a travel agency and a coffee shop, and the second floor was a reception area for Hoffen-Bayne. After an hour she moved to the upper tier of the parking ramp for the tall insurance building beside Hoffen-Bayne and studied the upper windows to determine which ones were small, functional offices for accountants, brokers, and consultants, and which ones were big pools for bookkeepers and secretaries. She paid special attention to the desirable corner offices.

At six P.M., when she saw people inside taking purses out of desk drawers and turning off computers for the day, she strolled along the quiet side street near the driveway and studied the men and women who came out and got into cars in the reserved-for-employees spaces in the parking lot. She wrote down the license numbers and makes and models, and matched the cars to the people she had seen in the windows.

Tall-Thin-and-Bald wanted to be noticed. He drove a gray Mercedes 320 two-door convertible that retailed for about eighty-five thousand and was too sporty for him. Woman-with-Eye-Trouble, who had the habit of putting on her sunglasses while she was still inside the office, drove a racing-green Jaguar XJ6, which was only about fifty thousand, but she was still a possibility, as was Old Weight-Lifter, who drove a Lexus LS 400, which sold for even less. Eye-Trouble might have chosen her car because it was pretty, and Weight-Lifter might be the sort of person who bought whatever the car magazines told him to.

Jane made four grids on a sheet of paper to represent the windows of the upper floors, labeled them "N," "S," "E," and "W," and made notes on each window about who had appeared in it and what went on when he did. A supervisor might pop in on a subordinate, might even deliver sheets of paper to the subordinate's desk, but when several people met in an office, it was usually the office of the ranking person.

An hour later, after the upper windows were dim but there were still people in the coffee shop and travel agency, she went into the lobby, took the elevator to the second floor, and stood outside the locked glass doors to the Hoffen-Bayne reception area. She was looking for a directory of offices posted on the wall, but there was none. The reception area was all smooth veneer and expensive furniture that made it look like a doctor's waiting room. There was no easy way into the complex, and there was a small sticker on the glass door that said "Protected By Intercontinental Security," and under that, "Armed Response." She didn't particularly want to bet that she could fool the sort of security system a company that handled money for a lot of rich people might consider a good investment, so she turned and went back to the elevator and took it to the basement of the building, on the level with the parking lot, and found a door with a NO ADMITTANCE sign. The door had a knob with a keyhole to lock it and it wasn't wired, so she had little trouble slipping her William Dunlavey MasterCard between the knob and the jamb and pushing the catch in. Inside the room were circuit breaker boxes and a telephone junction box. She opened it and studied the chart pasted inside the door. It gave the extensions of the various offices in the building, so she copied them and returned to her car.

She checked into a hotel two miles down Wilshire Boulevard and compared her office chart with the telephone extensions. Some of the offices must be the big ones she had seen through the third-floor windows, where people sat at computers and worked telephones in a pool. Nobody important had a single number with fifteen extensions. The offices she wanted were on the fourth and fifth floors, so she concentrated on them. She dialed each number and listened to a computerized voice-mail system telling her what part of the company it belonged to—investment, property management, billing, accounting—but not the name of the person. She used the information to eliminate more of the offices. The person who had been robbing the trust fund would have to be in a position to exert power over where the money was placed and how the company kept track of it. He didn't share an office, or send out bills for services, or manage real estate, or answer other people's phones. She consulted the résumés that Mr. Hanlon had sent her, and filled out more of the chart before she went to sleep.

The next morning Jane went to the Hollywood lot of the car-rental agency, told them Mr. Dunlavey didn't like the car he had rented in San Diego and that he had instructed her to exchange it for a different model. She drove out with a white Toyota Camry and sat on the side street watching the west side of the building while the Hoffen-Bayne executives arrived for work.

She watched and worked on her chart of the company for three more days. Each morning she turned in the car she had rented the day before and went to a different agency to rent a new one under a new name. Each evening she would choose one of the likely executives and follow him home when he left the office. Each night she slept in a different hotel in a different part of the city.

On the afternoon of the fifth day, Jane was reasonably sure that the man she was after was Blond Napoleon. His name was Alan Turner, and he had the office on the southeast corner of the fifth floor. This afforded him the best view of the city and made people walk a long way to get to him, past secretaries and intermediaries. The car he drove, a dark blue BMW 740I, cost about sixty thousand dollars. It was not the most expensive, but like only four others in the lot, it had a license plate holder from Green Import Auto, a leasing company in Beverly Hills. To Jane this meant that he was one of only five people who were entitled to company cars.

Whoever had been robbing Timmy would have needed to be high enough in the hierarchy seven years ago to make decisions about the Phillips trust's portfolio without much fear of second-guessing. He would also need to remain in that position long enough to see the cover-up through to the end. Of the five people who drove company cars and occupied the right sort of offices in the building, two had joined the firm within the past four years. Of the others, one was a tax attorney and another the head of the Property Management Division. There was nothing in either man's résumé to suggest that he had ever served in another capacity or had the background to handle a trust fund. The only one who had been with the company long enough and who had a specialty that sounded promising was Alan Turner, head of the Investment and Financial Planning Division.

Jane decided to test-drive a car from Green Import Auto. She selected a gray Mercedes with a telephone in it and drove directly to the side street below the southeast corner of the Hoffen-Bayne building. She waited until three o'clock, when even the important people were back from lunch meetings and the sun was on the west side of the building so that Turner's blinds would be open. She turned the corner off Wilshire and cruised toward the building, dialed the number of Mr. Hanlon, the salesman, and set the receiver in the cradle so she could use the speaker and keep her hands free.

"Hanlon," he said. She knew he was at his desk on the other side of the building.

"This is Marcy Hungerford. We spoke a few days ago, and you sent me some material." She pulled over and parked on the quiet, tree-lined street.

"Yes. Did you have a chance to look it over?"

"I did, and I think yours is one of the firms I should talk to." She wanted to make it clear there was no commitment. She was not in the bag yet.

"Good," he said. "I've been thinking about what you've told me, and I think I'd like to get you together with one of our partners for a talk." Salesmen didn't make decisions like that; partners did. He had told his boss about her call. "Are you back in Del Mar?"

"No," she said. "I won't be back for another week. I

just thought I should tell you I got your information and am still considering it."

Hanlon went on cheerfully as though he hadn't heard her. "The man I'd like you to meet is very experienced. He's been with the company for twelve years, and he's knowledgeable about all aspects of personal management."

Jane listened carefully. While she had been investigating them, they had been investigating Marcy Hungerford. The name had rung some bell or other. She had chosen well, but from here on she had to be cautious. They knew more about Marcy Hungerford than she did. She decided to stop flirting. It would do her no good to convince people Marcy Hungerford was an idiot. "Fine," she said. "I'll be happy to drive up there and meet him as soon as I'm back in California. Can you connect me with whoever keeps his calendar?"

"Let me see if he's free to talk to you himself right now. I know he'd like to if he can."

"Even better."

She heard a cascade of annoying music pour out of the speaker, and watched the man in the corner window. She saw him pick up the receiver. He talked to Hanlon for a few seconds, reached across his desk, picked up a file, opened it, and then pushed a button on his telephone.

"Hello, Mrs. Hungerford," he said. "My name is Alan Turner."

"Hello," she said. She started the car and pulled away from the curb.

"I understand you're considering us to manage your assets."

"Yes, I am," she said. She drove up the street away from the building, turned right at the corner, and kept going west. "I'm considering several companies. I'd like to find someone who will take responsibility for handling things."

"Well, that's what we're in business to offer," said Turner. "We have experts on the staff in every aspect of financial management, and—"

"I know," she interrupted. "Mr. Hanlon said the same thing. But let me explain. I want to know who would be the one person coordinating everything. I don't want to have to call thirty people every time I have a question."

"I understand perfectly. With your approval, I would manage your account myself. I don't do much of that anymore, but I still have a few."

"That's very kind."

"Here's what I propose. I'll sit down with you when you return from Palm Beach. We'll take an inventory of your current assets. I'll examine what you have and come back with a hypothetical portfolio that's sufficiently diversified to ensure you a good income. We can arrange to have it continue in perpetuity for your heirs, if you wish."

Jane had to be sure. "That sounds like a trust fund."

"That's what it is," Turner said. "In my experience, people who are busy—as I know you are, with your charity work and so on—don't want to waste their lives micromanaging their wealth. Over the years I've helped quite a few of our clients establish trusts, and so far we've done very well for them."

Now she was sure that they'd had Marcy Hungerford investigated. She had never mentioned charities. "What do you charge for all this?"

"Our commission is five percent of income," he said. "Of course there would be incidental fees from time to time for brokers, front-end loads on certain purchases, and so on, but you're familiar with those and they don't go to Hoffen-Bayne. They might be quite high in the first year while we're developing a group of haphazard assets into a coordinated portfolio, and there will be legal fees if you choose to establish a trust, but the costs taper off as the years go by."

"That all sounds good," said Jane. "What you've said in the last few minutes has done a lot to convince me that you're the one I'm looking for. I'll call you as soon as I'm back home."

"Wonderful," he said. "I look forward to meeting you."

"Goodbye," she said, and tapped the button to disconnect, then drove the Mercedes back to the dealer's lot. She looked at a few more models, then let the salesman know that she hadn't found anything she was really comfortable in. She got back into her rented Honda Acura and drove over the pass to the Hilton on the hill above Universal City and took another room. It was a comfortable hotel, and she didn't mind staying there a few days while she did the paperwork. After she was settled and had dinner she left instructions with the concierge to have both the morning and evening editions of the *L.A. Times* delivered to her room each day, and went for a walk.

She strolled around the complex of buildings at the top of the hill and across the parking lots to a row of pay telephones outside the gate of the Universal Studios tour. She reviewed what she was about to do. There was no way anyone could trace to Jane Whitefield a call made from a public telephone at a place that had millions of visitors a year. It was safe. With the three-hour time difference, she would catch him just after he had come home. She felt a little uncomfortable. She had told herself that she was doing it now because she was afraid of waking him up early in the morning, and there was no point in calling while he was out. But she also knew that if he had decided to do something other than come home from work, this would be the time a person might call and find out. She had no choice but to behave the way she would if she were trying to check up on him, and she hated that. She pushed a quarter into the slot and dialed Carey McKinnon's number. The operator came on to tell her how many more quarters were needed, and she dropped them in.

"Hello?" he said. His voice seemed a little thin, as though he were winded.

"Hi, Carey," she said. "It's me."

"Well, hello," he said. He sounded delighted, and she felt glad. "Are you back from your trip?" When she noticed he had not yet said "Jane," it occurred to her that there might be a reason.

"No, I won't be able to get through this job right away. I just felt like hearing your voice."

She wanted him to say "And I felt like hearing yours," maybe because if he said it she would know there wasn't another woman in the room with him. The thought made her feel contempt for herself. He said, "My sentiments exactly. I must have just missed you the other day. When I came in there was your message on my machine. When will you be back in town?"

"I'm not sure."

She heard the *beep-beep-beep* of his pager in the background. "Oh, shit," he said. "That's my pager."

"I heard it."

"Look, give me the number where you're staying, and I'll call you when I'm back from the hospital."

"Oh, I'm sorry," she said. "I'm out and I don't have it

with me. I'm never there anyway. I'll have to try you again in a day or so, when things cool down."

"Do that."

"Goodbye."

"For now," he said.

As Jane stepped away from the bank of telephones she had to dodge a group of Asian teenagers who swept past laughing and talking. She wished that she didn't have the kind of mind that always suspected deception. She reminded herself that it was ridiculous even to think of Carey that way—as though she had a right to expect that he would never see another woman. He had offered, and she had not agreed, had only said "We'll talk about it." There was no proof that a woman was in the room with him, anyway. She was just inventing a way to make herself miserable. As she walked back to her hotel, she wished that she hadn't known that when a pager was clicked off and then on again, it beeped to signal that it was working.

She spent the late evening trying to think about Alan Turner, but found her attention slipping back to Carey McKinnon. She was angry at herself for being suspicious, and angry at him for being the sort of person who made her suspicious. He was probably innocent, and if she cared about him enough to be this uncomfortable, what was she doing thousands of miles away from him, forming agonizingly clear pictures of what he might be doing with some other woman? She should be there. She was surprised by the strength of her urge to be with him. She wondered why it was stronger now than it had been yesterday. Was it because his voice had triggered some unconscious longing for him—maybe love, but maybe just some crude sexual reflex, the equivalent of Pavlov's dogs' hearing a bell and salivating—or because it had set off an even cruder instinct to gallop back and defend her mate from the competition? Twice she was tempted to call the hospital to see if he was on duty but fought down the impulse.

When the hour was late enough so that she could not imagine a good excuse to call any of Carey's numbers, Jane managed to remind herself of what she was doing in Los Angeles. She had decided it was necessary to find out who had been trying to kill Timmy Phillips. If that was true a week ago, then it was still true. Turner was the prime suspect, and anything she could figure out about him might save a little boy's life. Thinking about anything else was a waste of time. When she had reached this conclusion, she promptly fell asleep.

As the morning sun came up over the next ridge in a blinding glare, Jane laid all of her information about Alan Turner on the table of her room and studied it. She had Turner's name, the license number of the car he drove, the address of his office, and the address of his house on Hillcrest in Beverly Hills where she had followed him two nights ago. The résumé that Hanlon had sent to Marcy Hungerford said that Turner was a 1969 graduate of the University of Pennsylvania, and that he had an M.B.A. from the University of Southern California.

She forged a letter from Turner to the U.S.C. registrar's office requesting that a transcript of his graduate work be sent to the personnel manager of Furnace Financial, Ltd., in Chicago. The Furnace corporation was a business she had founded some years before. It had a genuine legal existence, but the ownership was cloudy and the physical plant consisted of a post office box that she had rented in a small Chicago mini-mall, with the arrangement that everything that arrived was to be sent unopened to another post office box in Buffalo. Then she called the owner of the little shop where the box was and asked him to call the Hilton when anything with a U.S.C. return address arrived.

As soon as she hung up she dialed Carey's number. When his machine clicked on, she tried to think of the right kind of message. She knew he wasn't working now, or she thought he wasn't. It occurred to her that if there had been a woman with him last night, she would still be there. She simply said, "It's Jane Whitefield." She paused to let him change his mind or go to an extension where the woman wouldn't hear. "I guess I missed you again." As she hung up, she closed her eyes and felt a headache building. All right, she thought. I said I would call him, and I've called him. Enough. I have work to do.

She drove to the Department of Motor Vehicles office in Glendale and filled out a form. On a line near the top, she provided the license number of the BMW Turner drove, and in the big space at the bottom she said he had scraped her car in a parking lot. The DMV answered with the name and address of the owner, which was only the leasing company Green Import Auto, but it also listed the lessee, Alan Turner, and included his driver's license number.

After only two days, the U.S.C. transcript arrived in Chicago. Jane asked the owner of the shop to open it and read it to her. From this she got Turner's Social Security number. With the driver's license number and Social Security number, she was able to have Furnace Financial request a credit report on Alan Turner.

The credit report told her he was paying a mortgage of one million, eight hundred thousand dollars to Southland

Mortgage. This must be the house on Hillcrest. He had several credit cards and paid the balances each month to avoid interest charges. He had checked the box on his mortgage papers that said "Divorced," which made things simpler: he didn't have a wife with a second income. But there was also a surprise. Turner was repaying another loan of six hundred thousand dollars to the Bank of Northern California. It was a mortgage on a second home.

She looked in the telephone book for the Bank of Northern California and found listings for several branches, as well as a Bank of Northern California Mortgage Services in San Bernardino. She called the mortgage office and asked for the credit department. Anybody who loaned money must have a credit department. In a second a woman answered.

"This is Monica Butler at the San Francisco office," Jane said. "I've got a loan application here from a customer who lists a mortgage from us already for six hundred thousand. I'd like to know what the property is."

The young woman said, "The name?"

"Alan R. Turner. Need his Social Security number?"

"No," the woman said. She was typing the name into a computer. If the person on the other end of the line thought you were from the same company, none of the privacy rules applied. She was merely transferring information from one internal file drawer to another.

"The property is at 1522 Morales Prospect, in Monterey."

"Do you have a zip?"

"Sure. It's 93940."

"Thanks." Jane hung up and wrote down the address. The picture she was forming of Turner was coherent and consistent: he made a lot of money and he was cautious and premeditated. He saved some by driving a leased company car. He used his high income and stability to take out big deductible mortgages on two of the most desirable addresses in the Western Hemisphere, so he probably didn't pay much in taxes. But those were relatively modest prices for their neighborhoods, so he wasn't taking big risks. He wasn't in love with debt, because his credit cards had never carried a balance to the next month. He didn't look like an embezzler. If he had been quietly robbing the Phillips trust fund for years, he must have had the foresight to know that some day a stranger might take a look at his assets. Either he was extremely sophisticated or she had chosen the wrong man at Hoffen-Bayne.

The following morning Jane rose before dawn, walked to the door of her room, picked up her copy of the *Los Angeles Times*, and unfolded it to reveal the second page, where the summary of major articles was printed. On the lower left side was a box that said, "Judge Seizes Hoffen-Bayne Records (See E-1, Business)." She had run out of time.

13

Jane had checked out of the Hilton and had her car on Laurel Canyon Boulevard by five A.M. She hadn't dared stop to read the whole article, but she had scanned it on the walk down the hallway to the desk, and took a longer look while she was waiting for the valet to bring her car to the entrance. The judge had been devious. He had issued requests for specific documents, which Hoffen-Bayne had dutifully provided a week ago. Probably he had done this to give them the impression that he was just going to take a cursory glance at a couple of carefully cooked annual reports. If he hadn't asked for something, they would have suspected trouble. Then, last night after business hours, he had issued a warrant and sent cops with a truck down to Wilshire Boulevard. She moved her eyes down the column of print, but could see no names.

She decided to avoid Wilshire Boulevard. The office would already have reporters and cops and, as soon as the clients got up and read their papers, enough panicky investors to keep them all busy. She needed to go to Beverly Hills.

She reached Sunset and turned right. Even at five in the morning the street was busy, but the cars were moving quickly. She made her way in the intervals between cars, the skyline in front of her dominated by enormous lighted billboards with pictures of pairs of giant actors looking stern and fearless, and actresses with moist lips the size of watermelon slices.

The judge had done his work. Timmy was, at least for the moment, as safe as anyone could make him. He had already told the authorities everything he knew. The judge had taken away the incentive for anybody at Hoffen-Bayne to kill him. It would be like killing a witness who already had testified. There was only Turner to occupy her mind now. She had calculated that she would have a few more days to study him, and her feeling of frustration surprised her. It wasn't that she had any real hope that she could do any more than the authorities could to get Timmy's money back. She wasn't even sure how she felt about the money. She had to fight the conviction she had been raised with that accumulating wealth was a contemptible activity.

This wasn't something that her parents had invented. It was an old attitude that had never gone away. In the old days no family ever built up disproportionate surpluses of food. Whatever they had was shared with scrupulous equality. Each longhouse was owned by the women of the clan, and each woman had a right to live there and raise her children and sleep with her husband when he was around. A man was a warrior and hunter, out in the forest for most of the year, and he seldom owned anything he couldn't carry. If he wanted respect, he would bring back lots of meat and plunder for the village. A person's status was a measure of how good he was at obtaining things to share, not how much he was able to take and hoard. After the white people arrived they advised each other that the way to find the leaders of the Iroquois was to look for the men in rags.

Whatever would happen to Timmy's money would happen whether she was here or in Deganawida. It was Turner she was interested in. She had to know if his careful accounting and his conservative, respectable manner of living had all been part of a scheme to disguise a greed strong enough to make him kill people.

She turned down Hillcrest and cruised slowly past Turner's house. She had to be alert and careful this morning. The richest parts of Los Angeles were guarded with a strange, subtle vigilance. There were small, tasteful signs with the trademarks of security patrols on every lawn, small, unobtrusive surveillance cameras on the eaves of the big houses, and lots of invisible servants watching. The sound of a helicopter overhead probably meant a cop was looking down with night-vision binoculars. An unfamiliar car parked in the wrong place, a stranger walking down the street, and particularly anybody doing anything before sunrise, were ominous signs to be remembered and reported.

She drove across Sunset onto the slope on the north side, parked her car on a side street next to a medical building in a space that was shielded from the intersection by a big tree and a Land Rover, and ducked down in the seat while she changed into her sweat suit and sneakers. She pulled her hair behind her head, slipped a rubber band around it to make a ponytail, and began to jog slowly down onto the flats.

The sidewalks here were wide and even, and the street was lined by two long rows of coconut palms. The air was warm for early morning, and she could hear traffic above and below her but saw no cars driving down

Hillcrest yet. She ran slowly and easily, less to keep from pulling a muscle than to keep anyone who saw her from looking twice. A woman trotting painfully along a residential street at dawn was just another local girl in the dull business of keeping her waist and thighs attractive; a woman loping along like a track star was something else.

Jane took her time and looked closely at the houses. Few of them showed any interior lights at this hour. The garages were all hidden far back behind the houses at the ends of long driveways, and nobody left his car parked on the street. When she approached Turner's block she slowed to a walk, as though she were catching her breath.

The house had lights on behind the drawn blinds. She watched the windows for a few seconds and glanced at her watch. It was five-thirty now. When she looked up, one of the lights had gone off. She began to jog again. If he was turning lights off, he must be coming out. She passed the house, keeping her head forward but moving her eyes to the left to scan the house and the yard. As she came abreast of the house, another light went off.

She saw the newspaper lying on the front porch. As she trotted on down the street she wondered about it. By now there was no chance he didn't know that his office had been raided. If he hadn't been behind his desk at Hoffen-Bayne when the cops came in and started padlocking filing cabinets, then somebody certainly would have told him. Reporters would call him. Was it possible that he wouldn't bother to read what the newspapers said about it the next morning?

She stopped running again at the end of the block and looked back at the house as she crossed the street. Two lights were still on. She started moving again, this time down the street toward Wilshire, glancing back now and then to see if anything had changed. Maybe he had gone out in the night to buy the paper as soon as it had come off the presses. No, that didn't make sense; the newsstands carried only the early edition that had been printed the previous afternoon, before the raid.

She turned and ran toward her car. The sun would be up before long, and there would be people out even in this quiet neighborhood. Inside her car she quickly changed into a pair of jeans and a blouse.

She drove back down onto Hillcrest. As she passed the house, the other two lights went off. She checked her watch. It was exactly six o'clock. She was positive now that the lights were on timers. The ones they sold in hardware stores had crude dials on them, so it was difficult to set them for any time but an hour or half hour. She had always used them in her house when she went on a trip, and had solved the problem by setting the present time on them not to correspond with what her watch said. Turner wasn't as good at this as she was. He might be a thief, but he had not learned to think like one. He had not even timed them to be sure they didn't click off before the sun was up.

Still, it was conceivable that he had set them but hadn't left yet. She stopped at a small convenience store with an iron grate across the door, walked to the pay telephone, and dialed his number. There was no answer and no machine to record a message. She hung up after ten rings and got back into the car. As she started it, she checked the rearview mirror and saw a car coming that had lights on the roof like a police cruiser. It had blue and yellow stripes, and the shield on the door said "Intercontinental Security." She pulled out and followed it at a distance. The car swung up and down a couple of side streets above Sunset, and then came down to Hillcrest, gliding along, the driver glancing casually at all of the houses with blue-and-yellow security signs. He pulled up at the curb in front of Turner's house and got out. He was young and broad-shouldered and wore a tight uniform like a cop's with a gun belt that made him hold his arms out a little from his sides as though he were carrying two buckets. He opened the gate, ran a flashlight over a couple of side windows, and picked up the newspaper. Turner was gone.

Jane drove on, turned left on Sunset Boulevard and continued west to the entrance for the 405 freeway near U.C.L.A. This was the way Turner would have come after he had heard the news. He could have turned south toward the airport, but she was sure he had not done so. He was a conservative, judicious man. He had taken the second ramp, the one that got him safely out of town but didn't incur the risk of appearing to flee the country. He had gone north to his house in Monterey.

14

Jane came up over the hill that separated the city from the San Fernando Valley and edged to the right onto the Ventura Freeway, then stayed on it as far as Santa Barbara before she stopped for breakfast in the restaurant of a sprawling hotel complex along the beach. By the time the food was cooked she was too impatient to eat, so she had the waitress put it in a Styrofoam container and took it with her in the car. North of the city at the Santa Barbara airport, she turned in the rented car and took a commuter flight to San Francisco, then rented another car there to drive down the coast to Monterey. It was early evening when she checked into a small motel a mile inland from the ocean, showered, and wrapped herself in a towel.

She sat on the bed and dialed Carey McKinnon's number, then hung up before it rang. She had been waiting, listening to the static while the telephone company's computers threw switches to move the call across the country to Carey's house, and she sensed in herself a feeling that was not right. She had not been calling because she wanted to give him a message of love before he dropped off to sleep, or even to soothe herself with the sound of his voice. These were the only legitimate reasons for calling Carey tonight. If the eagerness she had been feeling was morbid curiosity or the grim satisfaction of confirming a suspicion, then the only decent thing to do was leave him alone.

She opened her suitcase and looked at her clothes. She decided that evening in Monterey was an occasion for basic black. She put on a black turtleneck sweater, a matching jacket, and black pants, then tied her hair back. The accessories were what would make such an outfit. She laid out the few items of female paraphernalia she had brought and made her selections. She fastened her hair with a black ring and a thin five-inch-long peg that had a T-shaped handle at one end and was sharpened at the other. Before she put the perfume bottle into her purse she opened it and sniffed cautiously. It had a soft wildflower smell with a little touch of damp earth that tickled the nose a little. It was a mixture of mayapple and water hemlock roots that she had mashed and strained into a clear concentrate. Eating the roots was the customary Iroquois method of suicide.

For her feet she chose a pair of twenty-dollar black leather Keds. They had gum soles like sneakers, but the soles had no distinctive lines or patterns. They were merely plain, flat, and rough, a texture that could make it hard to distinguish the prints they left as a human track, let alone identify them as the prints of a particular woman's shoe.

She left the lights on in her motel room in case she returned, but put her suitcase in the trunk of the car in case she didn't. She made her preparations carefully because she could not have said what she was preparing for. As she started the car and pulled out of the lot, she began to feel uneasy. If she had seen another woman adorning her hair with a spike designed to be driven into a person's chest, or popping a vial of hemlock extract into her purse, she would have said that the woman was on her way to kill someone. People who brought along weapons without knowing why had a tendency to find out why after they arrived.

She ran a quick inventory of the thoughts she had about Turner. She suspected that he was a man who stole from children, but she had not discovered any evidence that he had ordered the deaths of Timmy and his parents, or told anybody to kill Mona and Dennis rather than let them into the courtroom. She wanted to watch him and study him. He didn't seem to be a physical threat, and she was not suddenly feeling the urge to go and supply herself with a gun; that would have been a bad sign. The poison proved nothing. Over the years she had promised clients that she would die rather than reveal where she had taken them. To say this without keeping within reach the means to accomplish it would have made it a lie.

Jane drove down Morales Prospect past the address and took a long, careful look. The house was set far back on the deep lot, partly concealed by a few tall pine trees that had been left standing when the house was built. The second floor was fake Tudor, with a high, steep mansard roof that didn't go with it, and the ground floor had a brick facade about six feet high. There were dim lights on in the second-story windows, but the bottom-floor windows were dark. Even the porch light was off. As she passed, she could see that the house was sheltered on three sides by the remnants of the pine grove. The trees ran right up to the edge of the driveway and nearly touched the garage.

She drove up the road looking for a place to leave her car. A half mile farther she found a closed gas station with five or six cars lined up along the side waiting to be fixed. One of them had its hood off and in its place was a tarp of heavy-gauge plastic taped down to keep the sea air out of its engine. She pulled into the lot with her lights off, parked next to this car, and moved the tarp to her own hood.

She walked back along the road, keeping in the shadows of hedges and trees inside the property lines of the big front yards so that any headlights unexpectedly shining on her would fall on her black hair and black clothes and not on her face and hands. But this part of Monterey was a winding seventeen-mile scenic route, so people probably drove it in the daytime when they could see it.

In ten minutes Jane was standing among the trees in the side yard of the house. She felt the soft, cushioned layer of long needles on the ground and smelled the pine scent in the dark, still air. She made her way to the garage and looked in the window. She could see the gleaming finish of the black BMW inside. This was the place where Turner had come to wait out the scandal, leaving the questions and cameras to his lawyer. She walked slowly and quietly around the house, staying back among the trees.

She studied the lower windows, then the upper ones. She scanned the eaves and gutters for spotlights that might automatically come on if she made a noise, but she saw nothing that worried her.

She wanted to see Alan Turner. She returned to the spot where she felt most sheltered by the trees, at the back corner, and watched the lighted upper windows on two sides of the house. There was no glow of a television set, no shadows on the ceiling from anyone walking across any of the rooms. She felt a strong urge to see what he was doing and what he looked like tonight.

Maybe she had come too late, and he had lain down to rest with the lights on and fallen asleep. He had driven much farther than she had, and had probably done a lot of it at night, so he would be tired.

She felt drawn to the light. When she walked to the side of the house to peer into a window, she saw the little yellow-and-blue sticker of Intercontinental Security. It made her take a step backward while she tried to analyze the uneasiness this gave her. It had begun to seem that every building she had seen since she started looking into Timmy's problems had one of these stickers on its window. Alarm systems didn't surprise her—she had one herself—but California seemed to be blanketed with Intercontinental stickers. Had it been that way for years without her seeing it?

But of course Turner's houses would be protected by the same company that Hoffen-Bayne used. He probably hid the cost of the alarm systems for both houses in the monthly fee for Hoffen-Bayne. She decided that her uneasiness was only the result of having her attention focused on the signs. If somebody she knew got a disease she had never heard of, suddenly she would notice articles in the newspapers about it and overhear people talking about it until it seemed that the whole world had been infected.

She pushed the security company out of her mind and forced herself to think about the sticker in a way that was of more immediate use. It warned her that Turner had an alarm system. Whatever interior traps and gadgets the system had, they would probably be turned off if he was still up and walking around, or he would risk setting them off himself. The perimeter circuits would certainly be turned on.

She studied the building for its weakness. The alarm system would protect the windows and doors. The high, steep roof didn't have skylights or big vents, and if he were in an upstairs room, he would hear her walking up there. She looked down. This house was like most in California. The ground never froze, so they had no basements. Houses were bolted to three-foot foundations with a crawl space under the floors for pipes and wires. Near the side door by the kitchen was a little wooden trap to cover a two-by-three-foot concrete access well. She lifted the cover off quietly. As she looked down she had a momentary foreboding of spiders and rats, but she pretended there were no such things. She crawled under the house and pulled the trap back over the opening.

Beneath her was bare, powdery dirt. It was dark under the house, but she could see moonlight coming through little screened openings placed at intervals in the foundation. She found the gas pipe from the kitchen overhead and followed it slowly toward the center of the house, making out thick drain pipes and thinner water pipes here and there. Finally she reached the place where the gas pipe jointed and went upward. There was a square opening in the floor beside it about three feet wide.

She reached up to touch the place where the opening ended. It was a big square fabric filter. She pushed up on it and tilted it, then brought it down under the house with her. She reached up again and felt the row of burners. There was only about a foot and a half of space between the business part of the gas furnace and the floor, but she estimated that she could probably fit. She felt carefully around the inside of the furnace until she found the panel that slipped off so the filter could be removed and cleaned. That must be the front.

Jane placed her fingers on the lip and the top of the panel and slowly pushed upward. The panel slid up a quarter inch, when suddenly there was a flash and a click, and the pilot light came on. The burners just above her head began to hiss as the gas came out of them. She ducked down quickly and lay on her back as the gas ignited and the level blue flame spread across the top of the row of burners. Now she could see in the weird blue light. She could tell that she had estimated the shape and structure of the furnace only slightly wrong. She studied it, moving her head from side to side and lifting it as far as she dared.

There had to be some kind of safety button to kill the furnace when the door was off so that it didn't start up and burn the house down. As she searched, the blower motor went on and the fire grew hotter. She couldn't let it run for long, or all the metal around it would get hot too. She kept her head low, slipped her fingers under the bottom of the panel, and pushed upward again. The panel lip was freed, and the furnace went off. Carefully she pushed the panel higher until it came off, then leaned it on its side to keep from making noise, and lay down again.

A few minutes later she judged the air was cool enough to let her reach up through the space where the panel had been and feel around. There was a wooden door in front of the panel: the furnace must be in a space disguised as a closet. She ran her fingers up the side of it until she felt a hinge.

She sat on the ground and waited until she could touch the burners with her fingers before she made her attempt. She squatted cautiously, rose to a crouch, straightened to raise the upper part of her body into the furnace, reached out the front to find the doorknob, and opened the door a crack. She pulled herself up, slithered under the burners and out the front of the furnace, crawled out of the closet, and closed the door behind her.

She was in a dim hallway with a bleached oak floor and a long row of small framed drawings of sailing ships on the white walls. As she looked down the hall she could see the foyer. There was an alarm keypad on the wall near the front door. A small red light was glowing to indicate that the system was armed. At the other end of the hall was a staircase. If she herself had installed the security system, this was where she would have put an interior trap. Whatever a burglar stole down here, you didn't want him getting up those stairs where the bedrooms were. She stepped slowly to the side of the staircase, grasped the railing, and sidestepped between the posts up along the outside of it. She was ten feet up, just below the center of the staircase, before she found the electric eye mechanism. It was a foot above a step, so a crawling intruder couldn't slide under it, and even one who took three steps in a stride would break the beam. There were probably pressure pads under the carpet on some of the steps in case an intruder saw it in time.

She kept outside the railing beyond the top of the stairs and then climbed over the railing into the hallway. There might be other traps on the second floor, but if Turner was up here, this alarm zone was probably turned off.

There were lighted rooms on both ends of the second-floor hallway. The house was absolutely quiet. She could hear no movement or snoring or the shifting of a person in a chair. She wondered for a moment if she had been lucky and entered while he was out, but then she remembered the car in the garage.

She looked at the glowing doorway of each room and

chose the one to her left. It was slightly closer to the stairway, and if she had to run she didn't want to have Turner three steps closer to the only way out. Slowly she edged along the hallway with her shoulder almost touching the wall. When hardwood floorboards creaked, it was usually the ones in the center.

At the doorway she leaned out just far enough to use the dark windows in the room as mirrors to search for Turner. When she found him she jerked backward. She had been looking for a human form, and when she found it lower and closer to her than she had expected, her reflex was to duck back quickly to evade the blow or the shot. But even as her body was protecting itself, the feeling had already turned into something else.

His blond hair was wet with blood, and under the body, the thick beige rug had soaked up the first of it and saturated, then let a pool of it form and spread. She could see that the outer edge of the pool was already drying into a dark maroon ring, the carpet tufts hardening into twisted bristles. She craned her neck to look for the gun, and found it where it was supposed to be, beside the right hand. She knew enough about the way policemen treated the scenes of suicides to know it was a bad idea to enter the room. If she lost a strand of hair or a fiber from her clothes, she would be somebody they wanted to talk to.

She leaned inward far enough to verify that there was a discoloration that looked like a powder burn on Turner's right temple around the entry hole. The other temple was pressed to the carpet, and she decided it was just as well. The exit hole would be bigger and harder to look at.

It hadn't occurred to her that he would kill himself. If he hadn't doctored the records well enough he was about to be revealed as a thief, but a lot of people in his business had suffered that kind of publicity, and a fair percentage of them had never gone to jail. If he had been likely to be charged with the murders it would have made more sense, but the authorities had made no progress on the first ones in over two years, and they hadn't even been able to hold the men who had broken Dennis's neck and thrown Mona down the stairwell. Nobody was offering those men a deal in exchange for his name.

The raid on Turner's office must have made him panic. She looked down at him and felt something like sympathy for his fear and his forlorn death, but then she decided that she was only feeling the immediacy of it. The sweat and blood were still fresh, and the smell of his fear was probably still trapped in the air of the room and had set off some basic physical reaction in her brain that was stronger than the disgust he had aroused when he was alive.

She took off her shoes and stepped back along the same path that she had taken to reach the door, shuffling her feet a little to obscure any invisible marks her sneakers had made. At the stairway she hesitated and looked at the second room on the far end of the hallway. Why was the light on in there too? She reminded herself that he was beyond caring about electric bills, but then why had he turned off all the lights downstairs?

As soon as she was at the door, she could see the two sheets of paper on the desk. They were placed on the surface in the pool of light from the desk lamp like an exhibit. She stepped into the room.

They had been typed on the computer in the corner of the room and printed on the printer beside it. She looked at the second sheet, the one with the signature. All it said was "I take full responsibility for my actions. Alan Turner."

Then she looked at the first page. It began, "This is my last message to the rest of the world. When you read it I'll be gone, out of your reach." She had never seen a suicide note before, but somehow she had assumed they were addressed to family members or friends, like personal letters.

"The reason I have decided to end my life is that I have not been able to resist the temptation to steal from one of my accounts. I believed Timothy Phillips would never be found alive, so I was harming no one. Later it became apparent that Timothy Phillips was not dead. The people who had been posing as his parents were sending letters, and I knew that if I allowed them to go on, I would be caught. I went to Washington, D.C., where the letters were coming from, and agreed to a meeting. I hired two men to follow the couple from the meeting and find out where they were living with the boy. I am not certain, to this day, what I would have done if they had followed my instructions, but they did not. They formed some plan of their own, probably to take the boy and use him to take control of his money. Whatever it was, it failed. The next thing I knew, the supposed parents were dead and the boy had disappeared. I regret having proceeded in this fashion. Because I hired those men, I was, and am, technically guilty of arranging two murders. I should mention that none of my associates or colleagues benefitted in any way from my actions, and none of them had any knowledge of my theft or any of the things I did to cover it up. I do not know the names of the two men I hired to find the boy in Washington. I met them in a bar and made the deal in the parking lot outside. There is nothing more to say."

Jane studied the sheet without touching it. The printing went right to the bottom of the page. Then there was the second page with "I take full responsibility for my actions" and the signature. The handwriting experts would certainly find that the signature was genuine. It was only the first page that she suspected was a forgery.

She had sensed that it was odd to write a suicide note on a computer, but now she could see the purpose of it. Once Turner was dead, they had simply gone into the file, deleted whatever had been on the first page, typed a new one, and printed it out. Computer printers placed an extra step between the typist and the paper. There were no keys to hit unevenly, no distinctive characteristics to reveal that one page had been typed by Turner and the other by someone else. Maybe he had signed a blank sheet before they shot him, and they had simply run that through the printer too. It didn't matter. He had been shot in the right way and fallen in the right way. Everything was in the right place. The security system was on, so the police would assume there was no way anyone could have come in, killed him, and left. Unless they found something that wasn't perfect—a wrong chemical residue on his right hand, or a different set of prints on the brass casings of the bullets—he was a suicide.

She stood still for a moment. She could feel that the man who had done this was the one who had fooled her at the courthouse. Turner probably had earned his death, but he wasn't the one she should have been thinking about all this time. The one to worry about wasn't the inside man who took a share and didn't ask enough questions about what was going to happen if the plan didn't work. The one to look for would be the one who would still be left standing if everything went wrong. He had been in this room. If she had been smelling fear, she now knew it had been fear of him. His cunning had arranged everything around her to disguise his presence, but the perfect positions of the objects in the room only made his presence more pervasive.

Jane did not stop to form a clear, logical plan about what she was going to do. She simply knew that whatever arrangements the enemy had made must be to his benefit. She snatched up the forged suicide note, walked to the room where the body was lying, picked up the pistol, put it into her belt, and slid down the banister to the ground floor. Then she made her way back through the furnace to the crawl space, closed the closet door above her, replaced the metal panel, and crawled back out from under the house.

Within ten minutes she was back at the gas station taking the plastic tarp off her rented car. She dropped her room key in the mail slot at the motel office and drove south. She didn't know the enemy's name and she didn't know where he lived, but now she knew something about him. He wasn't some accountant who had hired a few head-bangers to block a courtroom so his embezzling wouldn't get noticed by the authorities. He was a pro.

15

Jane drove for the rest of the night. As soon as she was over the last big hill into Los Angeles County at Thousand Oaks, she ate breakfast at an enormous coffee shop surrounded by brown gumdrop-shaped hills. Just as she was taking her first sip of coffee the clock reached seven and men with heavy machinery began assaulting the mounds, shaving the tops to make level building lots.

She waited in a shopping mall until noon and then checked into a brick hotel in Burbank with a glass elevator that ran up the outside of the building to give future guests a view of whatever was going to be built in the empty, weed-tufted lot under it. She was glad that whatever was in the master plan for the lot had not yet been started, because she needed to sleep. She closed the curtains, undressed, and turned off the lamp. She knew that the dreams would probably come, but she was too tired now to fight them. She lay in the bed staring up at the single red light of the smoke detector on the ceiling, then relinquished her will and slept.

In her dream she found herself kneeling on a bare earth floor in a dark enclosure. Her ears told her that the space was about fifteen feet square. As her eyes slowly became more used to the dark she could see the texture of the inner side of the elm bark that had been shingled together to make the walls and roof of the ganosote. It was a large one built in the old style, about a hundred and twenty feet long with compartments like this one on either side. She counted ten cooking fires at intervals down the center aisle. She could see dark shapes of men, women, and children huddled at the fires or walking past them.

One of the children pushed aside the bearskin that was hanging at the east end of the longhouse to cover the door, and she had to look down to avoid the glare. She knew from the bright sunlight that it must be morning. When the child scampered out and the bearskin swung shut again she didn't raise her head because she was thinking about what the light had shown her. She was wearing a leather skirt and moccasins, and she could feel that the reason the bare ground didn't bother her knees was that they were protected by a pair of leggings. She reflected in a detached way that all of her clothes were soft deerskin, and this confirmed her impression that the day that was beginning was in the Old Time.

She could see that around her neck was a necklace woven from fragrant marsh grass, and she reached up to touch it. Every few inches there was a little disk of marsh grass covered with shell beads. She could smell the fresh, grassy scent, and she knew that the perfume made the smoke, cooking meat, and the twenty or thirty bodies in the ganosote easier on her nostrils.

She heard a noise and turned to see that behind her there was the big shape of a man on the lower platform along the wall of the compartment, and that he was stirring, about to wake up. She didn't know who he was, but stored on the platform five feet above him were her things—the extra moccasins she would use to replace the ones on her feet now, the elm bark gaowo tray she used to prepare corn bread, her collection of ahdoquasa with the bowl ends polished smooth for eating soup and the handles carved in the shapes of men and women embracing. She knew he must be her husband, but he stayed asleep in the shadows with his face to the wall because it was not time for her to see him yet.

She heard someone calling her name outside, and in the logic of dreams, she knew that the voice was the reason she was here. She stood up and walked past the fires to the bearskin flap. A strong hand gripped her arm, and she turned. A man whose face she did not quite see in the dim light said in Seneca, "If you don't want to dream about the dead, you don't have to. If the women sing the Ohgiwe, they'll leave." She knew this voice.

"I know, Jake," said Jane. She lifted the corner of the bearskin and ducked out into the light.

"Jane!" said a voice. It was harsh and high, not quite human, like the screech of a parrot. "Jane!"

She looked around her, and her eye caught a flash of deep blue above her on a maple tree, and then another flitted across the open air from an old sycamore. It flew in spurts, a dip and a wing-flap to bring the bird up, then a dip and a wing-flap and claws clutching the branch of the tree beside the first one. Jane could tell they were the two scrub jays she had captured in California.

The two birds dropped to the lowest branch of the maple just above her. The male tilted his head to the side and glared at her with one shiny black eye. "Jane!"

"What?" she asked.

The female jay hopped to reverse her position on the

branch, her head where her tail had been, and leaned down. "We did what you asked," she said. "We took Dennis and Mona to Hawenneyugeh."

"Thank you," said Jane. "But you have to go home now. You can't survive in this climate, and winter is coming."

The male shifted back and forth on the branch nervously, and she could hear its claws scratching the bark. "We came for you."

The jays eyed her without moving. Jane felt a small, growing fear. "Am I going to die too? So many people, all dying for nothing."

The female dropped to the grass at her feet and jerked her head from side to side to bring first one eye and then the other to bear on Jane. "It's not supposed to be *for* anything," she said. "It's what we are."

"What we are?"

"Hawenneyu, the Right-Handed Twin, creates people, birds, trees. Hanegoategeh, the Left-Handed Twin, makes cancer, number-six birdshot, Dutch Elm disease. For every measure, a countermeasure: Hawenneyu creates the air, Hanegoategeh churns it into the cold wind; Hawenneyu makes fire and houses, Hanegoategeh makes the fire burn the houses."

"Are you here to tell me it's my turn to be used up?" asked Jane.

"To warn you. If you want to be alive and breathe the air and drink the water, then look and listen. Nothing has changed since the beginning of the world. You're still walking through wild country. No sight or sound is irrelevant. Learn about your enemy."

She studied the two birds. "Who is my enemy?"

"Think about how he works," said the female jay.

"He's been killing people," Jane said. "There's nothing special about it at all. It's just brutal: cutting up the Deckers—"

"Without leaving any sign in the house that a little boy had ever lived there," the male reminded her.

"How about Mona and Dennis?" she asked. "He hired some men to beat Dennis to death and throw Mona down a stairwell."

"He waited until you had made your preparations for one building, and got the case moved to another. You had to go to a new place where a dozen men were waiting for you and court was already in session."

"And what about Alan Turner?" asked the female jay.

"What about him?" Jane asked.

"We know how you got into Turner's house past the alarm system and out again. How did he do it?"

"I don't know," said Jane. "I suppose he rang the doorbell. Alan Turner let him in. They must have known each other."

"You're not listening," said the female jay. "Anybody could get *in* by ringing the doorbell. How did he get *out* without tripping the alarm after Turner was dead?"

"How?" she asked.

Jane awoke and listened to the sounds of the cars on the freeway a few blocks away. Rush hour must have begun, but then she remembered that the term had no meaning around Los Angeles. There were cars clogging the roads every hour of every day. She sat up and looked around her, then stood and walked into the shower.

She had only needed some sleep. She still didn't know the man's name, but while she slept she had figured out something else about him. He might have gotten into the house in Monterey without setting off the alarm because Turner had let him in. But the only way he could have gotten out and left the alarm on after he had killed Turner was to know the alarm code.

16

Ellery Robinson opened the apartment door and looked out past her with wary eyes. "Come in," she said quietly. "This isn't a neighborhood for standing in a lighted doorway."

Jane stepped inside and watched the thin, hard arms move to close the steel door and then turn the dead bolt.

"I been waiting for you," said Ellery Robinson. "I knew you saw me in jail because I saw you. How did you find me? I'm not in the phone book."

"I went to your old apartment and asked around until I found somebody who still knew you. . . . You're in trouble again."

"No big thing. My parole officer thinks I have an attitude, so he forgot to write down when I came to see him."

"You don't have an attitude?"

Ellery Robinson shrugged her thin shoulders. "When a black woman gets past the age where they stop thinking about her big ass, they remember they didn't like her very much to begin with."

"Can you do anything about it?"

"He turned out to be unreliable, so his reports aren't enough to send anybody to jail anymore."

"He must have been really unreliable."

"Yeah. While I was in jail I heard they caught him in his office with a Mexican girl going down on him. He's been getting what he wanted regular like that for years. All he had to do to get them deported was check a box on a form, so they did a lot of favors."

"Does he know who set him up?"

For the first time Ellery Robinson smiled a little, and Jane could see a resemblance to the young woman she had met years ago. "Could be anybody. Everybody knew."

Jane sat in silence and stared at her. She had aged in the past eleven years, but it seemed to have refined and polished her. Ellery Robinson tolerated the gaze for a time, then said, "How about you? Have you been well?"

"I can't complain."

"You mean you can't complain to me, don't you?" said Ellery Robinson. "You're thinking I should have gone with you."

"I don't know. Nobody can say what would have happened."

"Don't feel sorry for me. I had a life, you know. My sister Clarice and I had one life. When I was in prison I would sit in the sun in the yard and close my eyes and follow her and the baby around all day with my mind. The women in jail thought I'd gone crazy, that I sat there all day in a coma, but I wasn't there at all. I was living inside my head."

"You don't regret it?"

"I regret that I'm a murderer. I don't regret that he got killed. He needed it."

Jane nodded. "You doing okay now?"

"I'm contented. I know what's on your mind. It's that woman in county jail, isn't it?"

"Mary Perkins?" said Jane. "No. She's far away now."

"What, then?"

"I know people hear things—in jail, the parole office, places like that."

"Sometimes."

"What have you heard about Intercontinental Security?"

Ellery Robinson's clear, untroubled face wrinkled with distaste. "If you're hiring, hire somebody else. If they're looking for you, don't let them find you."

"They seem to have a lot of business."

"Oh, yeah, it's a big company. And it's old, like Pinkerton's or Brinks or one of them. I think they used to guard trains and banks and things. For all I know they still do; I'm not a stockholder."

"Have you heard anything about burglaries in places they're supposed to protect—as though they might be fooling their own alarm systems or something?"

"No. What I hear most about them now is they hunt for people."

"What sort of people?"

"The usual. Skip-trace, open warrants, wanted for questioning, runaways. Somebody jumps bail, the bail bondsman is on the hook. Some clerk takes a little money out of the till and runs. The police don't look very hard, so the company hires Intercontinental."

"What's different?"

"The ones they bring in seem to fall down a lot. Maybe a broken arm, maybe a leg. Maybe their face doesn't look too good."

"It's an old company. Did they always have that reputation?"

Ellery Robinson shrugged. "I didn't always know

people who got chased. Then I was away for a few years. It's since I got back that I've been hearing things."

"Who have you been hearing them from? Can you help me get to one of them?"

The little woman leaned back on her worn couch and looked up at the ceiling for a moment. She seemed to be searching for names and addresses up there, but Jane could tell that she was rejecting some of them for reasons that she would not reveal.

The young man stood beside a car in the darkness. He was tall and heavy, with a jacket that was too thick for this weather and baggy blue pants. Jane could see that there was a streetlight directly above him, but the lamp was a jagged rim of broken glass.

Ellery Robinson followed the angle of Jane's eyes. "The street dealers shoot them out at night, and the city replaces them in the day. Everybody gets paid." She stopped walking and held Jane's arm. The young man looked up the block for three or four seconds, then down the block. When he was satisfied, he came away from the car and walked across the sidewalk onto the lawn.

Ellery Robinson looked up and said to him, "This is the woman." Then she turned to Jane. "He won't hurt you." Then she turned and walked away across the packed dirt of the big gray project toward her room.

Jane turned to the young man. "Thank you for coming."

The young man started walking, and she stepped off with him. "Got to keep moving or everybody starts to notice you're not going about your business."

"All right."

"She said you want to know about Intercontinental."

"Yes," said Jane. She waited for the logical question, but it did not come. He didn't consider it his business why she wanted to know, just as Ellery Robinson had not taken it on herself to tell either of them the other's name.

He said, "I worked for them."

"How long?"

"About two weeks." He anticipated the next question. "In October. They put out ads in this part of town. They wanted store security for two big malls in time for Christmas. You know, they didn't want a couple of white kids in uniforms in front of a store on Crenshaw. They'd just get hurt."

"What happened?"

"They made me a trainee. That means they don't have to pay regular wages. They put me through a lie detector test, a couple of days in a classroom, and turned me out. I worked the malls for a week and a half."

"Why did they fire you?"

The young man's eyes shot to hers and then ahead again. "Security check turned up my priors. Couldn't get bonded."

"What did you find out before you left?"

"Now you're not going to believe me, right?" he asked. "I got priors, and I'm a 'disgruntled former employee.' "

Jane looked up at the sky, then sighted along the wall of the complex. "It's a cold, clammy night for L.A. It'll probably rain soon, from the way it feels. And you may not believe it, but I hardly ever find myself in this part of town after midnight in any weather."

"I can believe that," he said.

"If I thought you were going to lie to me, I'd be pretty stupid to be here, wouldn't I?"

"Yeah."

"Then tell me what it was like."

"They're looking for young men with strong motivation and they'll give them the skills to succeed. Like the army. They got this guy who comes in and tells you how to be a thief in a big store so that you know what to look for."

"Did he get it right?"

"There were plenty of people in that room who could tell you for sure, but I wasn't one of them. I think it was pretty close, though, because they were all listening. Probably got some new ideas for the off-season."

"The skills to succeed. Can you tell me anything about this guy? Who was he?"

"His name was Farrell. Sort of an old guy with gray hair that's all bristly like a brush and spit-shined shoes. They called him the training officer. After he told us how to spot thieves, he told us what to do about them."

"Take them to the back of the store and call your supervisor?"

"Yeah," he said. "He says the system doesn't do any good. They get a court date and in a day they're back for more. So the supervisor would take them someplace and scare them."

"How scared?"

"Farrell says that comes under initiative. The company judges supervisors on the results."

"What are the results?"

"He says there are three kinds: the ones who don't need it and are doing it for some kind of kick, the ones in a crew that sells it, and junkies. There's no way to make any of them stop, but you can make them go to another store next time."

"Did you get to see any of this?"

"Once. A woman got caught with a bag that had a big box in it with a trapdoor cut in it, and she was shoveling stuff into it. The supervisor took her in the back for a while, then shoved her out the loading dock door. She ran."

"I've heard this before. Stores do it themselves. What else did you see?"

"The next week my background check comes in, so I'm out. I turn in my blues and go home. Two days later I get a phone call. It's Farrell. He says he's sorry to hear what happened, but maybe he can do something for me. I got initiative and motivation and I'm not afraid to do what needs to be done. He says sometimes there are jobs for people who can't make it through a background check. I'd still be working for Intercontinental, but they'd pay me in cash. Kind of an undercover job, and it paid a lot more."

"Did he say what you would be doing?"

"I'm twenty-two. Never had a job before because I'm dragging a five-page rap sheet. Got two convictions. Aggravated assault—did three for that in youth camp. Assault with a deadly weapon—did three more for that in Soledad. I figure he was looking for a brain surgeon."

"You said there were a lot of people in the training class who had the same problem. Did anybody else get the same offer?"

"I don't know."

"What did you tell him?"

They reached the sidewalk on the other side of the complex. He moved to the outside and looked carefully up and down the street before he ventured out of the shelter of the big buildings. "I told you I couldn't get another job."

"So you signed on."

"He had me come to another office. Not the big place where they hire and train people. This one was out in Van Nuys. There were eight or ten men hanging around—white guys, black guys, a couple of Mexicans. Everybody dressed good, but not really doing much. The sign on the door said 'Enterprise Development.' "

Jane remembered the men at the courthouse. They had all been wearing suits or sportcoats, and none of them had been carrying anything that could connect them with Intercontinental Security. "Where in Van Nuys?"

"The address is 5122 Van Nuys Boulevard. Big building, small office."

"What did you do there?"

"Farrell came and talked to me for a while."

"What did he tell you?"

"Pretty much what anybody tells you when you're doing something you get paid in cash for. If something goes wrong they'll slip you bail money, but if you tell anybody anything, there are a bunch of them and only one of you."

"And he still didn't tell you what he wanted you for?"

"Yeah, he did," said the young man. "Hunting."

"What?"

"That's what he said. The way it works is, the company has a list of people they want. The company does whatever is legal to find them. That's all in the open. It's a big company with offices in fifty places and a lot of people on the payroll. But then there's some cases that are off the books. Like maybe a guy disappears at the same time as a computer chip or a famous painting or something. The company knows it, they know he's got it, or he's got the money from it. Somehow he got away with it."

"So they hunt him."

"Yeah. The rest of it was just about the head guy."

"What about him?"

"How he did all of it. He went to work in the L.A. office a few years ago and set all this up. He was born off in the woods someplace way north of here, and he's a tracker. He thinks like a hound. Once he's got the scent, he never gives up. Farrell says he used to go after killers all by himself just for the kick it gave him. He gets a rush out of it, like a hunter."

"When?"

"When what?"

"When did he go after killers?"

"Before. When he was a cop."

Jane felt increasingly tense. "What's his name?"

"Bearclaw."

It wasn't exactly a surprise, but she felt a sensation like an electric shock. "Barraclough?"

"B-A-R-R-A-something. He's—"

"I've heard of him," Jane interrupted. She tried to clear her mind of the thoughts that were crowding in. She could almost see Danny Mittgang's face eight or nine years ago when she had asked him why he was running. He had not said the Los Angeles police wanted him as a material witness; what came out of Danny's mouth was "Barraclough." He had actually begun to sweat and gulp air. The name was already so familiar in certain circles that he had expected her to know it.

She had heard it many times after that, and each time there was something odd about the story. A fugitive's friends who had refused to betray him the first time they were questioned talked to Barraclough. A middle-aged man who had committed a white-collar crime would uncharacteristically forget there was no evidence against him and burst out at Barraclough with guns blazing. Barraclough would use information that could have come only from a wiretap to find a suspect, but no wiretap evidence would be introduced at the trial. She had filed the name with a few others, policemen in various parts of the country who were willing to do just about anything to catch a suspect. But the difference between Barraclough and the others was that when his name was mentioned, the person who said it was always afraid.

Jane tried to concentrate. She was not likely to get a second interview with this young man. "How did you get out of the job?"

"No problem. I told Farrell I didn't want in."

"Why not?"

"I didn't like him."

"It was the job you didn't like, wasn't it? The first one he wanted you to do?"

The young man shrugged. "Ellery said you might be interested in the picture they gave me, and I just told you I got no job."

Jane held out her hand. In the palm were two fresh green bills that had been rolled into her fingers since she'd come out of the shadows to meet him. They unrolled enough so that he could see the hundreds in the corners.

He reached inside his jacket and pulled a photograph out of his breast pocket. He handed it to her and then gently plucked the two bills off her palm.

Jane held the picture up, trying to catch the dim glow of the distant street lamp. She didn't want to wait to know whether it was one of the Christmas snapshots the Deckers had mailed to Grandma or one of the family mementos the killers had taken from the Washington house. She caught a flash of blond hair, and held it higher to be sure. It wasn't a picture of Timmy at all: it was Mary Perkins.

17

Mary Perkins had spent most of her month in Ann Arbor learning about Donna Kester. She had discovered that Donna was not comfortable in the apartment that Jane Whitefield had helped her to rent. It was not Jane Whitefield's fault, although she was tempted to sweep up whatever annoying particles of blame were lying around and heap them on her. Mary had assumed that Donna Kester was going to be someone who would like the long, clean lines of the modern apartment complex. It reminded Mary of the hotels where she had stayed for most of her adult life.

But as the winter came on, the building seemed hastily built and drafty, as though the carpenters had left something undone that she couldn't see. The exercise room that the tenants shared was a big box with a glass wall where women a lot younger than Mary went to display the results of many earlier visits to young men who seemed to be too intent on lifting large pieces of iron to notice what was being offered. The pool in the courtyard promised more of the same in the distant summer without the chance to hide the mileage under a good pair of tights. And the dirty snow that had drifted over its plastic cover began to contribute to her feeling that summer wasn't something that was still to come.

As Donna Kester explained her position to herself, the place wasn't congenial. She moved closer to the university and rented the top floor of a big house that had been built in the 1920s. It was the sort of house where she had grown up in Memphis, with a lot of time-darkened wood in places where they didn't put wood anymore, and a layer of thick carpet that covered the stairway and muffled the creak and was much cleaner at the edges than at the center.

Her apartment had a small, neat little kitchen and a bedroom with a brass bed in it that wasn't a reproduction of anything, but wasn't good enough to be an antique. The closet was small, but it was big enough for the sort of wardrobe that Donna Kester was likely to acquire. The living room had a bad couch and a good easy chair that was aimed as though by a surveyor directly at a twenty-year-old RCA television set that picked up only two channels she had trouble telling apart. But the two channels had forecasters who did a fair job of predicting the weather, and this was about all she required of them for the moment because it let her know what to wear while she was out looking for a job.

Mary began to feel more comfortable as Donna Kester soon after she moved into the old apartment. She had no trouble suppressing the landlords' curiosity with a vague reference to a divorce. In the future, whenever they had a question in their minds about her lack of a work history and shallow credit record, she could be too sensitive to talk about it. They could chew on the divorce and come up with plausible answers until they found one that satisfied them. It sometimes seemed that Donna Kester knew everything about people that Mary Perkins knew, only it hadn't cost her as much.

Donna walked into the hallway, threaded her new scarf into the sleeve of her big goose-down coat, stuffed her new gloves into the pockets, and hoisted the coat onto the peg. She sat down on the steps to take off her boots, and felt the distressing sensation of having the melted snow from her last trip soak through the seat of her pants. She stood up quickly, set the boots on the mat, and carefully made her way up the stairs in her socks. She felt unfairly punished. She thought she had learned about tracking snow on the steps early enough. The carpet would have dried by now if there had been heating ducts near the entrance at the foot of the stairs.

If she owned this place, she would damned well have a contractor in by tomorrow noon. She would put a big old brass register right by the door where a person could get hugged by that breath of hot air as soon as she made it inside, and then leave her coat and boots in front of it to get toasted before she went out again. She had a brief fantasy about buying the house from the Monahans and getting the contractor on the phone before the ink on the deed was dry.

She reached into her purse and grasped her key. That made her feel better. It was the big old-fashioned kind that was a shaft of steel four inches long with an oval ring on one end and the teeth on the other. It looked like the key to a castle and it made her feel safe. She had some justification for the feeling. The lock set into the thick, solid door looked about the size of a deck of cards, with big steel tumblers and springs that snapped like a trap when she locked it, and it was easy to see that it had been in there for a long time. If there had ever been a break-in they would have replaced it.

She reached the top, put her hand on the yellowed porcelain doorknob, pushed in her key, and felt the door swing open. The lights were on. She turned and tried to step back down the stairs as quickly and quietly as she could, but she knew she was making too much noise—already had made too much noise just coming in and climbing the stairs—so she began to take the steps by leaning on the railing and jumping as many as she could to land with a thump.

She burned with a hatred for her stupidity. When she had felt the cold wet spot on the stairs she should have known someone else had been here. It wasn't as though it were a faint clue; it was a warning sign practically branded on her ass. She regretted all of it: leaving the sprawling, noisy, busy apartment complex for this old house where they didn't even have to think hard about how to get her alone because she was always alone; letting herself rent a second apartment at all, because showing the false documents twice raised the risk by exactly one hundred percent; trusting like a child to big locks and keys—no, hiding the way a child did, not by concealing herself but by covering her own eyes with her hands.

As she reached the bottom and realized with a pang that common sense required that she race through the door into the snow without stopping for her boots, the voice touched her gently.

"It's me," said Jane Whitefield. "Don't run. It's only me."

Mary stopped with her face to the door. She turned and looked up. She could see the silhouette of the tall, slim woman in front of the dimly lighted doorway at the top of the stairs. The shape was dark, a deeper shadow, and for a second a little of the fear came back into her chest like a paralysis in her lungs. Then the woman at the top of the stairs swung Mary's door open and said in the same quiet voice, "Sorry to startle you."

Mary climbed back up her stairs slowly and deliberately because she wanted to let her heart stop pounding. The way Jane had said it was an invitation to join a conspiracy. People who were startled jumped half an inch and said, "Oh." They didn't vault down twenty-foot staircases and dash into the snow in wet socks. That was what people did who were terrified, running for their lives. We'll let your cowardice pass without comment, and we'll call it something else. That was what Jane was saying. No, it was even worse than that. She knew it wasn't merely cowardice. It was the only sane response for a woman who was guilty of so much that any surprise visitor was probably there because he wanted to put her in a bag. That was what Jane was passing without comment.

Mary reached the top of the stairs and stepped into her living room. She looked around for Jane but couldn't see or hear her, which made her remember the strangeness about the woman that had always irritated her. It was that erect quietness that made other people feel as though they talked too much without getting anything in return, like they were emptying the contents of their brains into a deep, dark hole, where it wasn't deemed enough to amount to much. She drifted around like she was the queen of the swans, and it was okay with her if anybody with her suspected she thought they were dumb, short, and pasty-faced and their voices were too loud.

Mary heard the sound of the teakettle steaming in the kitchen; then it stopped, so that was where Jane must be. She felt tension stiffen the back of her neck and shoulders.

This was her place, and there was some primal insult in having another woman walk in and go through her cupboards. She hated owing this woman so much that she had to endure it.

Mary moved toward her little kitchen just as Jane came out with the tea tray, already talking. "I'm really sorry I had to come in like this. It would make me angry if anyone did it to me, but it seemed best. In the first place, I didn't know you well enough to be able to predict whether you were likely to have gotten your hands on a gun. You've had plenty of time to do it."

Mary felt the words dissolve what remained of her confidence like a sugar cube in a rainstorm. She had been here a month, and it had never occurred to her to obtain the most obvious way of protecting herself. The decision she would have made was by no means certain, but that didn't help; it made her even more frightened, because she had not given it even enough thought to reject it.

But Jane was going on, and Mary hadn't been listening. ". . . didn't want to get my head blown off, and I figured if your landlord heard a woman coming up the steps he would assume it was you. I've been very careful not to cause trouble by coming here. Nobody followed me and nobody had a chance to see me outside waiting. I saw you coming up the sidewalk, so I made tea." She held out a cup so Mary could take it.

Mary sniffed it and said, "It's different."

"I picked it up in L.A.," said Jane. "It's mixed with blackberry leaves. I've got a weakness for nonsense like that."

Mary sipped. At least this woman had not come in and put her hands into the cupboards looking for things. The teakettle and the water were in plain sight. She resisted the feeling. Whatever this woman wanted, she was not going to get it by dropping a teabag into a cup of water. She smiled. "Me too."

Mary's smile was like a cat purring while it rubbed its fur against a person's leg. Jane could see that the smile had not just been practiced in front of a mirror. It had about it the cat's ease and grace that could only have come from bringing it out and using it to get what the cat needed. She looked around. "I like your apartment," she said.

Mary longed for her to say something insincere about the furniture.

"You got everything right," said Jane. "It would be pretty hard for somebody to get all the way up that stairway if you really wanted to stop him. The building looks like a single-family house from the outside, so nobody would look for a stranger here. That's the important thing. Not what you'll do if they find you, but being where they won't look."

"How did you find me? Or were you here all the time watching me?"

"Why would I do that?"

"I don't know. Maybe to see what I did." Mary realized that she had not said anything. She resolved not to make this mistake again. "To see if I was good enough at it to have a chance."

Jane said, "No, I don't play games."

"Then you changed your mind about me." Without any reason at all, Mary thought.

"No again," said Jane. "I expected you to be good at it."

Mary was tired. She had spent the day trying to get personnel managers to give her a competitive test of business skills when all they wanted was references, then to give her the benefit of the doubt based on her ability to speak knowledgeably, and the promise that references could be obtained, and finally just to give her a break because she was pleasant, well-groomed, and eager. Now she was sitting in a pair of pants with a wet seat. "Let me try to be more direct," she said. "You helped me, and I thank you for that. Then you walked out on me. Rather mysteriously, I might add. Now you're back. You tell me I played a good game of hide-and-seek, but here you are. You seem to have had no trouble finding me, or opening the lock to my door to get in and make yourself a cup of tea. I've never had any difficulty believing you're better at this than I am, but now I'm not just awed, I'm scared to death. So what do you want?"

Jane put down her tea. "You shouldn't be scared to death. I found you because I knew where to look. If you had been stupid, you would have left Ann Arbor, put yourself in the airports and hotel lobbies again, and inevitably found your way to one of the places where they're looking. I knew you weren't stupid, so I was pretty sure you must still be in this town. So what would you be doing? If you had wanted to give up on life you would have stayed put and done nothing. A person can sit in the right locked room forever without getting found if she has enough to pay the rent. I figured you would be too lively to go that way, so I tried the job route."

"What's the job route?" Mary asked.

"I knew you had the sense to figure out that the more you do with a fake identity, the better it gets because after a while it's not exactly fake anymore. You're not the only woman in town with records that only go back a few years. Pretty soon it will take a lot of digging to detect whether you're entirely rebuilt or just went through the usual changes—a couple of marriages that brought new names, a couple of moves from one state to another, a career change or two. Having eliminated the possibility that you had left or gone into a coma, I knew you would be applying for jobs. It's the best way to start a new life."

"That was enough?" asked Mary.

"The biggest and safest employer in Ann Arbor is the university. I called the personnel office and said I was a member of a faculty committee trying to hire someone to do the accounting and clerical work for a big research grant in the medical school."

"Why that? Why not something else?"

"Faculty members aren't hired by the university personnel office. They're hired by the faculty, so there was very little chance she would look for a personnel file on me and not find it. Medical schools are semi-autonomous, so I could play an insider without knowing anything about her operation. I asked her to send me copies of applications with a bookkeeping background, since I figured that would be your strength. I asked how long it would take to bring them to my office. She said a day or two, so I offered to come over and pick them out myself. That way I didn't need an office."

"You got this address off my application. God, it's easy."

"Not that easy," said Jane. "Nobody knows what I knew—your new name, the city, and where you'd have to apply for work if you wanted any." She stared at Mary Perkins over the rim of her teacup. "Not even Barraclough."

Mary felt her spine stiffen. She considered her options. She could pretend the name had made no impression on her, and later find a chance to slip away quietly. She could create some kind of disturbance—throw the cup at

Jane and run. But even if she got out the door, the only way of taking the next step was to fall back on the name and the credit that Jane had given her. She wasn't ready. She should have been ready. "How do you know that name? I never told you."

"Why didn't you?" asked Jane. "You told me you didn't know who was looking for you."

Mary Perkins's mind stumbled, held back from the conclusion it was about to reach. That was right. She had come to Jane Whitefield, and Jane Whitefield kept nagging her about who it was. She hadn't known. She couldn't have been working for Barraclough. At least a month ago she couldn't. "I wanted you to help me," said Mary. "I only provide the arguments for what I want. You have to supply your own arguments against."

"All right," said Jane. "Then let's take the whole issue off the table. I have decided to help you."

"In spite of Barraclough?"

"Because of Barraclough."

"Do you know him?"

"I've seen his work." She looked at Mary closely. "Has he ever seen you?"

The question didn't make any sense unless the way Jane Whitefield wanted to make money was to sell someone else to Barraclough and say she was Mary Perkins. "I suppose he has lots of pictures of me."

"Not pictures," Jane said. "Has he actually looked at you face-to-face?"

"Is that important?"

"Yes. Tell me."

"We never met," said Mary Perkins. "When I got out of the federal prison eight months ago, he somehow heard about it. He knew where I was living. How he got that I don't know. They said it was going to be a secret to help in my rehab—you know, help me fit into the community, keep my old cronies away, and all that."

"He used to be a cop. He knows how to use the system. He didn't come for you himself?"

"He sent two men," said Mary Perkins. "They explained to me about Barraclough."

"What did they tell you?"

"He's the director of the Los Angeles office of Intercontinental Security. He's got a huge organization and a lot of power, and connections with every police department. You can't get away from him and you can't fight him. He had read about me."

"Read what?"

"Everything. Newspaper reports, the transcript of my trial, the investigation reports. I don't know how he got those either. He had decided that I had a whole lot of savings and loan money hidden someplace. He wanted it. I couldn't call the police and say he was taking it because I wasn't supposed to have it."

"You told me the pitch. You just didn't tell me where you heard it. Since you're still running and they're still chasing, you must have gotten away. How?"

"They didn't put a gun to my head and say 'Pay or die.' I told them I didn't have it. But they said Barraclough knew I did because he had followed my case." She chuckled sadly. "You know how prosecutors are. They rave around in front of the jury, flinging enormous, impossible numbers around. This is how much is missing from savings and loans in this great, tormented state of Texas. This is the woman caught with ten dollars of it. All that nonsense doesn't simply go into the jury's subconscious; it goes into the transcript. Even if your lawyer proves it's silly, once it's been said it exists. It had convinced Barraclough I had some insane amount of money—like fifty million."

"So Barraclough sent them to pick you up and take you with them, right?"

"What else? If I had that kind of money I couldn't haul it around in a suitcase. It would take a couple of freight cars. It would have to be in a numbered account in Switzerland or someplace. They said they'd have to hold on to me until I had led them to the accounts."

"What was the up side?"

"Does this sound like it has an up side?"

Jane said, "When it was all over, what did they promise to leave you? Would you have any money left, or just your life?"

"They said Barraclough had done this quite a few times before. He just took half from each one he caught and let him go."

"Did you believe them?"

Mary Perkins smirked. "Do I look younger than I am, or what? It was like having a man ask you to take off half your clothes."

"What happened then?"

"They each took one of my arms and led me outside to their car. It was a two-door, so you had to kind of squinch in behind the front seat. They had the passenger seat already tipped forward when they opened the door. They had turned off the dome light so it wouldn't go on when the door opened. I remember looking in and thinking, I'm going to die. I had just read one of those articles they have in magazines about serial killers and rapists, and it said whatever you do, don't get in the car. Once you're in, nothing is up to you anymore; it's up to them. They pushed me in and I started crying."

"Because you thought you were going to die?"

"Knew it. I knew I would die if I didn't do something. The crying was all I could think of. It made them nervous and nasty. One of them said if I didn't stop he'd hurt me, so I stopped. I could see that made them get overconfident. It was a long drive, and they had been waiting outside my apartment for hours. They had to make a pee stop. They were talking about going to a gas station, but they had a full tank, so they didn't want to stop and have the gas guy stare at them and maybe remember they had a woman with them. So they waited until they were on the Interstate and pulled into a truck stop. One of them was going to go in, and then the other while the first one stayed with me. I kept looking for a chance to get in there, so I could scream my head off, even make one of them hit me, but they didn't give me any chance. I tried saying I had to pee too. I tried saying I had to change a tampon. I begged, I promised."

"How did you manage it?"

"Did I mention it was a two-door car?"

"Yes."

"They kept the motor running so they could get away fast if something went wrong. I waited until the first one got back. He was the driver. He comes to the left door to open it, and the other one opens the right-side door to get out. I pushed the driver's seat forward, flopped over on it on my belly, set the transmission in gear, ducked down, and punched the gas pedal with the palm of my hand. The car goes. Not real fast, just jerks ahead and coasts at maybe ten miles an hour. The one trying to get into the driver's side gets his foot run over. The other one jumps back into his seat. The car moves in this sort of stately pace right into the front of the restaurant—*crash!* When it hit, it kind of jammed me head-first under the dashboard onto my elbows with the brake pedal pressing on my forehead and the steering wheel holding my butt down and not enough room for a somersault anyway. The one in the seat kind of belly-flopped next to me, only his face hit the glove compartment."

Jane frowned. "Why are you making this up?"

Mary Perkins looked angry, but she seemed to be holding her breath. Finally she let it out. "I'm not sure. I guess I wanted to sound brave."

"What really happened?"

"A Highway Patrol car pulled in beside us. I was too scared to even look at them. The cop saw I had been crying, so he knocked on my window and asked if there was something wrong. I told the cop I was turning myself in—that I left Los Angeles in violation of my parole."

"Why did you tell him you were on parole?"

"I thought it was a stroke of genius. If I said I'd been kidnapped, they'd keep me there to testify. They could do it; I really was out on parole. Even if I did get these two convicted, what good was that going to do me? They might not have been telling the truth about Barraclough, but they were working for somebody. On their own, these two couldn't have known all that about my trial transcripts and everything. They were maybe twenty-one or twenty-two years old, and dumb."

"So what happened?"

"I figured the C.H.P. would just ship me back to L.A. for a lecture, and when that was over I could hop on a plane and disappear. Only wouldn't you know it, when they identified these two characters, they both turned out to be convicted felons, so instead of a little scolding, I get to do ninety in L.A. County Jail. Consorting with convicted felons is apparently more serious than going out of town without telling your parole officer."

"That was what you were in for when you saw me?"

"Yes. They let me out two weeks early, or else those guys would have had me before I got to the airport. But they must have a way of knowing when somebody is released early."

"Not them. Barraclough does." They sat for a time in silence, sipping their tea. The cold wind outside the old house was stronger up here on the second floor. The snow was falling harder now, as it sometimes did after nightfall, and the white flakes came tumbling into the light and ticked the window as though it were the windshield of a moving car.

Mary Perkins said, "What do you know about Barraclough?"

Jane stopped watching the snowflakes and turned to her. "He's not what they all think he is. They think he's a hunter, so he's entitled to hunt. That's the chance you take: if you run, there will be somebody like him who gets paid to bring you back. But he's not that anymore. He's a cannibal."

"What do you mean?"

"He's not working for the system anymore, catching people and bringing them in and then getting his reward. He's living by gobbling people up."

"Who else?"

"The last one I know about is an eight-year-old boy."

"Why was he after a little boy?"

"The boy inherited some money and disappeared. Barraclough heard about it and killed at least four people just because they were between him and the boy—killed them just to get them out of his way so he could get the money."

"Did he get it?"

Jane shrugged. "The lawyers still have to do their audits and studies and sort out at least eight years of paper. When they finish, they'll probably learn enough to charge an accountant who's already dead with breach of trust or something. They'll also find out that the money is gone. They don't know that yet, but it is. Barraclough would never have killed the accountant if he didn't already have it."

"Why did you come back here?"

"Because I was one of the people who let him do it. I don't want him to do the same thing to you."

18

The night was cold and the oil furnace hummed in the basement two stories below them. Jane sat quietly in the corner of the room looking out the window and watching the feathery snow falling, first to fill in the icy ruts on the road and then to lay a blue-white blanket over it. No cars passed on the street to disturb it, and nobody had been out to leave human footprints, so it began to seem that she and Mary Perkins were the only ones left, adrift in a place where there was no motion and no time.

Mary stirred and walked into the kitchen. After more snow fell, Jane could smell food cooking and hear plates rattling onto the table. The roasting smell grew thicker in the air, and steam that carried the scent of vegetables fogged the window. There was the creak of the oven door opening and then the thump of it closing. Mary's footsteps reached the doorway and she said, "Time to eat."

On the table were a roasted chicken, asparagus, carrots, and potatoes, an excess of food cooked absentmindedly without regard to the number of people at the table. They ate sparingly and with formality. When they were finished they cleared the table and washed the dishes without speaking. They were like two strangers stranded together in the only way station in the empty wilderness, surrounded by hundreds of miles of howling winds and drifting snow—not because they had decided to be together but because there was no other shelter.

Mary walked into her bedroom for a few minutes and came out to set a pillow and a thick quilt on the couch, then went inside again and closed the door. Jane went back to the window to watch. The snow fell for another two hours before she stood up and walked to the couch, pulled the quilt over her, and fell asleep.

In her dream a light, powdery snow was falling while she trotted ahead of her companion through the forest. It was cold, but she didn't feel the cruelty of it because she had worked up a light sweat. She ducked her head under spidery branches frosted with snow, knowing that if she bumped one, the snow would shower off onto the ground. Then pursuers would read that as clearly as a track, and the wind would be slower to cover it.

They were making their way south from Ann Arbor and she was watching for the rivers that fed into Lake Erie. First would be the Raisin, then the Maumee, then the Sandusky. This forest was wild country. Hunters from tribes from every direction came to get bear, deer, and beaver in the winter and passed through it in the summer on their way to kill each other. It had been full of armed men for a thousand years.

She listened to the breaths of the woman trotting along behind her, and at each breath there was more of her voice, more of a cry. Jane stopped and looked back. Mary Perkins had slowed down to a stagger, too tired to plant her feet in the trail Jane had broken for her, and now and then meandering to waste her strength fighting the deep drifts. Jane walked back in her own tracks and held Mary's arm as they walked. Mary tried to say something, but Jane pulled her near and whispered, "They could be close, so save your breath. Nothing does us any good but moving."

Mary didn't try to answer, so she returned her attention to the trail. It was important that they cover as much ground as they could while the snow was still falling to hide the signs of their passing. As soon as she had completed the thought, the snow stopped. The air was frosty and still, and their feet made loud crunching sounds each time they stepped on the unbroken snow.

The ones who were following them would be able to keep up a fast pace, running in their footsteps in the flat places where the going was easy, and avoiding the depressions where their tracks had sunk in deep. Jane was always looking ahead, using the glow of the moon on the snow to search for any irregularity in the terrain that she could use to hide their trail—a thicket or a fallen log or a frozen streambed leading to the next river.

Far behind, she heard the first call of the hunters. "Coo-wigh!" reached her in the still air, and it was answered by a whistle somewhere closer and to their left.

"We've got to run now," she whispered to Mary Perkins.

They stepped into a jog with Jane at the front again, keeping her strides short to push aside the snow and make the going easier for Mary. She heard more whistles, and then the report of a rifle off to the left, and there were faint voices behind. She stepped into a deep drift and fell, then scrambled out of it and saw the stream. They ran along it for about a mile. As Jane came around a bend she saw the platform. It stood alone on the bank, a row of poles lashed ten feet above the ground between two saplings. She could see that its surface had something on it, so she hurried to the thicker sapling and began to climb.

"What are you doing?" hissed Mary impatiently. "They're coming."

"We can't outrun them," Jane whispered. "They never get tired and they never give up. All you can ever do is fool them."

The sapling was smooth and half frozen, with a layer of frost on the northwest side that held the snow to it, but she hoisted herself up high enough to see what was on the platform. There was a haunch of venison with the hide still on it, and a fat chunk of flesh that could only be bear meat. Some hunter had stored it there to keep it frozen and high enough to be out of the reach of animals. Then she found the two pairs of snowshoes. She tossed them to the ground and dropped beside them.

She knelt in the snow and tied one pair on Mary Perkins backward, so the long narrow shaft was at the toe end. "Stay here. Don't move," she said, then ran along the streambed and into the woods where the hunters' trail began. She tied her own snowshoes on backward, made her way back to Mary Perkins and said, "Come on."

They stepped along more easily now, the snowshoes holding them on the surface of the snow. Jane followed the stream to the right for a hundred yards to the first place where the low plants penetrated the snowpack enough to complicate their trail, then turned right again, toward the east. They made a trail that looked as though it led in the opposite direction and belonged to the hunters who had cached their game on the platform.

When the first sunlight caught them, they were in a flat, open valley. Their trail stretched behind them for miles, and as soon as the sun was high enough to stir the morning wind, much of it would be blown away. She said to Mary Perkins, "Just one more run, to get out of the open before they see us."

They began to run due east, where Jane could see a row of evergreen bushes tall enough to hide the shape of a standing woman. She was tired now too. They had been moving silently for the whole night, never speaking for hours at a time, only concentrating on the awkward business of walking in snowshoes. They could see the end now, and it made Jane run faster. As soon as they reached the shelter of the bushes they would be able to sit and rest, maybe even sleep in turns while the wind blew across the valley and erased the shallow marks of their snowshoes. "Faster," she said to Mary. Everything would depend on how they behaved for the next few minutes. They ran until their breath came in short gasps and their legs were numb.

The sun was rising now right behind the row of evergreens, glaring through the upper branches and making it hard for Jane to focus her eyes on them to tell how far they were. She clenched her teeth and kept running, and then they were there. Jane dragged Mary between the first pair of trees, then five more steps into thicker cover where the trees were small and close together, and they both let themselves collapse into the soft snow.

Jane lay there, breathing deeply, feeling the cold flakes against her cheek but not caring. She started to raise herself to her elbows, and her eyes rested on the bushes. All around her, they began to topple over. The men who had been holding them let go, and they fell to the snow with a low, whispery, ugly swish. All of the bushes seemed to change into men as warriors stood up from behind the clumps of brush they had tied into blinds or shouldered aside the small trees they had stuck into the snow.

Rough, hard hands clutched her arms, a heavy, leather-clad body threw itself across her legs, and another pressed her face into the snow so that she nearly smothered. They bound her hands behind her, dragged her to her feet, and jerked her ahead. One of her snowshoes came off, but when she tried to stop and look down a push that felt like a punch propelled her forward, so she limped along a few steps before the other one came off too. She tried to glance behind her to see what had happened to Mary, but a hand on the small of her back shoved her on with such force that for an instant she saw the sky.

They marched them to a path that led up over the hill into the next river valley. As Jane climbed, she tried to get her strength back, but they kept her moving too fast. She heard a language that meant nothing to her. The sounds were gruff, guttural, and alien. When she reached the crest of the hill her heart stopped for a moment, then began to beat hard.

Stretched out below was a squalid, sprawling settlement that seemed to have been laid out by a madman. There were a few longhouses that looked as though Hurons or Eries had built them with no intention of living there long, interspersed with Algonquin wigwams made of bark and thatch, a few hide tents like the wandering plains people had, and in the center a clump of shanties made of boards. It was as though enemies of all of the wars of the Nundawaono had somehow survived in de-based remnants and gathered here for the winter hunt.

As she stumbled down the steep path to the huge collection of ramshackle dwellings, she could see small shapes of people below, their shadows long in the bright dawn sunlight. One of them pointed upward and yelled something, and then men began to stream out of the shelters and gather in the center of the village. She could see them talking and pointing, and she could feel their excitement growing until, when she was dragged to the edge of the village, their voices rose in a shout that was harsh and deafening, full of hatred and glee. It grew louder as she moved closer to it, until she could feel her stomach vibrating with it, and the men started to fire their guns into the air, a ragged *powpow pow powpow*, like popcorn popping.

They prodded Jane and Mary across the dirty, mud-caked snow between the huts and pushed them into a big pen made of upright pine logs sharpened at the tops. Jane looked around her and saw to her surprise that there were dozens of other people already inside—men clinging to their wives and children, trying in vain to reach around all of them with their arms, other men who looked as though they had run the gauntlet on the way into the little pen, with limbs broken and faces streaked with blood from blows above the hairline, women with eyes swelled shut and missing teeth.

"What's going to happen?" asked Mary.

Jane said, "The fighting has gone on forever. So many people get killed that the main reason for it now is to get prisoners to adopt."

"Adopt? We're grown women."

"When people are killed they capture someone to take their place—their name, their work, their family."

The gate across the pen opened and about fifty warriors streamed in, painted and armed as though they had just returned from battle. They were agitated and angry, some of them in a frenzy, dancing from one foot to the other like boxers and shouting in the incomprehensible languages of enemies. One by one and with reluctance, they took notice of something behind them and stepped aside to let the one Jane had been watching for pass among them to the front.

Jane hung her head like the captives around her to give her a chance to study him without attracting his attention. She looked from his feet upward. He was big and muscular, wearing a clinging, whitish leather shirt that seemed to have been stitched together from many small pieces. Around his neck and shoulders hung a gateasha of six rows of small white wampum beads. When she forced her gaze to move upward, she nearly fainted.

He was wearing a Face. It was a scalp mask, painted bright red, with round staring copper eyes and the clenched teeth that made it resemble both the rage of battle and the ghastly grin of a rotting corpse. It was terrifying to see a Face here. She could tell that this was an old Face, the features that a supernatural being had shown to some virtuous Seneca ages ago in a dream. The Seneca had carved to free the Face from the trunk of a living basswood tree, given it presents of tobacco, rubbed it with sunflower oil, and fed it the same mixture of cornmeal and maple sugar that the warriors ate on the trail to battle. It didn't merely represent the supernatural being; it *was* the supernatural being. It gleamed with power strong enough to cure disease and change the weather, but on this man that power became the force of evil and witchcraft and death.

The Face approached and stared at her with its round, empty eyes. Jane could see now that the necklace was made not of little white shells but of human teeth. As he moved on, she realized with revulsion what the leather must be: strips of skin flayed from human beings. The Face walked around the pen, stopping in front of each captive to turn its round-eyed, unreadable gaze on him for a second or two, then moving on.

Finally the Face came back to where Jane was standing. The Face stopped and pointed at Mary. At once a warrior appeared out of the mob and poured a bucket of black, greasy paint over Mary Perkins's head. The paint streamed down to her shoulders and ran along her arms to her fingertips.

Mary gasped and sputtered. "Why did he do that? What is it, some kind of joke?"

"No," said Jane. She could feel waves of nausea that started in her chest and moved down to grip her belly.

Mary shivered with cold. "It must be an initiation, right?" Her voice was tense and scared now, and a little sob was audible in it. "Why me?" she wailed. "What do they want me to do?"

Jane tried to speak, but what she would have to say was impossible to put into words. The black paint was the sign that a captive had been selected to be burned.

19

Jane awoke in the darkness with her heart pounding. She walked to the window. The snow had stopped sometime during the night, and now the sidewalks and streets were white and still, but in the east the sky had changed enough to tell her there was no point in going back to the couch. She raised her hand to touch her forehead and rubbed away the beads of sweat that had formed there. She had been denying what she knew about Barraclough, and the knowledge was fighting its way to the surface in dreams.

She moved quietly into the kitchen and put the coffee on. Then she sat and listened to Mary waking up and remembering and making her way toward the smell of the brewing coffee. The door opened and Mary walked out into the kitchen, poured a cup of coffee, and stood at the sink to drink it. "I've been thinking," she said. "I've been on my own most of my life and I think I can stay out of Barraclough's way if I don't do anything stupid." It was a question.

"It can be done." Jane sat still. It was time already. She would have to work up to it gradually, tell Mary what she knew and let her draw her own conclusion. "You just have to avoid doing anything stupid."

"Like getting my picture in the papers," Mary offered.

"Right," said Jane. "You might want to keep it off things like credit cards and driver's licenses too. Barraclough is the regional head of a very big detective agency, so he can probably find a way to have your picture circulated. You know, a reward for a missing person."

"I guess I can," Mary said. "And keep from getting arrested."

"Or fingerprinted."

"That's what I said."

"You've got to keep from being a victim too. If your house is burglarized or your car is stolen, they fingerprint the owner so they can identify prints that aren't supposed to be there. Some states take your prints for a driver's license. And a lot of employers require it; if you need to be bonded or licensed or need a security clearance, it's hard to avoid. Most companies hire a security service to handle the details and report the results—a service like Intercontinental."

Mary Perkins glared at her. "You're trying to scare me."

"Yes," said Jane. "It's better. I don't want to hear you sometime saying, 'Why me?' "

"All right," said Mary. "What else?"

Jane stared at the wall. "Well, they're not just passively waiting for you to turn up. They're searching. I know that because I talked to somebody who was hired to help. But the easiest way is to get you to come to them. You know—an announcement in the paper says some rich aunt of yours died and the following eighty people are named in the will. Or the help-wanted section says there's a job for a blue-eyed woman age thirty-four and a half and five feet four and seven eighths who's good at arithmetic. Or a personal ad says a wealthy widow with a

large secluded mansion wants a roommate: a quiet female nonsmoker from the South who plays cribbage, or
whatever else you do but not everyone does. Barraclough
is perfectly capable of renting houses in the ten most
likely places and having ten women sit there for a month
waiting for you to show up."

"He'd do that?"

"Sure," said Jane. "It's quick, it's easy, and it's
cheaper than the alternatives."

"What are those?"

"Well, you have a history. There are people you were
close to. They'll go see them. Maybe watch to see if you
come for a visit, or maybe bully them into telling what
they know. If you ever left clothes anywhere when you
started running, they'll have translated the labels into
places where you might buy the next batch. The more expensive they were, the fewer places to buy them, and
they know you'll need spring clothes or risk standing out.
They'll also use them to construct a projection of how
you're likely to look now, so they don't miss you in a
public place: exact height, weight, style, and color preference. Then there's chemical analysis."

"What do they have to analyze?"

"If you wore perfume or cosmetics when you wore the
clothes, they'll identify them and add them to your profile. If you love Thai food or going to the zoo, they'll
know that too."

"That's crazy."

Jane shrugged. "No crazier than having people meet us
in airports all over the western half of the country. Intercontinental is an enormous detective agency, much bigger than most police departments. There isn't a city in
the country that doesn't have a crime lab with a trace-

analysis section. There's a machine called a gas chromatograph that vaporizes whatever substance they find and identifies it. There's no question Intercontinental has one, and probably an emission spectrometer and an electron microscope. If you're in the business of tracking people for money, that stuff pays for itself quickly."

"You're making it sound hopeless."

"Not hopeless. It just takes some thought."

Mary protested. "But there are thousands of people in this country nobody can find."

"Millions," said Jane.

"Well, who are they? You can't tell me they all get caught."

"It depends on who's looking for them and how hard. A lot of them are divorce fugitives: the man who doesn't want to pay alimony or the parent who loses custody and takes the child out of state. Somebody else runs up a debt or embezzles a few bucks. Unless the person is foaming at the mouth and shooting people at freeway rest stops, the only ones who are very interested are the local police back home. Then there are a few million illegal aliens. There's not much reason to look for them because nobody gets any benefit from finding them. There are also personal cases: some woman breaks up with her boyfriend and he threatens her. There's practically no place where the police will do anything to help her, so she moves away and changes her name. There are millions of people hiding under assumed identities, and the reason most of them don't get found is that nobody's looking."

"What you're saying is that if anybody tried, they would."

"No," said Jane. "What I said is that it depends on who's looking and how hard."

"You think I'm going to get caught, don't you?"

Jane hesitated. "You can take that chance, or you can choose to take other chances."

"What does that mean?"

"He's not going to give up. He has lots of trained people at his disposal in offices all over the country, and he can probably dream up a charge to get the police looking for you too, if he wants to. If you learn fast and never make a mistake, he might not find you." Jane looked at her closely. "Or you could make a mistake—intentionally."

Mary's eyes widened and the color seemed to drain from her face. "You want to use me for—"

"Bait. Yes. What he's doing isn't just evil; it's also illegal."

"I can't. I don't have the money. You're wrong. He's wrong."

"It doesn't matter. He thinks you do, and he wants it. That makes him predictable, and that can be turned into a weakness. Your chance of trapping him and getting him convicted might be better than your chance of hiding from him."

"No. I won't do it." Mary looked at Jane defiantly.

"Suit yourself."

"Are you leaving this morning?"

"I said I'd help you get settled."

"But I told you I wouldn't do it. You can't use me as bait."

"I heard you."

For the next six days, Jane Whitefield waited. When Mary woke up she would find the quilt folded neatly and stowed beside the couch. Jane would be in the middle of the only open space in the small living room going through the slow, floating movements of Tai Chi.

On the sixth day, Mary Perkins said, "Why do you do that?"

"It keeps my waist thin and my ass from getting flabby."

Mary repeated, "Why do you do that?"

"It helps me feel good. It keeps me flexible. It helps me think clearly and concentrate."

"Don't worry," said Mary. "I'll shut up."

"You don't have to," said Jane. "Part of the idea is that after a while the body makes the movements flow into each other without consulting the conscious mind much."

"What's that one?"

"What do you mean?"

"They all have names, right?"

"Oh. 'Cloud Hands.' " Then her body was in a radically different position without much apparent movement. " 'Golden Cock Stands on Leg.' " Her body continued to drift into a changing pattern of positions.

Mary watched for a long time. "Where did you learn to fight?"

"By fighting."

"No," said Mary. "I mean fight like that."

"This isn't exactly about fighting. It's about not fighting. Your opponent is fighting, but you're watching. He attacks, but you've already begun to yield the space. He strikes, but you're not really there. You only passed through there on your way to somewhere else. You bring his force around in a circle, add yours to it, and let him hurt himself."

"The mystic wisdom of the mysterious East."

"It's practical. I'm a very strong woman, but no matter

what I do, I'm going to be smaller than any man who's likely to try to hurt me. If I fight him for the space between us, I'll get hammered. He's using one arm and maybe his back foot to throw the punch. I'm bringing my whole body into one motion to add force to his punch and alter its direction just a little. For that fraction of a second I have him outnumbered."

Mary put on her coat, walked toward the door, opened it, turned, and said, "You should have let your ass get flabby. It might have made you more human." She went out and closed the door. That night she came home late and tiptoed past Jane on the couch.

Two hours later Jane opened her eyes and acknowledged that she had heard Mary come out of her room again. It was three A.M. and she was sitting in the big easy chair staring at Jane.

Mary said, "You're trying to wear me down. You're staying in the corner of my room and not saying anything to convince me, just putting yourself in front of my eyes wherever I look so I'll have to think about it."

Jane said, "You've spent time with people who take what they want."

"I was one of them."

"Then you can predict what Barraclough is thinking as well as I can. You don't need any arguments from me."

Mary sat back in the big chair with her hands resting on the arms. "Why haven't you mentioned the little boy?"

"Why should I?"

"I've lived by convincing people to do stupid things they didn't want to do, so I know how it's done. The little boy is an overlooked resource. Here I am, unmarried and alone, and anybody who is alive can feel her biological clock ticking away. I've reached the age where women start getting too many cats. The little boy is alone and probably scared. Barraclough has already robbed him, and now he'll kill him."

"Will he?"

"You know he will, and that's why you're here. If the kid's dead, the cops will run around bumping into each other for a couple of months and then forget him. If he's alive, there's always the chance that Barraclough will wind up sitting in a courtroom across the aisle from an innocent ten-year-old."

"Not much chance."

"But as long as the kid is alive, there's also the chance that he'll live another ten or fifteen years and find out who killed his four best friends and left him broke. Barraclough will be thinking he doesn't want to wake up some night and find a young man who looks vaguely familiar holding a gun against his head." Mary waited a few seconds. "So why didn't you mention him again?"

Jane sat up and stared at her. "People are killed every day. Why would I imagine you would pick him out of all the thousands and say, 'You're the one I've chosen. I've trained myself since I was a baby to ignore the screams of the dying because if I let even a little of the sound in I couldn't hear or think of anything else. But for you I'll risk my own life.' "

"You're right, I wouldn't." She leaned forward. "But not saying it is the argument, isn't it? I'm supposed to think of doing it, and if I think of it, I have to admit a second later that I'm not the kind of person who does that, and wonder why not."

"I apologize for telling you about him."

"But he's the reason why you're doing this, isn't he?"

"There's not much more I can do for him. I was in a fight, and all of the people on my side except Timmy are dead. That's all."

"I don't suppose the money has anything to do with it."

"For me? Not this time."

"You're above that kind of consideration."

"Hardly," said Jane. "I have enormous expenses. But money is not a pressing problem. Once you have what you need, it's hard to get yourself to lean over a cliff to reach for more. And I can't even spend what I have. A fancier house or a lot of expensive jewelry raises my profile and maybe gets me killed."

"Then why does this kid's money matter to you?"

"Or your money either? It's important only because it's what Barraclough wants. He uses it to grow stronger. I don't want him to succeed. I don't want to feed him."

"Why do you care?"

"I'm the rabbit, he's the dog. I run, he chases. He's good at it, and he's getting better. He's using Intercontinental to recruit young guys with nothing much to do and criminal records that make it unlikely that anybody else will ever pay them to do anything. He's picking out the ones with a certified history of violence and training them to hunt."

"We're finally getting down to a reason that means something. You're afraid he might get to be a problem, aren't you? Not just to people like me, but to you."

"He already is. If I let him get stronger, eventually he'll kill me."

Mary slumped back in her chair and breathed a deep, windy sigh. "At last. Thank you."

"You haven't changed your mind, have you?"

"No, but now maybe I can sleep. You're no better than I am."

When Mary came out into the living room again it was nearly noon. She looked at Jane and her face seemed to deflate. "You're still here."

"Even if you won't help me get Barraclough, it's still to my advantage to make sure he doesn't get you."

"How long do I have to live like this?"

"After we get you working, it will be easier," said Jane. "We'll study the other women here—shop where they shop and buy what they buy. Everything you do has to keep your head down where there are lots of other heads."

Mary looked as though she were considering it. "How long do I have to do this?"

Jane shrugged. "The longer you do it, the safer you'll be. Most women live quiet, private lives, and most women are basically happy. It helps to make new friends and be part of a community. If you look at the way your friends live, you'll feel better, and that will keep you from getting lazy."

"Lazy?"

"The average person sets an alarm to get up early, goes to work, has a little leisure time, sets the alarm, and goes to bed. The weeks get long, and people don't get paid what they deserve. There will come a day when you can't get your mind off some fantasy—a week in the Bahamas, or maybe only a dress you saw in a magazine. It doesn't matter what it is. Live within your means. I mean your visible means."

Mary's face turned hard and her eyes glittered. "I'm not sure I understand."

"Don't touch the money that's in Zurich or Singapore."

"I told you: there is no money." She stared at Jane for a long time, waiting for the contradiction.

Jane sat motionless and returned her stare evenly. Finally Mary angrily jumped to her feet, threw on her coat, and walked out the door. When Jane heard the dull thump of the door at the bottom of the stairs, she stood up, put on her coat, and prepared to go out too. She had a lot of work to do.

20

The Detroit–Wayne County airport was only twenty-
six miles east of Mary Perkins's apartment on Route
94. The flight was not even three hundred miles, so when
Jane Whitefield emerged from the gate at O'Hare, the
clock on the wall said 3:10. The taxi took her to the State
Street mall and she walked two blocks along East Madi-
son Street. On another day she might have had the taxi
driver leave her farther away, but last night's snow had
reached Chicago by morning, and today the wind was
picking it up and moving it along between the big buildings in horizontal sheets. Most pedestrians were just
scurrying across the open to get from one building to another, and she saw none who might have followed her.

She reached the Bank of Illinois before four o'clock
and was behind the counter in a quiet cubicle opening her
safe-deposit box within five minutes. Months ago she
had come to Chicago to pay the bill for the Furnace corporation's post office box, shop for clothes, and store
Catherine Snowdon's papers. She took them out and
studied them. Catherine Snowdon had a birth certificate,
a driver's license, a Social Security card, a Visa card, and
an ATM card from the Bank of America in case she
needed cash. Jane examined the other papers in the box.

That left only Wendy Lewis, Karen Gottlieb, and Anne Bronstein. She examined their papers to reassure herself that she had not let any of the expiration dates go by. Then she put them back under the savings passbook and the nine-millimeter Beretta pistol, closed the box, and rang for the lady who would go with her to return it to its slot in the vault.

A guide needed more insurance policies than any of her clients, but she could spare Catherine Snowdon for Mary Perkins. She would hide the Catherine Snowdon papers with ten thousand dollars in cash somewhere within walking distance of Mary's apartment in case she had to bail out.

Jane caught a cab from the Dirksen Building on West Adams and flew back to Detroit to do some shopping. At a Toys "R" Us she found a toy called Musical Moves. If the child stepped in the right places on a brightly colored mat, he could play a tune electronically. Jane would redirect the wire so that instead the pressure on the mat would send current to a small lightbulb. Two would be better—one mounted inside the apartment and one somewhere outside—maybe in the mailbox, if it could be done without alarming the letter carrier. If the bulb was lit, Mary Perkins would know that somebody was in her apartment waiting for her.

At a hardware store she bought the tools, wires, electrical tape, and a rope ladder designed for getting out a second-floor window in an emergency. She decided these purchases would be enough for the present. Mary had a lot to get used to in a short time, and she would be less likely to make mistakes in a crisis if she wasn't distracted by complexity.

Jane stopped at a pay telephone and dialed her own

number. She heard the telephone ring four times and then heard her own voice. "Hello. Please leave a message at—" Jane quickly punched in her two-digit code, then heard the machine rewind. It seemed to be taking a long time. Then there were a couple of clicks and Carey McKinnon's voice.

"Jane? It's Carey. I know you're probably calling in for messages, and this is the only way I have to reach you. I'm sorry I had to go back to the hospital the other night. Give me a call when you can—at home or the hospital or my office. If I'm in surgery or something, leave me a number where I can reach you." The machine's computer voice said, "Tuesday, ten-fifteen A.M."

Carey's voice came on again. "Hi, Jane. Just me again. It's been a few days and you still haven't called me. Am I imagining that you said you would? I'm in my usual haunts." "Saturday," said the machine, "two thirty-six P.M."

The next one said, "I'm beginning to think you're mad at me or something. If you are, please call me up and yell at me. Two weeks is a long time to sit around wondering." "Friday, six fifty-two P.M."

Jane hung up the telephone and then dialed Carey's number. When his machine came on, she said, "Hi, Carey. It's me. I'm sorry I couldn't get back to you. This job has turned out to be just awful. I'm trying to help a woman make her business profitable, and her business is promoting products all over the country. I've been in more airports than . . . a couple more than my suitcase has, anyway. I always seem to be strapped into an airplane seat when you're home, and then we have to sit down and run figures for the next meeting the minute we're in a hotel, and get to the meeting by breakfast time. Enough whining. I'm not mad at you. I'll call you when

I'm home." She caught herself before she said "I love you" because he had never said it to her, but then she felt foolish for being petty. She changed it into "I miss you," then hung up. She tested the sound of it in her mind and decided it was true, as far as it went. She did miss him.

There had been two or three friends in college who had known that she had a knack for hiding people, but Carey McKinnon had not been one of them. Each year thereafter it would have been harder to tell him, but that was not why she had avoided it. She had been saving him for herself. She needed to keep home a safe place where she could talk to people who cared about her and forget that the next day she might have to take a fugitive out of the world. But she had planted a lie that had grown thick enough to choke her. Now that he had asked her to marry him, she could barely stand to talk to his answering machine.

As she stepped off the curb, she realized that the only solution she had thought of was to perpetuate the lie—tell him the profession she was quitting was the consulting business—and not admit to him that she was not the person he thought he knew. She would only be doing what she had taught dozens of other people to do—pick the life you want and lie fifty times a day to get it—so she felt ashamed that the prospect seemed so empty and hopeless to her.

Then she recognized that she was thinking about it as though she had decided to marry Carey. She had not decided. The time to decide about marriage was when you had reason to assume you would be alive on your wedding day.

Jane took a bus back to Ann Arbor and got off at the university. She did not begin the walk down Huron Street back to the apartment until after midnight. She had taken a longer time than necessary to give Mary Perkins a day alone. The more time Mary had to think, the better she would be.

As Jane walked up Huron in the cold, still air, listening to her feet crunching the snow, she began to hear another sound, far off behind her. It started low and quickly moved up an octave a second until she recognized it as a siren. She walked along, listening to it grow louder and closer, until she heard it pass her on a parallel street. A minute later, she heard another set of sirens coming toward her from somewhere ahead and to her right.

She watched the intersections ahead and saw the blinking lights of a fire engine swing around a corner and head out Huron Street. After another block she began to smell the smoke in the air. It was a thin, hanging haze like the smoke from somebody's fireplace in the windless night. She began to walk faster, and at the next corner she turned down a side street. It was a two-alarm fire so far, and there was no point in walking into the middle of a lot of firemen and policemen after midnight carrying shopping bags. At the first corner she turned right along the street behind Huron and hurried on.

When she was still two blocks from the big old house where Mary lived, she could see the sky suddenly begin to glow. She dropped her bags and broke into a run. It must be the house. As she ran up the quiet residential street, she began to see other people coming out of apartments and houses and walking toward the fire.

When Jane turned back onto Huron, she could see the trucks lined up in front of Mary's house. The coats of the firemen were glowing, their wet helmets reflecting the flames that were now coming out of the lower windows and licking up the wooden clapboards toward the upper floor.

Jane forced herself to slow her pace to a fast walk, looking carefully at every human shape illuminated by the fire. She tried to recognize one that might be Mary, already almost certain that she would not see her. The fire didn't make sense unless they had made a mistake and killed her. They had set a fire not because it would fool a coroner—Farrell, the training officer, would have taught them that much—but because fire got rid of fingerprints and fibers, and because water and firemen's boots obliterated footprints.

She moved into the curious crowd and began to study the faces of the people who had gathered in a big circle around the fire. She wasn't looking for Mary anymore; she was looking for any face that she had seen before.

She heard the loud *blip-blip* of another siren and saw another set of lights sweep around the corner and stop at the curb thirty feet behind a fire truck. The new vehicle was an ambulance. Jane moved toward it, weaving her way between spectators who were so intent on the fire that they seemed to be unaware of her passing.

She edged closer to the ambulance and watched the two paramedics haul their collapsible stretcher out the back and rush, not to Mary's house but up the other side of the hedge to the lawn of the house next door. Jane felt a tiny resurgence of hope that she could not suppress. Maybe that was where the firemen had taken the victims—out of their way and out of danger—and if the paramedics were in a hurry, they must believe they had a patient waiting for them, not a corpse.

Jane followed the paramedics. They hurried up the

lawn until they reached a pair of firemen in gas masks who were kneeling over somebody lying prone on the snow beyond the hedge. One of the firemen had an oxygen tank on his back like a scuba diver, and he was holding the mask over the face of the person on the ground. Jane held her breath as the four men slid the victim onto the stretcher. When they lifted it to unfold the legs, she let her breath out in disappointment. The person on the stretcher was wearing a black rubber turnout coat and high boots. One of the firemen must have collapsed from the smoke.

She turned away and looked at the house. The top floor had caught now, and she could see the flames eating their way through the inner walls. In a few minutes the roof would collapse into Mary Perkins's apartment and the killers would have accomplished what Barraclough's training officer had taught them to do when things went wrong.

She watched the firemen straining to hold the hoses steady while they sprayed enormous streams of water into the upper windows. She glanced at a couple of firemen coming around the house carrying long pike poles. Their faces had dark, grimy smoke stains around the eyes and on the foreheads where their masks had not covered, their coats and pants glistened with water and dripped on the snow as they trotted toward their truck. She whirled around in time to see the four men pushing the stretcher toward the back of the ambulance. The injured fireman's turnout coat wasn't wet. He had been in there long enough to succumb to the smoke, but he didn't have a drop on him. The two firemen who had been kneeling over him were dry too.

Jane moved quickly in a diagonal path toward the

ambulance, keeping her eyes on the stretcher. They had the tie-down restraints strapped over a blanket they'd draped over the turnout coat, and the mask still over the face. She couldn't see the hair because they had a pillow under the head and their bodies shielded it from view. As they reached the lighted street she stared hard at the side of the blanket, where a couple of the victim's fingers protruded an inch. The red, whirling light from the fire truck just ahead passed across them and glinted off a set of tapered, polished fingernails. It was Mary Perkins.

Jane stepped around the front of the ambulance, slipped into the driver's door, and crouched on the floor. She heard the back doors open, the sliding of the metal wheels of the stretcher, and then the back doors slammed. She climbed into the seat, threw the transmission into gear, stepped on the gas pedal, and veered away from the curb to avoid the fire engine parked thirty feet ahead.

Then she straightened her wheels and roared down the block. She glanced in the rearview mirror. The four men took a couple of steps after her, then seemed to see the futility of it and stopped in the street. Before she turned the corner at the first traffic signal she looked again, but she couldn't see them anymore.

She drove fast for five blocks, letting the siren clear the way for her, and then turned into a smaller street, flipped off the flashing lights and siren, and went faster.

"Mary!" she called. There was no answer. It occurred to her that the gas in the fireman's tank had probably not been oxygen. It could as easily have been medical anesthetic. If it was, Mary was about as likely to die as recover. Jane drove on for another minute, then pulled the van to a stop in the lot behind a school. She ran to the back of the ambulance, opened the door, climbed inside, and looked down at Mary. She could see that her eyes were wide open, and then they blinked.

"You're alive after all," said Jane. She pulled at the oxygen mask and saw that it was held by a piece of elastic behind the head, so she slipped it up and off. There was a wide strip of adhesive tape across Mary's mouth. She undid the top straps on the stretcher.

Mary quickly sat up and fumbled to free her own feet. She was sobbing and shaking, and kicking at the strap so hard that her own hands couldn't hold on to it. Jane undid that strap too. "You'd better take the tape off your own mouth," she said.

Mary clawed at it and gave a little cry of pain as she tore it off. "They trapped me!" she sobbed. "There was no other way out." She shook the heavy turnout coat off, and Jane could see they had slipped it over the jacket she had put on to escape the fire. "There was smoke, and they banged on the door, and they looked like firemen. One of them gave me an oxygen mask, and—"

"I know," said Jane. "Come on. We've got to get out of here."

"Can't you just keep going?" Mary looked at the driver's seat, willing Jane into it.

"No. We're already pushing our luck. They'll be looking for the ambulance. I assume it's stolen, so the police will be too." She pulled Mary to her feet, pushed her out the back door, and said, "Run with me."

Mary stood against the ambulance. She took a step in the fireman's boots, her beige pants bloused over the tops just below her knees, then stopped and pulled her jacket around her. "I can't."

"Try," said Jane simply. She slung her purse across her

chest and started off across the lot at a slow, easy trot. After a few steps she heard Mary running too.

Jane jogged onto the broad back lawn of the school. It seemed to be a high school because all of the athletic fields were full-sized and elaborate, with wooden bleachers beside them. The grass under the snow was level and clear, with no chance of any unseen obstacles. Even better, there were tracks on it where she could place her feet. When she was in the open away from the building she could feel the wind blowing tiny particles of snow against her cheeks. Now was the time to set a quick pace, before some cop arrived to find the ambulance. She waited until she thought Mary Perkins was warm and loose, then lengthened her strides a bit. The playing fields were an advantage because she could lead them out a quarter of a mile away on a street far from the path of the ambulance. But while they were out here they would be the only black spots on an ocean of empty white snow.

She looked over her shoulder at Mary and saw that she interpreted the look as permission to slow down. Jane turned ahead again and quickly worked her way up to a comfortable lope. She listened to Mary's footsteps and timed her breathing. She was not used to running, but she seemed to be doing it.

When Jane reached the goalpost at the end of the football field, she stopped and ran in place until Mary caught up. She said, "We'll be able to walk as soon as we reach cover," and started off again. This time it seemed to be a soccer field because it was longer. She could discern what was at the end of the school property now. There was a high chain-link fence, and beyond it some tall, leafless trees. She ran ahead to look for the gate.

She found it in a few seconds, but it had a thick chain

and a serious padlock on it. She looked back to see Mary
struggling to catch up. She could see that there were
tracks all over the field. Unless kids had changed a lot
since she was in high school they would never walk an
extra quarter mile just to get around a fence. She moved
along the fence and saw the answer. There was a city
parking lot beyond the fence, filled with plows, dump
trucks, tractors, and a forage harvester parked beside a
building that looked like a warehouse. The parking lot
was empty of cars, but it was clear of snow because they
had used the plows to push an enormous pile of snow up
against the fence nearly to its top eight feet up.

Mary came up behind her, breathing deeply but not in
distress. Jane said, "How are you at climbing fences?"

"Take a guess."

"I'll help you," said Jane. "All we have to do is get to
the top. We can walk down." She took Mary's arm and
pointedly placed her hand on a chain link above her head.
She began to climb, and Jane waited for the moment to
come when she decided she couldn't do it.

Mary stopped. "I don't think—"

Jane reached up, put both hands on her thighs, and
boosted her higher. "Do the work with your legs. Toes in
the spaces, step up. Just use your hands to hold on. Step
up. Good. Step up." She climbed up after her, and when
Mary reached the intimidating part, where the packed
snow was above the top of the fence, she said, "Step up,"
held on to the fence with one hand, and pushed Mary
hard with the other so that she rolled up onto the mountain of snow.

When Jane reached the top and flopped onto the snow
she found Mary still lying there, breathing deeply and
trying to get her heart to slow. Jane sat up for a second,

then ducked down and burrowed into the snow. "Stay down," she said.

A beam of light moved across the field. Jane could see it pass above their heads, lighting up thousands of tiny snowflakes that had been blown into the air by the wind. The police car was beside the ambulance, so the beam widened in the thousand feet of empty fields and became enormous, but it was still so bright that she could see the line of adhesive the tape had left on Mary's cheek.

Mary asked, "Is it—"

"Cops," said Jane. "In a minute they'll shut the light off. When they do, don't move."

The light swept across the field, came back, continued around the horizon, and then went out. "Rest," said Jane. "Use this time to rest." They lay in the darkness and she listened. Suddenly the light came on again, swept over their heads, and shot back and forth around the field. She listened for the sound of the engine, but it didn't come. Finally the light went off. "Okay," said Jane. "Now we move." She sat up a little, slid down the hill, and waited while Mary followed.

They hurried to the far side of the lot, where the gate to the street was, and stopped. This gate was locked with the same kind of padlock and chain as the first one. She looked up at the fence. It was as high as the first, but it had coils of barbed wire strung along the top. They couldn't go back because the police wouldn't leave until they had a tow truck hooked up to the ambulance. She looked around her. There were sure to be cutting tools in the low building at the side of the lot, but breaking in would be harder than getting over a fence, and at least the fence didn't have an alarm. There were trucks, tractors, and plows all over the place, but even if she managed to hot-wire one of them to crash the gate, the sound of the engine would bring the police car across the field in twenty seconds. Then her eyes sorted out the strange shapes at the other end of the yard.

"All right," she said. "I hope you're strong, because I'll need your help."

She ran to the corner of the little compound, past the swing sets stored for the winter and the playground merry-go-rounds and over to the slides. The first two had frames of welded steel pipes that made them too heavy. The third was made of thin fiberglass in the shape of a tube, and Jane could lift the end of it by herself. They dragged it to the fence, lifted it so that the ladder was on their side and the tube went over the barbed wire and out to the street. "Want to go first?" asked Jane.

Mary climbed the ladder, slipped her legs into the tube, and flew out the other end onto the snow. Then Jane slid down and fell in the same spot. Mary was impatient to get away from the fence now, but Jane said, "If we don't move it, the cops will figure it out without having to get out of their car. Help me." They pushed the tube back over into the compound, then started down the street.

"Where are we going?" asked Mary.

"The university."

They jogged the last mile in silence. Jane set the pace again and listened for Mary's footsteps. She glanced at her watch. It was after two A.M. now, and even close to the university there were no pedestrians. Twice she saw headlights far down the street and pulled Mary with her into the dark space between two houses until the car had passed. When they finally reached the university campus, Jane slowed to a walk. She heard Mary's footsteps hit hard for two or three more steps, and then they sounded softer and slower too.

Jane walked on, studying the buildings for a long time. Finally she pointed to a long four-story building. The name on the facade was Helen Mileham Hall. Jane stopped a hundred feet away. "That wouldn't be a bad place to get out of the cold."

Mary Perkins said, "What is it?" She was so exhausted that her voice sounded almost detached.

"I think it's a women's dormitory," said Jane.

"It's the middle of the night. Won't it be locked?"

"Of course," said Jane. She wished she hadn't mentioned the cold. They were both heated from their run, but the night air was already beginning to dry the sweat on her face and leave it numb. The front door was out of the question. It led into a reception area that looked like a hotel lobby. She could see that there was an intercom and some kind of electronic locking system on the glass door. She supposed she had been in the last generation of coeds who had curfews, so probably there was no old bat to take the names of girls who came in late, but the world had gotten more dangerous for women since then, so they would have something worse, like an old bat in a guard's uniform with a .357 Magnum strapped to her hip. She walked around the building once looking for the fire doors while Mary waited. Then she heard the sound of the dryer.

As Jane walked toward it she walked into her memory. When a girl was eighteen and away from home for the first time, nights like this came now and again. The term papers and the laundry had piled up at about the same rate, and it was a Friday night near the end of the fall semester. The music and the shouting in the dorm had died out, but she wasn't ready to lie in the dark yet because even though morning would come with nauseating punctuality in a few hours, she was still eighteen and restless. She would convince herself that what she was doing was eminently practical. She could use all the laundry machines at once if she had enough quarters, and the silence and the solitude would make the term paper better.

The girl was sitting across from the dryers with her feet on a chair, underlining passages in a textbook. The laundry room was hot and humid from the washers and dryers, and she had the door propped open to let the steamy air out.

Jane hurried to the corner of the building and beckoned to Mary. Then she moved to the wall of the building, stepped close to the door, and looked at it. There was a crash bar that pulled a dead bolt out of a hole in the floor, and there was a standard spring latch that fit into the jamb. She opened her purse, pulled six dimes out of her wallet, and leaned behind the door to reach out and slide them into the hole in the floor. Then she came over to Mary and whispered, "What did you do with the tape they put over your mouth?" —

"What?" whispered Mary.

"I didn't see you throw it away. Where is it?"

Mary said, "I don't know. I guess I . . ." She reached into her pocket. "Here it is." It was in a wad.

Jane took it, stepped far back from the door and away from the light, came back to the doorjamb, and stuffed it into the hole where the latch would go when the door shut. Then she beckoned to Mary and they both went across the dormitory lawn to sit on a curb and wait.

In fifteen minutes the girl's dryers stopped and she folded her clothes, kicked the doorstop up, and closed the door slowly and quietly. It was almost three in the morning and she didn't need a couple of hundred neighbors waking up angry.

Jane waited a few minutes longer before she opened the door, pulled the adhesive tape out of the doorjamb, dug the dimes out of the hole, and pulled Mary inside. She shut the door, and they made their way up the back stairs to the second floor, away from the public areas to the long corridors lined with students' rooms. Jane walked quietly through the halls of the dormitory, looking at the doors of all of the rooms. At each corner she stopped and listened for other footsteps, but she heard none. Finally she stopped at a door where there was a folded note taped at eye level. She pulled it off carefully and read it.

> Cindy—
> Your mother called like eight times!!! I told her you were in the library. Call her as soon as you get back from Columbus.
>
> Lauren

Jane slipped the Catherine Snowdon credit card between the doorknob and the jamb until she found the plunger, then bowed it a little to push the plunger aside and open the door. Before she closed it behind Mary she put the note back. Cindy was going to need time to prepare a comforting story for her mother.

Jane felt for the single bed by the wall, pulled the thick blanket off it and draped it over the rod behind the curtains so that no light would escape, then turned the switch on. She went to the closet and studied the clothes for a moment, then started taking things out. "She's about your height, but she wears her tops big." She tossed a sweater on the bed. "Put it on." She took off her own blouse and slipped another sweater over her head. Then she glanced at Mary's rubber boots. "Those aren't going to help us either. Try some of hers."

Within a few minutes they were both dressed in Cindy's clothes. There was one short fall coat and one University of Michigan jacket. It was reversible, so Jane pulled it inside out and put it on. There were places where she could still pass as a college girl, but a college was not one of them. She counted a thousand dollars out of her purse and set it on the desk. "Sorry, Cindy," she wrote on Cindy's pad. "I needed clothes." She turned to Mary. "You look good, considering. Let's go."

Jane led Mary out through the laundry room, then found the Student Union by walking toward the center of the campus. The Ride Board was something she remembered from her college days, and she found it in a big hallway off the entrance. There were index cards posted in long lines on a cork bulletin board. She ignored the "Ride Wanted" cards and looked closely at the "Going to . . ." cards. Most of them offered rides for Thursday night or Friday, so they were obsolete already. She selected one that said, "Going to Ohio State. Leaving for Columbus Saturday 5:00 A.M. Return after game. Share driving and gas. Doug," and gave a phone number. She glanced at her watch. It was four A.M. now. If Doug wasn't an idiot he was at least awake. She walked to the pay phone across the hall and dialed the number.

At five o'clock the car pulled up in front of the Student Union. Doug was big and smiled easily. He was the sort of boy who would shortly flesh out and play a lot of golf. His two passengers were a surprise to him. While he was driving from his room to the campus he had planned to say he was glad that they had turned up at the last minute because he loved company. He also liked making a road trip without having to pay all of the expenses himself, but better than either, he liked women. He liked looking at them and hearing their voices and smelling the scents that hung in the air around them. When he saw the two women walking down the steps of the Student Union he thought that this was turning out to be a very fortunate day. But when they got into the car and the light came on he realized that they were old. They weren't old like somebody's mother, but they were still too old to be any more interested in Doug than his female professors were.

Near the ramp for the 23 Expressway at Geddes Avenue, Doug started to signal for a turn into the all-night gas station, but the dark one said, "Can we stop for gas later? There's nobody on the road now and we can make good time. Later on we'll be dying to stop."

Doug could live with that. The gauge said they had half a tank, so it didn't really matter. But for a second it seemed to him that she had some other reason for not wanting to stop until she was out of Ann Arbor. It was as though her husband was cruising around looking for her or something. They didn't stop until Toledo, and then the dark one insisted on paying for the gas and driving the next hundred miles.

It turned out that the one in the back was a graduate student in the business school. She had worked for ten years and then decided to go back. She was asleep most of the time. The dark one was a lot more talkative. She was a friend of the graduate student, and had talked her into going down for the game. Maybe she wasn't really that talkative, because afterward he couldn't remember learning anything else about her in the four-hour drive. Maybe she had just prompted Doug to talk and smiled a lot.

When they were on the outskirts of Columbus, the dark one announced that they still had to go scrounge tickets to the game, because she had talked Alene into coming at the last minute on a whim. She had him drop them off on the Ohio State campus so they could check the bulletin boards for offers of unused tickets.

Doug hated to relinquish the fantasy he had been developing for four hours, revising and refining it at each turn in the long road. He had envisioned himself ending up in a hotel in Columbus with the two older women, celebrating Michigan's victory on a king-sized bed. But he had not been able to invent any plausible set of circumstances that might lead to the fulfillment of this fantasy, nor could he imagine how one went about proposing such a thing. He left them with a regret that hung about him until later in the day, when he met a girl named Michele who called herself Micki with an *i*. She had seen him on the Ohio State campus with the two older women and convinced herself that there was a melancholy sophistication about him. He did not think about the two older women again until Sunday night, when he was driving back to Michigan with Micki. It had occurred to him that they might not have been able to get tickets to the game, but he would not have guessed that instead they had bought airline tickets from Columbus to Boston under assumed names and disappeared during the stopover in Cleveland.

21

Mary lay on her bed in the motel room and listened to the airplanes passing overhead. She had already unconsciously perceived their rhythm. They would growl along for four minutes somewhere far beyond the eastern end of the building, then roar overhead and into nothingness. There would be a pause of forty-five seconds before she heard the next one growling and muttering at the starting line.

Mary was tired of waiting for the question. She turned her head to look at Jane. "It was the medical records," she said.

Jane was sitting at the round table under the hideous hanging lamp sorting small items she had taken from her purse. There was a lot of cash, and cards that seemed to have been taped to the lining in rows. "What medical records?" She didn't look up.

"You were the one who made me think of it. I wanted to do it the way you would. I went to a doctor in Ann Arbor. I asked for the form people send to their old doctors to get their records forwarded. I signed it and changed the doctor's address so they would send it to me."

"Why did you do that?" asked Jane. "Do you have some condition that needs to be watched?"

266

Mary Perkins shook her head. "It just seemed like the right thing to do—to have them. Now, before something happened. I was going to change my name on them and bring them to the new doctor on the first visit. I couldn't think of a reason why a woman my age wouldn't have records somewhere, and I knew I could never make some up. And they're confidential; they're supposed to be protected."

Jane sighed. "They are. The address where they're sent isn't."

"Oh. But how did Barraclough's people get it?"

"There are a lot of ways. You pose as Mary Perkins's probation officer and ask. Or you get a person hired to work in the office so she can watch for the right piece of paper to come in the mail. They might have wanted a copy of your records anyway to see if you had a condition that meant you had to keep seeing one of fifteen specialists in the country, or needed a particular kind of surgery or something. They could even do the same thing you did: send a note from a real doctor requesting the records. The old doctor's secretary would say they'd already been sent to such and such an address. I don't know, and it doesn't matter very much. Did you get them?"

"Get what?"

"The medical records."

"Oh. Sure." She looked uncomfortable. "They got burned up."

"Good." Jane went back to her sorting. "It's one more avenue Barraclough had that he doesn't have anymore."

Mary's voice began in a quiet tone that was low-pitched and tense, as though she were flexing her throat muscles to keep her vocal cords from tightening. "They started the fire while I was asleep in the house, you know. They didn't do it so nobody would know they had been there. They made me come out to them because they were dressed like firemen who were there to save me. I couldn't see their faces, just the masks and helmets and raincoats."

"I know," said Jane.

"I'm not trying to tell you what happened," said Mary Perkins. "I'm trying to tell you what happened to me." She said more softly, "To me." She stared at Jane's face for a reaction, and what she saw told her Jane was waiting. "I'm new at this," she said again. "For you it's like herding cattle around. It's not just taking care of them; it's making sure they don't stampede off a cliff or eat poison or drink so much water that their stomachs rupture."

"There's nothing to be ashamed of," said Jane. "They had you. It wasn't something you imagined."

"They do that too. They talk softly to the cattle and say, 'Come on, girl. It's okay.' But it's not exactly true and it's not exactly for the cow's benefit." Mary took a deep breath. "I'm not used to being the only one who doesn't know things, and I'm not used to this way of looking at the world. I guess I should have had enough imagination to figure out what it was like. I once knew some people slightly who were supposed to be very tough, but I never saw any of them actually *do* anything. I keep looking back and wondering how I ever got from being eighteen and smart and pretty all the way to being twice that and having men I never saw before burning me out of a house."

Jane shrugged. "You told me how it happened."

"No," said Mary Perkins. "No, I didn't. I told you

what happened to some savings and loan companies. Not what happened to me."

Jane stopped sorting and began to string together credit cards and licenses with strips of adhesive tape. She did not dare look at Mary for fear there would be something in her eyes that gave Mary permission to stop talking.

"In the summer of 1981 I was twenty-two. I had just graduated from Florida State. I was good at interviews—I could tell that they liked me—but I couldn't seem to get a job. I remember coming home and closing the door to my bedroom upstairs. I would take off my outfit and hang it up carefully so my makeup wouldn't ruin it when I flopped down on the bed to cry. Then I would get newspapers from other places and write letters to answer the ads. Finally in October I got a job. Winton-Waugh Savings in Waco, Texas, wanted a management trainee. I went to work in the loan department at just about the time when things started heating up. I remember I was making two hundred and seventy-two dollars a week. Pretty soon I started noticing that a lot more money was coming into the bank, and a lot more going out as loans. That was the start."

"What did you do?"

"I went to a party." Her face had an ironic smile, as though she had thought about it so many times that she expected Jane to understand. "The bank had a giant bash for its big customers, and I got introduced to some of them. There were men there who had tens of millions of dollars. And I was with them, talking futures and options with them as if I was one of them. There was one in particular who was really nice. His name was Dan Campbell. Not Daniel. When he signed papers he wrote 'Dan.' He had everything: a big house in Houston, a cattle ranch in Oklahoma, and a plane for flying back and forth. I knew all about them because the loan papers were in a filing cabinet right behind the desk where I sat every day.

"There was this big candlelight dinner on tables set up in the bank lobby, and dancing. I'd never seen so much liquor, all the bottles lined up on this portable bar with the lights behind them so they looked pretty, like perfume bottles or something. When the formal party was over and most of the people went home, the night wasn't over. There was a small private party just for maybe twenty people like Dan Campbell in the executive suites down the hall. We all started in Mr. Waugh's office, but people wandered out into the garden outside the sliding door and into some of the other offices, carrying their drinks. Somehow Dan Campbell and I ended up in my office. After a few minutes he switched off the light and locked the door. A person would have had to be retarded not to have it occur to her that if we didn't make any noise people would never know we were in there."

"You don't have to tell me this."

"Yes, I do," said Mary. Her face was set and insistent. "So then Dan Campbell is saying, 'Come on, Lily. Just touch it. I promise it won't bite.' I was not an innocent young thing. I don't want to give you that impression or imply that I was drunk or something. I wasn't left breathless and swept off my feet by a charming older man. If I was dazzled by anything, it was by being near all that money. Also, I liked him and was impressed with him, so I did it.

"The next day I was back at my desk as usual, feeling a little bit amazed when my eyes would happen to fall on some particular piece of furniture, and then a little depressed and foolish, and in comes a delivery guy with twenty-four long-stemmed red roses in a beautiful crystal vase and puts them on my desk. I see them, and for a second I think maybe I wasn't just this stupid girl who got talked into something. Maybe this was just what I had convinced myself it was for a few minutes last night when I forgot it was the bank that took me to dinner. Then I opened the card, and it was signed by Mr. Waugh, my boss. There was a check for a thousand dollars from the bank that said 'Employee Incentive Bonus.' "

"Did you quit?"

"No," said Mary. "I didn't. I started to, I thought about it, but I didn't do it. You hear a lot about people doing that, but you don't see it much. People say they walked out, threw their jobs away or something, but at least they have their principles. But it's almost never like that. It almost never happens right away, just like you never think of the clever thing to say to somebody when it would have mattered. And I couldn't think of a way to tell Mr. Waugh I resented getting a check for it without coming out and announcing exactly what it was that he and I both knew I had done. I decided I wasn't about to face that conversation, and there was nothing else I could do to change things. All I could do was cash the check and go on with my life.

"The bank was growing then, and pretty soon I'm not working in the loan department, I'm a loan officer. Mr. Waugh tells me we've got to go on a business trip to Houston. I remember the flowers and get all upset, but there just isn't a way to get out of it. By now I understand why the bank needs to move money in and out, and my job is to keep the money going out, and that means meeting with customers. And there were two other women going: Mr. Waugh's assistant and another loan officer.

The pay was getting better and better, and I was learning a lot, so I didn't try to get out of it."

Jane could tell that Mary was not lying now. She was trying to push away the excuses. This was a confession.

"We meet with a group of twelve investors who have formed a limited partnership for a real estate development. You know, right now I can't even remember what they were calling it, but it was the usual thing, something like Sunnydale Vistas or Meadowgrove Heights. Anyway, the first session is in an office they've set up near River Oaks. Not *in* River Oaks, of course, but close enough so people would smell money on their business cards. Things were really tantalizing in that first session. We've got the chance to lend them sixty million, maybe more later. They're willing to keep it deposited until they need it, with the interest in escrow offsetting our costs—which are nil—and release times tied to what gets built. Then we were supposed to go out and see the land. It was near La Porte, right by Galveston Bay. The plans called for canals, with boat slips for each house, malls, and all that.

"We don't drive, though. We go out to get the best view on this big boat that's leased to the company's sales department for impressing the customers. We see it through binoculars and talk business until dark, but still no papers get signed. We have a catered dinner, and still no agreement comes out of Mr. Waugh's briefcase. It just degenerates into a cocktail party on the upper deck. Everybody's talking about money and their favorite things that it buys and how great they're all doing. They're getting tipsy and optimistic. Pretty soon I start to hear music coming from somewhere down below, and laughing and loud talk. One by one, people start to disappear. It goes on awhile until it's just me and Waugh and maybe three of these investors. It's getting cold up on deck. I say to Waugh, 'Maybe I'll go down below.' He says, 'If you like.' So I make my way down those steps in the dark in high heels carrying a martini."

"The others didn't go down?"

"One did. I had to help him, because he was getting drunk. So I go down and open the door to this big room they called the saloon, and the music is deafening. What I see at that moment makes me drop my drink. It's Waugh's assistant. Her name was Marla. She's dancing, doing a strip for these four investors, and I do not mean a tease. When I came in she was already down to her panties, and she's got her thumbs in the waistband, as though they were about to move south. I start to back out, but the drunk behind me pushes me in, and Marla sees me. She kind of wriggles over to me without losing a beat, puts her arm around me with a big smile, yells into my ear, 'Come on. Get with the party,' and starts pulling me into the saloon with her. I pushed her arm off me and said, 'Stop it. I'm not some hooker.' "

"What happened?"

"She got really angry—shot me a look that would knock a pigeon off a telephone wire—and said, 'Don't kid me, honey. Who do you think made out your last bonus check?' But then there's one of these investors behind her, and he's impatient for the show to go on, and he pulls the panties down to her feet. She grins, steps out of them, kind of sticks out her rear end, gives it a little wriggle, and starts to dance with him. I turn and walk out of the saloon. I don't know where to go. I open the door to one of the staterooms, and there's the other loan officer. She's doing one of the investors on the bed while a couple of others watch. I shut the door, go back up the hallway toward the steps, and there's Mr. Waugh. He opens the door of the saloon so he can glance in, and I can see that Marla has gone way beyond the strip. It's an orgy. He opens the door a little wider, holding it for me to go in first. Then he sees the expression on my face, kind of shrugs, and goes inside. I spend the next four hours alone up on that freezing deck."

"Did he fire you?"

"No. I took a plane back by myself and came in Monday morning to find the loan papers, all signed, on my desk. All of a sudden the account was mine and I had to make the deal work—get it through the loan committee and the lawyers, and set up the schedules, and all that. And I had to make out the bonus checks: ten grand each. Nobody said a word about it. Marla was invisible for weeks. The other loan officer—her name was Kathy—was no friend of mine. She never spoke to me again. I started looking for jobs. The bank was growing out of control by then, so we were all busy enough not to have to look right at each other."

"Nothing else happened?"

"About a month later, I come into work and there are these strange women in the office. Both of them are young—twenty or twenty-one—and gorgeous. Marla comes in with them, and her face is absolutely empty. She says to me, 'We're really running short of space around here. Mr. Waugh wants you to move back out to your old desk to make room for the new loan officers.' Out front was the pool of low-level clerical people and beginners. I cleaned out my office—pictures, plants, and paper clips—carried everything out, and put it all on my old desk, and something happened. I knew they wanted me to quit, and I wanted to quit, but up until then I had also wanted to outlast them, take whatever they had to offer for as long as it took and then end up with a better job somewhere else. I had been operating on the theory that I made them more uncomfortable than they made me. But it was too much. I closed the desk drawer and walked into Mr. Waugh's office. He was on the phone and he said into it, 'Excuse me. I have something I have to take care of. I'll call you right back,' all the time with his eyes on me. He hung up. I said, 'You didn't have to hang up. I just wanted to say goodbye.' I reached over the desk and shook his hand and said, 'Thank you for hiring me.' He was surprised. I thought at first that he was just relieved because it wasn't a horrible scene, but before I was across the lobby I realized that all along he had been expecting me to come around."

"You didn't have another job. Where did you go?"

Mary Perkins gave a sad little laugh. "I went nowhere. I couldn't find another job in town. I couldn't find one anywhere, so I moved to California. Just getting there took about the last of the money I had saved. I was out of work for six months. I was twenty-four, looking better than I ever have in my life because I didn't have enough money to eat regularly. I'm not trying to make you feel sorry for me. The fantasy I had wasn't about getting a nicer place to live and having enough food. It was getting rich—really rich. I had been on the party boats, done the big real estate deals, and flown in the private planes, and I wanted them again. So I thought of how to get them, and I got started."

"How did you get started?"

"I used to spend a lot of time at the unemployment office, and I got used to seeing the regulars. One was a guy who had tried to talk to me. You have to picture this. There's a guy about forty, in there to collect his unemployment check, and he sees a woman who turns him on, so he goes up to her and tells her not to worry. He's a successful contractor, and as soon as spring comes he's going to be doing more big projects and he'll hire her. But he was good-looking and cheerful and, oddly enough, he wasn't stupid, so I decided to get to know him. I went into the unemployment office and smiled at him. When he hit on me, I said, 'Why don't you take me out for coffee?' We walked out to the lot, and he's driving a three-year-old BMW with a brand-new lock on the trunk. I'd had enough experience making loans to know that locks don't wear out in three years. They get drilled out because the original owner didn't hand over the keys. It turns out that even though he's a liar, he really does have a contractor's license, but no capital, no crew, and nothing going for him. He was perfect."

"Perfect for what?"

"I had decided to use what I knew about savings and loans. I promoted him from contractor to developer. I was his wife. We called ourselves the Comstocks or the Staffords or the Stoddards. We would go to a new city where nobody knew us. Sometimes we'd rent a house in a quiet, upscale part of town and do nothing but get to know our neighbors. Eventually there would be somebody who would invite us to his club, or to a summer home, or just to a party. Once we were accepted, the bankers would find us. Sometimes all it took was to let our new friends know we were happy there and wanted to buy a fancy house. By 'eighty-three a lot of savings executives were dying to lend a couple of million to just about anybody who wanted it for something as normal as a house, and they listened for leads."

"What then?"

"It varied. Sometimes we'd get somebody to sell us a hundred-thousand-dollar house for a million, kick back five hundred thousand, and leave town on the same day. The best was when we got to know the savings and loan executive and his wife—saw them socially. I would find a way to get the man alone—happen to go alone to the place where he always ate lunch, or drop in to see his wife on a Saturday afternoon when I knew she would be gone. I would convince him that he was so irresistible that I didn't plan to try. If that worked I would turn it into a full-blown affair and concentrate on making sure he didn't want it to end just yet. Eventually the subject of my husband's real estate development would come up. I would say he was considering moving to another state and doing the project there because the local money people didn't see the potential. Bobby would get his loan. When Bobby didn't make payments, the bank would issue a new loan to cover the interest, or buy into the project. I learned all the tricks that a banker could think of just by watching these guys trying to keep Bobby busy and stupid."

"It always worked?"

Mary Perkins shook her head. "Nothing *always* works. But I designed it so that if the banker wasn't interested, the worst he could do to me was to tell my husband. But if he once sunk it into me, that option was gone, and he was in for the ride of his life." She stopped and stared at Jane. "You're thinking that I invented a scheme to turn myself into a whore, don't you? To do what I wouldn't do for Mr. Waugh."

Jane shrugged. "I'm not in the habit of making that kind of judgment."

"Well, that's exactly what I did. At one point I was doing both the husband and wife at once, and the three of us were conspiring to keep Bobby too busy to notice by pumping money into his business. Of course I had to keep Bobby happy too. We were living as a married couple, and I couldn't have him going off tomcatting around the country club. This went on for about three years."

"What ended it?"

"I got enough money and enough inside information to do the stunts I told you about. It was essentially the same, except that Bobby had enough to retire, so I let him. I would get the loan myself, and would default on it myself, but first I made sure that Cyrus Curbstone had seen enough of me so that he didn't want my loan brought to the police."

"How did you get caught?"

"I bought a savings and loan," Mary said. "Big mistake. I thought I knew more than I did. I didn't know when to set fire to the place and get on a plane."

"Why are you telling me all this now?"

"I want you to know," Mary said.

"Know what?"

"Why I held on to the money when I was caught and the feds wanted it back. Why I told you I didn't have it when I needed your help and any sane person would have given it up to stay alive. It wasn't because I needed to have a lot of money hidden someplace where I'll probably never see it again; it's because of what I had to do to get it."

"But why now?"

"Because now that I know enough to want to give it up, I can't give it up. He wouldn't take it and let me go, would he?"

"No."

"He would take it and insist there was more, and when I couldn't give him any more, all he could do was kill me."

"Yes."

"And he'll never give up, will he?"

"No," said Jane. "He won't."

"And if I go to the police and tell them he's been chasing me, what I'm telling them is that he might be trying to steal fifty million dollars. That's no crime, but I'm admitting that I still have it. I'm the only one who will go to jail, and he'll still be free to kill me."

"Fifty million dollars." Jane returned to taping her cards into the lining of her purse. "You'll make good bait."

"Yes," Mary said, "I will."

22

When Jane and Mary left Cleveland they were carrying suitcases that were much larger than they needed to hold the few outfits they had bought, because they had more shopping to do in Chicago. The first item they selected at the electronics store was a small video camera with automatic focus and a zoom lens. The second was a directional microphone. The brochure that went with the microphone described the wonderful capability it offered for recording bird songs without coming close enough to disturb the little creatures. The copy obviously had been composed in order to protect the company from becoming a co-defendant in some criminal proceeding. Jane tested a number of voice-activated tape recorders, and when she had settled on the best, she told the salesman to write up a bill for two.

While he was busy doing this, Mary whispered, "Why two?"

Jane answered, "Because I don't think having a conversation with Barraclough is something I'll want to try twice if the first recorder doesn't catch every word."

Jane bought a used Toyota in Chicago under the name Catherine Snowdon. It was five years old, had one previous owner who had kept it greased, oiled, and main-

tained, but it had a sporty red exterior. She drove it off
the lot to a one-day spray shop and had it painted gray
for five hundred dollars. Then she picked up Mary at the
motel and turned west onto Route 80. It was winter now,
and if they were going to travel by road, it had to be a
big one.

For six days they drove the interstate through Daven-
port, Des Moines, Omaha, Grand Island, North Platte,
Cheyenne, Salt Lake City. Just before Reno they turned
south down 395 along the east side of the Sierras to the
desert. Jane checked them into a motel in San Bernardino
near the entrance to I-10, rested for a day, and studied the
maps of Los Angeles County. The next day she drove to
the Department of Motor Vehicles, reported the sale of
Catherine Snowdon's car to Katherine Webster, a resident of Los Angeles, and picked up a set of California
plates.

She spent two days driving the freeways until she
found the spot she wanted, right on the western edge of a
confusing knot of interlocking entrances, exits, and over-
passes on the Ventura Freeway. If a person drove east, he
would immediately come to the fork where half the lanes
swung off onto the San Diego Freeway, then divided
again to go north toward Sacramento or south toward
San Diego. After another mile or two, there was another
junction where some lanes went north on the Hollywood
Freeway but most swung southeast toward the city. Another mile and there was another fork, with some lanes
continuing southeast and the others bearing due east
toward Glendale and Pasadena. With a small head start, a
car heading eastward could be very hard to follow.

Every mile on the Ventura Freeway there was a little
yellow pole with an emergency telephone on it. The

small blue marker above the pole Jane chose announced that it was number 177.

That night in the motel Jane tested the equipment. At two A.M. she drove back into the San Fernando Valley. She parked the car on a quiet side street in Sherman Oaks just north of Riverside Drive and walked the rest of the way to the little hill that elevated the Ventura Freeway above the surrounding neighborhoods. She had to lower the equipment over a fence and then climb over after it.

She was hidden from the street by thick bushes, and from the freeway by a low metal barrier along the shoulder. The barrier was supposed to keep a runaway car on the eastbound side of the Ventura Freeway from careening down the hill into the front of somebody's house, and judging by the depth of some of the dents and scrapes, it probably had. She trained the directional microphone carefully across the freeway on a spot twenty feet from call box number 177, then adjusted the breadth of its field until it picked up very little street noise. She threw a stone at the spot and watched the reels of the two tape recorders turn when it hit, then stop again. She set the video camera on automatic focus and aimed it at the same spot. She switched everything off, carefully covered all of the equipment with leaves and branches, then went down the hill, over the fence, and back to her car.

Jane and Mary stayed at the motel for two more days. They rehearsed, memorized, and analyzed until it began to seem as though everything Jane was planning had already happened and they were weeks past it already, trying to recall the details.

"How long do you stay?" asked Jane.

"Ten seconds. Fifteen at the most. Just long enough to pop out the tapes."

"What happens if he pulls out a gun?" Jane asked.

"I leave."

"What if he puts it to my head?"

"I ignore it. There's nothing I can do to stop him, so I leave."

Early each morning they drove along the Ventura Freeway past call box 177, studying the flow of the traffic for ten miles in both directions. They memorized the fastest lanes, practiced making an exit just beyond the junction with another freeway and then coming up a side street to emerge on the new freeway going in another direction.

"Can't you just call him up and record what he says on the phone?" asked Mary.

"No," said Jane. "He's the regional head of a big security company. His phone will have sweepers and bug detectors that even the police can't buy yet. Besides, he won't say anything that will put him away unless he sees you."

On the third day at four in the afternoon Jane White-field went to a pay telephone in Barstow and made the call. "I want to speak with Mr. Barraclough," she said. "Tell him it's Colleen Mahoney from the courthouse. I have something he wants to talk about."

"Can you hold?" said the secretary.

"No," said Jane. "I'll call back in two minutes. Tell him if he's not the one who answers, he's lost it." She waited four minutes, then dialed the number again.

This time a man's voice answered. It was deep, as though it came from a big body, but it was smooth, clear, and untroubled. "Yes?" he said.

"Is this Mr. Barraclough?"

"Yes, it is." He held the last word so it was almost singsong.

"This is—"

"I know who it is, Jane," he said. "I heard that's what you like to be called. What can I do for you?"

Her mind stumbled, then raced to catch up. He was far ahead of the place where she had thought he would be. "I have Mary Perkins," she said.

"Who's Mary Perkins?"

"I'm not recording this," she said. "Your phone isn't tapped."

"I know it isn't."

"Then do you want her?"

"If you have her, why do you need me? You like me all of a sudden?"

"If you weren't tracing this call, why would you ask so many stupid questions?" Jane asked. "I'll call this number at five A.M. tomorrow. If you meet me alone and unarmed, you'll get a peek." She hung up, picked up Mary, and drove to Los Angeles, where they rented two identical white cars, then left the gray Toyota at the Burbank Airport. They spent the night in a motel in Woodland Hills.

At four A.M. Jane parked her rented car on the street she had chosen below the freeway, climbed the fence to turn on her camera, microphone, and recorders. Then she drove west to the big coffee shop in Agoura and at exactly five A.M. used the pay telephone outside the door.

"Yes?" said Barraclough.

"It's me," she said. "In twenty minutes I'll be at the lot on the corner of Woodley Avenue and Burbank Boulevard in the Sepulveda Dam Recreation Area. If you're not there I'll keep going."

"Wait," he said. "I didn't get those streets."

"Then rewind the tape and play it back," she said, and hung up.

Twenty minutes was an enormous stretch of time for a man like Barraclough. Jane thought about all of the preparations he would have made already. He would have all of the trainees on the special payroll of Enterprise Development already awake and standing by. He would have some pretext for using Intercontinental Security's facilities and equipment too. Now he would be frantically ordering all of them into positions around the Sepulveda Recreation Area. No, not frantically: coldly, methodically.

She had selected the meeting place carefully. It was the sort of spot a person might choose who had some fear of ambush but no understanding of how such things happened. It was free of people in the hours before dawn, a flat open lawn that had been built as a flood basin with a vast empty sod farm on one side, a golf course on the other, and nothing much but picnic tables and a baseball diamond in between. The place gave the illusion of safety because she could see a second car coming from half a mile off. So could he, but all he had to do was block two spots on Burbank Boulevard and one end of Woodley and she was trapped.

Jane left the Ventura Freeway and continued eastward on Burbank Boulevard. It would still be another hour before the sun came up. At exactly 5:20 she was driving beside the golf course, and as she came around the long curve, she saw his car. It was a new, dark gray Chevrolet parked beside the road on the small gravel plateau above the empty reservoir. She could see the little stream of exhaust from the tailpipe that showed her the car was running. She took her foot off the gas pedal as she approached, and coasted to a speed of under ten miles an hour. She made a left turn onto the lot, then pulled up ten feet away from his car and stared into the side window.

It was difficult to tell how tall he was when he was seated in the car, but he gave her the impression of being big. His hands on the wheel were thick and square-knuckled, and his shoulders were much wider than the steering wheel. The white pinstriped shirt he had on seemed a little tight on his upper arms, the way cops wore theirs. He was obviously wearing it without a coat to make her believe he had actually come unarmed.

She looked directly into his face. The corners of his mouth were turned up in a wry half smile. She reminded herself that she had known he would try to rattle her with some intimidating expression, maybe the poker player's look when he raised his bet: my money's on the table, so let's see yours. But his face set off a little burst of heat in her chest that rose up her throat into her jaw muscles. She could not turn away from the eyes. They were light, almost gray, squinting a little because of the false smile, and watching her with a disconcerting intensity. They took in her fear and discomfort, added his savoring of it, and reflected it back to her. His mind was focused utterly on her, on what she was feeling and thinking. His eyes revealed that he felt nothing except some vicarious glow from the anxiety he could inspire in her.

It was time to lose whoever he had brought with him. Jane stamped her foot on the gas pedal and the car's back wheels spun, kicking up gravel. It fishtailed a little as one wheel caught before the other and then it squealed out of the lot onto Burbank Boulevard. She drove to the east, took the ramp onto the San Diego Freeway at forty, and sailed into the right lane at sixty-five. She checked her rearview mirror to be sure he was coming, and saw the gray Chevrolet skid around the curve and shoot off the ramp toward her. She kept adding increments of speed while she held the car steady in the center lane.

She watched the mirror so she could spot his helpers coming up to join him, but no other car on the freeway was traveling as fast as theirs were. She checked the cars ahead, but none of them did anything out of the ordinary either. She waited until the last second to cut back across the right lane to the feeder for the Ventura Freeway, then stayed in the eastbound lane until it was almost too late before she cut across the painted lines to the westbound ramp. She looked into the mirror again, not to confirm that he was still chasing her but to be sure that no other car could have followed him.

She drove westward until she saw the telephone with the blue "177" painted above it, then turned on her emergency flashers and coasted along until she made it to the shoulder and stopped twenty feet past the call box. She got out of her car and walked to the spot where she had aimed her directional microphone and camera. She saw his headlights after five seconds, then the turn signal, and in a moment he was rolling up along the shoulder of the road to stop behind her.

He swung his door open on the traffic side, got out as though he were invulnerable to getting clipped, and walked up to her. His arms were out from his sides, but he was carrying something in his hand. She stepped backward to the door of her car. He saw her move and seemed to understand that she was preparing to bolt. He set the object on the ground and stepped back.

Jane kept her eyes on him as she stepped forward and picked it up. It was a small box with a metal hoop and a thumb switch. She recognized that it was a hand-held metal detector like the ones they used in airports when somebody set off the walk-through model. She ran it over herself from head to foot, then tossed it to him and he did the same, turning around so she could see there was nothing stuck in his belt. The little box didn't beep.

Barraclough's eyes scanned the area around him in every direction, returning to her face abruptly now and then to see if she reacted. He said, "Mind if I look in your car?"

"Go ahead," she said. "Mind if I look in yours?"

The mysterious smile returned. "No." He watched her as he took a step toward her rented car. She never moved. He said, "You driving or am I?"

She said, "I'm not getting into a car with you."

He looked around him again, as though this meant he needed to do a better job of searching the middle distance for witnesses. He said, "What made you panic back there?"

"That's not what I want to talk about. I say it was a trap, you say it wasn't, I say you're a liar."

His smile seemed to grow a little. "What do you want to talk about?"

"You've been chasing Mary Perkins, I've been hiding her. Now I'm ready to sell her."

He squinted a little as he studied her face. "Why?"

She returned his stare. "I've been at this a long time. A lot of people would be dead without me."

"I've heard that," said Barraclough. "Sometime I'll get you to give me a list."

"No, you won't," she said simply. "Mary Perkins isn't the sort of person I want to risk my life for. She's not worth it. I gave her a chance and she disappointed me. I know that she's got a lot of money. You seem to think you can get it. I'm not interested in that kind of work."

Barraclough tilted his head a little to watch her closely. "You know what will happen when I have her?"

"You'll end up with her money. I also know that if you have her she's not coming back to ask me how it happened."

"That's true," he said.

She took a deep breath and blew it out. She had done it. He had agreed on tape that he was going to take the money and kill her. "This is a one-day sale," she said. "Tomorrow she goes up for auction. You want her or not?"

"I want her."

"The price is three million in cash. You hand it over and I give her up three weeks later. I know you'll mark it, so I need time to pass it on before you start tracing."

A laugh escaped him abruptly, as though a small child had surprised him by saying something unintentionally profound. "Done," he said. "Of course, that's assuming I get to see her in person so I know you can deliver."

"You can," said Jane. "She'll be along any minute."

"Here?" he said. She could see his mind working. He wanted to get back to his car to retrieve the weapon he had hidden, but he had not yet thought of a way to do it without Jane's noticing.

"There," said Jane. She pointed across the ten lanes of the freeway at the white car just like hers gliding onto the shoulder on the eastbound side. "That's her now." Mary Perkins's car rolled to a stop just at the spot Jane had shown her. "She'll get out of the car so you can see her. Then she'll pick up something I left for her in the bushes over there. She thinks you're a wholesaler who sells me stolen credit cards and licenses." Jane watched Barraclough's hands. "You're not trustworthy, so I can't pay you until she has them." Mary got out of the car and stepped over the barrier into the bushes.

Jane let her eyes flick up to Barraclough's face. "Well?"

"Hard to tell," he said. "She's so far away."

"Nice try," she said. "I saw you start to drool the second she opened the door. You get one more peek."

Mary Perkins came back out of the bushes. Jane could see the bulge of the tapes from the video camera and the recorders in her purse. Mary nodded and Jane stepped away from Barraclough, closer to her car. Now was the time when it would occur to him to hold her.

Barraclough was smiling again. His arm straightened and he waved happily at Mary Perkins.

"What are you doing?" Jane snapped.

He turned to face her, but his arms were poised in front of him. He looked like a fisherman about to make a grab for a hooked fish. "Just waving to the lady. We don't want her to think I'm not a friendly wholesaler."

Jane's body tensed, not certain whether to run for the car or attack him. He was signaling someone, and it wasn't Mary. What had she missed? She jerked her head to the left to look back up the freeway—and saw the man Barraclough must have been waving to. He stepped out of the bushes and ran back along the shoulder just at the entrance ramp. In another two steps he disappeared around the curve.

He must be getting into another car that had been idling out of sight beside the entrance ramp. Now she saw its lights come onto the freeway and they seemed to jerk upward into the sky before they swung around and leveled on the pavement ahead of it. The car accelerated toward Jane and Barraclough, its right tires already on the shoulder as though it were going to obliterate them.

Jane waved her arm at Mary. "Go!" she shouted.

Mary seemed to be transfixed by the sudden arrival of

an unexpected car. She stared across the ten lanes of the freeway and watched the red car rushing up the westbound side toward Jane, knowing it was time for her to leave, but not knowing how.

Jane screamed. "Go! Go! It's a trap!" She started backing toward her parked car, the adrenaline making her legs push too hard so she half walked and half danced, trying to watch the car bearing down on her and Mary and Barraclough at the same time.

Mary dropped her keys, bobbed down to pick them up, then got into her car. Jane took one more look at Barraclough and hurried to the door of her own car.

The headlights of the car Barraclough had summoned dipped down as it decelerated suddenly, moved past Barraclough, and then pulled over. As it slowly moved up behind Jane's car, her heart began to pound. Its headlights went out, the driver's door opened an inch, and the dome light came on. The one in the passenger seat was Timothy Phillips.

Barraclough opened the other door, pulled the little boy out onto the shoulder of the freeway and yelled, "Hey, Jane! How about a trade? Is he worth it?"

These were the first words loud enough for Mary to hear across the freeway. She started the engine and shifted to Drive, but her eyes were on the activity going on across the freeway. The little boy must be the one Jane had told her about. Who else could he be? He was scared, straining to get closer to Jane Whitefield, but the big man in the white shirt had a grip on his thin arm and it was hurting him. Anybody could see it was hurting him. Headlights settled on them, grew brighter and brighter, and then flashed past. Were those drivers blind? Couldn't they see that something horrible was happening?

The knowledge slowly settled on Mary that none of the drivers knew who the big man was, and you had to know that. They probably thought he was a father who was afraid his son might stray too close to the lane where their cars were speeding past. There was only one person here who had any idea of what she was looking at.

Mary turned off the engine, got out of the car, and stood on the shoulder of the road. She could see Jane ten lanes away, caught for a second in the headlights of a speeding car, staring back at Mary, her mouth wide open and her arm in motion, waving her back into the car. Her voice reached Mary faintly across all the lanes, but whatever it was saying was only a distraction.

Mary was concentrating, so there was no room for Jane's voice. She waited for a moment while a truck barreled past and the hot, sulfurous wind from its passing tore at her clothes and stung her face. Then she stepped onto the hard pavement of the freeway. She walked at a normal pace. She never stopped to wait on the dotted line between two lanes, because anything that was not in motion might blend in. It would take only a second of blindness for a driver going sixty miles an hour to travel eighty-eight feet and kill her. She made it across five lanes to the middle island and rested her fear for a moment inside the barrier before she could face walking across another five lanes.

Now Jane was much closer, and Mary could see the anguish on her face. "Run! Go back!" Jane shouted. Mary was disappointed. Jane simply didn't understand.

Mary looked across the last five lanes at Barraclough. They stared into each other's eyes, and she could see that he understood. He pushed the little boy back into the red car that had brought him, then ran back along the edge of the freeway and got into his big gray car.

Mary Perkins's eyes never left Barraclough after that. She could see him glancing in his rearview mirror as he pulled out into the traffic, then crossed over one lane, then another, then another. He had already gone far past her, but she walked in his direction patiently, watching him take the last two lanes and stop far ahead of her on the center island where she walked. Then she saw his back-up lights come on, and he began to move in reverse on the center margin to meet her. She had never seen anybody drive backward so fast. Oh, yes, he had once been a policeman. They all learned how to do things like backing up on freeway shoulders.

Timothy Phillips looked out the window of the red car and watched Jane staring in horror at the other lady. But as the man who had brought him here started the car, Timmy saw Jane's right hand move down beside her leg and beckon to him.

Timmy got the passenger door of the red car half open before the driver lunged across the seat and clutched his shirt to drag him back. The sudden movement was enough. Jane flung the driver's door open, delivered a hard jab to his kidney, and snatched the key out of the ignition.

The driver turned with a pained snarl and started out the door after her. Jane retreated toward the front of the car. The driver heard the boy opening the door behind him again just as his foot touched the ground. He yelled, "Stay there or I'll kill you," but half turning his head to say it made him a microsecond slower. Jane had time to take a running step and deliver a hard kick to the driver's door.

The door caught the driver's leg just above the ankle. He winced at the pain, pivoted with his hip against the door to keep it from coming back at him, and rolled out onto the ground. He scrambled toward the rear of the car to lure Jane into an attack. All he had to do was get his hands on any part of her and swing her onto the freeway.

As she advanced a step, he did his best to look as though he were hurt and vulnerable. He got her to take three quick steps toward him while he hobbled backward, preparing to grasp her and roll back to add momentum as he propelled her into traffic. Jane took one more step, slipped into the car, slammed the door, and hammered down the lock buttons.

The man heard the engine start as he dashed toward her. Just as his fingers brushed the door handle, the rear wheels spun, bits of loose gravel shot out behind, and he had to step back to keep from being dragged out into the traffic as the car shot past him.

23

"**F**asten your seat belt, Timmy, and don't be scared," said Jane. She drove as fast as she dared, threading her way between slower vehicles and accelerating into the clear stretches. Even half an hour before sunrise there were beginning to be places where knots of cars jammed all the lanes at once. She turned off the freeway at White-oak, then shot under the overpass and up the eastbound ramp. The traffic was heavier heading into the center of the city. She had intended this as an advantage for Mary, because the slow, close-spaced stream would make it hard for even a superior driver to catch up with her. Now Jane was fighting the inertia herself.

She glanced down at the dashboard. The gas tank was full. Of course it would be. The car didn't seem to have a radio, but there was a black box about the size of one mounted in front of the shifter on the hump for the drive-shaft. "Tell me what happened," she said. "How you got here."

Timmy shrugged. "They brought some of my stuff. You know, from the apartment where Mona and I lived in Chicago. There were things they wanted me to identify that belonged to Mona. Then there was another box with some of my clothes and things. The next day I tried to put on my good shoes, but I couldn't get one of them on because your note was crumpled up in the toe."

"My note?" Once again Barraclough had been thinking faster than she had. Timmy's location had been kept secret, but the Chicago apartment had not. Barraclough had known that the F.B.I. or the Chicago police would search it. Because he had been a cop, he had also known that after they had preserved and labeled everything that could be considered evidence, there would be a lot left. They would release some of Timmy's belongings. Barraclough had even known that if nothing else got to Timmy, his best shoes would. He was going to have to look presentable in court.

"Yeah. So I called the phone number on your note, and the lady told me you weren't home but to call again when I could. And she asked me what the address was. I thought that was kind of odd, but she said you forgot to tell her. So last night when I called, she told me you wanted me to meet you."

Jane held herself in check. It wasn't Timmy's fault. For over two years he had been surviving by following whatever incomprehensible directions some adult— Morgan or Mona or Jane—had given him. "What else did she tell you?"

"That you told her if I could make it to the door by the garden, I could crawl along between the bushes and the house and slip right through the hedge to the next yard without anybody seeing me. You were right about all of it. Nobody saw me go. Then I walked over two streets, found this car right where she said it would be, climbed in the back seat, and lay down to wait. After a long time that man got in and we drove off. He said we were going to meet you."

Jane groped under the seat and beneath the dashboard, and then realized it was a waste of time. If there had been a gun in the car it couldn't be anyplace where the driver could have reached it or she and Timmy would be dead. Barraclough had made sure the assignment had stayed specific. Probably what he had feared most was not that Jane would see a gun and call the meeting off. He would be more afraid that his court-certified violence-prone trainee would show his initiative by using a gun where Mary might get hit.

She studied the inside of the car. "Did you see the driver use this black box?"

"Oh, yeah," said Timmy. "He said it was how he knew where we were going to meet you. See?" He pointed at a dial on the top that looked like the face of a compass. Jane was on a long, straight stretch of freeway, and she could see the needle was moving.

"Timmy," said Jane. "I didn't send the note. If I ever come for you again, I won't send a note or make a telephone call either. I'll make sure you see me. Don't go to some woman with dark hair who waves from a hundred feet away. I'll be up close, so you can tell."

He looked alarmed. "You're taking me back?"

"I can't drive you to a policeman's house in a stolen car," said Jane. "I'll have to drop you off in a safe place."

Jane leaned forward a little to glance at the black box. The needle was moving again. They had swung around to the east, just as she had. She had only the vaguest idea how direction finders worked. There was some kind of transmitter in Barraclough's car, and the black box received the signal and pointed out the direction it was coming from. But what could the range possibly be? A mile? Five miles? As though the machine had read her thoughts, the needle wavered, then swung to a straight vertical position and stayed there. It had already lost touch with Barraclough.

Jane maneuvered through the crush of vehicles. At any minute Barraclough or one of his lieutenants would know that she had the car, and they would take the necessary steps to find it. Probably they would report it stolen and let the police catch her for them. She had only one way to avoid the police. She drove to the parking structure at the Burbank airport.

She parked beside the gray Toyota and took the car keys from under the bumper. For a moment she considered ripping the black box out of the red car and trying to install it in her own car. But by now Barraclough certainly knew she had it. If she got the direction finder to work, eventually she would find that it was following a transmitter Barraclough had placed where she could be ambushed. She ushered Timmy into the gray Toyota and drove out of the parking ramp.

Ten minutes later Jane dialed a pay telephone and listened to Judge Kramer's voice. "Hello?"

She said, "Judge, it's me. Do you know for sure that your phone is not tapped?"

"I have it swept every day. No bugs so far. What's going on? How did you get this number?"

"Listen carefully. I'm with Timmy. They found him and lured him out. They know I've got him back and they're about to start looking for us, if they aren't already. I'm leaving him in the waiting area of the emergency room at Saint Joseph's Hospital in Burbank. He's faking a stomachache, so they'll have to keep him at least long enough for a doctor to be sure it's not his appendix.

The guard inside thinks I'm calling his father to say we got here. Say that's who you are when you come for him."

"But what—"

"He'll tell you. Bye." She hung up and looked in through the glass doors of the emergency room at Timmy for a heartbeat, then hurried to her car.

As Jane got back on the freeway she had to struggle against the feeling that Barraclough was simply too smart for her. Every time she tried anything, he seemed to have anticipated it and brought it back to bear on her. She pulled off the freeway and made her way to the quiet side street in Sherman Oaks. She climbed the fence with a growing dread. She made her way up the little hill and crouched beside the freeway. The rented car was still where Mary had left it, and across the freeway she could see hers too. She moved to Mary's car, looked in the windows, then under the seats and mats and in the glove compartment. Barraclough had won again. When he had produced Timmy, Mary had gone to him with the tapes still in her purse.

Jane forced herself to move. She slipped away from the freeway, leaving the camera, microphone, and recorders in the brush. She climbed the fence and drove out to Riverside Drive. Everything depended on her ability to use time efficiently now.

She glanced at her watch. It was six-thirty A.M. and the sun glinted on the windows ahead as she drove west. She tried to think of all of the facts that carried with them some bit of hope. Timmy was alive. Barraclough would never have kidnapped him if he had not expected the driver to take him somewhere and kill him quietly as soon as Barraclough had Mary. Mary was also alive, and would stay alive as long as she was able to keep from giving Barraclough the last dime she had stolen. This thought led Jane in a direction she did not want to go, so she forced herself away from it. Even the black box might help. If Barraclough thought Jane had it, he would try to use it to trap her. This would take some of his time and attention, and anything that accomplished that would help to neutralize the enormous advantage he had.

Jane had an advantage too, and she began to concentrate on it. There was no way that Barraclough could know that the young man she had met in the housing project had told her about Enterprise Development. He had said 5122 Van Nuys Boulevard. She turned right on Van Nuys Boulevard and watched for the building.

When it came up on her right, she could see the car Barraclough had been driving. It was parked on the street near the side door of the small, four-story building. Jane took a breath and felt the air keep coming and coming, expanding in her chest with a feeling of joy. Maybe Barraclough had finally done something foolish. She had assumed he would take Mary to a safe house somewhere. Maybe he had gotten overconfident and stopped at Van Nuys Boulevard to direct the search for Jane. Maybe the driver of the red car had not been heard from yet and Barraclough assumed she and Timmy were dead. Even as she formulated the idea she knew it was impossible. Barraclough had stopped here just long enough to change cars. She pulled her car around the corner out of sight, then went across the street into a coffee shop.

She waited in the coffee shop and watched Enterprise Development for half an hour before a man came out the door of the building. She checked her watch. It was exactly eight. Something prearranged was going on. The chance that someone would happen to emerge from the building on the stroke of the hour was exactly fifty-nine to one against. As the man approached Barraclough's car she studied his wiry gray hair, the razorsharp crease of his pants, the cocky toe-out walk and impeccably shined shoes.

He must be Farrell, the one who called himself the training officer at Intercontinental but who ran the undercover operation out of this building. He took a set of keys out of his pocket, pretended to look down to select the right one while his eyes scanned the block, then got in and drove off. Jane was confused for an instant. Of all the people Barraclough had working for him, Farrell was the only one she had been sure would not be here. He would be where Mary was.

Jane made up her mind quickly, hurried to her car, and drove after him. She had gone only a couple of blocks before she noticed the second car. It was black and nondescript, with one man in it. She turned off Van Nuys Boulevard, then left up the parallel street and watched her mirror, but he didn't follow. She pulled back onto Van Nuys Boulevard two blocks behind him. When Farrell turned right on Victory Boulevard and he followed, she realized that the black car had not been following her; it was following Farrell.

After the turn Jane pulled a little closer to the black car. Even if he was the star graduate of the police auto-surveillance team he couldn't follow a car ahead of him and watch his own back at the same time.

Then Farrell's gray car reached its destination. Jane watched the second car pull to the curb ten feet from the entrance. She drove another two blocks before she parked and watched them in her rearview mirror. Farrell was returning Barraclough's gray car to the agency from which it had been rented. A few minutes later he emerged from the little building, walked out to the street, and got into the black car with the other man. Jane drove around a block to come out behind them on Van Nuys Boulevard. They continued south only as far as the Enterprise Development building and turned in at the parking lot.

Even as Jane winced with frustration and disappointment, she knew she had been right. Farrell was the one Barraclough trusted to manage his separate under-the-surface operation. He was the one to select and recruit young thugs, deliver pep talks, and give them the skills to do his hunting. He was the one who talked about potential, initiative, motivation, and all the nonsense that made them think that whatever qualities they had gone to jail for were now going to make them rich. He was the specialist in the psychology of brutality. He would be the one person Barraclough was sure to want with him for the interrogation of Mary Perkins.

24

Mary sat on the bare, ridged, metal floor of a van. The bumps of the pavement were regular, and she was beginning to get used to them now. Her spine was jarred by the *ba-bump* as the front wheels, then the back, went over each crack, then paused and went *ba-bump* again. She had felt a moment of relief when they had dragged her out of the car, but before she had taken a step under her own power they had pushed her into the back of the van and put the bag over her head. It was a burlap sack that had been sprayed with several coats of black paint so she couldn't see through it. The bag went over her head and down her arms to her elbows, and then unseen hands cinched it at the neck. It looked like the black hoods convicts wore in old photographs of hangings—no holes for the eyes or nose, just a gap at the mouth for breathing.

Her heart had stutter-started when she saw it, and then just when she had begun to sense that it wasn't what it looked like, she had felt them pulling her wrists together behind her. This made her remember the article in the magazine about doing anything you could before you got into the car, because afterward it was too late. She had struggled then to save the use of her hands, but she knew she had already missed her best chance to accomplish an escape. She resisted only because her fear was jumping around inside her and making her body move. With the black-painted hood over her head, any one of the three men could have tied her hands while the others went away.

The van was white. She had seen that much before the hood went on. For some time thereafter, while the white van turned sharply a couple of times to topple her over onto the floor, then gathered speed, she wondered why she was no longer afraid. It took her more than an hour in the solitude and darkness of the black-painted hood to detect that it was because none of this was happening to her.

The distinction was a delicate, slippery one that had to be grasped carefully and not squeezed too hard. She was here feeling movement and hearing activity, but even before they had put the hood on, the sights had been distant and the sounds hollow. This didn't feel real. She had been afraid this was going to happen for such a long time that she knew the way it should have felt. It wasn't happening to her; it must be happening to someone else.

The van turned off the big road with the regular cracks on it and went more slowly. Now and then there would be a sharper bump, maybe a pothole, and the hard floor of the van would abruptly jolt her. It was not the bumps that bothered her; it was the fact that the van was moving more slowly, the way people drove when a trip was nearly over.

For the first time she became conscious of everything about the hood over her head. It was hot and rough, and the petroleum smell of the black paint was nauseating. She could feel an itch on the side of her cheek, but her hands were fettered behind her. She tried rubbing the side of her face against the metal strut beside her, but the fabric was so rough and prickly that it seemed to spread the itch from her hairline to her chin. Then the van hit another pothole and the jolt knocked the strut hard against her cheekbone. She let out a little cry and felt tears welling in her eyes.

She hoped the men had not heard it. She knew they had, so they must be aware of her weakness now, staring at her with critical, unpitying eyes while her hope deteriorated into a bitter wish that she had not been so stupid. The physical pain in her cheek kept insisting that she examine it, so she stopped resisting. She allowed herself to contemplate it and to wait for it each time her heart beat and then experience the throb. It was a small pain, only one of the bumps that the body was made to take, but it brought her bad news: this wasn't happening to somebody else. It was happening to her. She had filed somewhere in the back of her mind the information that a person in this situation might have to face some physical violence. Now she could not ignore what her common sense told her: that the pain was not going to be incidental, but was the whole purpose of this trip. They were taking her someplace to hurt her profoundly. It wasn't going to be her standing outside of herself and watching the tall man slapping her once across the face so she didn't really feel it. She was in a kind of trouble that made her heart release a flow of heat that went up her throat and got trapped under the hood with her so that it felt as though her head were in an oven. She could barely breathe, gasping in air through her mouth and tightening her neck and shoulders to bring the small mouth hole they had cut in the hood closer. The hood was wet now from the humidity of her breath, but this didn't seem important.

Every sensation was uncomfortable and unpleasant, and her mind couldn't choose only one to think about.

The van turned and tipped her against the wall again, but she didn't dwell on that either. She was consumed by the fear of the pain that was to come.

As Jane watched the office building on Van Nuys Boulevard she searched her mind for other ways to get Mary back. It was mid-morning already, and there had been no further sign of Farrell. She longed to call the police and get them to find Barraclough. The reasons she couldn't do so flooded into her mind. Barraclough would take time to find even if the police did everything right, and usually they didn't. Even then there was no way they could do anything without talking to somebody who worked for Intercontinental or showing up at one of their offices. If Barraclough had a few minutes of advance warning, Mary would disappear forever.

Barraclough would be taking Mary to a safe house somewhere. The property would probably be a place Barraclough owned, but there would be no way to use his name to find it. He had been in the business of kidnapping people for some time now, so his routine would be practiced and efficient, field-tested and refined. The only reasonable way of finding the place where Mary was being held was to get Farrell to lead her there. That was not going to be simple. She thought of trying to find another Intercontinental car with a direction finder installed in it. But this meant figuring out what car Farrell would drive to the safe house, hiding a transponder inside it, and teaching herself how to operate the receiver. Then she would be stuck behind the wheel of a stolen car, probably for some distance. It wasn't a plan; it was a fantasy.

Any preparation she tried to make now would involve taking her eyes off Farrell's door for at least an hour, and in that time he could have a sixty-mile head start in any direction. She would just have to keep him in sight for as long as it took and hope that he would lead her to Mary.

She kept her car parked a block away and around the corner, out of sight of the windows of Enterprise Development. She watched the building, first from the diner across the street, then from the inside of a bookstore two doors away. After she had leafed through every book near the front window twice, she walked to the thrift store across the street and picked over the used clothes. She chose two hats, a tan jacket, a black sweatshirt, and a pair of sunglasses. She put them on the floor of her car and went to eat dinner at the hamburger franchise on the far corner, where she still had a good view of Enterprise Development.

She knew that every thought she had, every movement she made that wasn't directed toward Farrell was a waste and a danger, but she couldn't keep Mary in the back of her mind where she should be. Each time she thought she had her mind focused on Farrell, a few seconds would tick away and the mere passing of time would remind her. A lot could happen to a person like Mary in thirty seconds, enough horror to last an eternity.

Each hour passed so slowly that she couldn't remember what she might have been thinking or doing before the last one, and the meeting on the freeway seemed to have happened weeks ago. She had stared at the office doors and windows for twelve hours, and still Farrell had not emerged.

Something must have happened that she had missed. At ten P.M. she began to prepare herself to enter the building. He might have walked out the door while she was in the ladies' room of the diner hours ago and gotten into a car that someone had brought to the curb for him. That could be why none of the cars parked near the building had been gone when she returned to the window. Maybe she had seen him go. He could have changed clothes with one of his trainees—something simple and rudimentary like that—and fooled her. He had spent his life perfecting the skills of searching and following, and there was no reason to imagine he had not seen all the ways of hiding and deceiving.

This was the other thought that she couldn't seem to get out of her mind. The reason Barraclough had Mary was that he had known what she would do and Jane had not. No, it was even worse. Mary had never met Timmy. He couldn't have known that she would walk into a fire for him. What Barraclough had known was how Jane would react. He had known that she would have to choose one of them, and the one she would choose was the one he had no further use for, the one he could kill.

She dumped her unfinished food and wrappers into the trash can by the door, slid her tray onto the stack, and walked across the parking lot toward the dark stretch of the street where she could cross without coming under any lights. She could hear footsteps on the sidewalk behind her as she stepped into the street, but she had to use this chance to see the building from a new angle, so she ignored them for the moment. She looked up at the building as she crossed, and through the window she saw Farrell. He was sitting behind his desk talking on the telephone. She reached the sidewalk on the other side of the street, stopped walking, and felt her calm return for a second before she remembered the footsteps.

Maybe the footsteps had been behind her when she

came out of the restaurant and she had been so distracted that she simply had not heard them. She began to walk and listened carefully; there were three sets of shoes. She felt as though she had put her foot on a step and it had fallen through. She had been so busy watching the office that it had not occurred to her that Farrell might have a few trainees on the streets outside. She walked along more quickly until she could use the darkened window of a store to get a look at their reflection. The three didn't fit the pattern at all. One of them wore a baseball cap backward and all three wore baggy pants and oversized jackets. They looked about seventeen or eighteen years old, and not seasoned or desperate enough for Farrell.

She had told Carey she had been mugged in Los Angeles, and now here she was, being considered and evaluated for a mugging in Los Angeles. It was simply out of the question tonight. It was not going to happen.

She took a moment to collect her thoughts, then suddenly turned on her heel and walked toward the three boys. They slowed down and spread apart on the sidewalk. When she stepped directly up to the one in the center, he stopped, not sure what he was going to do, but certain he didn't want to bump into her. "Hold it, all three of you," she said. "I want to talk to you."

The other two stopped, looking at her warily with half-averted faces. "What?" said the one on her left.

As she looked at the three unpromising young men, the idea came to her fully formed. The only question was whether she could convince them. "Are you doing anything tonight?" she asked.

The one on her right said, "We're not doing anything," with no inflection. He didn't know whether she was accusing or inviting, but either way that was the right answer.

Jane reached into her purse and they all tensed to move, as though they expected her to douse them with tear gas, an event that was probably not out of the question on these streets at night. She ran her fingers along the lining of her purse and found the Katherine Webster identification packet. She flashed the business card at them. "Katherine Webster, Treasury Department," she said.

"We didn't do nothing," said the one in the center.

"I didn't ask," she said. "I want to know if you're interested in working for a few hours."

"Doing what?" He was very suspicious now.

She pointed up at the lighted window of the Enterprise Development office. "There's a man in that office who's a suspect. In a while he's going to get into a car and drive out of town. You follow him, I follow you. If he spots you, turn off and go home. If he doesn't, you follow him to wherever he's going, you call a number, leave the address on the answering machine, and go home."

"Why us?" said the one on the left.

Jane quoted from an imaginary field manual. "If in the judgment of the investigating agent it is useful to deputize or otherwise employ private citizens in order to avoid detection by the surveillant, he or she is authorized to do so." She waited for a moment while they deciphered this, then said, "You don't have to do it. I can pay you per diem and a performance bonus if you work out."

"What does that mean?" asked the one on the right.

"A hundred dollars each to cover your expenses on the drive. That's the per diem. It means 'per day,' and you don't declare it on your tax return." She caught the amused glance from the one in the middle to the one on the left when he heard that. "Another two hundred each if he doesn't see you. You could each make three hundred before the sun comes up."

"What makes it worth that?"

"He's armed, he's dangerous, and he's smart. If he stops, you've got to keep going. Don't get yourself into a spot where his car is stopped and so is yours. He'll probably kill you."

The three looked at each other. There were a few shrugs and head tilts, but no smirks. The part about killing seemed to have raised their level of interest considerably. She had forgotten for a moment about seventeen-year-old boys. There had never been a moment in human history when anybody hadn't been able to recruit enough of them for a war. She reached into her purse again and said, "The per diem is in advance." She started to count the bills in front of them.

The one in the middle said to the one on the right, "You want to use your car or mine?"

"You have two?" asked Jane.

"Yeah," said the one in the middle.

"Use them both and you each get an extra hundred."

Mary was leaning against the tiled wall of the shower stall in the big first-floor bathroom of the farmhouse. They had finally left her alone, her right wrist handcuffed to the shower head so that she could never quite sit down. She tried to stand on her own, but she felt faint and unsteady. This was probably why they had chained her that way. If she fell she would hurt her arm, but she probably couldn't kill herself by hitting her head on the tiles.

When she looked down at her legs she could see the bruises were already a deep purple, and the welts were red and swelling. She had tried to kick out at them, but they had not grabbed her or tried to wrestle with her; they had simply clubbed the leg that came up at them, and when she kicked out again they would hit it again, until finally she couldn't get the leg to kick.

The two men had not spoken, even to each other. They went about it in a cold, impersonal silence, like people in a slaughterhouse working on an animal. They left the hood on her head the first time, but not because they didn't want her to see their faces; it was because they had no desire to see hers. Desire had nothing at all to do with it. The next time, when she was thinking that maybe it was better that she couldn't breathe, because dying was just going to sleep and being awake was every nightmare she had ever had, they took the hood off. She could see them doing it, their faces intent but detached, whatever they were feeling not comprehensible to her as emotion. Their faces were not like the faces of men having intercourse, but unself-conscious and empty, as though no other human being were present. She had always thought of rape as a crime of hatred, or the sick pleasure of exerting power over somebody who was helpless. But this didn't seem to bring them even that feeling of triumph; they were just using what was there because it was there.

At first she cried and screamed. She said, "No, please. You're hurting me." The one who was holding her tightened his grip, but the one who was doing it to her didn't pay any attention at all. He didn't seem to be able to understand. Her voice was the call of a bird or the bark of a dog, something he could hear but that carried no meaning at all.

When they left they chained her to the shower, still naked. She tried to take what was left of herself and put it back together, but she couldn't. She was torn apart, a lot of fragments that she couldn't seem to collect. After a long time she started to think again. Her mind kept ticking off an automatic inventory of hurts and injuries that kept being the same over and over, as though it were establishing the boundaries. Then she began to imagine herself telling Barraclough what they had done to her, and saw him decide to kill them for it. She was valuable. But even while she thought about it, there was a small, nagging voice somewhere just below hearing to remind her that she wasn't important. She wasn't really worth anything at all.

It was midnight when Farrell emerged from the back door of the building. He walked a hundred feet to the rear of the parking lot, opened the trunk of a dark sedan at the rear of the lot, took out a large hard-sided briefcase, and then turned and walked back into the building.

Jane waved to her lookout and pointed at the front entrance, then started her car. A moment later, Farrell came out the front door. A young man drove up to the curb in a white station wagon, got out, and stood on the sidewalk while Farrell took his place behind the wheel. Jane watched the boys she had hired. The lookout had been in the narrow space between two buildings, and already he was gone. He had waited long enough to see the car Farrell was driving, and now he was in the back of the building getting into his companion's car.

When Farrell started off and turned right, she saw the boys' black Trans-Am already on the right street, crossing the intersection after him. The second car, a sedate-looking brown Saturn, only joined in after she had counted to eight. She turned around in order to avoid passing the office building, went down the side street, and joined the convoy three blocks later.

She followed the three cars onto the freeway, fell back a quarter mile, and watched the Saturn's taillights. She had given the boys a short course on following cars while they waited for Farrell to move, and now she watched them work. On a freeway all they had to watch Farrell for was an exit. They stayed well back from him. When there were packs of cars on the road ahead they moved up and hid among them. They didn't change lanes when he did. They waited, showing a clear preference for the right lane, where it was difficult for him to notice them, and other cars entered the freeway and slipped in to put a new set of headlights in his mirror for a few minutes.

After they were north of the city and the traffic thinned out a bit, the second car passed the one in front and stayed there until it was possible that Farrell was getting used to the new set of headlights, and then it dropped to the rear again. Jane drove conservatively, watching the taillights of her decoys and holding herself in reserve. She was beginning to feel a little more hopeful now. Every minute that passed, Farrell would come closer to accepting the conclusion that he had not been followed.

Mary had been left alone in the shower stall for hours. She had begun to spend long periods trapped in her own mind. She would try to strengthen herself. "I did this. I chose to trade my life for the life of a little boy. This is the best thing that I have ever done. It's the best that any human being ever does. I'm past the decision, the part where I'd have been weak if I had thought about it, so no matter what happens to me now, I can't fail. I can do this." But there was another feeling, one that didn't respond in its own words. It was just like an echo that revealed the hollowness of the sounds Mary was making. She was a fraud. She was not brave enough. It was self-deception. She had stepped off a cliff and now as she was falling she was regretting it more every second. Then she would wonder. Priests said that if a person made a pure unselfish act of contrition at the very last moment, she would be forgiven, her whole life validated retroactively. But what if she did make the promise, the sacrifice, and then wanted to take it back much more sincerely with every single breath? She wished she had died before she had ever had that moment of madness.

Then there were sounds outside the door, men's voices, big heavy feet on the floorboards, and she tried to stand without holding on to the wall, but she couldn't. It wasn't that she was hurt, but her muscles didn't want to contract when her mind willed them to. They were quivering and weak.

When the door swung open she felt an impulse to scream, but even her throat was paralyzed. Just a harsh, raspy "Huh" came out. The man came into the room and closed the door. It was Barraclough. She cringed and tried to disappear into the corner of the shower as he walked toward her. She tried to cover herself with the one arm she could use.

After a moment she realized that he was paying no attention to her. He walked across the tile floor, looked around, and stopped. He seemed only to be making sure she was alive. Then to her surprise he turned to go.

"Wait," she said. "Don't you want to talk?" She was fighting the fear that he was going out to let the other two come in again.

He said, "What do you want?"

"They raped me," she tried to say, but her face seemed to collapse and shrivel inward, and she couldn't control her voice, so it broke into a sob.

"Don't waste my time," he said. It sounded like a warning. It didn't matter what they did to her because she wasn't a regular person anymore, a being who had the right to keep anything as hers, even her body. She had thrown her rights away. She was a criminal and she had been caught. She longed to change that, or at least hide it from him.

"Look, this has been a mistake. You seem to think I'm somebody I'm not. I didn't do anything or hurt anybody." She pointed to the door. "They hurt me. But I can understand; they didn't know they weren't supposed to. I'll just forget that it ever happened. Like a bad dream. We'll never mention it again. You let me go—anywhere you like. Drive me someplace so I don't know where this house was."

He looked at her with an expression that froze her. It came from a vast distance. It seemed to detect everything at once: her abject fear, her guilt, her lying—no, not just that she was lying but that she was a liar. His expression showed that he knew all of it, and that it inspired disgust and contempt. For the first time he even seemed to contemplate her naked body, but not with lust. It was the way a god would look down at it from a great height. She was dirty, bruised, covered with sweat, and throbbing with pain, a small, unremarkable female creature who would have been unappetizing at any time but was now filthy and cowering.

It made her desperate, as though she were standing alone on a shore and the ship was drifting farther away.

"I'm not naive, and I know you aren't. Sure, I have money. That's what you want, and I've got it. You seem to forget, I didn't get caught. I came to you. Why do you suppose I did that? I know you want some money from me, but I also want something from you. I took lots of banks for lots of money while the time was right. And I wasn't alone. I know people you haven't even heard of who took a whole lot more than I did. I can bring them to you. I can deliver them here."

His expression didn't change, and it made her more desperate.

"You'd really be making a mistake to waste a resource like me." She was sweating and horrified at how unconvincing she sounded, but she couldn't stop, could only go on like a drowning swimmer. "I took the Bank of Whalen for six million dollars on a piece of land I'd bought for half a million a month before. I'm a moneymaker. When I bought out Harrison Savings, I used their own money to leverage an option on a controlling interest and then made the bank pay back the loan as an operating cost. I can do all of it again." His face didn't change. "I can do new things because a person who knows how to make money will always know."

When he turned toward the door and took a step, she tried to stop talking, but she couldn't. "If you don't want to get into business, I understand. You want it quick and clean and simple. So take me to a bank. Any major bank can do an electronic transfer. I'll get the money, hand it over, and everybody can go away."

He was at the door now, and she waited for him to turn and look back at her so that she could read his features. Maybe there would be something false in his expression to let her know that he didn't really intend to kill her. He opened the door without hesitation and walked out.

Jane drove through the night thinking about the station wagon far ahead of her. She knew all of the reasons Farrell had chosen it. There was something benign about station wagons. The drivers were people who hauled kids around and had houses in the suburbs. They were also useful because if you put a good tarp down in the cargo bay you could carry a fairly stiff corpse without breaking any joints or doing any cutting.

Maybe Mary had already broken and told them how to get her money. It took time to do that to a person, but she wasn't coming into this fresh. She was already exhausted and disoriented when she first saw Barraclough. She had been in prison for a month, and then spent the next month running and hiding, getting burned out of a house, and then running some more. The belief that had been nurtured in the human brain that a person could endure physical and psychological torture without revealing secrets was probably accurate. The notion that more than one person in a thousand could do it was idiotic.

Mary had one advantage. She was smart enough to know that within an hour of the moment when Barraclough had her money, she would die. It might make her hold out for an extra couple of hours. There was no doubt in Jane's mind that at some point Barraclough would make dying seem like an attractive alternative to whatever was happening to Mary, but first she would offer all of the stalls that she could imagine—lies, promises, con games. As long as she kept trying new ones instead of giving in and telling the truth, she would keep breathing.

Farrell had driven deep into the San Joaquin Valley.

Some time in the past hour the signs marking ways to go east to Bakersfield and Tulare had ended and been replaced by signs for Fresno. Suddenly Jane caught the flashing of taillights ahead as the two follower cars tried to slow down without getting closer to Farrell's station wagon. They slowed to forty and Jane let herself glide up behind them in time to see Farrell turning off the highway.

She watched the first car take the exit ramp to go up the road after Farrell. The sign at the top of the ramp said MEN-DOTA 20. When Farrell stopped at the lighted island of a gas station, the boys drove past, then pulled over to wait a quarter mile down the road while he filled up his tank. Jane drove up the road, stopped ahead of the boys, and kept her eyes on Farrell's car as she hurried to the driver's window. She held out a handful of hundred-dollar bills. "Here," she said. "This is far enough. Pay your buddies."

The boy protested. "This can't be the end of the road."

"For you it is," she said, and stepped back to her car.

When Farrell had paid the gas station attendant and gotten back into his car, he drove a mile down the road to a motel. Jane watched him go into the lighted office, then come out with a key and go into a room. She pounded the steering wheel in frustration. This wasn't it. He was going to sleep.

Two hours before dawn Mary almost fell asleep. She woke up with a start, gripped by the feeling that she was falling, and slapped her hand against the side of the shower stall to hold herself up. The second day began for her at that moment. She was feeling a dread so deep that there was no difference between the dream and what was happening. The ground was coming up faster and faster, and when she hit she would be dead.

An hour after dawn she saw the doorknob turn. When the door opened she saw it was Barraclough. He was naked too this time. He unlocked her handcuff and left the key in it, turned on the shower, and held her under it for a long time, turning her this way and that as though he wanted to be sure she was clean enough. Then he turned her face to the wall. He never spoke. He just put his foot between hers and kicked each of her feet outward a little so she would know, and put a hand on her back. This time she did not struggle. She stood stiff and still like a dead person while he forced himself into her. After a few moments he slapped her buttock hard with one hand, then grasped her wet hair in the other and gave it three hard tugs. Slowly, a little at a time, she understood what he wanted and began to move her hips with him.

After he had finished with her, he turned on the shower again, washed himself as though she were not there, then turned the water off, refastened her handcuff, and left the room. As soon as the door closed, she began to cry. She had no idea how long it went on, because time was no longer something that had meaning. Finally the tears simply stopped and she was gripped by a fully formed, uncontrollable anger. She wanted them to come in. Her fingers clutched at the air, wanting to claw their eyes. Her jaw clenched, her mouth salivating at the thought of biting a throat and clinging to the man while the others tried to tear her loose.

The anger left her as abruptly as it had come, but as she leaned against the wall in the shower again she discovered that the anger had left something inside her. It was small and hard and clean like the scar from a burn. She studied it, touching it the way her tongue might touch a little sore in her mouth, over and over until it knew the place and the pain and the shape. She knew what she was going to do. Of all the people this might happen to, Mary had the best chance of carrying it off. She had a good head for numbers.

A few hours later Barraclough returned with the tape recorder. He plugged it in at the outlet by the sink for electric shavers, then turned it on. Mary watched him warily. Now must be the time when he was going to get her to talk. But then she heard a sound like the swish of a car going by, then several of them at once, then Jane's voice saying "You've been chasing Mary Perkins, I've been hiding her. Now I'm ready to sell her."

"Why?" That was Barraclough.

"I've been at this a long time. A lot of people would be dead without me."

"I've heard that. Sometime I'll get you to give me a list."

"No, you won't. Mary Perkins isn't the sort of person I want to risk my life for. She's not worth it. I gave her a chance and she disappointed me. I know that she's got a lot of money. You seem to think you can get it. I'm not interested in that kind of work."

"You know what will happen when I have her?"

"You'll end up with her money. I also know that if you have her, she's not coming back to ask me how it happened."

Barraclough stared at Mary for a moment, then turned and walked away into the rest of the house, the part where people who were free could walk.

Mary tried to laugh. She wanted Barraclough to hear her laugh, but it was so low and empty that he couldn't have heard it. She knew why he had played the tape. She was supposed to think that Jane had really been selling her. But how could he expect her to believe that? She had been in on the plan from the beginning.

But then she thought about what she had heard, and she knew. He was playing it to let her know that Jane had caught him on tape, and that she had thrown the evidence away. She was so stupid that she had forgotten to leave the tapes in the car when she had gone to him. She had forgotten there were any tapes. He would have been caught and convicted of her kidnapping, rape, and murder except for her unbelievably stupid mistake. She felt burning humiliation and shame. She was going to die a horrible, slow, degrading, painful death and the last thing she would remember was that she had let her killer go free.

It was another hour before she moved beyond herself and thought about Jane. "Mary Perkins isn't the sort of person I want to risk my life for. . . . I gave her a chance and she disappointed me." The reason Jane sounded so convincing on the tape was that she was telling the truth. Mary knew how to lie, and she had lied the same way. "She's not worth it." Even Barraclough, who caught liars for a living, was fooled because the words were literally true. Then the last part came back to her. "I know if you have her she isn't coming back . . ." That was true too. She was here, chained, injured, and hungry, and it was going to go on and on until she was dead.

For the next six hours Mary tried to work out a way to kill herself. The shower door had been taken out, and they had been too smart to leave the hinges. She experimented with the handcuff to see if there was a way she could get the chain across her throat to hang from the shower head, but the effort hurt her wrist terribly and there was no way to bring any pressure on her windpipe. At some point they would have to feed her, and there would be something—a glass, a knife, or even a china plate—that she could use to slash and stab herself.

But in the end she realized that she was not going to do it. If she killed herself, she would leave the hard, cold, perfect nugget of hatred inside her dead body, stranded like a virus. She had to stay alive to use it.

25

Jane waited until she was positive that Farrell was asleep, drove the mile back to the gas station to fill the tank of her own car, and returned to the motel. She was so exhausted that she was afraid she would doze off and wake up hours later to find Farrell's station wagon gone. She walked close to his car and looked in the windows. For a moment she considered hiding in the cargo section in the back and letting him drive her to Mary, but dismissed the idea. He would have a gun, and she would probably wake up about the time he flipped off the safety to fire it into her head.

Then she saw something lying on the dashboard, a yellow, crumpled piece of paper. She moved closer and recognized that it was a receipt from an American Express card. It was so wrinkled that she could barely read the machine printing on it. She took her pen and a receipt from her purse and wrote down the information—the name David R. King, the expiration date, and the thirteen-digit number—then walked to the pay telephone at the convenience store across the street.

She looked at the back of Catherine Snowdon's American Express card and dialed the number printed on it.

"Customer Service," said the voice. "May I help you?"

Jane said, "Yes. I'm afraid I have a problem and I guess you can tell me what to do. My husband's wallet has been lost, and his American Express card was in it."

"Account number?"

Jane read it off her receipt.

"Expiration date?"

"Next August. He's in the hospital. There was an accident and they brought him in, and his wallet somehow disappeared. I don't know if—"

"I understand," said the woman gently. "We'd better not take a chance. I'm going to cancel the card as of now. He'll be receiving a new one in the mail in a couple of days with a new number."

"But what happens if somebody else has it?"

"That's all explained in detail on the back of your statement. Basically you have nothing to worry about. You did the right thing by calling. Thank you very much. I hope your husband recovers quickly."

"Thank you," said Jane. She took some time walking back to the motel, formulating the details of her story.

She opened the office door with an air of authority and looked around. It was a bright morning already, but the young man behind the desk looked as exhausted as she felt. The hair on the back of his head was standing out in tufts from lying back in his chair while he watched a dreadful dubbed movie on the small television set beside him. At the moment several muscular men in fur kilts were swinging clumsily at each other with swords and taking a terrible toll on the columns of the Parthenon. He stood up and leaned his elbows on the counter. "May I help you?"

"I'm Kit Snowdon," Jane said. "American Express Fraud Division. I'm afraid we've got a little problem."

The young man switched off the swordsmen behind him and looked as though he were glad she had come along. "How can I help?"

"You have a gentleman staying in Room 4 who is in possession of a stolen American Express card. He would be registered under the name David R. King."

The young man was shocked. "But I ran his card on the machine. There's got to be some mistake."

"Run the numbers again." She allowed her voice to betray a tiny portion of the impatience she was feeling.

He picked the receipt out of the drawer, pushed a few buttons to get onto the phone line, then punched the numbers in. After a few seconds the machine rattled off a message from the central computers in North Dakota or someplace. He looked sick. "They want me to confiscate the card."

"The computer always says that. We haven't had a computer beat up yet," she said. "Ignore it."

"But—"

"If you ran the card before, you must have gotten a look at him. Did he look like somebody you want to take a card from?"

"No." He shook his head solemnly, then looked at the telephone on the counter. "Should I call the police?"

Jane sighed wearily. "I'll lay it out for you. He's been traveling for two days. He has two other cards and he's got some charges—maybe fifteen hundred by now. If I apprehend him, he gets charged with petty larceny. If I can get him without making a legal mistake and if the company lawyers follow through, he gets ninety days— tops. If I follow him another day or two and he gets the bill up over three thousand, then it's grand theft, forgery, maybe possession of stolen property, and the judge gets to swing hard. In fact, he has to."

"What do we do?"

"I've been following him for two days," said Jane. "I'm asleep on my feet. I want you to check me into a room and watch his door while I get some sleep. The minute you know he's awake, ring my room."

"What if he checks out? Should I slow him down?"

"Don't do anything you wouldn't normally do, except this time buzz my room. That's all." She handed him the Catherine Snowdon credit card.

The kid slid it across the slot of his machine and handed it back to her with the key. "I'm sorry I messed up with the authorization. I was positive—"

"You didn't mess up," said Jane. "He altered the magnetic strip to change one digit, or the machine would have said 'Tilt.' The real pros know how to do that. Just be sure he doesn't slip away. If you go off duty, make sure the next guy knows what to do."

She went into her room and slept in her clothes. The call came in the evening. When she picked up the receiver there was nobody on the other end. He must be in the office, so the boy could do nothing but press the button for her room. She was on her feet instantly, standing by the window. His station wagon was still in the lot in front of Room 4. She slipped out her door, turned away from the office, walked around the building, got into her car, and followed Farrell down the street past the freeway entrance. He pulled into the parking lot of a supermarket, got out of his car, and walked into the store.

Jane looked at her watch. Some of the mystery of his movements was dispelled. It was eight-thirty P.M. He had left his office in a clean car at midnight and driven through the rest of the night. When he was positive he had not been followed, he had slept through the day in the motel room under a fake name. If he was wrong about being followed, probably the pursuers would have made a move of some kind while he slept. If they had lost him somewhere during the long drive, he would have been invisible for a whole day, while they were forced to widen their search to places he had never been, dispersing and exhausting themselves.

Now he was sure he had nothing to worry about, and he was going grocery shopping. That made sense too. They could not have known they were going to be using the safe house. They probably didn't visit it often enough to keep fresh food there. When Barraclough had gotten Mary, he had simply changed cars and driven her up here.

There was another side to what Farrell was doing, and it made her feel anxious again. He had efficiently changed himself into a nocturnal creature. Jane had taken a few people out of the world who had been held by someone who wanted information, and they had told her what it was like. The captors would wear them down for days, alternately abusing and ignoring them, depriving them of sleep and food until some chemical imbalance occurred and they began to lose themselves in a depressive psychosis that seemed to bounce erratically from guilt to anger, but hopeless guilt and anger. The tormentors who understood the process would begin their final interrogation when the mind was weakest and most vulnerable, between two and five in the morning. Tonight when Mary woke up, starved, exhausted, and probably injured, there would be a new face. He would be fresh and sharp and tireless, and by now it would seem to her that he could read her mind.

Jane could see Farrell through the front window of the store filling a shopping cart. The moment was going by, and when it was gone there would not be another. She got out of her car and walked toward the station wagon. She could see his overnight bag on the seat, the crumpled receipt from the motel on the dashboard. She moved out of sight behind the truck parked beside the station wagon and watched the window of the store until she saw him move around the shelves at the end of the aisle. Then she walked to the front of his car, pretended to drop her keys, and knelt down to pick them up. While she was kneeling she slipped her hand under the front bumper and stabbed the lower radiator hose with her pocketknife, stood up, and walked on to the corner of the building where she could see the checkout aisles.

She watched while the clerk ran Farrell's groceries along the conveyor belt and past the cash register, then put them into bags. The first had quart-sized bottles on the top. The second had round bulges of fruits and vegetables, double-bagged in smaller sacks inside. The third had cartons of orange juice, milk in a plastic jug, and a box of cereal. She turned and made her way back to the truck parked by Farrell's car.

She waited while he slipped his key into the driver's door lock and electronically released the rest of the locks so he could load his groceries, then put the three bags in the cargo bay. He finished, then turned to push his cart back to the collection rack, twenty paces away.

Jane moved along the right side of the car to the back seat door, slipped the rubber band off her ponytail, doubled it, opened the door, slipped the rubber band over the catch in the door lock, then eased it shut again. Then she moved back around the truck out of sight and made her way back to her own car.

Farrell drove out of the lot and turned east across the flat farm country toward Mendota. Jane glanced at her watch, walked into the store, and bought a can of cola and a box of plastic straws. Then she got into her car, waited three minutes, and drove out after him. She could picture what was happening. When the station wagon's engine started, the water pump began to circulate the coolant, taking the water from the leaky bottom radiator hose, while some of it drained from the hole. As soon as the engine reached its optimum temperature, the thermostat would open. He would go a few miles before his temperature gauge went wild, because the expansion tank would empty, keeping the engine cool until that coolant too drained out the hose onto the road.

She drove down the dark road until she saw the car pulled over on the right shoulder. She turned off the road, killed her lights, and watched. There was no sign of him. Far ahead along the road a truck pulled over to the side and she could see him caught in its lights for a moment, waving it down. He climbed into the truck and it drove toward her. She turned on her lights, pulled back onto the road, and passed it, but as soon as it was out of sight she turned around and drove back to Farrell's car.

She opened the backseat door, took the rubber hair band off the latch, and pulled up the button on the driver's side to unlock the tailgate. She had thought it through carefully on her drive, so she had no decisions to make. She put a tiny slit in the plastic milk jug, stuck a plastic straw into her perfume bottle of water hemlock and mayapple, put her finger over the end, inserted the straw into the milk bottle, and let it drain into the milk. Then she moved the gummed price tag to cover the slit.

She did the same to the cartons of orange juice. The flat packages of meat were an experiment because she had no idea what cooking would do to the chemical composition of the clear liquid, but the holes in the cellophane wrappings were easy to hide, so she used them. She was confident about the bottle of scotch because the alcohol would hide any taste. She found the cap could be opened and reclosed by peeling the blue tax stamp off with her knife instead of tearing it, then pasting it down with a little spit. She was certain that even if a bit of the food was intended to reward Mary for talking, the scotch was for the men. Alcohol made people too reckless to be afraid and too stupid to remember, and it dulled pain. She left the vegetables alone because they would be washed and boiled, but she made a tiny incision in each of the apples and pushed the straw far enough into the depression at the bottom to reach the almost-hollow core, so the poison would come out as juice and the white of the apple would not be discolored by contact with the air.

When the perfume bottle was empty Jane closed the tailgate, went to the driver's side, pushed down the button to relock all the doors, and then drove her own car a mile down the road to wait for Mary Perkins's interrogator to return with a new hose for his radiator.

26

It had been nearly forty-eight hours since Mary had walked across five lanes of the Ventura Freeway and gotten into the car. She did not know this because time had already become one more thing that had to do with other people. Sometimes so much happened in a very short time. If one of the men hit her, the bright sharp suddenness seemed to explode into pain and wonder, then bleed on into the next several hours, slowly tapering down into something she knew but didn't feel.

At first she had been most afraid of permanence. There was some instinct that told her it didn't matter if they gave her a sensation that made her scream, not because having it happen so many times had made her used to it but because it left something. It was like dividing her in half. Each time they did it, half of her was gone. Then they would divide the half, and she would be smaller, but no matter how many times they hurt her, some tiny fraction of her would be left. Even if all that was left at the end was the size of a germ, someday it might grow back. But if they blinded her or crippled her, her eyes or legs would not grow back. She had a deep animal urge to keep her body intact.

But even this feeling was faded now. She had gone

from fear to despair. She could not force herself to imagine a future. The past was all lies, arrogance, and deception, and she could not think about her life as separate events now. Even Mary Perkins was more filth she had made up and smeared on herself. She was Lily Smith, and she was sorry.

Sometime after the little window high on the wall in the bathroom turned dark again, a man she had never seen before walked in carrying a briefcase. He was older and had gray, bristly hair. He wore a gray suit with a coat that seemed a little too tight in the shoulders, and a pair of shoes that looked as though he polished them a lot. She thought of him as Policeman. He brought with him a straight-backed chair that appeared to be part of a dining room set and sat down on it.

He watched her with eyes that looked serious and alert, but there didn't seem to be anything else behind them. He had no predatory gleam, no cold contempt. He was simply waiting. She wanted to please him, to deal with this new person and win him over to her side.

She began slowly and logically because she had failed so miserably with Barraclough, and this one seemed even more touchy, more likely to dismiss her and go away. "I would like to find a way to make this end." She tried to sound ingratiating, but her voice came out toneless and monotonous.

He pursed his lips and nodded, as though he were giving her permission to go on. "I know."

She ventured a little further. "Nobody has asked me any questions."

He shrugged. "There's no hurry."

This was like a weight tied to her. "Why?"

He said, "We destroyed the tapes you made of the meeting on the freeway—"

"I didn't do that," she interrupted.

He raised an eyebrow as a warning. She winced, forcing herself to keep silent. That was how she had earned Barraclough's contempt, and if she did it to this one, her last chance would be gone. They both knew she was an accessory to the crime, so she accepted it.

He said, "Your girlfriend Jane wrote you off. She turned up yesterday at the L.A. airport. Operatives followed her to Chicago." He opened his briefcase and lifted out a big plastic food-storage bag with a seal on the top like the ones they used for evidence. Inside was a long shock of shiny black hair. He placed it back in the briefcase. "It seems to me that there's nobody else who even knows that you're missing. You've been traveling under false names for some time."

She had not realized until now that she had been living on the assumption that Jane was alive. If she was gone, then Policeman was right. Enduring a day or a year made no difference because nobody in the world knew she was gone. There was no possibility that she could ever leave this room. She repeated, "Is there any way that I can end this?"

Policeman looked at her judiciously. "It all depends on you."

A tiny hope began to return. It was from a different source this time, and it seemed more genuine than imagining that Jane could convince the authorities to break down the door to save her. Now that Jane was gone, she could see how foolish she had been to think of it at all. She said, "What do I do?"

He said, "Let's talk."

"All right."

"Tell me what happened the day you left the Los Angeles County Jail."

"I took a bus to the airport. Then I saw Jane."

"What color was the bus?" He asked her questions without appearing to listen to the content of the answers, just watching to see if she was lying.

"What name did you use in Ann Arbor?"

"Donna Kester. Jane picked it. She had cards and things in that name."

"Where did you go when you left there?"

"Let's see. Ohio. We hitched a ride with a student to Columbus, then Cleveland. The Copa Motel."

"Did you pay cash?"

"No. Credit cards. She had lots of credit cards, all in different names."

"What name did she use at the Copa?"

"I'm not sure. I think it was Catherine Snowdon." She told him the addresses of the hotels and motels, the agencies where they had rented cars, the routes they had driven—everything that came out of her memory. She wanted to please him. He seemed to be rooting for her, hoping she would pass. He wrote nothing down, but he seemed to be listening for mistakes. Each time a detail struck his ear as wrong, he would interrupt.

"How did you get into a women's dormitory at night? They're locked." It would always be something irrelevant, but it would be like a slap because it made her remember something else to prove she was giving him everything.

Finally, when the questions didn't bring any new answers, he stood up and took a step toward the door.

"Wait," she said. "Don't go. I've done everything, given you everything. What do you expect me to do?"

Policeman opened his briefcase again, pulled out a blank piece of paper, took a black felt-tipped pen out of his shirt pocket, closed the briefcase, and set the pen and paper on the chair. Then he walked to the shower, unlocked the handcuff from her wrist, turned, and walked out the door. She heard him locking it behind him.

She could not believe her good fortune. She stepped unsteadily to the chair. She started by printing the names as neatly as she could: Bahamas Commonwealth Bank; Union Bank of Switzerland; Banco de America Central of the Cayman Islands; International Credit Bank of Switzerland. The names themselves brought back the numbers, clear and fresh and clean in her mind, because numbers always were.

When she was finished, she left the pen and the paper on the seat of the chair and went back to her shower stall. After a long time, Policeman came through the door, picked up the chair and the piece of paper, and walked out the door.

It took them a few hours to do whatever they had needed to do to verify that the accounts existed. Then Policeman came in with Barraclough. This time Barraclough carried the papers. They were bank-transfer authorizations. Across the top was the name of one of her banks and the account number. Across the bottom of each one was the account where all of the money was going: Credit Suisse 08950569237. Her hatred clutched the numbers to her and clung to them as though they were the eyeballs of the men in the house.

When she was finished signing the papers they took them and walked out of the room without speaking to her. She had a strange sense of relief now. Her body felt light, as though she could dance or just rise up into the air. She held the numbers in her head and played with them like colored billiard balls that clicked when she moved them. Oh, eight ninety-five, oh, five sixty-nine, two thirty-seven. No fours or ones. First letters, O-E-N-F-O-F-S-N-T-T-S. 08950569237.

Jane sat in the dark and studied the gravel drive beside the house. There were the white station wagon, a white van, and a dark gray Dodge that looked like the same model as the red one they had used to bring Timmy to the freeway meeting. The small white house looked as though it had once been a real farmhouse where a family had lived and worked the broad flat fields around it, probably back in the thirties.

Jane knew she was going to have to do everything as quickly as she could. In an hour or two the sun would be up and one of them would look out a window. She had left the car a mile away by the side of the road, so there was no chance of using it as a blind.

She moved a little closer to the house, slowly and quietly, watching for signs that they had wired the grounds somehow. She had seen a beige box on the back side of the gate that she guessed was a motion sensor, and she had given the long gravel drive a wide berth because of it. She had come in across the empty field and seen nothing electronic since then.

She had imagined the safe house would be something big and fancy and in proportion with Barraclough's ambitions. But if Barraclough owned such a place, he wasn't going to make the mistake of committing crimes there. This house was small, unobtrusive, and run-down.

He was too smart to have the fantasy that he could make any building impregnable. This one looked as though he expected to just walk away from it one day. His protection wasn't the delusion that he could keep the police out if they wanted to get in; it was the high probability that they would never try.

As soon as Jane saw the van she knew she was going to have to look inside it. If Mary was dead, they would not leave her body in the house for long. They would wrap it and place it in the back of the van so they could clean the house without any worry that there would be new blood when they moved it. The inside of a van could be washed with a hose. She moved quietly to the back of the van and looked in the rear window. The floor was lit enough by the moonlight through the windshield for her to tell there was nothing big enough on the floor to be a corpse. She could see the spare tire fastened with a wing nut on the right side just inside the rear door. She tried the door handle and found it unlocked, so she reached inside and searched around the tire by touch. When she found the tire iron she took it out and slipped it into her belt, then closed the door quietly and moved back out into the field.

She selected a spot a hundred feet from the house where the alfalfa had grown to about ten inches. Since the farm had not been worked for decades, the land had not been plowed and the thatch from other seasons lay thick on the surface. The tire iron was thick and heavy, and the chisel end that was designed for taking off hubcaps dug through it easily and reached rich, soft, black dirt only an inch down. She broke the earth and softened it, then took off her black sweatshirt, loaded double handfuls onto it, and used it as a sack to help her spread the dirt around the field in the deep grass. When the trench was longer than she was and ten inches deep, she gathered the tufts of alfalfa and thatch she had removed, lay down, and began to bury her legs.

The dawn came slowly, while the low fields were still blanketed with wet fog. It was still half an hour before sunrise when she heard the front door of the house open. She lay still in her shallow grave with the blanket of alfalfa and thatch covering her to her neck, then the sweatshirt above her head with a layer of cut alfalfa over it. She clutched the tire iron. There were two sets of heavy footsteps on the front porch. She heard them clop down the wooden steps, then followed the quiet crunches on the gravel. She heard one car door slam, then another. Then there was the hum of an engine. She listened as the wheels rolled on the gravel toward the highway.

Jane lifted her head only far enough to see that it was the dark gray car that was gone, then lay back for a few minutes considering the implications. Two men were gone. It could mean that they had come to the end of Mary Perkins's interrogation and that she was dead. She decided this was not likely. There would be the body to worry about. Barraclough had more understanding of human nature than to leave the body and the cleaning entirely to some underling, and he certainly wouldn't send his trainees on an errand while he did the messy, stomach-turning work himself. He would supervise while at least two of them wrapped the body, put it in the van, and took it somewhere far from here, then buried it deep. Mary was alive.

Two men were gone. Jane waited for twenty minutes, listening for sounds from the house, before she moved. Jane had to use this time to find out where Mary was and how many men were still in the house. Quietly she rolled over in her trench and crawled out the end of it. She slipped to the side of the house, put her ear against one of the clapboards, and listened. She heard music. In a moment it stopped and she heard the muffled cadence of speech, but it was loud and exaggerated like the voice of an announcer, and then the music came on again. She moved to the front of the house and checked the window. The living room was almost empty. There were two chairs, an old couch, and a portable television set on a coffee table. She followed the sound of the radio around the house to the kitchen door.

She listened for a few minutes, but there were no other voices. She slowly stepped up beside the door and let one eye slide close to the corner of the screened window. Inside were two young men. They were lying on the floor beside the kitchen table. One of them was clutching his belly, and his mouth was open as though he were trying to scream, but his eyes were staring without moving. The other was facing away from her, but he too was still. She could see that they had begun to eat breakfast. Cereal and milk were spilled on the floor, and on the table were two empty glasses with little bits of orange pulp residue almost to their brims.

Jane swung her tire iron and smashed the small window over the door, reached inside and turned the knob. Neither of the men moved. She walked past them into the living room and quietly climbed the stairs to the second floor, holding the tire iron. She looked in the door of each room and saw only four empty, unmade beds. She descended the stairs again and found a closed door off the hallway. She tried the knob, but it was locked. She pushed the flattened end of the tire iron between the jamb and the door at the knob, lifted her foot to step on the lug end to set it, then pushed with all her strength. The door gave a loud creak and then a bang as it popped inward, bringing a piece of the woodwork with it.

The sight of Mary was worse than the sight of the two men Jane had poisoned. She was naked and bruised, one eye swelled so that it was nearly closed, her lips dry and so chapped that when her mouth moved a clotted wound at the corner cracked and a thin trickle of blood ran down to her chin. She didn't seem to have the strength to stand up, so she started to crawl across the bathroom floor toward Jane.

Jane stepped to her and put her arm around her waist to lift her to her feet. "Come on," she said.

"They said you were dead." Jane could barely hear her.

"I'm not, and you aren't either. We have to hurry. Where are your clothes?"

"I don't know." She was seized with tremors, and it was a moment before Jane heard the rest of what she was trying to say. "Just get me out."

"Stay here a minute," said Jane, and quickly went into the kitchen to search for car keys. They were lying on the counter. As she snatched them up, she sensed movement behind her.

Mary was reaching for the bottle of milk on the table. "No!" Jane said sharply, and knocked it to the floor. Mary cringed and stared at her without comprehension.

"I poisoned everything."

Mary seemed to notice the two men on the floor for the first time. They had died in terrible pain and convulsions, and their faces were so contorted that they didn't look quite human. She seemed to marvel at them. "They look so young," she said. "I thought they were older." Then

she seemed to remember something she had known before. "The devil is always exactly your own age."

"Come on," said Jane. "We'll forget the clothes for
now." She dragged Mary out of the kitchen and onto the
porch. She tried the car key in the van, but it didn't fit. It
opened the white station wagon, so she eased Mary into
the passenger seat, started the engine, and drove up the
driveway. "Here," she said, and put the black sweatshirt
on Mary's lap. "It's dirty, but it's better than nothing. Put
it on."

Jane drove the next mile staring into her mirrors and
up the road ahead for signs of Barraclough and Farrell.
When she reached the place where she had parked the
gray Toyota, she pulled the station wagon up to it, put
Mary in the back seat, and drove up the road. She said,
"Keep down on the seat and rest. Whatever you do, don't
put your head up. Do you need a doctor right away?"

"I don't want one," said Mary. Her voice was raspy
and brittle, but it was beginning to sound stronger.

"We'll get you some clothes and some food as soon as
we're far enough away. Nothing's open yet."

"Just get the clothes. I can eat on the plane."

"The plane?"

"I have to go to Texas."

Jane felt a reflex in her throat that brought tears to her
eyes. She didn't want to let pictures form of what they
had done to Mary, but there was no way to avoid thinking about it. She wasn't dead, because her heart was still
beating and she could form words with her bruised
face, but she could easily spend the rest of her life in a
madhouse.

"Ask me why."

The voice was self-satisfied and coy, almost flirtatious.

Now Jane was going to have to follow Mary down whatever path her deranged mind was taking. She owed her a thousand times more than this tiny courtesy. "All right. Why?"

"Because I can remember numbers."

Jane tried to keep her calm. "I know, Mary. I noticed you were good with numbers the first time we talked. You're an intelligent, strong woman, and you're going to be okay." It was a lie. She was not going to be okay. Jane had done this to her. Barraclough had taken the bait and chewed it up.

"They finally made me give them the money I stole."

"I know," said Jane. "There's nobody who wouldn't have done what you did. Forget the money."

"Let me finish," said Mary impatiently. "They knew I had stolen it from banks, but they thought I did it by being an insect or a rat or something who crawled in and took it. It didn't even occur to them that the reason I could do it was that I know all about the business, and that I was smarter than the people I took it from. They filled out bank-transfer slips. They listed my bank account numbers and the number of the account where the money was supposed to go. I signed them all, one after another, so I saw it six times."

"Saw what six times?"

"There's no need to write it down. I can close my eyes and read it any time I want. 08950569237. He's transferring all the money into his bank account at Credit Suisse in Zurich. He has a numbered account, and that's the number. I captured it."

27

As Jane drove, Mary lay on the back seat talking at the roof of the car. "It has to be Dallas."

"Why Dallas? You told me once that you couldn't go there because people knew you."

"And I know them," said Mary. "They have you, and you have them. It's like the tar baby."

Jane tried to choose her words carefully. There would be nothing accomplished if she managed to nudge her own agitation into hysteria, but Mary had to know that it wasn't over. "I killed those two men back there. Barra-clough wasn't there."

"Yes," said Mary. "He's in San Francisco."

"How do you know that?"

"That's where the big West Coast banks have their main offices. What he's doing right now is riding the jet stream, and you can't get on it very easily in some branch office in Stinkwood, Minnesota. All they can do for you is to ask the big offices to do it for them, and he can't fool around all day and let all those people know what he's doing."

"What do you mean by 'riding the jet stream'? Is he flying to Switzerland?"

"No," said Mary. "That's way too slow. Stock exchanges, bond markets, commodities, currency, the treasury securities of a hundred countries go up and down a hundred times a day. Some tyrant is shot in South America, and before the ambulance reaches the hospital, billions of dollars from Hong Kong are already buying up copper and coffee beans in London and New York. Barraclough isn't going to travel to Europe and then to the Caribbean to hand six tellers withdrawal slips and collect fifty-two million dollars. He's got to move the money the way big money moves—electronically, in thin air. Bonn, Paris, London, New York, Chicago, San Francisco, L.A., Zurich, Melbourne, Singapore, Hong Kong." After a breath she added, "Dallas."

Jane tilted the rearview mirror to get a glimpse of Mary on the back seat. She was bloody, bruised, and exhausted, but she seemed to be describing something that was real. "You mean you want to try to get your money back? Is that what this is about?"

Mary Perkins gave a quiet cough, and Jane realized that it had been a kind of mirthless laugh. "You told me before and I didn't get it, did I? You have to strip yourself clean. Lose everything: friends, clothes, medical records, your name, even your hair. The money was the last thing to go. That's gone, Jane. I had to give it to him, and I put it right in his hands so I could see which pocket he stashed it in."

Jane dressed Mary in a pair of blue jeans because the welts and bruises on her legs were so bright and angry that a dress would not have covered enough of them, and it was impossible in the small store in Gilroy to buy any other kind of women's pants in a length that fit an actual, living woman. The blouse was off another rack in the same store, a plain blue shirt that would attract no attention and was big enough to let her shrink inside it without having much of the fabric touch her skin.

Jane left the car in the long-term lot in San Jose because Mary insisted there was no time for a more elaborate arrangement. "Get me to Dallas," she said. "After that I don't care."

"What don't you care about?"

"Anything."

Mary ate and drank on the plane, then slept the rest of the way to Dallas. At the Dallas–Fort Worth airport, Jane rented a car. As she drove it out of the lot, she asked, "Where is it?"

"Bank of Sanford, corner of Commerce and Field. Turn left here."

"It must be almost closing time," said Jane. "But we may be able to catch your friend coming out."

"We don't want to catch him coming out," said Mary. Her voice was still even and low, as though it were an enormous effort to talk. "We'll catch him on the way in. Everything happens at night."

They waited in the bank lobby until Jane saw that each customer who approached the wide glass doors hurried to give the nearest handle a tentative tug to be sure they weren't locked, then stepped inside with a small sigh of relief, and then during the walk to the tellers' windows, looked up at the clock built into the wall.

At one minute before four a man about forty years old with hair that was combed straight back to emphasize the gray hair at his temples entered the bank. He wore a lightweight suit that had a slight sheen to it, and on his feet were a pair of brightly shined shoes that it took Jane a second to recognize as cowboy boots.

"There he is," said Mary Perkins. She stood up quickly, but the barely audible groan she gave showed that it had cost her something. She stepped in front of the man. "Hello, Gene," she said. "It's me—Mary Perkins."

The man looked at her, puzzled, while he inhaled once, and then puffed the breath out when he remembered. His eyes shot around him in a reflex, as though he were checking to see who was watching. He said uncomfortably, "Well, now, Mary. How are you these days? I heard you had some problems a while back."

"Yes, I've been away," said Mary. "I can see that you're thinking I don't look like the experience did me any good. You're absolutely right."

The man's brow wrinkled a little to tilt his eyebrows in sympathy, and his mouth forced itself into a sad smile. "Well, I can see it's behind you now, and that's the main thing."

Mary said, "Do you still have an office? I'd like to talk to you about some business."

The man reflexively leaned back away from her. "Mary, you have to understand that things don't work the way they once did. It's nice to see you, but—"

Mary turned and nodded to Jane, who was still sitting in the overstuffed chair next to the marble table where the pens were chained. She stepped forward to join them, but she didn't smile. Mary said, "This is Katherine Webster from the Treasury Department. This is Gene Hiller, my old friend."

The man looked from one to the other. "Now wait a minute," he said. "What's going on?"

"Don't worry," said Mary. "If your time is coming, I don't know about it. Let's talk."

Jane began to open her purse and fiddle with the little

black wallet, as though she were about to pull out a badge.

Gene Hiller looked around him again, then said quickly, "This way."

His office was small, a place where he could hang his coat while he was out in the computer room. As soon as they were inside, Mary closed the door and stood in a place that made it impossible for him to sit behind his desk where he felt safe. Jane could see that Mary had once been very good at this.

"Here it is, Gene," she said. "I've made a deal with Katherine here. I'm going to give the money back voluntarily." She seemed to notice the sweat forming on his pale forehead. "I'm not—confirm this for me, Katherine—not expected to testify against anyone who may have had anything to do with any of the illegal activities in which I was once engaged."

The muscles in his shoulders seemed to relax so that his neck actually got longer. "What . . . brings you here?"

"It seems I can't go to Zurich, pick up a check with a lot of zeros on it, and fly back here to hand it over." She gave Jane a sarcastic smile. "There's very little trust left in the world."

"I see," said Gene, but all he could see was that in Mary's mind Jane represented what was stopping her.

"My attorney tells me that in order to get past the judge a week from now, it has to be voluntary, and apparently spontaneous, as evidence that I feel remorse and have been rehabilitated sincerely. I can't appear to have bought my way out with the Treasury Department. This puts me in a serious bind. Consequently I have to ask old friends for help."

The threat was not wasted on him. If for some reason

she could not give them the money, there was something else she could give them. "What do you want me to do?"

"An electronic transfer," she said. "Receive the money, then send it on a second later. Write this down, and get it right. Credit Suisse, 08950569237. If they need a transfer request, I'll sign one and you can fax it. If they ask for verification tell them I've furnished identification. The name I used was James Barraclough."

Gene looked at her for a moment. "Want to tell me why you put a false name on a numbered account in a Swiss bank?"

Mary said, "I'm rehabilitating myself these days, not giving anybody lessons."

His eyebrows slowly began to rise. He smelled something. "Where exactly do you want these funds sent?"

Mary took a deep breath and blew it out. "Turn on your payroll computer and punch up the account number where you send the money for federal tax withholding. Can you do that?"

"Sure. What then?"

"Transfer all of the money from the Swiss bank into that account without ever having it appear on your computers as a transaction received by this bank. Give it to the I.R.S."

She looked at Jane Whitefield. Her eyes were wet and red and hot. "You think that will do it?"

Jane nodded solemnly.

Gene Hiller took the paper and walked into the computer room. There was a screen with a long list of transactions he was supposed to monitor—money the Federal Reserve was lending the bank overnight, money the bank was moving into accounts all over the world to cover investments it had made during the day, adjustments to the accounts of the various branches, like water being poured from a pitcher to even out the levels of a hundred little cups.

Gene ignored these and went to another terminal, typed in the name of the Swiss bank and waited while their machine signified that it had heard and recognized his machine. Then he told it he had authorization to close a numbered account and transfer the money. He typed in the number and waited. After a moment he said, "You sure this number is right? It doesn't usually take this long."

"It's right," said Mary firmly. "Tell them again."

As he prepared to do it, something happened. Letters and numbers appeared on the screen to fill in blanks. He stared at it for a moment, then looked up at Mary. "Jesus, Mary, two hundred and six million dollars? You stole two hundred and six million?"

Mary almost smiled. "No, Gene. I only stole fifty-two. The rest I inherited. Send it now."

Gene typed in the number of the Internal Revenue Service account and tapped his return key. Before his fingers rebounded from the keyboard, the money was gone. He stared at the screen as though he were having trouble believing what he had seen, and certainly couldn't believe what he had done.

Mary said, "Probably nobody is ever going to ask you about this, but if they do, you don't know a thing. You didn't do it. That's part of the deal I made. There can't be any way in the world for anyone to get a penny of it back." She patted his shoulder. "That means you too, Gene."

"I'm not that stupid," he said. "Anybody who asks the I.R.S. to refund his two hundred and six million dollars is going to get a lot of things, but none of them will be a check."

"Right," said Mary. She leaned down and gave him a peck on the cheek. "Thanks, baby. Now I'll leave you alone for the rest of your life." '

She walked out of the computer room with her head high and her shoulders back. Jane could tell that she was in pain, but she stood erect until Hiller had let them out the fire door and they were around the corner getting into the car. As soon as she sat down the strength seemed to go out of her, and her head rested on the seat.

"Mary?" said Jane. "You okay?"

"It was better than I ever dreamed. All the time I was in that house I was so scared, so hurt, that I thought he had opened an account just to take my money. But you have to open a numbered account in person. How could he do it that fast? He had me, but he had no place to put my money except in the account where he kept all the money he had stolen for years. I got to take every penny he had and pour it all into a sewer."

28

Jane drove fast across the flat plains of northern Texas. The night was just beginning, and she knew that she would need to use this time well. The trip from California to the Texas bank had taken them all day.

She tried to imagine what Barraclough was doing now. She was convinced that Mary knew enough about money to be reliable in her guess that Barraclough had driven to a bank in San Francisco that morning. He and Farrell could not have returned before about noon to find Mary gone and his two trainees dead.

He would have found Farrell's white station wagon by one o'clock and figured out that Jane and Mary had gotten into another car. Then he and Farrell would have spent more time disposing of the two bodies, cleaning the farmhouse of evidence that a woman had been held there, and removing any objects or prints that connected him with the property. That still left him with a van and two cars, with only Farrell to help him drive. He needed at least one person, perhaps two more people, he could trust to drive the vehicles back to Los Angeles. The most likely candidates would have to come all the way up from Enterprise Development in L.A.

She guessed that Barraclough would have been finished with all of this by nine or ten in the evening, about five hours after the time when all of his stolen money had disappeared. She said, "Is there some way Barraclough would know his account in Switzerland was gutted?"

Mary didn't answer. Jane glanced over her shoulder and saw that she was curled up like a child, asleep on the back seat. The question would have to wait. Probably the bank would send him some kind of written closing statement.

Jane couldn't risk going back to the airport and flying Mary out of Dallas tonight. If Barraclough had the presence of mind to ask for confirmation that the gigantic deposit he had made was credited to his account, he would be told that his account was closed. Even if the Swiss bank didn't know that the transfer to the Internal Revenue Service had been initiated in Dallas, there would probably be a way to find out. She had to assume Barraclough would have people searching Dallas before the sun came up.

She looked at Mary again, then returned her eyes to the road. She had been holding down the feelings for days, but now she let them surface. What she had done was unforgivable. She had used this woman for bait and let the beast have her. All she could do now was try to preserve what was left. Whatever had been holding Mary together—the delay of physical sensation that came from shock, or maybe merely the energy of sheer hatred—had apparently drained out of her now. Before she had fallen asleep she had been weak and vague enough to make traveling a risk. Jane would have to get her indoors before morning. She used the last eight hours of darkness to run north out of Texas and up the short side of Oklahoma.

It was still dark when Jane bumped up off the road

onto the smooth asphalt surface of a gas station and turned off the car's engine. She heard Mary sit up in the back seat, so she turned around to watch her squinting and blinking at the lighted island, then reach up to run her fingers through her hair. Jane watched her slowly begin to remember. She was suddenly agitated. "Where are we? Why are we stopping?"

Jane chose to answer the first question. "Miami, Oklahoma."

"Where are we going?"

Jane was glad to hear the annoyance in Mary's voice. It was a vital sign, like a pulse or a heartbeat. "This is it for now. It's safe here."

At a little past nine A.M. they walked into the gift shop in the Inter-Tribal Council Building. The young woman who was cleaning the display case turned and smiled, then went back to her work. Jane waited until the woman sensed that she wanted to talk. She looked up from her work, let her eyes rest on Jane for a second, then said, "I'll bet you're here visiting relatives."

Mary smiled involuntarily.

"Yes," said Jane. She saw Mary's face turn to hers in surprise. "I was hoping to catch Martha McCutcheon here."

"Oh, Seneca," said the woman.

"That's right," said Jane. She held out her hand. "Jane Whitefield."

The woman took it and smiled. "Rowena Cloud. Ottawa."

"I'm very pleased to meet you," said Jane. "Is Martha in the back?"

"Martha hasn't been well this week," said Rowena Cloud. "She has arthritis bad in the winter, and it's been bitter cold for a couple of days, so she might be in bed. She didn't mention anything about going anyplace. If she's not home, though, come on back. You can stay at our house. I can give you directions, and the key is over the door."

"Well, thank you," said Jane warmly. "We'll go see if she's up to visitors."

As they walked down the street, Mary asked softly, "Are you really an Indian, or is that some kind of assumed identity too?"

Jane looked at her, amused. "Think I could fool her?" She opened the car door and waited while Mary eased into the seat, then started the car and pulled out onto the road.

"How did she know? You have blue eyes."

"This is Indian country. She's seen about every kind of Indian there is, so she's an expert. There are reservations all around us."

"Seneca?"

"Some. The Iroquois all lived in New York State in the beginning. But there were some Seneca and Cayuga families who used to go into Ohio every fall to hunt. After the Revolutionary War they didn't see any point in going home. They were on reservations at Lewistown and Sandusky until they got pushed out in 1831 and sent to Oklahoma."

"But this isn't your hometown?"

Jane shook her head. "Not me. My family stayed in New York." She watched Mary closely. "Look, Mary. There are going to be a few things you see and hear that won't make sense to you. Like that girl back there saying we could stay with her, when she had never laid eyes on us before."

"It did seem a little odd," said Mary.

"Smile a lot and ignore anything that seems unfamiliar. I didn't want to bring you here, but we've run about as far as we can for now. Barraclough already knows I killed his men, and pretty soon he'll know you took all his money and gave it to the government. He's going to be searching, and this time he won't let anything distract him. He wants us dead."

"I know that," said Mary.

"A few of the people here know me. Most of them don't. A few are—in the way that we figure these things, not the way you're used to—relatives. We need to get you to a doctor, and we need a place to rest. This is it."

They left the car parked on the road and walked along a path to the trailer park. It took Jane a few minutes of searching before she found the mobile home she remembered on the very edge of the lot. There was a small stenciled sign on the door that said "MCCUTCHEON." She knocked quietly and listened.

The door of the mobile home opened and an old woman in a cardigan sweater and a flowered dress stood in the doorway three steps above them. Her long straight hair was thick and gray, tied back in a tight ponytail as though it belonged to a much younger woman, but her mouth was toothless and her jaws were clamped together so her chin nearly touched her nose. She said simply, "Hello."

Jane spoke to her in Seneca. "My name is Jane Whitefield, Grandmother. Do you remember me?"

The old woman squinted, smiled happily, then said in English, "Just a minute." She went away and came back with her false teeth in. "I remember you, Granddaughter," she said in Seneca. "I'm glad to see you again."

Jane said in English, "This is a friend of mine, Mary Perkins."

The old woman scrutinized Mary in mock disapproval. "Not another anthropologist."

"No," said Jane. "She's only a safecracker."

Martha laughed happily. "Dah-joh." She repeated it in English, stepping back to make way. "Come in. I'm having trouble with the lock on this door. Maybe you're the one to fix it."

Jane and Mary climbed the wooden steps into the tiny, neat kitchen. Mary could see that the television set was on in the living room, but Martha seemed to notice it at the same time. She reached into her sweater pocket, pulled out the remote control, aimed it carefully, and killed the machine. She said, "Sit down, sit down. I'll get you something."

Mary drew a breath to say "We just ate," but Jane touched her arm and gave her head a single shake.

Corn bread, honey, and strawberry and blueberry preserves appeared so suddenly and with so little preparation that Mary instantly perceived that this was another of the things that she must simply smile at and not question.

Jane and Martha walked out among the dry, frost-flecked flower stalks in the garden and spoke to one another in Seneca. "What happened to her?"

Jane had come here because it was the only place she

could think of in this part of the country where she could trust people absolutely, but when the question came she could not relinquish her old habits. She quickly manufactured a story, but when she looked into the old lady's eyes to begin, they seemed already to have penetrated the lie. Telling it would be a waste of time. "She was kidnapped. She had money that wasn't hers. Some men wanted it. They tortured her. She hasn't said so yet, but they raped her."

"Did the police catch them?"

Jane shook her head. "We couldn't even call the police. She's done too much. She'd end up in jail and the men would find her there and make sure she never got out."

"What's a Nundawaono girl got to do with that kind of business?"

Jane looked into her eyes. "It's what I do. Fugitives come to me and I guide them out of the world."

"Why?"

Jane laughed a sad little chuckle. "Because if I didn't, they would give me bad dreams."

"I'll bet a lot of them do anyway," said Martha. She looked at Jane with her bright old eyes and shook her head. "People like me—the old longhouse people who believe in the visions of Handsome Lake—we're always saying the young have forgotten everything. So the one day I stay home from work my own great-grandmother comes to my door. I should learn to shut up. Now I have to help you take care of her, don't I?"

Jane said, "You're a clan mother. You must have learned enough in all those years to make a decision by yourself."

"Has she been to a doctor?"

"Not yet. I'm going to call a doctor friend of mine and

have him use his connections to get us one who won't call the police when she walks in."

"I know one who will see her today. Leave her to me," said Martha.

A few days later, Mary opened the trailer door and walked outside to find Martha standing alone in the weeds. The old woman was already looking at her, as though she had been watching the door and waiting for it to open. "Come on," she said, and began to walk.

Mary Perkins caught up with her. "Where are we going?"

"No place. I've been walking like this for seventy-five years, and if I stop doing it, I'll stiffen up and die."

They walked along in silence for a time. Every few minutes Mary found that her steps had started to move toward the highway without her thinking about it, and she had to correct her course. Martha showed no interest in the road. She kept walking straight through the weeds. After a time Mary noticed that Martha's dress was hemmed precisely a half inch above the weeds so that it didn't get caught in brambles or pick up seeds. "How about you?" the old woman asked. "Have you decided yet?"

"Decided what?"

"To die."

Mary walked a long time. "I don't know. Sometimes I think it's already happened and I missed it. I don't know exactly when. I was beyond noticing things by the time Jane came. After that I concentrated on staying upright long enough to do something I had promised myself to do. That's over now, but nothing has come to take its place."

Martha walked along in the weeds. The cold made the dry stalks snap as her feet pushed them aside to touch the snow. "Each time I walk through here it's different. In four months this will all be wildflowers. Tiny white ones, lots of blue and gold and pink, all mixed together. There are about four hundred acres here that nobody has farmed since I was a kid, and the flowers grow like crazy."

"I'd like to see that," said Mary.

"Then you're not dead yet."

Mary walked stiffly, not paying much attention to the rattling stalks of the weeds. "Maybe that wasn't me. It's been so long since I used my real name that it doesn't sound like me anymore. Maybe Jane didn't tell you, but that's why this happened."

"Whatever you did, what was done to you wasn't the punishment. It was only something else that happened. Now something else will happen."

"That's my problem. It's not that I don't know what will happen, or that I'm afraid. I can't even think of anything that I would like to happen."

"Maybe you need some help. You could spend the rest of your life going to see psychiatrists."

"I take it you don't approve."

"It's okay with me. Some people like drugs, and I think a lot of them just like getting dressed up and having a place to go where they're expected at a certain time."

"Right now I can't see any difference between that and anything else that people do."

"Maybe Mary Perkins got so torn up that she isn't worth much anymore. Maybe you didn't like her much to begin with. Forgive her, because you know that she's suffered. Love her, because you traveled together and shared secrets. Then end her life and bury her."

"Kill myself?"

"Unless you still want to see the wildflowers."

Mary studied her carefully. "You made that up about the wildflowers, didn't you?"

Martha nodded. "Of course I did. This is all thistle and buffalo grass. I'd like to see some wildflowers, though. Most winters I find that's all that's necessary."

Jane waited until Martha McCutcheon had gone to work at the store, then sat beside Mary on the steps of the trailer.

"I didn't ask you to talk much about what happened because I didn't want to upset you," Jane began. "Now I need to."

Mary's voice was tense, but she said, "Okay."

"They probably asked you a lot of questions—things that didn't seem to make any sense, right?"

"Yes. It was the older one, most of the time. It was like he was trying to see if I was telling the truth. Where did we meet the guy to get a ride in Ann Arbor? What did we eat—"

"Names," Jane interrupted. "Did he ask you about the names we used when we were running?"

"Well, yes." She seemed to sense she had made a terrible mistake. "I told them. I was so scared, so tired—"

"It's okay," Jane said. "It's okay. Just think back. Are there any names you know that you left out?"

"No."

Jane nodded and stood up. "You didn't do anything wrong. I just needed to know."

The "older one" must be Farrell. He had waited until she had reached the lowest point and then asked her all of the questions. The answers would have given Barraclough what he needed now. Barraclough could take something as trivial as the room number of a hotel on a particular date, approach the right clerk in the right way, and get the name Jane had used and her credit card number. If the hotel happened to be one that bought its security from Intercontinental, then they would give it to him without any fuss. Whenever Barraclough wanted to, he could be Intercontinental Security Services.

Jane spent the next few days watching the horizon. The flat, empty fields on all sides should have made her feel safer, but the endless sameness induced a panicky agoraphobia in her. She would sit at Martha McCutcheon's kitchen table for fifteen minutes at a time, staring into the west down the highway, then move to another window to gaze to the south across the winter-bare fields.

On the fourth night she heard a noise and sat up in bed, not waking up, just awake. From the other wall of the trailer Martha McCutcheon whispered, "It's the wind." After a moment she said in Seneca, "Have you thought about what you were going to do if it weren't?"

"Always," Jane whispered. She stood up, put on her coat, and walked outside the trailer into the field and away from the lights of the trailer park. She sat in the weeds in the dark and listened to the wind. It was cold and wild, coming across the plain in sputtering gusts and eddies. She had a scared feeling that it carried something that she couldn't quite hear. It might be something that she would have been able to identify if the air had been calm, and it might be something she should not have been near enough to hear at all, something the wind had brought from far away.

Either way it was the same sound. It was car doors slamming, men's feet trampling the stiff, frozen weeds, the metallic clicks as shotgun slides pumped and pistol magazines locked into place. She looked up into the sky and tried to discern the constellation of the loon that the old runners had used to navigate as they moved along the Waagwenneyu at night, but it was hidden behind trailing clouds.

When she looked back at the little camp, she could see it through Barraclough's eyes. It would not be hard to find the right trailer, with the shiny new car she had rented in Dallas parked beside it. Ordinary .38 ammunition would pierce the trailer wall. A rifle round in a big-game caliber could go through both walls and kill somebody behind the trailer from three hundred yards out. There was nothing in the flat, empty country that was big enough to hide a running woman.

In the morning Jane went with Martha on her walk. After a time, Martha said, "You're leaving today, aren't you?"

"Yes."

"You want something first, don't you?"

"It might not be safe here much longer. I want you to drive up north with her."

"Where?"

"Nundawaonoga." It was the Seneca word for the western half of New York State. It was like saying "Home." Jane added, "No planes, no buses, no credit cards." She held out a thick stack of hundred-dollar bills. "This will pay for a car."

Martha walked along in silence for a time, then took the money and slipped it into the pocket of her jacket.

"There are people up there I haven't seen in ten years. They'll be very glad to see me."

"Thank you, Grandmother."

Martha held Jane in the corner of her eye. "Why aren't you going with us?"

Jane shook her head. "He's not looking for her now. He's looking for me."

29

Farrell paced back and forth in front of the television monitor, the heels of his polished shoes clicking on the old hardwood floor of the Enterprise Development office. "Take another look at her." The picture on the monitor was dim and grainy. The sound had been erased. The woman had been caught in a telephoto lens standing on the edge of a freeway beside Barraclough. Every few seconds a car or truck would flash past in the foreground, shrunk by the lens to look smaller than the people beyond it. The woman was Jane. "Look at the shape of her face, the way she moves. Forget her hair and clothes. She'll change those. Study the things that don't change."

After ten seconds, the picture vanished in a wash of bright, popping static, and then the tape began to rewind. Farrell turned to his audience of young men. They were sitting on desks, leaning against walls, some even crouched on the floor near the screen. Assembled like this, they were an unprepossessing bunch, but he knew something about each of them that made him feel confident. During his years as a cop, Farrell had become very good at spotting a certain kind of young man early. "This is the only picture we have of her at the moment, but when we find something

365

that's a little clearer, we'll try to work up some still shots for you. Let's run the tape again."

As Farrell reached for the PLAY button he could hear the heavy footsteps on the stairs. He straightened as the door swung open and Barraclough walked in. Few of Farrell's trainees had ever seen Barraclough before, but they had just watched the tape, so none of them wondered who he was. Barraclough's empty gray eyes swept the crowd of young men. When a few of the trainees fidgeted involuntarily to correct their posture, the motion seemed to attract Barraclough's gaze to them. He stared, made some secret assessment, and moved on.

The tailored navy blue blazer and gray pants Barraclough wore had the simplicity and precise lines of a uniform. He turned away from the young men, slipped off the coat and tossed it onto Farrell's desk as a simple gesture to make it clear that this place was his, and turned back to them in his starched, Marine-creased white shirt. Strapped under his left arm was a Browning nine-millimeter automatic in a worn shoulder holster, carried muzzle-upward so it could be drawn with little movement. Attached to the strap under the left arm was an extra ammunition clip. The young men could see that this was not the gleaming, compact sidearm of a successful security executive. It was the weapon of a man who had been in gunfights with people who were now dead.

Barraclough judged that his silence had served its purpose. "Mr. Farrell has probably told you a little about me, but we should know each other better. Let me begin by telling you what I'm not. I'm not your friend."

A few eyes that had been hovering in his general direction shot to his face but found no comfort or reassurance there. "If you bring me what I want, I will give you what you want. Simple as that. Mr. Farrell is not your Boy Scout leader. I haven't been spending money on training to make men out of you, as though I gave a shit if you lived or died. I don't. I'm giving you the knowledge and experience to be useful to me. If you want to make something out of yourself, keep your eyes and ears open and you probably can."

A few of the young men seemed to mine some hint of hope from the notion that they could make something of themselves. He appeared to want to oblige them. "I'll even tell you how the business works. If you win, you get to have the prizes—the girls, the big house, the cars, people calling you 'sir' for the rest of your life. If you lose, you're dead. You may still walk around for a while before one of the winners happens to notice you, but that's just a technicality. Whatever you have is his. You're a failure, a victim, a corpse."

Barraclough looked at them with his empty, unreadable eyes for a moment, then spoke again. "I know at least some of you must have noticed that a couple of guys didn't come back after this last trip. I'm here to tell you what happened to them. They're dead. Mr. Farrell and I left them to guard an unarmed, incapacitated prisoner, and they let the woman you saw on the tape sneak in and poison their breakfast." He shook his head in amazement and chuckled. "If she hadn't used enough poison, I would have had to kill them myself."

A few of the trainees exchanged nervous grins, but Barraclough's smile dissolved. "That's the other part of our deal: I will always tell you the truth. If you're stupid, you're a liability. You won't just hurt yourself, you'll hurt me. I am not going to let that happen. Not for them, not for you."

He glanced at Farrell, who was standing near the door. "Mr. Farrell is going to give you specific assignments over the next day or two. But here's the short version. That woman is all I want right now. When I get her, I want her breathing." He nodded to Farrell, picked up his coat, and slipped it on as he walked out the door.

Barraclough went down the back stairs and across the parking lot to the next street, where he had left his car, and began the long drive to the Intercontinental Security building in Irvine. He could not keep his mind off that Jane woman. He wanted to tear her head off with his hands. She had blundered into his way when he was at the edge of a triumph, and the collision had obliterated years of small, painfully won successes: years on the police force, always working harder than the others, taking more risks, gradually building a reputation; more years at Intercontinental Security, always working tirelessly, always looking for a way up.

After he had come to Intercontinental, Barraclough had focused his attention on each of the divisions in turn: Home Security, Retail Security, Detectives. Slowly he had brought each of them up to modern standards, and the management team in Chicago had responded by making him Director of Western Regional Operations. But Barraclough had not been working for a promotion. He had always lived by his ability to see farther down the path than anyone else, and he had already moved ahead of Intercontinental's management. All of his efforts to revitalize the old security company were mere sideshows—preparations for what was to happen in the little Van Nuys office of the separate corporation he had formed called Enterprise Development.

Barraclough had designed Enterprise Development to

fit inside the skin of Intercontinental Security. Its costs were hidden within the giant company's overhead, its personnel culled from Intercontinental's applicant pool. When Enterprise Development conducted its business, a pretext was constructed so that the employees and equipment of Intercontinental's offices in twenty-six cities could be set to work identifying fingerprints, searching for cars, analyzing traces, performing surveillance.

Enterprise Development had been invented to specialize in exploiting a small and neglected group of criminals: the successful ones who had gotten away with large amounts of money. Some were already wanted by the authorities in the United States or elsewhere but were not actively hunted; others had not yet been discovered or were merely suspected. Some had been convicted and served sentences but had not made restitution. Barraclough used Enterprise Development to identify them, hunt them down, and turn them into cash.

In his first seven years of hunting, Barraclough had recovered over seventy-five million dollars. This had not been nearly enough, because the purpose of Enterprise Development was not merely to make its owner rich; it was a device for accumulating enough capital to buy control of Intercontinental Security.

Barraclough had made the next eighty million on only one find, the Timothy Phillips trust fund. Seven years ago he had decided that Intercontinental Security should obtain the Hoffen-Bayne account so that Enterprise Development could have a look at what was going on inside. He had not known about Timothy Phillips; he had simply realized that a company handling the personal fortunes of so many people was a good place to hunt. He had offered Intercontinental's services for a price that competitors could never match because the bid left no margin for a profit.

When he had placed security devices in the Hoffen-Bayne offices and the partners' homes, the customers had been interested in color and design, but circuitry had been beneath their notice. It had never occurred to people like Alan Turner that a little electronic box with glowing lights might be just about anything. It had never even crossed Turner's mind that if his security system had a little microphone he could talk into during an emergency, the microphone could also pick up what he said when there was no emergency. He had sat all day under security cameras and thought he was alone.

Once Barraclough had discovered the account Turner was stealing from, the money belonged to Barraclough. The man had been robbing clients for years, and all of the people who took salaries for catching thieves had missed him. Turner had been there for anyone to take, but only Barraclough had found him.

Barraclough had worked Mary Perkins with the same patience. Anybody could have read about her trial in the newspapers, as he had, but he had waited until the feds had taken their crack at her, and then he had taken his. The feds had come up empty, and Barraclough had walked away with fifty-two million.

His rage deepened. To have a woman like this Jane take it all away from him was more than an insult; it was a violation of the laws of the universe.

At ten o'clock in the evening, Farrell made his way across the polished marble lobby of the Intercontinental Security Services building, thinking about fate. Ten years ago, when he had been a cop for almost ten years and a detective for two, the captain had suddenly assigned him a new partner, a kid named Barraclough. After Farrell had watched him work for a few days, he had seen the future.

If Farrell kept on the way he was going, the best he could hope for was twenty years with the police department and a pension that wouldn't be enough to convince him that his life had been worth the effort. But ten years ago it was already apparent that Barraclough wasn't going to end up like that, and if Farrell stuck with him, he wasn't either. At thirty, Barraclough was entering his prime, and what he represented was a world that had no limits.

But tonight, as Farrell walked toward the elevator that would take him up to Barraclough's office, he was a little nervous. He had not been able to think of a way that this Jane woman could have found Mary Perkins except by following him to the farm. If he had figured this out, then Barraclough had too. No, he thought. He was not a little nervous. He knew Barraclough better than anyone alive, and he was deeply, agonizingly afraid. When he raised his hand to the elevator button, he saw it start to shake.

Farrell wasn't even sure what made him most afraid. A bullet in the back of the head had its attractions. It was quicker and kinder than most of the ways that lives ended. Slowly he identified what he feared most. He feared Barraclough's displeasure: not the bullet, but Barraclough's impulse to fire it, whether or not the trigger got pulled. This one lapse might have convinced Barraclough that Farrell wasn't like Barraclough—that he was just one of the others, a loser. After all these years, first teaching Barraclough and then following him, Farrell would be lost, abandoned and exiled from the light. He would be denied a share in Barraclough's future.

He stepped out of the elevator, walked to the big wooden door of Barraclough's office, and knocked quietly. No, that had been too quiet. Barraclough might think he was weak and used up, maybe even afraid. Fear disgusted Barraclough. Farrell gave a hard rap with his knuckles, then heard Barraclough call "Come in."

Farrell found him sitting behind the big desk. He only looked up long enough to verify who had come in the door, then went back to signing papers. He muttered, "The fucking home office is waiting on these reports. That's what they do. They sit in that building in Chicago and read quarterly reports. Talk to me."

"The lines are all in the water," said Farrell. "I finally got the last of the boys on their planes. With the ones we had out already, we should have two-man teams in fifty-six airports by morning."

"Are you sure they'll recognize her if they see her?"

"The ones who have seen her in person will. The tape from the freeway should help the others, but it's mostly on you." Farrell felt a chill. He had given in to some subconscious need to remind Barraclough that Farrell was not the only one who made mistakes. He tried to talk quickly, to get past it before the sour taste of it turned Barraclough against him. "But I've got people working on finding a decent picture of her from surveillance footage in the places we know she's been—stores, hotels, and so on."

Barraclough kept signing papers, then moving each one to a pile at the corner of his desk. He seemed to be listening, so Farrell went on. "I've got a couple of technicians traveling around with the teams trying to find her fingerprints where she touched something that might not have gotten wiped off: hotel bathrooms get scoured with cleanser, but prints might survive on a telephone receiver or on anything that was inside a drawer. Rental cars sometimes sit on the lot for a few days before they go out again. Fingerprints are still the best way to find out who you're really dealing with."

Barraclough frowned as he scrutinized a sheet that appeared to be covered with numbers, then wrote something on it and set it beside the pile of papers. He looked up, so Farrell said, "The credit checks on her fake credit cards come in once a day. So far she hasn't used any of them. I figure she's gone under somewhere to wait until Mary Perkins is healthy enough to travel again."

Barraclough looked down at his papers again. Something he was reading caused a look of weariness and impatience. "Is that it?"

Farrell said, "Just about. Of course I'm trying a couple of long shots. We know she met Mary Perkins in the L.A. County Jail. I hired a hooker to get herself inside and ask questions of the other prisoners, to get us a lead on where she lives."

"You said a couple. What else?"

Farrell gave an apologetic shrug. "Do you remember that guy who kept calling up bank tellers and saying he had their kid, so they'd leave money in a bag somewhere?"

"Sure," said Barraclough. "Ronny Prindle. That must be nine or ten years ago. What about him?"

"Well, there was something I tried that time that didn't pan out. I took one of the telephone tapes to a linguistics professor and asked him for an opinion of the accent. We caught Ronny Prindle before the report came back, but I remembered being surprised when I read it because the professor got it right. Prindle was from the east coast of

Maryland. So I cleaned up the tape we had from Jane and sent it to the same guy. He thinks I'm still a cop."

Barraclough smiled at the paper he was signing, and Farrell thought he heard a chuckle. "Every time I can't imagine why I'm dragging your dead ass around with me, you surprise me, and I remember. Let me know as soon as you hear from him."

Farrell's hands stopped shaking. He had bought himself more time.

Two days later Farrell hurried across the same lobby, pushed the elevator button, and walked into the same office. Barraclough looked up at him expectantly.

"She's started using the credit cards," Farrell said. "We got a Katherine Webster at a hotel in Saint Louis, a Denise Hollinger renting a car in Cleveland, a Catherine Snowdon in Erie, Pennsylvania—"

"She's heading northeast," said Barraclough. "Start moving people into her path."

Farrell's eyes twinkled. "It's done. Everybody we've got is either up there already or on a plane to northern Pennsylvania or upstate New York. I've got some strung out in rest stops along the big highways, some checking the parking lots of hotels, restaurants, and malls for the car she rented, others waiting at rental offices for her to turn it in. I've got some more—"

Barraclough interrupted. "Can you tell from the reports what she's doing?"

Farrell scanned the credit reports in his hands. "Pretty much what Mary Perkins told us she does. She alternates identities, so the same person never turns up two places in a row. She's paying the single-room rate, and the meal charges don't seem to be enough for two, so she's probably traveling alone."

"But what's she trying to accomplish?" Barraclough snapped. "Where's she going?"

Farrell smiled. "Well, let me tell you what the professor says." He moved another sheet of paper to the top and stared at it. "She's got a little peculiarity. Her lips don't quite touch when she says *m*, *b*, or *p*. He thinks that means she grew up speaking two languages, but it's not enough to tell him what the other one is." He moved his finger down the paper. "Oh, here's the part I was looking for. Her accent has what he calls an 'intrusive schwa.' It's a marker that places her in a narrow linguistic belt that stretches from Chicago east as far as Syracuse, New York." He shrugged. "If I had to make a bet, I'd say she's had enough and is going home."

It was only twenty hours later that Farrell returned to Barraclough's office, looking exuberant. "She's been spotted."

"Where?"

"She turned in the rented car at the Buffalo airport, went to the long-term lot, got into a parked car, and drove off. We had two guys there."

Barraclough glowered, his eyes narrowing. "They let her get away?"

"No," Farrell answered quickly. "They followed her to a house in a little town on the Niagara River between Buffalo and Niagara Falls."

"And?" Barraclough asked impatiently.

"She put the car in the garage and opened the door with a key," said Farrell. "It must be her house."

30

Barraclough and Farrell arrived in the Buffalo airport after midnight in the beginning of a snowstorm. The Nissan Pathfinder four-wheel-drive vehicle with tinted windows that Barraclough had specified was waiting at the curb with one of Farrell's trainees behind the wheel, but Barraclough stepped into the street to the driver's side and said, "Get in the back."

Barraclough drove the Pathfinder out to the slush-covered gray street and watched the wiper sweep across the windshield to compress the snowflakes into a thin, ruler-straight bar, then slide back for more while the defroster melted the bar away.

Farrell inspected and loaded the two pistols his trainee had brought for them, attached the laser sights, and tested the night-vision spotter scope he had brought with him from California. "Where is she?"

"You get on the Thruway up here and take it west. Get off at the Delaware exit and head north."

Farrell glanced at Barraclough to be sure he had heard, then back at his trainee. "What's the place like?"

"It's a two-story house. We didn't see any sign of anybody else. She went to bed just before I left for the airport."

"You mean her lights went out," Farrell corrected. "Who's watching the house?"

"Mike. Mike Harris."

"From where?"

"He's in a black Dodge. He's parked down the street, facing away, where he can see in the mirror the front door and the door that goes to the driveway."

Farrell felt a slight, pleasurable warmth in his chest. The boys weren't much to begin with—just oversized balls and a mean streak—but by the time he was through with them they knew how the game was played.

When they arrived at the street, Barraclough stopped the Pathfinder a distance from the Dodge. Farrell took out the radios and handed one to the trainee. "You remember how to use one of these, right?"

"Press the button to talk, keep the volume low when anybody might hear it."

"Good," said Farrell. "We're Unit One, you're Unit Two. Anybody picks up the signal, he thinks we're cops. No chitchat over the air."

Barraclough picked up the night scope and turned it on, then swept it slowly up and down the street. Houses, trees, shrubs seemed to burn with a bright green phosphorescence, but there were no signs of movement. He aimed it through the rear window of the Pathfinder. "Is that the house back there on the left?"

"Yeah."

"You been around the other side to check for other exits?"

"Sure."

"Did you check the houses around it?"

"Yeah. Couples with kids on one side and the back, an

old guy on the other. Curtains were open long enough so we saw people watching TV."

"Okay. Here's how it's going to be," said Barraclough. "Give Mike one of the radios and tell him to sit tight and watch. Then come back here and get ready to drive this vehicle. Farrell and I are going in. When we come out with her, pull up to the curb quick and pick us up. I want the burlap sack lying where I can reach it so we can get it over her head as soon as she's in the back."

The young man grunted his assent, then took the radio over to the black Dodge and got inside to talk to his partner.

Suddenly Barraclough hissed, "A light just went on. . . . She's coming out."

Farrell ducked his head below the window and spoke into his radio. "Heads down! She's out of the house."

Thirty seconds later Farrell heard a car door slam, an engine start, and the sound of tires on the wet pavement. He saw the red glow of taillights reflected on the dashboard. After a moment the glow receded.

Barraclough started the Pathfinder and pulled out into the street. Farrell said into the radio, "Change of plan. Unit Two, we're following. Stay behind us for now."

Barraclough swung the Pathfinder around the block and stopped with his lights off on the next street until he saw Jane's car pass under the street lamps of the intersection. The color was gray. It was an old Chevy—maybe a Caprice or Impala. "She's going too slow to be running." He waited another few seconds, glanced in the mirror to verify that Farrell's trainees had followed, and then started up after her.

"I'd sure like to know where she's going at this time of night," said Farrell. "She may have spotted the Dodge and decided to see if they'd follow her."

"I don't think so," said Barraclough. "If she had, she would have tried something like that while Mike was alone. If she saw him and us too, she'd have gone out the back window."

"Then what do you think she's doing?"

Barraclough shrugged. "She's been living like a scared rabbit for years. When she moves, it's nearly always at night. If I had to guess, I'd say she got a phone call."

"Mary Perkins?"

"Could be," said Barraclough. "But she might even be meeting new clients by now."

The gray car drove a few blocks, then turned left at the Niagara River. Barraclough waited for a long time before he turned after her. He had to be careful not to get stuck behind her at a traffic signal, where she would be able to get a good look through the rearview mirror.

When he could see her taillights far enough ahead, he gauged her speed and matched it. "She doesn't drive as though she's seen us. We'll wait until she gets to a dark, deserted stretch before we try to take her."

The road wound a bit to stay beside the big, dark river, then straightened and opened up into four lanes. Farrell unfolded the road map on his lap and checked it against street signs. After a few minutes he called the other vehicle on the radio. "Pull ahead of us now, Unit Two. We're going to fade into the background for a while. Give her lots of space and don't spook her."

The black Dodge followed Jane through little towns along the river, past a cluster of oil refineries, then onto the Thruway just before the Buffalo city line. Farrell studied the map, and as they approached each landmark, he would announce it. "There's a big park up ahead. Riverside Park. If she takes the exit, we might be able to pull her over there." She didn't. "Up ahead is the Peace Bridge over to Canada. That could be where she's heading." But it wasn't. The dark water beside them widened into Lake Erie.

Jane turned off the Thruway at Route 5 where it became Fuhrmann Boulevard and hugged the shoreline into the city of Lackawanna. Ahead of Farrell and Barraclough on their right loomed an enormous complex of old brick factory buildings behind a high chain-link fence. "What's that?" asked Barraclough.

"The map calls it the Gateway Metroport Industrial Center. It used to be one of the biggest steel mills in the world. I was here a couple of times in the early sixties, before it closed down. You couldn't breathe unless there was a strong west wind. It goes on like this for four or five miles." He stared through the high fence. "Looks like they're renting a couple of nooks and crannies of it to a few half-assed businesses now."

The radio crackled. "Unit One, this is Unit Two."

"Go ahead."

"We can't see her anymore."

Barraclough's head snapped to the right to stare at Farrell in intense concentration. "She must have made them."

Farrell spoke into the radio. "Is there any chance she just outran you?"

"No. We think she must have turned off on one of those little streets on the left."

"Then turn down the next one and circle—"

Barraclough snatched the radio out of Farrell's hand. "Negative. Cancel that. She didn't turn left, she turned right, or we would have seen her go across three lanes ourselves. Go back to where you saw her and look for railroad tracks."

Farrell held on as Barraclough swung the Pathfinder around on the icy street. What had Barraclough seen? They had been bumping over old railroad tracks for a long time. "You're thinking there's a way into the factory? But all the tracks lead smack into the fence."

"There has to be a line that goes in," said Barraclough. "They might have closed down the spurs that went to different parts of the plant, but to ship coal and ore in and steel out, there must be a regular railroad right-of-way. That doesn't go away just because something beside it stops making money. And they don't put a gate across it."

More than a mile back, Barraclough found the tracks. There was a functional-looking railroad-crossing light at a little rise just beyond a curve in the road. The big brick buildings on both sides of the boulevard would have obscured the view of her car just long enough for her to turn off her lights and coast up the tracks.

Barraclough turned the utility vehicle onto the railroad ties to straddle the tracks and slowly bumped along them. The tracks went only fifty yards into the dark shadow of the mill before they passed through a gap in the fence. "Here it is," said Barraclough. "She lives around here, remember? She's probably driven by here in daylight a hundred times." He wrenched the steering wheel to lurch off the tracks into the freight yard of the factory and waited until the black Dodge caught up.

Barraclough had already found her trail. The snow was clear and unmarked except for two deep parallel lines from a set of tires that ran deeper into the old steel mill. Barraclough trained his headlights on the tire tracks and sped up. He drove past a few small buildings in the complex that had new signs and recent paint on the doors, but as he went farther, immense brick buildings with dark windows loomed on both sides like the ruins of an abandoned city. He judged he had driven nearly a mile before he saw her car.

It was parked in the shadows on the lake side of a brick building, away from the distant lights of Fuhrmann Boulevard. Barraclough pulled to a stop when he was still a hundred feet away from it and let the Dodge pull up beside him. He said into the radio, "Watch the car and the doors of the building. We'll call when we need you." He handed the radio to Farrell and accepted the gear Farrell handed back: pistol, night-spotting scope, flashlight, nylon wrist restraints.

The two men stepped down from the Pathfinder and walked to Jane's car. Barraclough took off his glove to gauge the warmth of the hood of the car, then winked at Farrell happily. Then he studied the footprints leading from the driver's door. They led around the big building. Barraclough paused at the corner to draw his pistol, then quickly stepped beyond it.

He could see that the footprints led along the side of the building. He bent low to walk beside them, staying near the wall and keeping his head below the level of the windows. There were banks of thousands of little panes of glass along the side of the building, many of them broken and all of them opaque from at least thirty years of grime. The footprints led to a place where two of the panes had been hammered in and the frame had gone with them. "She must have heard us coming and gone in."

Barraclough looked ahead of him, but he could not see where the building ended. He stepped outward away from it to get a better view, then lifted the night scope to his eye, but he still could not see the end. The brick wall seemed to go on forever.

Farrell saw it too. "It's a big place. How do you want to work it?"

Barraclough peered cautiously through the broken window with the night scope, then pushed the switch to infrared. There was nothing nearby that gave off body heat. "We'll have to go in after her ourselves. We can't leave the cars unguarded, and if she can lose those two on an empty road, there's no telling what she'd do to them inside the dark building." He slipped the flashlight into one pocket, the wrist restraints into the other where he could reach them quickly. "When you see her, train your laser sight on her right away. She's not stupid; if she sees that bright red dot settle on her chest she'll forget about trying to outrun the bullet." He hoisted himself to the row of bricks that formed a sill below the missing windows, then squeezed himself inside.

When Farrell joined him inside the building, Barraclough drew his pistol again and turned on his night scope. They were in a huge, empty, unheated brick enclosure with a bare concrete floor, a fifty-foot ceiling, and a slight glow of stars above where panes of glass were missing. Barraclough turned his scope to the floor where Jane had entered. A few wet, snowy partial footprints led toward the other end of the cavernous room.

Barraclough walked beside the footprints, under an arch that was big enough for a truck to pass through, and beyond it into another high, empty room. To the right were a set of barn doors that must once have opened onto a loading dock.

They stalked through room after room. At each doorway they would pause, slip through the entrance low, and crouch a few yards apart around the corner. Barraclough would flick on his night scope, rapidly scan the space ahead for the shape of a woman, and only then venture to cross the open concrete floor. When they reached the end of the long building, they found a door open with snow just beginning to drift inside.

The footprints led to the door of another building. There was a half-rotted sheet of plywood on the ground that had once covered the empty upper panel of the door. Barraclough's heart was beating with excitement. They always made some mistake, and she had just made hers. She had gambled that she could drive into the enormous ruin of a factory, wait ten minutes, and then drive back up the river. Now she was alone on foot on a cold, snowy night. She was trying to hide in a complex that had been so thoroughly gutted that there wasn't anything to hide behind. She was running from two old cops who had been trapping fleeing suspects in dark buildings for half their lives. He would be able to see her in the scope as clearly as if she were in daylight, and she would be blind. Even the physical discomfort Barraclough felt as he entered the next building made him more eager. The air was frigid. The brick walls offered shelter from the bitter wind, but there was a chill trapped in the big spaces, and the icy concrete seemed to send a shock up his shins at each step. The cold would be much harder on her because she was alone and afraid. At some point she was going to come to a door she couldn't open, and he would have her. It was possible he would have to keep her alive for a month or two while she gave him what she owed him. She was a hunter's dream: a

woman who had made at least ten years of fugitives van-
ish. There must be dozens by now, most of them still hiding wherever she had put them. And what kind of person
had enough money to pay for that kind of service? Drug
dealers, money launderers, second-toughest gangsters,
big-time embezzlers. She had taken Mary Perkins away
from him, but she might easily have ten more like her. He
grinned as he walked through the darkened building; no
doubt about it, she was the girl of his dreams.

Farrell stopped at the next doorway and turned to him,
but didn't say anything.

"What is it?" Barraclough whispered eagerly. "Did
you hear something?"

"No," Farrell whispered apologetically. "But we've
been at this for over an hour."

Barraclough glanced at his watch. It was true.

Farrell said, "I think it might help if we brought the
two boys into this. We might want to have at least one of
them waiting for her at the other end."

Barraclough clenched his teeth to stifle his annoyance.
He didn't want to wait for people to move into position—
he wanted to finish this himself now—but Farrell was
right. She had already led them too far to have any hope
of getting back to her car. She was heading for the far
end of the factory. "Give me the radio."

He took the radio and pressed the TALK button. "Unit
Two, this is Unit One." He listened to the faint crackle of
static. He put the speaker against his ear but could detect
no voice. "Come in, Unit Two." He looked at Farrell, letting a little of his impatience show.

Farrell said quickly, "It's got to be the buildings.

There's a hell of a lot of brick and steel between them and us. Let me try it outside."

Farrell trotted to the next loading dock, slipped the bolt, and pushed the big wooden door aside so he could stand out in the open air. "Unit Two, this is Unit One. Come in." He listened to the static. "Unit Two, come in." In spite of the temperature, he felt a wave of heat begin at the back of his neck and wash down his spine. He knew his two trainees were probably in the car listening to a radio they had turned off by mistake. He walked back into the building and shook his head. "Nothing."

Barraclough's voice was quiet and cold. "Go back for them. I'll be up ahead somewhere."

Farrell handed Barraclough the radio, then set off to retrace his steps through the factory. After four steps, he broke into a run.

As he heard Farrell's steps receding behind him, Barraclough started into the next big room and turned on his night-vision scope. This building was different from the last. The big row of square enclosures built into the side wall must have been furnaces. The cement of the floor had holes at the edges of big rectangles where heavy machines had once been anchored, and overhead were networks of steel beams that must have held chain hoists, and brackets for vanished devices he could only imagine now. This place must have seemed like hell once, he thought—deafening noise, unbearable heat from the open-hearth furnaces, molten slag running into big buckets. He stepped close to the row of furnaces and shone his flashlight into each one as he passed it. He moved through room after room, seeing few relics, only traces that were less comprehensible than the stones of some ancient city dug out of the ground.

After half an hour the radio in Barraclough's coat pocket squawked and startled him. Farrell's voice said, "Unit One, this is Unit Two."

Barraclough crouched against the wall so the noise would not make him vulnerable and kept his eyes ahead of him on the portal to the next room. He pushed the button and said quietly, "Go ahead."

"I'm at the car," said Farrell. "The reason they didn't answer is that they're dead."

"How?"

"It looks like they left the motor running to keep warm. There's a hose running from their own exhaust pipe right back into the cab through the taillight. Looks like she cut the hose from under the Pathfinder."

Barraclough tried to sort out the implications. "Are all the cars still there? Hers too?"

"Yeah," said Farrell. "I don't know how she got all the way back here past us, but—"

Barraclough gripped the TALK button and shouted, "Then get out! She's still there!"

But Farrell had not released his button. Barraclough heard a swish of fabric as though Farrell were making a sudden movement, maybe whirling to see something. Whatever he saw made him voice an involuntary "Uh!"

Barraclough heard the report of the weapon over the radio. He had time to press his transmitter button and say "Farrell?" before the delayed reverberation reached his ears through the air. The sound was fainter this time, but without the speaker distortion he could tell it was the elongated blast of a shotgun.

Barraclough had already begun to put the radio into his pocket before he remembered there was nobody left to talk to. He hurled it into the darkness toward the corner of the big empty room. He was standing in a dark, icy labyrinth three thousand miles from home. The three men he had brought here with him were corpses. But the biggest change was what was standing between him and the cars. He didn't even know her real name, but he had thought he knew what she would do: she would run, and he would catch her.

He flicked on his flashlight and slowly began to walk away from the sound of the shotgun, his mind working feverishly. Where had the shotgun come from? She had not taken a shotgun off the body of either of the dead trainees, so she must have brought it with her. If she had, then she had known he was coming. This was not what he had expected at all.

Maybe she had not made a mistake and turned her car into the first place along the road that was big enough to hide it. It almost seemed as though she had been in this factory before. As Barraclough traced the logic backward, he began to feel more uneasy.

She had been shuffling credit cards and names for ten or twelve years. Why would she suddenly forget how it was done and take the chance of using accounts he might know about all the way to her own doorstep? Because that house in La Salle wasn't her own doorstep. He had not traced her to her hometown and right up to her house. She probably lived a thousand miles from here. He had followed her into an ambush—a killing ground.

Barraclough decided to run. The beam of his flashlight bobbed up and down wildly, making shadows that crouched in his path, then sprung upward to loom fifty feet tall. He had to remind himself over and over that there couldn't be anyone in front of him. What he had to worry about was behind him.

Was running the best thing to do? It was taking him farther away from the cars. But running made use of the only facts he could be sure of. He had heard the shotgun go off within a few feet of Farrell, so he knew where she was . . . no, he knew where she had been for the instant when she had pulled the trigger. His attempt to state it accurately invited doubts to creep into his mind, but he fought them off. She was half a mile behind him, he was sure. She had the shotgun in her hands, and she was walking through the dark line of empty rooms after him.

As he thought about her, a picture formed in his mind, and in the picture she was not walking. She had the shotgun in both hands across her chest, and she was running, taking long, loping strides. He increased his pace. The clapping of his boots echoed in the cavernous spaces and the rasp of his breath grew louder and louder. As he ran, he tried not to think about the shotgun. A double-aught load was twelve pellets, each the size of a .38 round. From across one of these big rooms they would hit in a pattern about twenty inches wide.

Barraclough calmed himself. All he had to do was keep her half a mile behind him and get out of this horrible place. As though a wish had been granted, his flashlight swept up and down the gray wooden surface of a door in the wall ahead of him. He dashed to it and tried the knob, but it spun in his hand without moving the catch. He pulled on it, but the door would not budge. He stepped back and ran his flashlight along the doorjamb. He could see a few puckered places in the wood where big nails had been driven in. He swept the flashlight's beam around him. The windows in this room were all twenty feet above him. When had that changed? Maybe the windows had been that way for the past half hour. He began to run back the way he had come. The windows in the next room were the same, and the room after that. But at the portal between the next two rooms he saw the doors of another loading dock.

Barraclough hurried to the doors, set his spotter scope on the floor, stuck the flashlight in his pocket, slipped the bolt, and tried to slide the door open. He strained against it, but it only wobbled a little on its track. He tried to remember: wasn't this what Farrell had done to open one of these doors? He turned on his flashlight again and ran it around the edges of the door until he spotted another bolt that went into the floor. He lifted it and pushed the door. When it slid open, he tried to feel happy, but the relief only reminded him how frightened he had been only seconds ago.

He stepped out onto the loading dock and jumped down into the snow. He felt a wrenching pain as his ankle turned under him and he fell across something hard and cold. He cursed himself. He had jumped onto railroad tracks. How could he have forgotten the railroad tracks? The loading docks didn't have flat paved surfaces for trucks; they were for loading steel onto freight cars.

Barraclough sat up and tentatively shifted some weight onto his ankle. It hurt, but he could tell it wasn't broken. He was grateful, glad to be alive. He wasn't going to be trapped; he could still make it. He slipped the pistol into his belt and walked to the left, toward the edge of the factory, the tall fence, and the street beyond. Then he saw Jane's car parked near the side of the next building. For an instant he struggled to fathom how he could have come out of the huge building right where he had started, but then understanding settled on him. She had not been running through the building at all. She had driven along the outside to wait for him here.

Barraclough hobbled toward the fence, gasping terror into his chest with each freezing breath. He threw himself against the high fence, clung to the links with both hands, and stepped up. He stretched his arm to clutch higher links, then tried to feel for a footing he could maintain with his injured ankle.

The blast of the shotgun slapped his left arm against the fence and deadened it. He was falling. His back slammed the ground hard and made him gulp air to reinflate his lungs. He tried to push himself up, but his mangled left arm would not respond, and he could see his dark, warm blood soaking into the snow. As he struggled to rise, it occurred to him that he had already heard the *snick-chuff* of the shotgun slide. "Stop!" he screamed. The weak, pleading sound of his own voice sickened him. He bent his legs under him, bobbed up, and turned to see her standing in the snow ten feet from him. She was only a dark, shadowy shape against the luminous snow. He waited for the roar of the shotgun, the splash of bright sparks, but they didn't come.

He gripped his injured arm with his right hand and pulled it painfully toward the center of his body. "Listen to me!" If he could just hide the right hand behind the left to get a grip on the pistol in his belt, he had a chance. "You need a way out of this as much as I do. The minute you helped your first felon to evade prosecution, you were meat on the hoof. Somebody—local cops, F.B.I., it doesn't matter who—was going to notice you and hunt you down." His fingers closed numbly on the pistol.

"Without a powerful friend, you're going to be some-body's dinner." He swung the pistol upward.

The shotgun blast blew through his chest. His body toppled backward to rattle the links of the fence, then lay still. "But not yours," said Jane. She turned and walked back through the snow to her car, put the shotgun in the trunk, and drove along the side of the building toward the gap in the fence.

31

Judge Kramer awoke from his dream. The house was dark, but the moon shone through the big magnolia tree outside his window, so small patches of gray-blue light fell on the bedspread. Something was wrong.

He heard the little voice and remembered that he had heard it in his dream and tried to ignore it. But it was all right. It was just the boy.

He swung his feet to the floor and walked out of the bedroom and down the hall to the guest room. He reminded himself that this was perfectly normal. A child who had seen what this one had was going to have night terrors. Kramer rubbed his eyes and struggled to wake up. He was going to have to be wise and strong and reliable. That was what this child needed right now. Adults came when you cried out in the night, and they told you everything was all right. If it wasn't all right, they damned well made it all right.

He stepped into the boy's room and said, "It's all right. Here I am, Timmy." He had barely uttered it when he realized he was wrong. The bed was empty. He looked around him. The boy was gone.

Kramer ran to the landing in time to see the triangular slice of moonlight appear on the floor of the foyer. The front door had opened. As he hurried down the first few stairs, he saw her step into the moonlight. "It's just me, Judge," said Jane Whitefield.

"What are you doing here?"

"I've come for Timmy."

"No," he said. He was shaking his head, but he knew she could not see it. "There are procedures for this. The law provides for it. You can't just . . ."

He could feel, not see, Jane Whitefield's eyes on him. "What does the law provide?" she asked.

"When it's safe, Children's Services will find him a suitable foster home."

"It's never going to be safe," said Jane. "Even if all the money is gone, there will be people who think more might turn up or who know how to get more just by using his name. Barraclough had a lot of people working on these side cases for him. They're still out there." She took a step with Timmy.

"You should know I have a gun." The judge reached into the pocket of his robe.

"So have I," Jane said. "I didn't bring mine either." She turned, took Timmy's hand, and then the slice of moonlight disappeared.

It was after midnight when Carey McKinnon turned his car onto the long gravel drive that ran up behind his old stone house in Amherst and parked his car in the carriage house that had, at some point in his grandfather's time, started being called "the garage." He swung the two doors closed and put the padlock on the hasp, not because any-one had ever tried to steal anything here but because the wind was cold tonight and by morning it would be strong enough to blow the old doors off their hinges if he didn't secure them. He had heard on the car radio that there was going to be another in the series of heavy snowstorms that had blown in, one after another, from the west, and he could already feel the cold front moving in.

Carey walked up the drive toward his house, looking down at his feet and trying to step in the spots where the snow had not drifted. He reached his front steps and stood under the eaves, stamping the snow off his shoes as he stuck his key into the lock, when he heard a car door slam. He looked over his shoulder at the street.

There was a person—a woman—walking away from her car across his front yard: Jane.

He stepped across the lawn to meet her. "Hey, I know you!" he said. "What happened—did your flight get grounded?"

She smiled as they met, and he tried to get his arms around her, but the brown paper bag she was carrying was between them, so he snatched it away and put his arm around her waist. "No." She stood on her tiptoes to kiss his cheek. "I'm home."

They walked together to his front door and he opened it. "Why didn't you call me? I'd have met you at the airport."

"Great idea, Carey," Jane said. "Then tomorrow while you were at work I could walk back there in a blizzard and get my car."

"Oh," he said. "Well, there must be some way that normal people do these things. I know some. I'll ask."

He flicked on the light and they stepped into the little old-fashioned entry. He set the bag on the bench, hung his coat on a hook, slipped hers off her shoulders and hung it beside his, then took her into his arms. They kissed in a slow, gentle, leisurely way, and then Jane put her hands on the sides of his face, held him a few inches away, and looked into his eyes. "You waiting for the wind to close the door?"

He shrugged, went to close the door, then came back and picked up the grocery bag. "Bring your laundry?"

She took the bag and pulled out a bottle of champagne. "There was a power failure in the store, so I thought this was Tabasco sauce. I figured you might be able to use it."

"A common mistake, but I can't launch the ship in this weather. Maybe we can drink it or something."

She reached into the bag again and pulled out a bouquet of white roses.

He looked at her for a moment, puzzled. Finally he said, "Oh, you brought my roses back. Thanks. It was getting to be about time, but I didn't want to say anything." He took the roses and sniffed them. "Held up pretty well, didn't they?"

"Remarkably," Jane said, but she barely got it out because he scooped her up and started to carry her toward the staircase.

He took her up the stairs, set her gently on the big bed, and began by taking off her shoes. He proceeded to undress her slowly. When he had finished, he sank down on the bed with her. He said quietly, "I love you, Jane," and before she could answer, his lips were on hers, and then by the time she could have spoken and remembered what she had wanted to say, words seemed unnecessary.

Hours later, Carey McKinnon awoke in his dark bedroom and moved his arm to touch her. She was gone. He stood up and walked down the hall. He found her downstairs, sitting on the couch in his big, thick bathrobe, looking away from him to stare at the fireplace. She looked tiny, like a child. He could tell she had heard him. "Hi, Carey," she said.

"What are you doing, figuring out how you're going to redecorate when your regime comes into power?"

"No. Come sit with me."

He walked down the stairs and sat beside her. He saw that she was not smiling. "What's wrong?"

She leaned over and kissed him, then said, "I've been thinking about your offer."

"You look like you've made up your mind."

"I have," she said. "One year from tonight, the tenth of January, you can set the date. If you'll give me some notice, I'll be there with something borrowed and something blue. If not, I'll just be there."

He grinned, but then his eyes began to look troubled. "Why a year from now? I mean, I guess what I want to say is, 'I'm happy. Ecstatic. I love you.' But what is there about it that takes so long? It's not as though we don't know each other."

Jane turned to face him. "I'm going to tell you a story. At the end of it, you'll say that you understand."

"I will?" he asked. "Then the year is to see if I really do understand. So it's that kind of story."

"I'm going to tell you about my trip."

EPILOGUE

In the spring of the year, as they had forever, Seneca women met at Tonawanda one evening at dusk to sing the Ohgiwe, the Dance for the Dead. Spring was the time when the dead came back. There were no drums, no rattles or flutes or bells, only the sad, beautiful voices of the women.

In the center of the big longhouse-shaped room, there were six lead singers who knew the ancient songs of the Ohgiwe best and had melodious voices strong enough to last through the night. They would sing the burden, and the women who danced along the walls of the longhouse would answer in chorus. Tonight the lead group included two who were not among the usual singers. One was Jane Whitefield, who had not been to Ohgiwe in some years, and the other was Martha McCutcheon, senior mother of the Wolf Clan in Oklahoma. She had been the one to sponsor Sarah Cartman in open council—not the Sarah Cartman everyone had known since birth, but the new Sarah, the one who had been adopted with her son, Timmy, in accordance with ancient practice.

The new Sarah Cartman danced along the wall in the circle with the other Nundawaono women. Six months ago she had been Mary Perkins. Six years ago she had called herself something else—maybe Stoddard or Stafford or Comstock—but she had done nothing under any of those names that she wanted to remember, so she did not think of them tonight. Instead, for a moment she anxiously wondered if she would be home in time to pack Timmy's lunch box for school tomorrow, then remembered that tomorrow was Sunday. When she had been Mary Perkins, she had neglected to develop the habits of mind that she considered necessary to a good mother, so sometimes she overcompensated. Still, she was becoming more comfortable as Sarah Cartman, and after a time she had even begun to feel safe. By then she already had a name, a job, a household to run, and a son to raise. Doing had made her Sarah Cartman; being was an afterthought. Through the long night, as her feet became accustomed to the dance steps and she repeated the words in the unfamiliar language, she began to forget that she had not always known them.

There were nearly a hundred other Nundawaono women, old grandmothers and young girls barely out of puberty, who danced for the dead on this night. Some wore modest spring dresses, as Sarah did. Others wore the traditional tunic, skirt, leggings, and moccasins, beaded and embroidered with all of the flowers that grew on the back of the great turtle that was the Seneca world. They wore them because women were the keepers and the source of life, the force that fought endlessly against the Being that is Faceless.

There were guests among the dead tonight too, and there were those in the longhouse who could feel their presence. The women sang the Ohgiwe for all of them together and for each in his own right. Some sang for the first Sarah Cartman, who had died in an automobile accident this winter at a young age. There was one who sang for Timmy Cartman's first parents, and for the couple who had taken him in and raised him. And she sang for Mona and Dennis, the lovers who had died in the fall.

The women sang the Ohgiwe and danced together as the grandmothers had, for the brave and the unselfish, for the protectors. They sang until dawn, when the spirits of the dead were satisfied and returned to their rest, where they would not be tempted to disturb the dreams of the living.

Jane walked purposefully across the casino alone, under the enormous crystal chandeliers, where she could be certain the two shadows would see her. She went into the lobby and stopped at the front desk to pick up her room key.

She made her way back across the casino and up into the bar that overlooked the long rows of green felt tables. She sat down at a table for two and waited. In the mirror above the bar she could see Pete's two shadows. The tall one was wandering around looking over the heads of the gamblers to see where Pete Hatcher could have gone. The second man was behind Jane and to her left, just at the perimeter of the bar, where he could slip away if he needed to.

She waited a few minutes for the barmaid to show up, then ordered a martini and a scotch and water, and watched the barmaid throw down two napkins, one in front of the empty chair, then head for the bar to get the drinks. The sight of two drinks on the tray coming back to the table seemed to make all the difference to Pete Hatcher's shadows. They were reassured, almost as though they were watching Pete. They might not know where Hatcher was right at this moment—the men's room, somewhere in the labyrinth of slot machines, where they had not looked for him—but they knew where he was going to be in a few minutes. The few minutes accumulated into a half hour, then forty-five minutes. The small shadow left to see if Pete Hatcher's car was still in the lot and came back to report to his friend that it was, but they weren't feeling confident anymore. Something was wrong, and they weren't yet sure what it was.

She glanced at her watch. Katie . . . she corrected herself: Miranda . . . had promised to transport Pete Hatcher out the stage door near the start of her act, so the show had given him a full two hours to make the Utah border. Jane's little pantomime of being stood up had bought him the third hour to get to Cedar City. His plane would be loading passengers just about now. It was time for Jane to start making herself disappear.

She left a twenty-dollar chip on the table and stepped out of the bar. The two men hesitated for a second, then followed. They had to give her plenty of room and try not to look interested. Jane walked toward the elevators, and she knew they had no choice but to follow. If they lost her, they had nothing. She took the elevator to the fifteenth floor, went into her room, kicked off her shoes, and called the garage. "This is Miss Seymour in Room 1592. I'd like my car right away, please." As she listened to the parking attendant's answer she was already stepping out of her gown.

She heard the doorknob rattle a little. She looked at the door, but it didn't budge. She could see the shadows of feet under the door. Jane kicked the dress under the bed, slipped on her slacks, pulled the sweater over her head, then heard a sudden thud. She looked at the door. The double-edged blade of a knife had pierced through the thin oak veneer of the hollow door beside the lock. She froze. An unseen hand worked the blade around a little and withdrew it. There was another dull thud, and the blade punched through again.

She snatched her purse, quickly slipped out through the curtains to the balcony, and quietly slid the door shut. She had misjudged them. They should not have been willing to take a chance like this yet. Maybe she had been too eager to get Pete out of sight and she had missed some sign, forgotten to ask some question. There was no way to fix it now, no time to think. She had to get out.

She had nothing with her. This was not the hotel where she had been sleeping. It was just the room she had rented to disappear from. In a few seconds those two would have the door open. She looked around her at the balconies of the other rooms. They were narrow and far apart, and even if she somehow managed to reach one of them without falling, she would only be in the next room. She leaned out as far as she could and looked down. On the floor below her there was a balcony just like hers, but it had to be twelve feet down.

Jane saw a thin wedge of light fan into her room as they opened the door as far as the chain would allow. She unclasped the leather strap of her purse, clasped it around the bottom of the vertical railing support closest to the wall of the building, tossed her purse to the balcony below, stepped over the railing, and lowered herself into the empty air. She was trembling with fear and awe at what she had done as she dangled there, six feet above the railing of the fourteenth-floor balcony. She wanted to drop but found her hands would not obey the command to open. It looked as though she would fall, scrape the outside of the balcony, and plummet two hundred feet to the pavement.

She bent at the hip and began a gentle swing. The first sweep brought her out away from the balcony and tipped her down a little so she had to look directly through all that empty night air at the tiny figures on the lighted concrete below. After a sickening pause at the end of the arc, she began to swing forward. When she judged that the balcony was under her, she let go.

She dropped and hit the concrete balcony hard, slid a little, and bumped the railing so it gave a low vibrating sound like a tuning fork. She turned and saw that the sliding door into this room was closed. As she stood and reached for the handle, she knew that, whatever else happened, she was not going to put herself outside the railing again. She tugged on the door and it wouldn't budge. She lay on her back, covered her face with her purse, and kicked out at the glass with both feet.

The glass gave a loud crack, but it didn't break inward. She went to her knees, lifted a long jagged shard out, set it beside her, then used her purse to push a bigger one inward. She crawled inside, hurried across the empty room, burst out into the hallway, ran to the elevator, and punched the button. But as she glanced upward she saw that the number lit up was fifteen. The elevator was coming down from above.

She turned and ran for the sign that said EXIT, slipped inside the door to the stairwell, and waited. The bell rang, the elevator doors parted, and she saw that nobody was inside. She ran for the elevator and got past the doors just as the big man emerged from the stairwell and dashed toward her.

She rode the elevator down to the garage level. When the bell rang she took a step toward the opening doors, but then the space was filled with a blur of moving flesh and gray fabric as the shorter man with the pink swine face charged inside the elevator. He slapped the button and used his body to block the opening while the doors slid together again, trapping her inside with him.

Jane predicted his half-formed strategy, because the small space made it inevitable. He had enclosed her in a tiny compartment, so he would sweep her into a corner before she could do much flailing and use the strength of his upper body to keep her there and stifle the screams. She put up both hands in a weak defense, half cringing before the blow, half supplicating that it wouldn't come. The man lunged toward her.

Jane's right hand jabbed out, more to stagger him than to do harm, but he was moving faster than she had expected. Her knuckles glanced off the bridge of his nose and into his left eye. His hands went up, too late, and Jane rocked back against the wall to deliver the kick to his knee that she had planned from the beginning. She felt the knee break; he dropped to the floor, gasping in pain.

She sidestepped past him and hit the OPEN DOOR button. As the doors slid open his hand shot out to grasp her ankle. His grip was so strong it hurt, tightening like the jaws of an animal as he pulled her toward him. She said quietly, "Think. If you drag me back in there alone with you and your broken leg, are things going to get better for you, or worse?"

She felt the hand slowly, reluctantly release its grip. The door closed, she stepped away, and hurried toward the valet loitering beside her rented car. She was already chattering. "It's here already? Gee, you guys are really fast. I'm sorry it took me so long. Thanks a lot."

She slipped a ten-dollar bill into the hand of the valet, threw her car into gear, and drove out along Bonanza Road and into the darkness to the west.

Jane drove out of the desert into Los Angeles while the morning traffic was still moving and the glaring sunlight was on the back of her car instead of in her eyes. The car was rented on a MasterCard that said she was Wendy Aguilar, so if someone in Las Vegas had seen the license number, then asking the right questions would lead the chasers to a fictitious woman who had disappeared in Los Angeles.

As she drove the rented car up Century Boulevard to return it to the agency, she spotted a convenient place to acquire a small extra measure of safety. She turned off the street beneath the tall white sign that towered above the car wash and stopped at the entrance to the tunnel lined with spraying nozzles and whirling brushes. She slipped out of the car and let the two men loitering nearby climb into the front and rear seats, steer it forward until the conveyor track caught the front wheel, then ride it through the tunnel to wipe the prints off every window and piece of chrome and vacuum the inner surfaces to pick up hairs and threads. Even if these men overlooked some trace of her and the clean-up crew at the rental lot missed it too, the process put two more people with their own clothes and hair and prints into the car. She used her ten minutes away from the car to stand in the shelter of the cashier's kiosk and watch the street to satisfy herself that no other car was idling nearby to wait for her.

When the men had finished, she pulled forward to the full-serve gas pump to have the tank filled, so any prints on the gas door or cap would belong to still another man. She drove the car around several blocks to dry it, crossed her own trail after a few minutes, and returned to the lot where she had rented it two weeks ago.

She took the shuttle van to the airport with six other people. It was always crowded in the morning at LAX because anybody who wanted to be on the East Coast by the end of the business day had to be in the air by eight. The shuttle van stopped at the loading zone, so she was only in the open for five quick steps, surrounded by men and women who were in as much of a hurry as she was. She had nothing but the canvas carry-on bag she had kept in her trunk.

Jane shopped for a flight on the television monitors on the wall as she walked. This time she decided that American Airlines Flight 653 to Chicago was the right one. From there she could go anywhere without much delay. Until a few years ago she would have paid cash for the ticket, because that gave her the option of making up a name. Now they checked identification on every flight. She rummaged in her purse and selected Terry Rosenberg's driver's license and credit card, because the name was common enough and wasn't definitely female. Years ago, when she had just begun as a guide and had seen these trips as a series of brief adventures rather than an accumulating succession of risks, she had sometimes made up names like those of heroines in romance novels. Dahlia Van Sturtevant had been one, as had Melinda-Gail La Doucette. Over the years she had slowly, painfully refined the whimsy out of her routines. A name like Terry Rosenberg might actually send a tracker off in the wrong direction: Destiny Vaucluse was a taunt.

She went through the metal detectors and walked to one of

the more distant ladies' rooms because they were less heavily frequented than the ones near the entrances and because nobody she met after the security check was likely to be carrying anything that would make killing her a neat, quiet task.

Jane washed off her makeup in front of the sink, dressed in a pair of blue jeans and a black silk blouse with a print of bright chrysanthemums, put on a pair of sneakers, threw her old clothes in the trash, and covered them with a newspaper she found on the counter. She let her long black hair hang loose and brushed it out, then put on fresh makeup and a pair of sunglasses. She inspected herself in the mirror, decided she looked as different from the woman who had been in Las Vegas as she needed to, and went out.

She bought breakfast and waited for her flight in the cafeteria, because fewer people could pass close by and look at her face here than in the waiting area. Every move Jane made while she was working was calculated to shift the odds a little more into her favor. Taking Pete Hatcher out of the world from a standing start had presented special problems and forced her to accept special risks.

Jane heard her flight announced over the loudspeaker, picked up her canvas bag, and walked toward the gate. She held herself with her spine straight and looked directly ahead, never allowing her eyes to focus on those of the other travelers, never turning away to give them permission to study her. She walked quickly, joined the line after it had begun to move efficiently but was long enough to include a lot of other people who would be more interesting for a bored observer to stare at than she was, and disappeared into the loading tunnel.

As soon as the plane was in the air, Jane pushed her seat back as far as it would go and closed her eyes. She had been anxious for two nights, trying to work out a path for Pete Hatcher that wouldn't lead him in front of a gun muzzle, then spent the third running. She knew she could sleep only fitfully now, because she had not dreamed in four nights and her mind was holding a jumbled backlog of jarring impressions that would plague her sleep. But lying with her eyes closed prevented other passengers from trying to talk to her, and that was another of her precautions. The road home was where the worst of the traps were, because she had already given dangerous people a reason to want her.